MW01172501

ANDALAYA

BOOK ONE OF THE EPIC OF THE SAGES

COREY RUSICK

ISBN: 978-1-961977-01-3 (Paperback)

ISBN: 978-1-961977-00-6 (eBook)

Copyright © 2023 by Corey Rusick

www.CoreyRusick.com

All rights reserved.

The story, all names, characters, and incidents portrayed in this production are fictitious. No identification with actual persons (living or deceased), places, buildings, and products is intended or should be inferred.

No part of this publication may be reproduced, distributed, or transmitted in any form or by any means, including photocopying, recording, or other electronic or mechanical methods, without the prior written permission of the publisher, except as permitted by U.S. copyright law. For permission requests, contact White Lake Press at www.whitelakepress.com

White Lake
—PRESS—

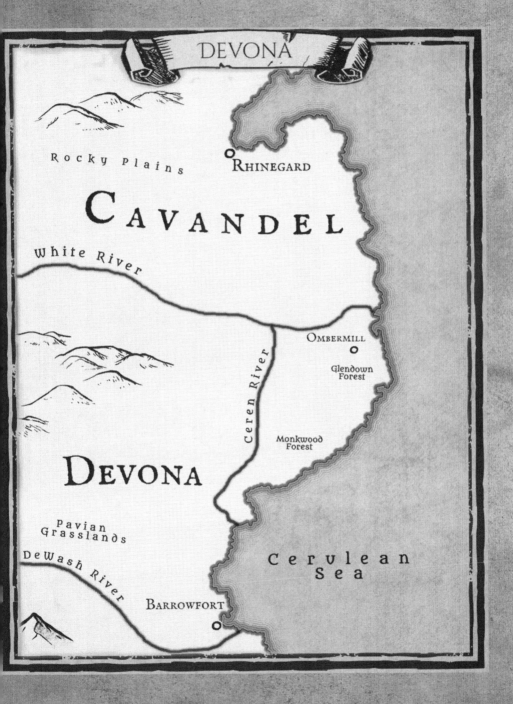

MAP OF IRIA

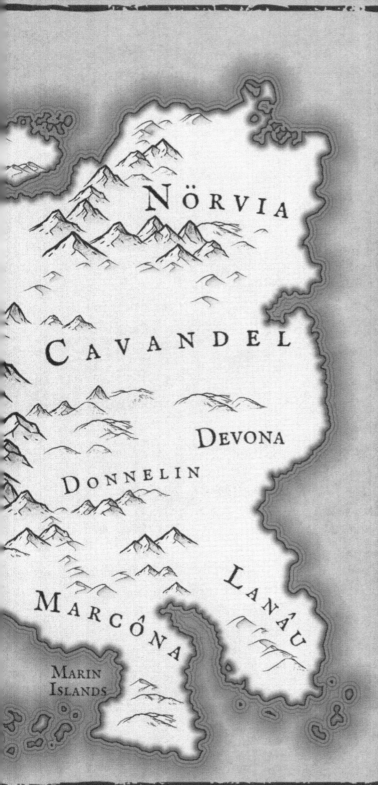

NÖRVIA

CAVANDEL

DEVONA

DONNELIN

LANAU

MARCÓNA

MARIN
ISLANDS

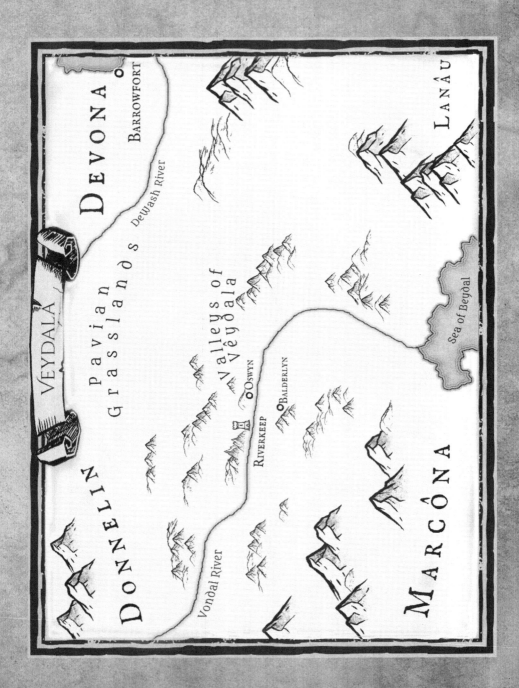

PART ONE

Narrator's Salutation

This story will undoubtedly seem incredible, or at least fantastic, and perhaps even naïve to those unfamiliar with the Epic of the Sages. I do not fault any man or woman who should read this account with a dubious mind. Even I still wonder at the thought of it all. How does one believe a tale about men who live for a thousand years? Men who levitate boulders and run faster than the wind? Such whimsical notions are surely beyond the confines of the rational mind. But to paraphrase the words of my mentor, the story which I tell is true in every whit.

This I can assure you with honor unsullied, for while this story is not my own — indeed, it begins many a century before my birth — I relay these events exactly as they were told from the mouths of those heroes who lived them. Many were the months I sat at the feet of those sages, giants among men, listening to their most wondrous history. While ensconced in their sacred city of Andalaya, they related to me the events of their lives in the most vivid detail, so much so that I could scarcely believe I had not witnessed these events myself. Those were joyous months indeed. Thus, it is now my hallowed obligation to share their story with the world, and may all the pains of Iria befall me if I fail to do them justice.

Having thus introduced the object of this endeavor, I am left with the dilemma of selecting the proper moment for our story to begin. I might begin as far back as the original founding of the Great Order when the mysteries of sagecraft were first discovered. Or perhaps I could begin a thousand years later when the great order fell and Iria plunged into an era of war and darkness. But as important as those events are to this story, they are before my patrons' time, and I have no firsthand accounts to relay to you.

I might instead begin with the origins of our heroes, their births and their families and their upbringings, all of which have been told to me firsthand. But these too would not suffice, for nothing of extraordinary significance transpired during their formative years, and I fear such a beginning would only dilute the magnitude of their story.

I shall therefore begin my account on the day when everything changed, the day that set in motion the chain of events that saved humanity.

CHAPTER ONE

THE HOUSE OF ROKA

42ND DAY OF WINTER, 896 G.C.

K ailem Roka had been underwater for five minutes, and his lungs began to burn. He simply ignored it. He still had two minutes before he had to surface, and he was determined to savor every second of it.

The bottom of the cove was a separate world unto itself. The water there was an idyllic temperature Kailem so adored, refreshingly cold without causing a chill. The gentle ebb and flow of the ocean rocked his body back and forth while the seagrass swayed in tandem. Critters of every color crawled among the coral below him, while sea creatures of every size and shape swam in schools around him. The fish darted about in perfect unison, as if possessed by a single mind, and Kailem had long pondered how such harmony was possible.

Here was Kailem's solace from the vexations that plagued him on the surface; not even gravity could reach him here. This was freedom in its purest form.

Seven oysters filled the mesh bag in Kailem's hand, a modest haul for the day, but he had time to find a few more. His elder brother, Mokain, swam a dozen yards ahead of him. The brothers could have easily purchased whole strands of pearls in the market, but there was something exceptional about a pearl found in the wild, a sentimentality that was beyond the reach of silver and gold. Kailem wondered how many oysters Mokain had found, and, more importantly, if it were more than he had.

Outside the Marin Islands, spending five minutes under the surface would have meant certain death for even the most vigorous of men. For a fully trained native of the Marin Islands, however, such a capacity was to be expected. Now, eight minutes was an impressive feat, one which both the Roka brothers had managed on more than one occasion. And although today was a contest of oyster finding and not of deep-sea diving, Kailem would never permit himself to surface before Mokain.

A short distance to Kailem's right, a sea turtle moseyed along without a care in the world. Kailem grinned. Sea turtles were one of the few creatures who enjoyed the peace and solitude of the ocean as much as he did. As a boy, he had once swum to a sea turtle, seeking to play with it, woefully ignorant of the power in a turtle's bite. When the young boy reached out to touch it, the sea turtle bit his forearm with such force that the beak hit bone; Kailem still bore the scar to prove it. Now, in the dawn of adulthood, he wisely left the turtle in peace.

Kailem spotted another oyster and retrieved it. That raised the count to eight, surely more than Mokain had found. Eight oysters would have to suffice, for the screaming in his lungs had grown too loud to ignore. He kicked off the sandy bottom and ascended the twenty feet back to the surface, exhaling tiny bubbles of air as he went.

Mokain sat on golden sand, as soft as powder, in front of his family's estate. He rested his elbows on his knees, with his net full of oysters between his legs, and worked his knife into the crease of an oyster shell. The beach had a gentle incline sloping into the turquoise waters of their cove, and from his vantage he could see the sandstone structures of other families' estates scattered along the coast of Suvara, the capital island of Marin.

Mokain cracked open his oyster and was disappointed to find no pearl within, so he returned it to his bag and moved onto the next. The odds of finding a pearl were one in a hundred, but their mother adored them. She always said it was a good omen, finding a pearl. Just a superstition, of course, but she swore by it all the same, so Mokain kept searching.

Out in the center of the cove, his younger brother finally surfaced. Once Kailem swam near enough to walk through the water, Mokain called out, "how many?"

"Eight," came his reply. "You?"

A smug expression spread across Mokain's round face. "Eleven."

Kailem rolled his eyes and groaned as he sat on the sand next to his brother.

"You spend too much time acting like a fish, little brother," Mokain said. "Not enough time searching."

"I know, I know," Kailem said. He shook out the water from his hair like a dog and spread open his mesh bag.

Mokain was taller and stockier, but Kailem had a more angular face and a longer torso. A faded scar adorned the left side of Kailem's jawline, the compliments of a rather aggressive sparring match with his older brother. Mokain was unparalleled in all matters of combat, which among Mariners was no small feat. At this point, he could scarcely find anyone to spar with him, apart from Kailem.

Kailem unsheathed his dagger from the side of his canvas trousers — the typical swimming garb in the Marin Islands — and pried open his first oyster.

Mokain eyed the Culmination Blade in his brother's hand. Kailem's ten-inch blade had intertwining knots carved into the polished steel. Those same intertwining knots were carved into the hilt with the Roka Family Crest at its center — a whale's fluke laid over a pair of crossed swords. The grip was coiled wire shaped perfectly to the contours of his hand. It was tradition to name one's Culmination Blade; Kailem named his dagger "Malua" after the old Marin word for peace.

"You couldn't find an oyster knife?" Mokain said with a shake of his head. He used his own oyster knife to crack open his third oyster.

"What's wrong with my dagger?" Kailem asked. "Malua works just as well."

"But it's your Culmination Blade, and you're dulling the edge on menial labor."

Kailem paused and looked at the dagger in his hand. Mariner steel was unlike any other, strong enough to withstand rigorous abuse while maintaining a fine edge, yet flexible enough not to shatter under extreme force. The Mariners' unique forging process left distinctive patterns like rushing waters in the steel and was highly regarded throughout all of Iria.

There was contrition on Kailem's face; his little brother had taken the rebuke harder than he intended. "I'm sure it's fine," Mokain said. "A dull blade can always be sharpened."

You see, Mariner training was legendary. It spanned from a child's sixth year to their seventeenth, and upon completion, the child would forge a new blade to mark their passing into adulthood. Every Culmination Blade was expected to be a masterpiece, a work of art as much as an instrument of death. So much went into forging a Culmination Blade that Mariners treated them like precious heirlooms rather than actual weapons, and most were even buried with it when they died. Kailem had chosen a dagger for his blade, a rare choice, to say the least.

His brother hesitated, then, as he had no alternative blades on hand, continued shucking oysters with his dagger.

"What time are you on duty?" Kailem asked.

Mokain checked the position of the sun. "Last watch before sundown. I ought to return to the barracks soon."

"Are you going to miss Amma's party?"

Mokain let out something between a laugh and a scoff. "Amma would drag me back home by my ear if I tried that."

Kailem laughed too. "You know, I think I'd pay to see that," he quipped.

Mokain shoved his elbow into him, which only made his brother laugh more. "Don't worry, I've made arrangements; I'll be there."

Mokain cracked open another empty oyster. "Do you know when Father's next voyage is?"

Kailem's posture deflated. "Tomorrow," he replied.

"Are you going with him?" Mokain asked.

Kailem worked the oyster in his hand and said nothing.

Although their family technically had titles of nobility, theirs was about the lowest-ranking house in Suvara. Any noble family unable to live off the value of their land was obliged to engage in commerce. In the Roka family, that meant selling spices to neighboring kingdoms on the mainland.

"Did something happen between you two?" Mokain pressed.

"No," he muttered. His hand slipped, still wet with seawater, and the jagged shell scraped his palm. "Rotting sard," he cursed. He tried to shake away the pain with little effect.

Mokain set down his knife and oyster. "No? Because for the first time in... I can't even remember, you missed family dinner. Father was quiet and sullen all night, but he asked about you. He wanted to know if I'd seen you, if you were okay."

Kailem kept his eyes fixed on his scraped hand.

"So, what happened?"

"We just argued, is all."

An awkward silence hung in the air, save for the sounds of crashing waves and the caw of a seagull overhead. Kailem looked up to see if the comment had satisfied him. Mokain stared back at him patiently. Kailem finally gave in.

"You know how Father has been hounding me to join his merchant voyages for months now?" His brother nodded. "Well, yesterday I finally told him I didn't want to be a merchant. I told him the family business was the duty of the firstborn, and it wasn't fair that it fell to me just because you have a promising military career. I said if he wasn't going to force you into it, then he can't force me into it either."

"I can't imagine that went over too well," Mokain said.

Kailem shook his head. "He started yelling at me, said I was foolish and lazy and ungrateful. Said I thought people should pay me to play in the ocean all day."

"Wouldn't that be nice?" Mokain said with a smile. When his attempt at levity fell short, he continued. "Father has yelled at you before; why was this time any different?"

Mokain gave him time to answer, and at length, Kailem confessed. "I don't know what happened, Moka. I just snapped. Until yesterday, I had never even raised my voice to him, but during the argument, I was shouting as loud as I could. The quarrel escalated, and he... he struck me with the back of his hand."

Mokain's eyes went wide. He could not imagine anyone yelling at their father, nor could he imagine their father striking his own son. Lord Roka didn't even treat their servants that way.

"That wasn't the worst of it, though," Kailem continued. "After he hit me, I pushed him back. I shoved so hard he fell. I couldn't believe it."

Mokain fumbled for words. "What'd you do?"

"We just stared at each other; not sure for how long. After that, I just ran."

"And you've been avoiding him ever since?"

Kailem nodded. He dug his toes into the sand, hoping the conversation would end.

"I can tell he feels bad about it."

"He should," Kailem returned with spite.

"And you know you should feel worse, right?"

Kailem huffed, shook his head, then nodded. "I'll figure out a way to apologize at the party tonight,"

Mokain patted him on the shoulder, and they returned to shucking oysters.

Mokain focused on the oyster in his hands, so he didn't notice when Kailem slipped his dagger back in its sheath. When his brother extended his hand to him, he looked up. Sitting on Kailem's palm was a perfectly round bead the size of a macadamia nut. It was the color of polished steel with a glossy finish that shimmered in the sunlight.

"Finally," Mokain said. Kailem let the pearl roll into his hand.

Mokain pinched the pearl between his fingers and held it up. "Beautiful color. Fine shape too." He returned the pearl to Kailem. "It's perfect. Amma will love it."

Mokain's praise made his little brother sit an inch taller. Kailem had already made a ring; after lunch, he would fasten the pearl on top and give the ring to his mother after the party that night.

Their parents had invited all the noblemen on their island to a formal celebration at their estate. Lord and Lady Roka had a grand announcement to make, something they had not even told their sons yet. Their mother had been planning the feast for weeks. Whatever the announcement was, a pearl ring was the perfect way to mark the occasion.

Kailem kept his eyes on the pearl as they climbed the stone steps from the beach to the backdoor of their estate. Draped over a bench, they found towels and fresh clothing laid there by the head servant, Tevano. The brothers dried their wavy brown hair and wiped away the crusted sea salt from their eyebrows and eyelashes. They slid a fresh tunic over their heads and tied the sash around their waists before entering the house.

Like most homes in the Marin Islands, the Roka Estate was an open, airy residence with sandstone walls and colorful ceramic tiles lining the floor, although the outer walls were more window than stone. The brothers found their mother in the kitchen preparing lunch with the help of two servants. Kailem sat on a stool and leaned his elbows on the preparation table.

"I trust you two are not tracking wet sand through my clean home," said Lily Roka. Their mother wore a smile all too familiar to the brothers, one that was thoroughly pleasant yet entirely serious. It was the type of smile only a mother could make.

"We would never dream of it, Amma," Mokain said, kissing his mother on the side of the head.

Kailem looked back at the footprints of sand they'd tracked in the hallway, but Tevano was already sweeping up the evidence.

Lily had the right amount of muscle tone to be both powerful and graceful, which was typical among Mariners. Her husband, on the other hand, was shaped like a gorilla, barrel-chested with large hands and a square jaw. That imposing figure served him well when negotiating trade prices. It was a wonder Kailem managed to shove him to the ground. He must have caught his old man off guard, or perhaps the weight of age had caught up with him.

The brothers were a fair mix of their parents, although physically Mokain took more after their father and Kailem, their mother; in personality, the opposite was true.

Lily wore a dress of hemp and linen fabric, elegant in its simplicity. In Marin, the wealthy showed their status through quality fabric and subtle embroidery rather than through ostentation. She slid across the table a plate of white fish and sweet potato, charbroiled and covered in a mango glaze.

"Mahi?" Kailem asked.

"Of course," she replied with a wink. She'd made his favorite. Kailem took a bite with his right hand while his left reached into a nearby basket and pulled out a piece of freshly baked flatbread.

"How was your swim?" Lily asked.

Kailem swallowed and replied, "Successful."

"Oh?" She sat across from him, encouraging him to say more.

Kailem couldn't wait to see the look on her face when he showed her the pearl. He was torn whether to show it to her then or wait until he fastened it to the ring, but before he could decide, his father walked into the kitchen wearing just a light tunic and trousers. The temperature in the room dropped several degrees. Lord Roka's eyes met Kailem's, and he set his jaw, his lips pressed into a line. Neither of them spoke.

Lady Roka looked from her son to her husband and back, then returned to the stove with a sigh.

"I expect you all to be ready to greet our guests tonight at sundown," said the lady of the house. Her words broke the staring contest and Lord Roka sat at the side of the table opposite his son.

"Unfortunately, Amma, I will be a few minutes late," Mokain said.

"What? Why? Did they change your shift? This has been planned for weeks. Why would they do that?"

Mokain shrugged and swallowed a bite of fish. "The order came from a general. They never give us a reason."

"But you will attend," she said, part question and part statement.

"I wouldn't miss it," he said, inhaling his last bite. He stood from the table and readied to leave.

Lily's shoulders slumped. "So soon?"

"I'm afraid so, Amma," Mokain said, hugging her.

Mokain looked at Kailem and nodded at their father. Lord Roka stared at his plate, eating in silence. Kailem nodded, and Mokain left for the barracks.

Kailem rehearsed different ways of apologizing in his mind, but he was at a loss about just how to broach the topic. His father wouldn't even look at him, he doubtless had no desire to talk to him either.

Several minutes passed in silence. Kailem moved the last few bites around his plate with his fork. Perhaps he should wait until his father was in a better mood before apologizing. The idea was appetizing, but he knew if he pitched that idea to Mokain, he would tell Kailem he was just being a coward. And Kailem *was* being a coward.

He opened his mouth to begin, then closed it again.

Don't be a pike, he told himself.

He opened his mouth again, but before any words could form, a sound shook through the kitchen. It was the sound of their front door breaking off its hinges. A ceramic plate slipped from Lily's fingers and shattered on the floor. Kailem instinctively gripped the handle of his dagger. A half dozen soldiers in studded leather armor marched down the hallway to the kitchen with swords unsheathed. Lord Roka stood to protest just as a second unit of soldiers marched in through the backdoor, tracking dirt and sand over the tile floor. Within seconds, a full squadron occupied their home.

A soldier threw Lord Roka against the wall, twisting his arm behind his back. Another grabbed Lily by the back of her dress and shoved her down on the preparation table with a disgraceful thud. When Kailem leaped to her defense, four soldiers surrounded him, the tips of their swords only inches from his neck. He clinched his teeth while soldiers clapped his parents' wrists in shackles.

"Lord and Lady Roka, you are under arrest for the murder of King Matala and Queen Liliuo," a soldier declared. The marks on his uniform said he was a lieutenant, the same rank as Mokain, although this man was at least ten years Mokain's senior.

"Are you mad?!" Lord Roka yelled with his head held high. "This is prepos-terous! Release us, immediately!"

The soldiers averted their eyes, unable to look at him.

"What about the boy?" one soldier asked. Kailem balled his fists, aching to use them.

The lieutenant looked him over. "Lord Vanua didn't mention the sons, only the Lord and Lady. Just leave him be."

The four soldiers surrounding Kailem sheathed their swords. Kailem reached out to his mother as the soldiers marched her past him, but a soldier batted his hand away.

"Go tell your brother," Lily called out.

Soldiers marched her down the hall behind her husband, leaving Kailem alone in the kitchen.

Kailem's heart pounded. His mind was a chaotic, incoherent mess. He stood in his kitchen, motionless, the inside of his skull a maelstrom of shock and rage and panic and dread. What in Iria had just happened?

The echo of his mother's words shook him from his stupor. *Go tell your brother,* she'd said. Kailem fled his kitchen and raced out the backdoor without stopping to put on his sandals.

He ran like a dog off its chain, his bare feet slapping against the cobblestones. The road held estates far more elegant than his own, and their residents emerged to see what the commotion was. Kailem ignored them. He kept pace until he had run the entire length of the capital city to Mokain's barracks.

He found his brother in the lieutenant's dorm, donning leather armor with metal studs.

"Moka!" he yelled through heaving breaths.

"Kailem?" Mokain set down his armor and steadied Kailem's shoulders.

"Mother and Father. They took them. Soldiers. They arrested them. Said they murdered the king and queen."

"What?!" Mokain yelled.

"What do we do, Moka?" Kailem asked, still gasping for air.

Mokain wasted no time. He didn't bother donning the rest of his armor, although he grabbed his side-sword before running from the barracks. His brother was close behind, and although Kailem had yet to fully catch his breath, he had no problem keeping pace.

The capital prison was adjacent to the barracks. Mokain marched through the front doors with the composure of a king and the intensity of a madman. When the sentry tried to stop him for the usual security checks. Mokain shoved him aside.

"Where are my parents?" Mokain demanded of the soldier at the reception desk.

"We... we don't have your parents here. Sir," the trembling soldier replied.

Mokain glared at the man.

"Honest, sir. You can check our prisoner log." The soldier pulled a thick ledger from a desk drawer and placed it on the table, a clear breach of protocol, but Mokain's reputation afforded him certain unofficial privileges. Mokain didn't bother to open it. Instead, he turned to Kailem.

"When they arrested them, did they say on whose authority it was?" Mokain asked.

Kailem thought back to the arrest. "They mentioned Lord Vanua."

"Lord Vanua?" Mokain scrunched his brow in thought.

Kailem followed his brother past the sentry still on the ground and out the prison doors.

The two brothers ran back through Suvara towards the palace in the city center.

The capital streets were never this empty. There should have been crowds of citizens flooding the streets, buying and selling wares and transporting goods. Even in the dead of night, there was always at least someone stumbling out of a tavern or an angry couple shouting from within their home. The only sound was the brothers' heavy breathing as they sprinted upon stone streets, their minds racing faster still.

This has to have been some mistake, they told themselves. Someone had made a grievous error, and the brothers would see they paid for it. They would reach the palace and set matters right. Soon everything would be okay, they were sure of it. They still ran like gazelles, regardless.

As they neared the royal palace, they heard a tumultuous noise up ahead. They turned the final corner and the city burst to life. A massive crowd filled the palace square and spilled out into the adjacent streets. Somehow, word of the arrest had spread faster than it should have. The screaming crowd was like the wind near the heart of a hurricane. People in the back stood on carts and even climbed on top of buildings to witness the spectacle on the palace steps.

The Royal Palace of Marin was a three-story mansion of alabaster stone, the largest and most elaborate structure in the islands. The palace steps were an entire story unto themselves that spanned the entire length of the structure. Atop those steps stood Lord Vanua working the crowd into hysteria. Instead of possessing the usual Mariner physique, Lord Vanua was plump and squat old man. He also happened to be the Royal Advisor to King Matala.

The brothers' parents, Lord and Lady Roka, were at the top of the palace steps, kneeling before him, their mouths gagged and their arms tied behind their backs. Beside them were four palace guards armed with side-swords and short spears, some of whom were under Mokain's command.

At first, the people were sparse enough that the brothers could maneuver around them, but as they moved closer to the palace, the crowd became so dense that the people couldn't have moved for them even had they wanted to.

The brothers shoved deranged men and women aside as they pushed their way forward.

The roar of the crowd was deafening. "Traitors!" someone yelled. "Murderers!" yelled another. This was no crowd drawn in by a scandal. This was a mob, and they wanted blood.

Lord Vanua was yelling some line of rhetoric, as he was known to do, but Kailem couldn't make it out over the rumble of the crowd. As if to accentuate some point he had made, Lord Vanua struck Kailem's mother with the back of his ring-laden hand. The mob roared in approval.

"Stop it!" Kailem shouted from behind Mokain. "Let them go!" The words burst out of him, despite the royal advisor having no chance of hearing him. But his yell had given them away.

"They're the traitors' sons!" someone yelled.

"Grab them!"

"Rotting sards!"

"Arrest them!"

Several townsfolk seized Kailem. They were people he had known his entire life, people who had dined in his family's home. Friends, teachers, mentors, regular clients of his father, people who at the very least should have given them the benefit of the doubt. How easily a good name can be soiled by a lie.

The mob had Kailem's arms restrained as they pulled at his hair and clothes, everyone wanting a hand in their twisted sense of justice. They took him almost to the palace steps before guards stepped in.

"I'm sorry, Lieutenant, we didn't have a choice," one soldier said as he pushed the townsfolk aside. "We're under orders from Lord Vanua."

Mokain ignored him and pushed his way toward the palace with Kailem close behind. They were stopped by guards who had formed a barrier to the steps by holding their spears parallel to the ground, pushing back the advancing mob.

"Let us pass," Mokain ordered.

"You know we can't do that, sir," one soldier said over the clamor of the crowd.

"You shouldn't be here, sir," yelled another. "Return to the barracks, please."

Mokain was about to push past them when he locked eyes with Lord Vanua.

"The traitors' sons have arrived!" Lord Vanua cried. "Guards, bring them forward!"

The guards obeyed the order with gritted teeth. Two guards took Mokain by either arm while another two secured Kailem. Mokain struggled against his own subordinates while they marched him to the middle of the palace steps with his brother close behind.

Kailem had not appreciated the size of the mob until he saw it from the palace steps. They were so tightly packed together that some could not raise their arms above their shoulders, or if they had, could not put them down again.

Kailem's parents had the fear of death carved into their faces. Panic shone in their eyes, beads of sweat dripping down their cheeks in the afternoon heat.

"What is this, Vanua?" Kailem yelled. "Release them! Now!"

"Your parents are traitors," Lord Vanua said. "They assassinated our king and queen!" The roar of the mob grew louder.

"You know us, Vanua," Mokain tried to reason. "Our parents are patriots, not traitors."

The bulbous man walked to a nearby guard and retrieved two blood-soaked daggers. "These blades were found in the chests of our king and queen, abandoned by the murderous cowards."

Another roar from the mob.

"Are these not your parents' daggers?" Lord Vanua asked. "The hilt bears the crest of House Roka."

"Those daggers could have been stolen," Kailem argued. "You know our parents; they aren't capable of this."

Lord Vanua continued. "When your parents were arrested, we found this letter in your father's coat." He held the letter high for all to see. "It is addressed to your parents bearing the royal seal of the King of Marcôna. He offers to pay them five hundred gold florins to kill the King and Queen of Marin."

The mob went feral.

Lord and Lady Roka fought to speak, but their gags were too tight. Kailem did his best to be heard over the thundering shouts.

"Our parents have a right to a trial, Vanua! This entire display is illegal!"

"These traitors forfeited their rights when they murdered our King!" Lord Vanua declared. The mob cried out in agreement.

"My good people of Suvara, what say you? Shall justice await while these murderers stand trial?"

"Nay!" the crowd yelled in unison.

"What need have we for further evidence? Are we not fully convinced of their guilt?"

"Yea!" came the reply.

"When would you see their sentence carried out?"

"Now! Now! Now! Now!"

Kailem looked out at the screaming crowd. He couldn't see the faces of those who were sickened by the display, couldn't hear those few dissenting voices drowning amid the tumult. All he could see were the rioters lusting for blood, Lord Vanua's thundering rhetoric having stolen all semblance of civility.

Lord Vanua nodded to a nearby guard who held a longsword the full width of Kailem's hand.

Mokain acted first. His right elbow met the nose of the guard on his right. The guard dropped his spear and held his face, blood oozing through his fingers. Before anyone knew what had happened, Mokain's fist struck under the chin of the guard on his left. The guard's head whipped backwards, and he collapsed to the stone steps.

Kailem was not a second behind his brother. He threw his head into the face of the guard on his left, knocking out the man's front teeth in the process. With his arms free, he thrust his elbow into the nose of the guard on his right, who was distracted by Mokain's escape; the guard rolled down the palace steps unconscious.

Mokain engaged two guards with spears. The guards stepped back and exchanged worried looks before advancing on their commander. An unarmed Mokain against two spearmen was a fair fight by any standard, and it left Kailem unguarded. He raced up the remaining few steps and across the landing to where his parents knelt. He was almost close enough to touch them when a guard tackled him from the side.

Before he could react, two more guards were on top of him. One held Kailem's hands behind his back, another pressed his knee between Kailem's shoulder blades, while the third held a spear tip a mere inch from his neck. More guards fell on Mokain as well. Kailem watched as they wrestled his brother to the ground and begged him to stop resisting.

Lord Vanua again gave a nod to the guard holding the side-sword. *This can't be happening*, Kailem thought. It wouldn't happen. Something would stop this.

Mokain. He always knew what to do. He would stop this; Kailem was sure of it.

Kailem met his brother's eyes; all trace of hope had vanished.

The executioner raised the blade high above his head. In a single swift motion, he slammed the blade down on Lord Roka's neck. The sound was something between a butcher slicing beef and a melon falling on stone. It was a sound the brothers would never forget.

Pinned to the ground by several guards, Kailem watched in horror as his father's head rolled down the steps, his mind unable to comprehend what he saw.

Lady Roka stared at her husband's lifeless body next to her with unimaginable pain in her eyes. Kailem saw something break in her, a sight he had never seen in his warrior mother. The executioner again raised his blade. Again, he swung it down.

Lady Roka's headless body collapsed to the ground next to her husband's.

A wave of nausea crashed over Kailem. Breath eluded him, and a hollow pit formed in his chest. The sight of his headless parents lying in their own gore before a cheering, gleeful crowd was more than he could bear. His stomach squeezed and the taste of bile filled his mouth. Tears leaked from his eyes, and a single, pathetic whimper escaped his lips.

Then his blood boiled. He thought he heard himself scream, but his mind was a blur and the sound was too far in the distance. Fueled by a hot, blinding rage, he threw off both the guards and burst to his feet, making a mad dash at Lord Vanua. For the briefest moment, he saw fear in Vanua's eyes as he barreled toward the putrid knave, and that fear gave Kailem strength. Then, within mere feet of his vengeance, four more guards managed to tackle him to the ground and restrain him, just as they would a raging bull calf. Even in Kailem's fury, there were just too many of them.

Lord Vanua looked at the two brothers subdued before him. The crowd had traded reason for vengeance; at this point, they would have agreed to anything he said. Better to have the brothers executed beside their parents and be done with it.

But the faces of the Royal Guard gave him pause. They had not fallen victim to his rhetoric, and Lord Vanua saw the conflict in their eyes. He couldn't know just how far they would let him break the law before they refused to follow orders. Or worse, before they turned against him. Knowing Mokain's reputation among their ranks, it was best not to push the men any further.

Lord Vanua raised his hands to the mob. "In the name of our beloved King, I declare that House Roka is hereby stripped of all titles of honor, that all lands and property held by House Roka are hereby forfeit, and that all surviving members of House Roka are hereby exiled from the Kingdom of Marin. In the name of our King, let it be so."

The mob cheered.

CHAPTER TWO

A ROYAL FEAST

24TH DAY OF SPRING, 897 G.C.

Kyra Arturri wore a scarlet gown to her betrothal feast. A daring color, to be sure. Scarlet was far too bold for so formal an occasion, but who would dare say such to the future Queen of Cavandel? The gown was made by the famed Norman Frode, of course, and the result was breathtaking. It hugged her hourglass frame in a perfect blend of tradition and innovation, revealing just enough skin to scintillate curiosity without courting scandal.

The twenty-year-old bride-to-be entered the Great Hall of the Palace of Rhinegard with all the pomp and circumstance befitting a royal event. At the appointed time, the royal herald announced Kyra's arrival, and a quiet reverence descended upon the Great Hall. Royal Guards pulled wide the double doors and a chorus of trumpets sang out as Kyra sashayed down the center aisle. The crowd let out audible gasps and hushed exclamations. Kyra savored the moment. The looks of envy from the women of the court had alone justified the gown's price. The looks of desire from their husbands were a bonus.

The Great Hall was more sublime than any structure to be found in Kyra's homeland. That was not to say ought against Devonian architecture; the Devonians were no less grandiose than any other kingdom of Iria. But the Palace of Rhinegard was a singular achievement. Stone columns the size of sequoias lined the sides of the Great Hall supporting an intricate system of arches upon the ceiling. Every surface in the Great Hall bore elegant carvings and flourishes, each of which was its own work of art.

Kyra took her seat at the High Table, raised on a dais before the two-thousand noblemen and women in attendance, and basked in the assembly's silent adoration. This felt natural. Royalty suited her.

She stole a glance at her fiancé, Prince Aedon, sitting on the opposite side of the High Table from her. How strange, she thought, that she should be denied a seat next to her fiancé at her own betrothal feast, but her mother assured her this was the custom in Cavandel. No matter the occasion, the King always sat in the center of the High Table, with his two most honored guests at either side. Tonight, that meant his son and heir on his right hand and Kyra's father, Lord Leonin Arturri, on his left.

Aedon was the second reason every young woman in the hall was jealous of her that night. Prince Aedon was carved out of pure marble. A firm set jaw and piercing eyes, with all the charm and poise a man of his breeding should exude. Any woman in the kingdom would have pulled out her own eye to be Aedon's wife, as long as she still had the other eye to gaze at him, but it didn't matter. He was hers, and all was as it should be.

Kyra ran her hand down the side of her gown. Although Norman Frode was technically the dressmaker, the design concept had been entirely her own. Layers of the thinnest satin and taffeta caressed her waist, topped with a layer of delicate lace. Where a traditional gown would have flowed out from the waist into a wide bell shape, Kyra's gown was tight around the hips and fluttered out to the ground like an unfurled rose. The bodice was cut low and slightly off the shoulder, giving just a glimpse at what only the Prince could have. She was a priceless gem, and her dress was the wrapping she came in.

It seemed every kingdom in Iria had at least a few representatives in attendance. That alone made this night an event to remember. Most were Cavender, as was to be expected, followed closely by Devonians. The various kingdoms of Iria mostly kept to themselves; Kyra's mother taught her to expect such division. Their cultures clashed, and this was a time of political unrest. Had it been from any other kingdom, most foreigners would have simply ignored the invitation, but no one ignored Cavandel.

A steady flow of dignitaries and well-wishers marched past their table. Her mother said she would have to learn all of their names if she were to "play the game" as she called it, but there would be time enough for that later. She hardly listened to anything her well-wishers said, mainly because they all said variations of the same sentiment. She simply gave each of them a gracious nod and a smile and kept track of how many times someone admired her dress. She was up to thirty-two now and they hadn't even served the main course yet.

A woman approached her mother, Lady Avalina Arturri, seated next to her. The woman was clearly from Donnelin; the Donnelish had no sense of fashion. The woman knelt and whispered into Lady Arturri's ear.

What in Iria is this woman doing? Kyra thought. Only their personal attendants and the Royal Guards were allowed to step on their side of the High Table. It was a matter of propriety as much as a measure for their security. Kyra had never seen this woman in her life, yet she presumes to approach them now, during the height of the feast. And why was her mother permitting this, she wondered?

Kyra noticed a small tattoo of a bird on the woman's wrists. Devonians weren't known for tattooing their skin, but she had noticed the bird on several of their servants' wrists back home as well. It must be an odd fashion choice sweeping through the servant class.

"Yes, milady," the Donnelish woman said after a brief conversation. She scurried away with the gait of someone who wanted to appear casual. Avalina resumed conversing with well-wishers like no interruption had occurred. Kyra rolled her eyes at her. She had no idea what her mother was up to, and frankly, she cared too little to find out.

She admired her own dress again. How long would it take before this became the latest fashion trend, she wondered? She would have to think of something new to stay ahead of the masses.

"Lord Baylor, what a pleasure to see you here," Kyra heard her mother say. "And Lady Baylor, thank you so much for coming."

Kyra looked up to see her mother speaking with the familiar nobleman and his wife, close personal friends of the family. The House of Baylor was a prominent family in Kyra's home country of Devona, and she had been dearest friends with Lord Baylor's eldest son, Edric, since they were children.

Edric appeared to be absent this evening. To Kyra's disappointment, their second son, whose name escaped her at the moment, was there instead, standing awkwardly behind his parents.

"And Kyra, by the moons, don't you look radiant this evening," Lady Baylor said. "And that dress, my... you've outdone yourself."

"You are far too kind, Lady Baylor." She paused, expecting Lady Baylor to ask more about her dress, who designed it and how much they had paid for it. When she did not, Kyra continued. "Your family appears to be one short; is Edric not with you?"

"Alas, Lady Kyra, he is not," Lord Baylor explained, "but he sends with us his warmest regards. Apparently, we've been too lenient with some of our tenants. They seem to have... forgotten their place, shall we say." He paused to let Kyra and Avalina chuckle. "In fact, I'm afraid Lady Baylor and I must take our leave after tonight's feast. We are returning to Devona to settle the matter."

"That is most unfortunate," Lady Arturri said. "I should have greatly loved to entertain the Baylors for a stay." Avalina's voice was flirtatious, as usual. She sounded that way whenever she spoke to friends. It was the same voice she used when she was manipulating someone.

"And we would love to return when this unpleasantness is settled, Your Highness," Lady Baylor said. Kyra grinned at the premature use of a royal address. "In the meantime, our son Osmund will be staying in Rhinegard for a time." She turned to usher her son forward.

Although Osmund was the same age as Kyra, she had never spoken more than a few words to him. He was a soft, small young man with a heart-shaped face, short loose curls of light brown hair, and spectacles over his dark blue eyes. At social gatherings, he kept to himself, ears deep in a book of some sort, while his brother Edric, a year his senior, was the paragon of congeniality and social grace.

"Hello, Kyra. Congratulations on your betrothal," Osmund said, giving a gentleman's bow. His words were deliberate and rehearsed, and he kept his eyes on the floor while he spoke. Kyra could never tell if Osmund had no interest in polite society or simply lacked the social graces to take part.

"Thank you, Osmund. And to what do we owe the pleasure of your extended visit?" Kyra asked.

"I'm here to study in the palace library. Rhinegard has one of the most extensive collections on the history of alchemy. I plan on writing a comparative analysis of various esoteric practices, such as alchemy, sagecraft..."

Kyra relaxed her shoulders but kept her courteous smile. If Osmund was going to be in the library, that meant she would be under no obligation to entertain him. *This boy can be such a bore*, she thought to herself. And was he still talking about his research? Why he thought she would care was baffling. Then she noticed a young woman a few paces behind him.

The woman was clearly a Shinda noblewoman, and by all the diamonds in her jewelry, not a wealthy one, at least by nobility standards. Diamonds were the poor woman's gem, completely lacking in color. Diamonds were also used in craftsman tools due to their superior hardness, and no self-respecting noblewoman wanted to be adorned in a craftsman's tool if she could help it.

The Shinda woman stared at Kyra's dress with envious eyes. Kyra's eyes met the woman's and immediately the woman looked away. That made thirty-three stolen glances. Kyra's smile became genuine.

She was suddenly aware of the silence in their conversation. "How truly fascinating, Osmund. I look forward to reading what you discover."

Osmund wilted. Kyra didn't bother to sort out the reason; she would never understand him. Osmund simply nodded and took a step back.

"Congratulations again, Lady Kyra," Lord Baylor said with a bow.

***

Osmund followed his parents away from the High Table to sit among the rest of the nobility. The Baylors fell somewhere in the middle of the Great Hall's hierarchy of honorable seating, inferior to those against the steps leading to the High Table yet superior to those seated in the back near the great doors. It was as high as a Devonian could hope for at a Cavander banquet.

The man across the table from Osmund was dressed in formal Cavander military regalia, a colonel based on the knots on his shoulders. His hands quivered ever so slightly, not enough to keep him from eating, but enough to be a burden. It was the war shakes. Osmund had read about the condition in medical texts. Men who had seen too much war never truly came home.

Osmund began silently listing off facts about the war shakes and other related maladies, as he often did when he felt out of place. While doing so, he looked to the High Table again. Kyra was the most beautiful woman in the kingdom; this was an undisputed fact by all who had seen her. And the Prince was the only eligible man more impressive than his elder brother, Edric.

Seated at the center of the High Table, in a chair a full foot taller than the others, was King Byron. When Osmund had walked past them, he had noted the Fang of Rhinegard, the ancient sword of Cavander kings, affixed to the King's belt. Osmund switched from recounting medical facts to historical ones.

Nearly 900 years ago, Cavan Kohel had worn the Fang in a military campaign unlike any the world had ever seen before or since. It began when an alchemist of the Kohel tribe devised a way to combine iron and charcoal into a revolutionary metal he called "steel". Where iron was heavy and brittle and bronze was expensive and soft, steel was strong, light, and cheap. Armed with steel weapons and armor, Cavan Kohel led an army that would subdue every land and tribe in Iria. It came to be known as the Great Conquest of Iria, and the people had even come to reckon their time by the year it began. Although Cavan Kohel's unified kingdom had not endured a generation after his death, the Fang of Rhinegard had continued at the side of every king of Cavandel since.

Servants hastened in and out of the banquet hall carrying the finest dishes that Cavander cuisine had to offer. One particularly cross old man in garb like a peacock, a Lanian by the look of him, lost his patience with a servant who failed to bring the precise vintage of wine he had demanded. He shoved the servant, sending him crashing to the stone floor behind Osmund. The sound of the fallen platter and the shattering of the wine bottle reverberated throughout the Great Hall.

Osmund looked at the fallen servant with pity. The nobility made it an un-spoken pastime to see who could make the most sophisticated demands of the servants, with extra points given to those who did so in the most pompous of ways. Osmund wouldn't go so far as to say that a commoner should be treated equal to a noble. That would be absurd, but he did believe that a nobleman should act nobly in his treatment of the common man. After all, had it not been the nobility of their character that earned them the name *nobleman* in the first place?

He leaned forward, about to help the servant to his feet, then he felt the eyes of his father upon him. He looked back to see his father glaring at him, disappointment beaming from his eyes. Lord Baylor was an acidic man that could wilt a rose with a single look. Osmund stared back at his plate and waited for the moment to pass.

***

Kyra sighed relief when the parade of well-wishers finally ended, leaving her to enjoy the evening's music and revelry. Representatives from each kingdom presented gifts to the royal couple while performers entertained with songs and heroic stories of Prince Aedon's ancestry. Kyra skillfully hid her disappointment that the attention was mostly on Aedon.

Drink was abundant. Flagons of wine and ale never saw their bottom before a servant replaced them. The progression of the evening could be measured by the drunkenness of the men in the hall. Decorum was slowly replaced by levity, especially among the Vangorians, who had little decorum to begin with.

Despite the drunkenness of the crowd, all became perfectly silent when the King of Cavandel stood to address them. He was a barrel-chested man with large hands and a salt-and-pepper beard. One hand held an oversized golden goblet of wine; the other hand gripped the hilt of the Fang of Rhinegard.

"My lords and ladies," King Byron bellowed. "We are here today to celebrate the impending marriage of my son, Aedon, to Lady Kyra Arturri of Devona. I recall with great fondness the day Prince Aedon was born, and what a blessed day it was for myself and for the kingdom. No father could be prouder of the man his son has become than I am of the young man who sits before you.

"And now, before you all, I, King Byron, son of King Walden of the House of Braise, Ruler of the Kingdom of Cavandel and all its protectorates, do here and now name my son, Prince Aedon, Master and Commander of the Royal Guard." A modest applause came from the assembly.

The King raised his goblet high in the air and declared, "to Prince Aedon and Lady Kyra!" The congregation raised their goblets and repeated the words.

How true the King's words were, Kyra thought. Aedon would be a mighty King, far greater than his father had been.

When the King sat, Aedon stood to speak. Most said Aedon was the spitting image of his father, but Kyra noted several distinctions. Aedon was taller than his father, by less than an inch, but still taller. He was clean-shaven where his father wore a ducktail beard; dressed fashionably where his father insisted on wearing a gaudy fur cape whenever occasion permitted. Leaner than his father, he lacked King Byron's signature barrel chest. But the most important difference was the eyes, a misty gray against his father's rustic hazel.

"My lords and ladies," Aedon began. "Under my command, we shall expand the Royal Guard and the City Watch, both in size and authority. With this expansion will come increased security and prosperity in Rhinegard, especially in our ports and places of commerce. To facilitate this expansion, I shall host a grand tournament. All those who advance beyond the second round of combat will be appointed to the Royal Guard. I mean to make Rhinegard the safest city in all of Iria."

The crowd applauded, purely out of obligation.

The Prince continued. "It is also my burden to announce that Lord Menden, who has served my father faithfully as First Officer of the Royal Guard for many years, has elected to retire with this changing of the guard. Few men in history have served the Kingdom as valiantly as Astor Menden. We are all the beneficiaries of his many years of unparalleled leadership. To Lord Astor Menden!"

The congregation lifted their goblets with the Prince and saluted the aged warrior. Some even banged their goblets and tankards on the table. Lord Menden, who stood in uniform behind the King, gave a gracious nod.

"And so, to replace Lord Menden, if it be possible to replace such a man, I have decided that the position of First Officer will be filled by the victor of the grand tournament."

At this, the Great Hall erupted with approval. The potential to win such a prestigious position gave this tournament real stakes rarely seen, and their enthusiasm was undoubtedly bolstered by the night's steady flow of ale and wine. Aedon's grin spread ear to ear.

"The tournament shall begin three weeks hence, on the 46th Day of Spring. We have already dispatched riders far and abroad. I will have Iria's greatest warrior for my First Officer."

The crowd continued to applaud as Aedon sat down. He looked over to his bride, who gleamed back at him and smiled.

He was hers, Kyra thought, and she was his.

Chapter Three

The Flying Manta

30th Day of Spring, 897 G.C.

"**K**ailem. *Kailem*. Awake, little brother. Our shift is starting."

For three weeks, the brothers had worked aboard *The Flying Manta*, a merchant schooner sailing between Barrowfort and Rhinegard. Kailem was so accustomed to sleeping in a hammock swaying with the sea that a shake to the shoulder hardly roused him.

"Just a few more minutes," Kailem said. He pulled his blanket to his chin and rolled away from his brother.

It was the eleventh week of their exile, and Kailem still relived his parents' execution every night. Recently, the dreams ended with Kailem wrestling away the executioner's sword and using it to cut off Vanua's head, and every morning, the memory of what had truly happened returned. The one bright spot was that he no longer awoke screaming. That had not gone over well with the crew.

Mokain lightly shook Kailem's shoulder again. "Come on," he whispered. "The sooner we start, the sooner we'll finish."

Kailem opened his eyes. It stung to hear one of their father's favorite sayings, and that sting was made even sharper by how similar Mokain's voice was to their father's, but it was a good sting. It kept part of their father alive somehow.

Something inside each of them had broken that day. And how could it not, having watched their parents falsely accused and beheaded before them? And they *were* falsely accused, neither of the brothers would entertain any notion to the contrary.

After Lord Vanua declared their exile, he had ordered the guards to take the brothers straight to the docks. The guards defied that order, instead allowing the brothers to first return home and retrieve some precious few belongings. The guards allowed them only as much as they could carry, which meant their Culmination Blades, some extra clothing, their largest coin pouches filled to the brim, and a few family heirlooms.

The brothers should have spent the voyage north confined to the brig, but their guards again had broken protocol and allowed them to walk the deck freely as they sailed. That day they had stood side-by-side on the stern as Suvara diminished in the distance, finally sinking under the horizon. Once they reached the Marcônish shore, the brothers disembarked as vagabonds, never to see home again.

Their first weeks as exiles were a low and dreary time for the Roka brothers, and I would not sully the honor of these great men with an unnecessary degree of detail regarding their darkest moments. I myself was shocked to learn of them, having been raised hearing only the stories of their greatness. Suffice it to say, they spent two months wandering from town to town. Most nights were spent at taverns drowning every memory, good and bad, in a river of lager and spirits and brawling with fellow tavern patrons. It wasn't long before they had spent every coin they had.

It was Mokain who finally came to his senses. He first put down his own tankard, which was no easy task, but it proved an even greater challenge for Kailem. Deprived of his sedative, thoughts of his parents invaded Kailem's mind. Never again would he hear his father's boisterous laugh or his many pearls of wisdom. Never again would his Amma sing to herself as she dressed her hair or watch, smiling as Kailem took his first bite of a meal she had prepared for him.

In these, his lowest moments, the memory of his parents' murder would return in vivid detail, a waking nightmare in the truest sense. He relived the sight of the executioner's blade, saw it pierce skin, sever bone, and spill blood.

Kailem screamed. He writhed upon the ground, begging for the escape only the drink could provide, but Mokain's resolve was unfailing. Eventually — and I shall not specify how long — Kailem learned to bear this burden sober. Let this be all that is said on the matter.

Having returned to themselves, the brothers bathed, sold their family heirlooms, and made their way east to the port city of Barrowfort. There, they hired on as sailors for the shipping company Cato & Sons. It had been difficult to find a captain willing to take on two foreigners with a dubious past, that was until they met Captain Gilroy. As a boy, the captain had seen the Mariner navy in action, so he jumped at the chance to add two Mariners to his crew. The brothers had worked aboard *The Flying Manta* ever since.

It was still dark when they stepped onto the main deck. Mokain's yawn proved contagious, and Kailem stretched out his arms to shake off his lingering sleep. A gruff sailor named Gregor rammed his shoulder into Mokain's as he walked by. Kailem clenched his fists and stepped towards him, but Mokain put his hand up to stop him.

The sailors on deck worked by the light of oil lamps, the stars, and two waxing moons. The greater moon with a yellow tint, called "Koa" in the Marin Islands, was half full, while the lesser moon of pure white, 'Tao' it was called, was only a quarter full. In the eastern kingdoms, they simply called them the gilded moon and the silver moon, respectively.

Mokain was assigned to crow's nest duty that morning, watching for hazards and enemy ships. Pirate ships were prevalent in the Cerulean Sea. Unfortunately, Gregor had the same assignment. Gregor was already ten feet up the shroud of the foremast before Mokain began to climb, yet Mokain reached the crow's nest first. He extended a hand to the old sailor, which Gregor smacked away.

"Enough of this, Gregor. I've suffered your hectoring for weeks now. What have you against me? I've done nothing to you."

Gregor stepped within inches of Mokain's face. "I'll tell ye what me problem be. Fer one, ye'r a sarding foreigner," he said with a scowl. "E'ryone on this ship be Cavander 'cept for ye and that brother a yers. Ye don't belong here." Gregor's muddled accent and appalling grammar were typical among sailors. He jammed his finger into Mokain's chest, then spat on the wooden boards at their feet.

"Second, ye'r taking posts that others ha' worked years for. Ye come aboard and the first day the cap'n makes ye a shipmate. I were a swab fer two years before I was made a shipmate. See Little Jay down there? He be a cabin boy fer o'r a year now."

"So, you hate me 'cause you reckon I ought to be a cabin boy? Gregor, I'm twenty-seven," Mokain said.

Gregor waved his hand. "The point be ye don't deserve to be a shipmate. Ye didn't earn it."

"Well, the Captain disagrees with you. Probably because my brother and I do the same amount of work it takes five of you swillbellies to do."

Gregor balled his fist, but Mokain stared him in the eye until the gruff sailor thought better of it. "Ye just watch out the starboard side and I'll take the port."

"Agreed," Mokain said. The two men walked to opposite sides of the crow's nest, neither completely turning his back on the other.

In the distance, grey clouds gathered on the eastern horizon. Mokain and Gregor both took concern. The clouds gathered slowly and were far in the distance, not worthy of raising the alarm just yet. Still, Gregor reached under his sweater and removed a necklace with a red stone disc at the end of it. Mokain recognized the amulet of protection, a palm-sized jasper gemstone polished and engraved with interlocking designs, carved by an alchemist and meant to keep its bearer safe during storms, fires, and floods. Sailors were a superstitious lot, even more so than the average commoner. Gregor stared at the darkening clouds and rubbed the crimson gemstone with his thumb.

Kailem was assigned to the top rigging. He climbed the mainmast and joined several sailors who were unfurling the mainsail to adjust to the changing wind speeds. The men all whistled and sang the familiar tune of *'How Long 'Til We Weigh Anchor?'* while they worked:

There once was a lady of the harbor, see,
And she held the eye of a sailor, three.
All bent the knee and his love decreed,
But a farmer wed did she.
Such be the life of a sailor, see,
There be none who know this better than me
Take me back where the wind blows free,
How long 'til we weigh anchor?
There once was a wife of a sailor, see,
And a greater beauty there could not be,
On leave he 'turned to his home with glee
But he found that home wast empty.
Such be the life of a sailor, see,
There be none who know this better than

me,
Take me back where the wind blows free
How long 'til we weigh anchor?

Kailem was grateful for the singing. Not only did it keep anyone from bothering him with their gibes, or worse, but it also swept the day along nicely. It was cold on the rigging, and the occasional gust of wind cut through him with icy malice. It made him long for the warmth and sunshine of the Marin Islands, for his life before that terrible day. But he'd never see his home again, and after what his people had done, he wasn't sure he'd ever want to.

With the sails set, Kailem climbed down to the main deck. Quartermaster Stel took him aside and tasked him with securing a loose jib sail at the front of the ship. The Quartermaster always gave Kailem the most dangerous jobs, a typical form of sailor's hazing. At first, it was because no one but the Captain liked him, but eventually the Quartermaster realized Kailem was a better sailor than any other shipmate in their crew. Unfortunately, the more dangerous assignments didn't earn him any extra pay.

Kailem crawled over the jib boom while the ocean rushed and sloshed underneath him. He locked his ankles underneath the boom and gripped the wooden pole with his thighs while he tied the jib sheet in a lark's head knot, just as his father had taught him. The spray of the ocean splashed against his feet as he worked, soaking his canvas trousers. Several times, the sea forced him to pause his work and cleave to the jib boom as the ship crested and fell over another swell.

With the jib sail secured, Kailem returned to the deck and wiped away the salt and sea spray that had crusted on his eyebrows and eyelashes. He spent the rest of their shift doing safety checks throughout the ship. When the bell signaled a shift change, Mokain climbed down from the crow's nest. Gregor climbed down as well, but his foot became tangled in the shroud; Mokain left him there to untangle it on his own. Captain Gilroy was on deck drinking his morning coffee while his First Mate gave him the morning report.

"Rokas, c'mere," the Quartermaster called. The brothers trotted up to the stout old man. "We be nearin' Rhinegard Harbor, boys. Should be there within a pair of hours. I'll be takin' my leave, be spendin' time with me youngans, so the Cap'n'll be needin' a new Quartermaster for the return. Gonna be needin' a new pilot as well. I recommended the two of youse and the Cap'n agreed. So? What say ye? Be interested?"

The brothers shared a series of glances that conveyed a full conversation on the matter, then turned back to the Quartermaster.

"We serve at the Captain's pleasure," Mokain said.

"Ah, na wonda the Cap'n fancies ye. I'll tell 'em he has his men."

Mokain and Kailem stood on the forward deck, wrapped in hooded cloaks cut after the Mariner tradition, down to their knees and open down the sides. They rested their elbows on the railing, their wavy hair swaying in the breeze, and took in the coastline as *The Flying Manta* sailed through the Cerulean Sea.

The southern end of the Devonian coastline had been covered in a dense forest, but as they had sailed farther north, that forest grew sparse and thin. By the time they crossed into Cavandel, the coastline was nothing but grass and stone. Limestone cliffs lined the beaches looking like a giant had cut the hills in half many eons ago and the ocean had rushed in to fill the space.

Within two hours, just as Quartermaster Stel predicted, *The Flying Manta* sailed into Rhinegard Harbor. Mokain and Kailem watched wide-eyed and awestruck as the capital of Cavandel came into view. The city continued in all directions without an end in sight, with towers that clawed at the clouds.

"I didn't know men could build cities this big," Mokain admitted. All Kailem could do was nod in agreement.

The tallest building in the Marin Islands had been the Royal Palace; it stood a mere three stories. Until today, it had been the largest building either Roka had ever seen. Now Kailem could spot a dozen buildings taller than the Royal Palace, and only part of the city was yet in view.

The Rokas descended the gangway with newly paid metal coins clanking in their pockets. The afternoon air was cold and humid, despite the sunny skies, and a salty breeze blew in from the sea. Sailors covered the dock, loading and unloading their vessels, and a dozen more docks just as crowded lined the harbor.

They passed Norvian sailors unloading bear skins and moose pelts, Lanian sailors carrying rolls of fine textiles, and Vangorian sailors carrying barrels of whale oil. No one could help but bump into each other. They reminded Kailem of sea lions fighting for space on an ocean boulder.

"Do you smell that?" Kailem asked.

Mokain sniffed the air and nodded. The city had a strange bouquet of foreign smells that the brothers couldn't distinguish, so all the scents mingled into a uniquely "Rhinegard" smell.

The longest and widest street in all of Rhinegard was the King's Ascent, a road leading from the harbor to the palace gates. It was the fastest, safest, and most practical route to the Royal Palace, and therefore was frequently traveled by wealthy noblemen and foreign dignitaries. The elevated stature of its commuters lent a high value to property along the road.

Despite its breadth, the King's Ascent was somehow even more crowded than the docks. Wooden booths lined the cobbled road where peasants bartered goods or sold them for coin.

"I never realized we were from a small town," Kailem said, taking it all in. Every few steps, another peasant thrust their wares in the brothers' faces. A basket of fruit, then sweaters and scarves, followed by fresh flowers and cloves of garlic.

A thin, disheveled girl in tattered clothes raced through the crowd like a fish swimming upstream. Her hair was a knotted mess the color of rotting carrots. She ran into Kailem's chest and would have fallen to the ground had he not caught her.

For the briefest second, she looked him in the eye. Her skin was pale as fresh cream, with the faintest sprinkling of freckles across her nose and cheeks, and her eyes were greener and brighter than wild clovers. There was panic in those eyes; Kailem saw it only for a moment, then she was gone, disappearing into the crowd.

A step behind her were three guards with the City Watch, shoving people aside like bears tromping through a mountain creek. The brothers stepped aside and watched as the chase continued out of view. The bustling crowd went back to their business as if nothing had happened. Mokain looked to Kailem, and they both shrugged and laughed.

Farther down the road, waves of heat assailed them from within a blacksmith's shop. The small room erupted with the smell of burning coal and the sound of a hammer on metal. A nearby apothecary shop filled with every kind of medicinal brew and alchemical elixir gave off a bitter, pungent smell. Outside a brothel, women in silk dresses with necklines plunging low on their bosoms called out to the brothers with sultry invitations.

Then there were the beggars. Miserable wretches sitting at the margins of the street with hands held out and heads hung down. One particularly pitiful man was more vigorous with his beggary; he went from person to person pleading for alms, nearly in tears. Within seconds, a guard with the City Watch shoved the beggar to the ground. The guard kicked the poor man as he tried to stand, then kicked him a second time, then a third, until the beggar finally managed to scamper off. The crowd didn't miss a beat.

Kailem met the eye of a young orphan. The boy couldn't have been more than ten years old, and that was being generous. His face was sallow, devoid of life and hope, his blank eyes staring forward. Kailem couldn't bear it. He reached into his coin pouch and placed a copper shilling in the young beggar's hand. The boy clutched it close against his chest.

The gesture caught the attention of every beggar on the street. A swarm of panhandlers surrounded them in an instant. The brothers had to push their way through the crowd until the swarm abandoned the chase.

"You just had to give him a shilling, didn't you?" Mokain chided.

"I know, I know. Sorry," Kailem said.

"Let's try this place," Mokain suggested. Kailem saw they had stopped in front of an inn with an adjacent tavern. A sign above the door read "The Weeping Wolf".

Leaving the cool Rhinegard air for the warmth of the tavern was like dropping ice into a boiling pot, and the brothers took off their heavy cloaks without delay. Wrought-iron chandeliers hung from the ceiling, bathing the tavern in yellow light. Long tables populated the center dining area, with smaller booths along the walls. Each booth had a pair of dividing walls for privacy. The brothers sat at a booth near the front.

"Youse from out of town, then?" asked a tavern maid. She was a middle-aged woman with greasy hair tied messily on the crown of her head.

"Are we that obvious?" Mokain asked with a smile.

"I'm afraid so, sweetness. I could tell from clear across the tavern, it's the hair that gives you away. Cavander men never wear their hair lower than their ears, and they certainly don't wear tunics with short sleeves. Not in Rhinegard, at least."

Before that moment, Mokain hadn't considered how peculiar they appeared. Most of the men in the tavern wore wool shirts with sleeves to the wrist and kept their hair short, many going so far as to shave it completely. The brothers stood out like sheep in a chicken coop.

"I guess we'll need some new clothes and a haircut then," Mokain said.

"Marcônish?" the tavern maid asked.

Mokain hid his confusion at her ridiculous guess and replied, "Marin Islands, actually." There were obvious differences between Mariners and the Marcônish; this tavern must not receive many Southerners.

"Ah! I've never met a Mariner before. Pleasure to meet you," she said with a grin. "So, how can I serve you boys?"

"I'll have a turkey leg, boiled potato, and a pint of your darkest ale."

"And for you, handsome?" she asked Kailem.

"Same, but swap out the potato for boiled carrots."

"With pleasure, back in a skip," she said with a wink.

Mokain reached across the table and congratulated his brother with a pat on his shoulder. Kailem rolled his eyes.

"I've been thinking about Vanua's accusation," Kailem said.

"You doubt they're innocent?" Mokain asked.

Kailem cocked his head and glared at him, then moved past the question. "Vanua said they found the note in Father's coat pocket, but Father wasn't wearing a coat when they arrested him," Kailem continued. "What I can't figure out is how they got those daggers, it's possible they—"

"Let's speak of other things," Mokain muttered.

Kailem was silent. For him, there was nothing else worth discussing, so he interlocked his fingers on the table and fiddled with his thumbs. At length, he asked, "Are you really going to cut your hair?"

Mokain ran his fingers through his dark, wavy hair. "It might be good to blend in a bit. We have enough trouble with the crew as it is." He took a handful of pine nuts from a bowl on the table.

Kailem looked around at the tavern patrons again. "Have you noticed how many carry weapons in here? And not just daggers and side-swords."

Mokain surveyed the tavern. Several men carried broadswords and battle axes. A few noblemen carried basket-hilted swords that had clearly never seen combat, and there was even a pair of Shinda warriors carrying scimitars.

The tavern maid placed two pewter mugs on the table, sloshing a bit of foam over the rim.

"Are your patrons always so well-armed?" Mokain asked.

She looked around and scrunched her chin. "I shouldn't say so. Not like this, anyhow. It's all for that tournament next week, innit?"

"Tournament?" Mokain asked with a perk in a voice.

The tavern maid nodded to a bulletin nailed to the adjacent wall. "The Prince is holdin' a grand tournament to celebrate... something or other, can't right remember now. He's offerin' quite a bit of gold to the victor though, isn't he? More than usual. But also, anyone that passes the second round is appointed Royal Guard, and the tournament champion will be the Prince's First Officer, so even men who are already on the guard are competin'. The bulletin there has all the particulars, if youse know how to read, of course."

"Interesting. Is the tournament open to anyone?" Mokain asked.

"I reckon so. Be that why so many foreigners have come. Right back with your food, then."

Kailem could see it in his brother's eyes; Mokain's mind was already set. "You're going to stay and compete, aren't you?" It was more a statement than a question. Mokain thought for a moment, then nodded.

"And what of avenging Amma and Father?" Kailem asked.

Mokain stared at the mug in his hand. "I've been thinking about that. I don't even know where to begin. Especially since we can't step foot on any of the islands without being thrown into prison. Plus, knowing Amma and Father, they would never wish us to spend our lives seeking vengeance. They'd tell us to go live and be happy."

Kailem's countenance darkened. "I'll be happy when Lord Vanua is dead, along with whoever helped frame them."

"Same," Mokain admitted solemnly. "I want to see Vanua's head on a spike, and I want every Mariner in Suvara to beg our forgiveness." Then Mokain took a deep, calming breath. "But remember what Father always said: living well is the best revenge."

Kailem knew his brother was right, as always, but he still needed Vanua dead.

"What do you think Amma's big announcement was going to be that night?" Kailem asked.

Mokain shook his head. "She never told me."

"Me neither. You know, half the people in that square were invited to her party," Kailem said. "They were supposed to be our friends."

His knuckles were again turning white against his pewter mug. Had the mug been made of glass or clay it would have shattered in his hand.

Mokain only nodded.

"So, living well for you is serving in the Royal Guard of Cavandel?" Kailem asked.

Mokain finished another pull of his ale. "I reckon it could be. Sailing, it's just not for me, Kailem. I trained my whole life to lead a combat unit. It's what I'm meant to do. This could be my chance to return to something familiar, to build a life for myself."

Kailem stared at the adjacent wall, his eyes unfocused.

"Why don't you stay and compete with me," Mokain suggested. He forced some cheer into his voice.

"I don't know, Moka. It sounds like the greatest fighters in Iria will be there. To leave a steady wage on the hope I can hold my own, that's quite a gamble."

Mokain shifted in his seat. "We don't have to win the whole tournament, though; we just need to survive the second round. Just imagine, the two of us serving in the Royal Guard together. How great would that be?"

The thought of it softened Kailem's stony posture. "That would be fun," he admitted.

"Ay, it would!" Mokain leaned forward. "We could make a name for ourselves, build a life here. And with a position in the Court, we'd probably meet people who could find who framed Amma and Father."

Kailem smiled, lost in the fantasy his brother had painted. But the smile soon faded. He shook his head. "It would never work, Moka. I like combat less than you like sailing; I'd be miserable in the Royal Guard. I... I have to stay with the ship." He fixed his eyes on the table. "I'm really going to miss you, though. I don't know if I would have survived the last few months without you."

Mokain was stung with guilt.

"So, you're going to stay a sailor?" Mokain asked. "Is that what you truly want?"

"It's the best option I can see. If the Captain makes me Quartermaster on this next voyage, it might not be long before I have my own ship."

"And you'd be happy living the life of a sea captain?"

Kailem shrugged. "I'm sure father would be proud if he knew I had command of a ship."

"Yeah, he probably would. Do you remember when he brought Lord and Lady Tasal home for dinner and had him explain how lucrative the spice industry was becoming?"

Kailem winced. "That was too awkward. Subtlety was never father's strong suit."

"Lord Tasal almost had you convinced, though."

"No, Lord Tasal's daughter almost had me convinced. Do you remember Maia? She was practically throwing herself at me."

"You didn't seem to mind."

"Didn't mind in the slightest." Kailem took another pull of ale and smiled. Those were happy times. Then he remembered seeing Lord and Lady Tasal, and Maia, in the crowd, screaming for his parents' execution. The memory soured.

The tavern maid placed their food on the table. "Here you are, my big strapping men." She looked directly at Kailem. "Now you just let me know if there's anything else I can do for you." She left with a wink, her hips swaying as she walked.

Kailem's eyes were the size of lemons. Mokain let out a boisterous laugh. Kailem would miss that laugh.

After supper, Mokain reserved a room with a single bed in the inn above the tavern. Kailem donated a portion of his wages, over Mokain's objections, insisting his brother's need was greater. The brothers found a clothing shop on the King's Ascent and purchased wool sweaters to replace their Mariner cloaks. Then Mokain had his hair cut short. When the barber handed him a looking glass to see the result, he grimaced.

"You look like an eel," Kailem teased. Mokain answered with a swift punch to the shoulder, which only made Kailem laugh harder. Mokain rubbed the back of his head the rest of the night.

When they returned to the ship, they shared Mokain's plan with Captain Gilroy. The old sailor tried every way imaginable to convince Mokain to stay, but it was all in vain. Kailem took the Quartermaster position, which came with a substantial pay raise.

Kailem followed his brother below deck while Mokain gathered his personal effects, which consisted of a coin pouch, a journal, his new sweater, and his prized possessions: his Culmination Blades. They were twin leaf-bladed swords, as elegant and agile as they were deadly. From point to pommel was the length of his arm, shoulder to wrist. They were shorter than any side-sword, but he preferred to fight in close quarters. He had named them Tao and Koa after the Old Marin names for the moons.

The brothers embraced at the top of the gangway.

"I'll come find you the next time we dock in Rhinegard," Kailem promised. "We should dock here every six weeks or so. We'll see each other plenty."

"Perfect, you can come find me at the palace guarding the King."

Kailem laughed with him. They passed a moment in silence, and Mokain saw the pain in his brother's eyes.

"You'll be okay, Kailem. You're a Mariner, and a Roka. You can do anything."

"You too," was all Kailem could manage in return.

Kailem's heart wrenched as he watched Mokain descend the gangway and cross the docks, leaving him alone on deck. At the end of the docks, Mokain turned and gave a final wave. Kailem waved back, and Mokain disappeared into the crowd.

Kailem had never felt more alone than he did in that moment.

Alone on the quarterdeck, Kailem's thoughts returned to his parents. What he wouldn't then give to go into business with his father. It seemed impossible he ever turned down the option to work daily at his father's side. He reasoned that if he could captain his own ship and become a merchant like his father, he could honor his father's memory.

How could it be that his last interaction with his father was shoving him to the ground, he wondered? He thought of all he wished he had said to him. If he could have returned to that day, he would have apologized immediately and begged his father's forgiveness. He would have told him what a wonderful father he was and how much he respected him, how he valued his father's wisdom and treasured all his many aphorisms. Kailem yearned to say it now, but his father was gone, and what good would it do to talk to the wind?

He reached under his collar and removed the silver pearl he had found that fateful morning. He had meant to turn it into a ring for his mother; instead, he fashioned it into a necklace with a thin leather strap. He had imagined giving it to her at the party that night. She would have immediately put it on, held it out for inspection, then put her hand on display for all to see. She would have clasped both of his cheeks, kissed his forehead as if he were still a child, told him how much she loved him, and reminded him that finding a pearl was a good omen. Something good was surely coming his way.

Instead, he had seen his mother's head cut from her neck.

He recalled the sound her head had made when it fell, the unbalanced way it rolled down the palace steps. Then he realized he'd just referred to his mother's head in his mind as an 'it.' A vile taste formed in his mouth.

His father was fond of saying, "some of our greatest fortunes at first seem like tragedies. You need only let time reveal the good in them."

But his father was dead. What good would ever come from that?

He tucked the pearl back under his shirt and went below deck.

CHAPTER FOUR

THE FUTURE QUEEN

31st Day of Spring, 897 G.C.

Kyra woke to the sun already well above the horizon. With her glass balcony doors shut and the fireplace still smoldering, her quarters were toasty and soothing. Ember, her pet fox, was still asleep at her feet. How odd she thought it was that Cavanders kept dogs instead of foxes. Dogs were such deplorable creatures, what with all their barking and drooling and rough housing, even the best of them were unfit for polite society. Foxes were far more regal.

She moved off her four-post bed and slid open the balcony doors, letting the cold Cavander air flood her room. Ember woke to the cold and squeaked out her disapproval, but Kyra ignored the fox. It was refreshing to stand there in her nightgown, letting the chill air wash over her.

The royal palace stood atop Palace Hill, the tallest peak within the city walls. From here, Kyra could see Rhinegard Harbor and the entire southern half of the city. The second tallest hill was at the southernmost edge of the city, Meager Hill, they called it, atop of which sat the King's Arena where Prince Aedon would soon hold his tournament.

The buildings in Rhinegard were peculiar from those in her native Devona. Back home, where forests abound, they constructed homes almost entirely of timber, all save for the very elite who built with stone. In Cavandel, however, timber was a scarce commodity. "The Rocky Plains" the region was called, and thus even the commoners built with gray sandstone and thatched roofs, all save for the very poor who built with mud bricks. From high on her balcony, the dark thatch stood out from the gray stone like freckles on the city. Kyra had fallen in love with this ancient, magnificent city, and soon it would all be hers.

"Your ladyship, the cold will make you ill!" a woman called.

Kyra turned to see her handmaiden, Martina, carrying new logs for the fire. Martina had been Kyra's handmaiden since Kyra came of age.

"You worry too much, Martina," Kyra said. "Sometimes a little cold air is just what the body needs."

"I don't know about that, but as you wish, your ladyship. I'll build a fire, all the same." Martina bent down next to the hearth and constructed a new fire over the smoldering coals. Ember leaped from the bed and rubbed against Martina — a thank you for the fire — then curled up in front of the hearth. Her fur coat was the same vibrant orange as the flames crackling beside her.

"Your parents sent me with a word, your ladyship. They wish for you to join them in the palace gardens for a luncheon."

Kyra exhaled and watched her breath turn to mist. "Very well, then." She turned her eyes from the balcony's panoramic view of the city and slipped off her nightgown. "I'll wear the blue gown, I think. It will match this cold Cavander morning."

"Excellent choice, milady." With the fire started, Martina went to the wardrobe to fetch the dress and undergarments.

As Martina helped slide Kyra's undergarments over her head, Prince Aedon walked in unannounced. Kyra's heart swelled. In his formal military uniform, one would think he could command the world with a snap of his fingers.

Kyra's parents had arranged this marriage before Kyra was old enough to speak, and she could scarcely believe it was finally happening. With the marriage announced and the wedding date set for the First Day of Autumn, she was now a permanent resident of the palace. And above all, she was actually in love with her intended. It was all so close she could taste it, and it was truly delectable.

Kyra noticed Aedon admiring the outline of her figure visible through the sheer fabric and her arms shot up to cover herself.

"My Prince, how dare you barge in here like this! I am not decent!" Kyra exclaimed. Martina scrambled to hold up a sheet and cover her lady.

Aedon lay down on Kyra's bed with his hands behind his head. "You have nothing to cover, my bride, that I haven't seen before."

Although Kyra had yet to give herself fully to the Prince, they were never timid in their affection. Kyra grinned as she crossed the room.

"Your 'bride', am I? I like the sound of that." She tossed her hair to the side and leaned down to kiss her prince. The First Day of Autumn could not come soon enough.

Martina averted her eyes, unsure how to react. Aedon held Kyra close as they kissed. Such passion was entirely improper. Kyra ought to be reprimanded, but Martina dared not be the one to do it. She took a silent step back, just to be safe.

Kyra pulled away and returned to Martina's side. "Continue," she instructed. Martina slid her lady's blue gown over her head and began lacing up the back.

"And to what do I owe your visit this morning, Aedon?" Kyra asked. Ember leaped back on the bed and crawled on Aedon's chest to solicit some ear rubs.

"I wanted to make sure you were taken care of today. I'll be preparing for the tournament most of the day, so I'm afraid I'll be unavailable." Aedon continued petting the fox while Kyra sat for Martina to comb her raven black hair.

"You're too sweet, my Prince, but I assure you, I can survive a day without you there looking after me. I'm having lunch with my parents in the garden, then I'm playing cards with some ladies from the Court this afternoon. Softer, Martina."

"Yes, milady," Martina replied, although she wasn't sure how she could comb any softer. There hadn't been a single pull on Kyra's hair, so she slowed her strokes just to be safe.

"And how are the ladies at Court treating you?" Aedon asked as he scratched Ember's chin.

"We all get on splendidly; in no time at all, we'll become bosom friends," she said. The truth was, she intimidated most of the ladies at Court. Their relationship was less a friendship and more like the crocodile who allows the birds to pick its teeth. It felt more natural to Kyra that way.

"Treating you like anything less than their future Queen is unacceptable," Aedon declared.

"Mmm, Queen Kyra. I like the sound of that as well," Kyra said. She gave him a smoldering look through the reflection in her vanity mirror.

Aedon stood from the bed. "As well you should; it suits you." He leaned down to kiss the top of her head.

"Take good care of her, Martina," Aedon said. Then he patted Martina's backside. Martina froze. Her eyes darted to her lady's reflection in the mirror, looking to know how to respond. Kyra wore an amused grin, so Martina continued brushing.

The walk from her quarters to the palace gardens was a pleasant one. The palace was ancient. Every square inch of the grounds was carved and painted with meticulous detail, from the tiles she walked on to the ceiling frescos above her. Everything was gilded, or silver-plated, or jewel encrusted. But she had come of age with such luxuries at home, albeit not quite so extravagant, so the opulence of the palace did little to impress her.

No, what truly made her walk a delight were the people she encountered, or rather the deference they paid her. Everywhere she went, staff and nobles alike stepped aside and bowed as she passed. She saw more than one woman wearing a poor imitation of her gown from the betrothal feast.

Well, that didn't take long, she thought. Fortunately, she already had several ideas for new designs that would keep her ahead of the trend.

Kyra met the King while passing through the Grand Corridor, his usual entourage of servants, advisors, and sycophants close by.

"Your Majesty," Kyra said with a curtesy. Byron returned a bow, then clasped her shoulders and kissed her cheek.

"You've created quite the stir in my Court, Lady Kyra," Byron noted.

Kyra tilted her head.

"The dresses, my dear. I fear that with you here, fashion in Cavandel will never be the same. You have quite the eye for style."

Kyra blushed. "Thank you, Your Majesty. If it pleases you, I could turn my eye on that cape of yours."

Byron adjusted the cape on his shoulders. "I am certain nothing should please me less, my dear. I look far too dashing in it, and a fur cape will never be out of fashion." Byron stood tall and raised his chin, posing like his portrait that hung nearby.

"If you say so, Your Majesty," Kyra teased. "I was just on my way to luncheon with my parents."

"Well then, I shan't keep you any longer. Give your parents my love." The two exchanged a formal bow and curtesy and Kyra excused herself to the gardens.

A table had been prepared under a gazebo in a secluded corner of the garden surrounded by blossoming cherry trees and multicolored hydrangeas. Vines of jasmine grew up and around the gazebo and sprouted fragrant white flowers.

Serving towers filled the center of the table with fruit tarts, soft cheeses, and Norvian langoustines wrapped in smoked salmon. Trays of butter and various flavors of marmalade surrounded a fresh loaf of bread.

Her parents, Leonin and Avalina, already sat at the table. Leonin was a tall, gangly man with a hawkish nose, whereas Avalina was on the shorter side and as curvy as a noblewoman could grow before she might properly be called "plump". They waited in silence for the servants to finish setting the food and for their daughter to arrive.

"Welcome, Kyra, have a seat," her father instructed. Neither of her parents stood when she approached, and they said nothing further while the servants filled her wine goblet. The servants then took two steps back from the table to await further instructions.

"Leave us," Leonin instructed. The servants frowned at each other. It was their duty to remain by the Lordship's side throughout the luncheon, waiting at his beck and call. They looked to Avalina, who confirmed the order with a wave of her fingers.

"How is our prince doing this morning?" Avalina asked once she was sure they were alone. Kyra selected a fruit tart from the serving tower.

"Brilliant to the point of perfection," she said. She couldn't have hidden the glee in her voice if she had tried.

"You know what we ask, Kyra," Leonin said in a low voice. "What is his stance on peace with neighboring kingdoms?"

Kyra set down her fruit tart. "We haven't discussed it. There hasn't been a good time yet," she confessed.

"Kyra," her father said flatly, setting down his wine. "You cannot possibly conceive the extent to which we have invested in this plan. We have operatives working in every corner of Iria. We have teams of alchemists developing new weapons. You think it's a simple task coordinating so many men and women across so vast a land? And all we've asked of you is to steer the Prince in the right direction."

They had people working outside the kingdom, Kyra thought? And what did he mean by "operatives"? She realized just how little she knew of their plans, and frankly, she didn't want to know. She told herself it was because the less she knew, the less they could force her to participate, but deep down, she knew that made as much sense as when children shut their eyes and think their parents can't see them. No, the true reason, which she would never admit to herself, was that she knew it was an ugly business her parents engaged in, and she had no stomach for ugly things.

"What does it matter?" Kyra said. "He's not the king yet." She spread a thin streak of butter on a slice of bread, wishing the servants were still here to do it for her.

"King Byron is proving to be even more stubborn than we expected. I reckon it will take the Prince joining our side to sway him," Leonin explained.

"Then I will make sure he does," Kyra promised, "but it will take time. It may rouse suspicion if I broach the subject without a cause."

"I don't think you appreciate the urgency of the situation, my dear," Avalina said. Her words were unusually cold and without affection. "Our plans leave us exposed. The longer we wait, the greater the odds we will be caught. If they catch us, they will certainly execute your father and I for treason. You will either be executed or sentenced to rot your life away in a dank prison cell. The best you could hope for is to be exiled into a life of poverty. Either way, marriage to your beloved prince would be out of the question."

Kyra put down her slice of bread.

Avalina continued. "In case I'm not being sufficiently clear, let me simplify it for you. Your marriage, your life, and the fate of our house all depend on the Prince opposing any peace agreement at the next council meeting. Understood?"

Kyra nodded.

"And we can count on you to make this happen?" Leonin asked.

Kyra nodded again.

"Good," he said.

"It is a fine line you must walk, Kyra," Avalina said. "You need to build the Prince's confidence so that he feels no need to listen to anyone else's council, but you also need him completely dependent on *your* council."

"It's a line that only a woman can walk," Leonin added. "Understood?"

"Yes, father," Kyra said. Her head was down, looking at nothing in particular.

A rustling sound came from the path to the gazebo. Kyra and her parents turned to see a small servant girl with a tray of canapes standing close enough to have been listening. She couldn't have been more than fifteen years old, with curly blonde hair and a dense constellation of freckles splattered across her nose and cheeks. The poor girl was terrified, and she slowly turned to leave.

"No, no. Come here, child, it's quite alright, I assure you," Avalina said in her sweetest motherly voice. Lady Arturri never spoke a word that wasn't first dipped in honey, at least not in public, anyway. This was the mask she presented to the world. The frightened girl inched towards their table.

"What is this you've so kindly brought us?" Avalina asked.

"Ca... canapes, milady, with pork belly and ap... apple glaze," the girl said.

"Ah yes, one of my favorites. I request this dish at every luncheon, in fact. Thank you for bringing it to us. You clearly perform your duties well. And what is your name, my darling?"

"Kris, milady," the servant girl said.

"Kris, what a lovely name. Beautiful in its simplicity. We took a similar approach when we named our daughter 'Kyra'. You must have wonderful parents."

"They are both gone, milady. Taken by the blue fever," Kris explained. She had yet to make eye contact with anyone at the table.

Avalina brought her hand to her chest. "Oh, you poor thing. Well, as long as I'm in this palace, I'll see that you are cared for. Every girl needs a mother in life. How does that sound, child? To have the mother of the princess looking after you?"

"Goo... good, milady." Kris smiled but continued to stare at her feet.

"Very good. Now, I have a special task for you, my dear. Will you do it for me?"

"Of course, milady."

"Such a wise young girl, I can see we will be fast friends. The task is a simple one, but one of great importance to me. Do you know where our quarters are? Near the top of the West Tower?"

Kris nodded.

"Well, our floors have not been scrubbed in quite some time, and that is entirely unacceptable. Now, I know this is no fault of yours, my darling, but still, the work must be done. I want you to go straight to our quarters and begin scrubbing. Don't go anywhere else or speak to anyone, other than to fetch what you need to clean. I expect it should take you several hours to do it right. Simply remain there and continue working. If anyone gives you trouble, you tell them I ordered you to do it and if they have a problem, you send them straight to me. Say nothing else. Understood?"

"Understood, milady," Kris said with relief. She gave an awkward and off-balance curtsy, as if it had been an afterthought, then raced to do as instructed.

"What a sweet girl, such a pity," Avalina said. She took a sip of wine from her goblet.

"Indeed," Leonin said, standing from the table. "I will send word to Daron; he will take care of her."

Chapter Five

The Traveling Assistant

31st Day of Spring, 897 G.C.

K ailem awoke at dawn with the first light shining through the porthole next to him. He looked over at Mokain's empty hammock; it was the first time in three months his brother hadn't been there when he awoke.

He joined the other sailors in the galley and waited for breakfast, one ladle of oatmeal with a tablespoon of molasses and a fried egg. The handful of empty spaces at the tables were quickly claimed, and none of those empty spaces had a friendly face beside it. Kailem decided to eat, standing in the corner. It didn't matter. This would be his last meal in the galley.

"Officer on deck!" the first mate called.

The galley hushed as the men stood at attention. Captain Gilroy entered, followed by the ship's remaining officers, and addressed the crew.

"As you all know, Quartermaster Stel has taken his leave. In the meantime, I've promoted Kailem Roka to be our new quartermaster. I know he's new on our ship, but on *The Flying Manta* we promote on merit and not seniority. I expect you to give him the same respect you gave Stel. That is all."

Captain Gilroy never used five words when two would suffice, and Kailem admired that. He and his officers left the galley as quickly as they had arrived, and before the door had even shut, the crew began to glare and grumble. Kailem shoveled another bite of oatmeal in silence.

They spent that morning loading cargo for the return voyage to Barrowfort. As the new quartermaster, Kailem oversaw the work. If the men had hated him before, this promotion only made it worse. It would make for a miserable voyage if he couldn't win them over. What would Mokain do, he wondered?

Kailem decided his brother would earn the goodwill of his men by helping them with their duties, so he hauled crates up the gangway alongside them. So far, it hadn't helped.

A sailor the same age as Kailem — Lars, they called him — climbed from the lower deck just as Kailem carried a crate of salted beef to the main stairs. Lars laid his shoulder into Kailem as they passed each other, nearly causing him to drop his crate. The shove was just light enough to feign it had been an accident.

Kailem felt his temperature rise. His first instinct was to throw Lars over the rails and into the harbor, but that would do nothing to help him win over the crew. As difficult as it was, he said nothing.

Captain Gilroy grabbed Lars by the hair and threw him to the deck. The surrounding crew all stopped and watched.

"Mr. Lars, if we had been at sea and you'd pulled a stunt like that, I'd have hoisted you on the foremast and given you forty lashes myself," the Captain said, his voice like gravel. "When your superior walks by, you step aside and let him pass, and if you graze against him, you bow your head and beg forgiveness. Now beg."

Lars stared at him for a moment, unsure if the Captain was serious. Captain Gilroy's eyes bore into him like a stonemason's drill. Lars returned to his feet and dusted his palms.

"I beg ya pa'don, Quartermaster," he grumbled with his head held high.

"Beg better," the Captain barked. "Or I'll give you them lashes, anyway."

Lars took a deep breath, then lowered his head. "Please forgive me, sir. I must'a forgot maself. Won't happ'n again."

Captain Gilroy looked to Kailem. "Do you accept his apology, Quartermaster?"

Kailem looked from the Captain to Lars, then back again. He was keen to say no and see the insolent sailor lashed. Maybe the Captain would even let Kailem be the one to give the lashings. But Kailem thought better of it and nodded.

"Be sure it doesn't happen again," the Captain ordered. "Now, back to work."

The Captain grabbed Kailem's arm above the elbow and spoke into his ear. "You let the men walk over you like that, and they'll mutiny before we set our sails. You're an officer on my vessel now, Roka. Demand the respect you deserve. Can I count on you?"

Kailem silently chided himself. "Aye, Captain."

The Captain released his arm. "I know I can. Now that's the last crate you carry. Your job is to see to it that all these slags do their jobs, and you can't do that if you're doing their job for them."

Kailem nodded. He carried his crate below deck and placed it with the others, continually berating himself. Mokain would never have problems with his men. He would have earned their respect with a single speech.

Some crates in the far corner were knocked over, and he looked around for a sailor to stack them. He was alone, so he did it himself.

While he stacked the crates, a rustling came from the back corner. It clearly wasn't a rat, nor the creak of wooden boards. He looked behind a stack of crates and saw a frightened young woman, perhaps only a year or two younger than himself. She cowered in the corner, her knees pressed to her chest. She was dirty and malnourished, green-eyed and dressed in sweat-stained rags. Her hair was a light mahogany, greasy and tangled with knots. Her eyes pleaded for him not to say anything.

Then Kailem recognized her. It was the girl he had seen the day prior running from the City Watch. She was likely a criminal; he should report her to the Captain. Looking at her, though, he couldn't help but feel pity for the young woman. If she could manage to stay hidden until they set sail, then perhaps Kailem could convince the Captain to not throw her overboard should someone else discover her during the voyage. He raised his hands as if to say, 'tis none my business' and returned to the main deck.

While ordering sailors about, a carriage arrived on the docks. Anyone could see this was not a merchant's carriage. It was drawn by two horses, rather than one, and it was painted black with gold trim and carved with flourishes around the doors and edges. When the carriage came to a stop, the driver hurried to open the door for the nobleman. Then, both driver and footman carried the nobleman's traveling chest down the dock. The two men strained under the weight of it.

As they approached *The Flying Manta*, Kailem could see the nobleman appeared to be in his early twenties, likely no older than he was. The man looked as natural on the docks as might an octopus on a mountaintop. The young nobleman wore velvet trousers, a blouse with billowing sleeves, and a silk vest. His driver and footman lowered his trunk to the dock with a thud. The nobleman tipped them a silver penny each, and the two returned to their carriage.

The young nobleman was short and soft, with a round face and honest eyes. He adjusted his spectacles as men worked around him, considering what to do next. He looked up and down the ship and then around the harbor, his polished boots glued to the dock.

"Gregor," Kailem called, "why don't you go down and greet our new friend there, see what he wants?"

Gregor looked to see what the new Quartermaster meant. "He's a passenger fare," Gregor said. "Rented a cabin fer passage ta Barrowfort, didn't he."

"Well, then go introduce yourself and see if he needs a hand."

"Ay, sir." Gregor grumbled.

Gregor descended the gangway, letting each step of his weathered boots land with a thump. "Ye our passenger?" he asked.

"I am, indeed, my good man. Sir Osmund Baylor of Devona." Osmund gave him a gentleman's bow, barely more than a nod of the head. Gregor ignored it.

"Well, yer cabin be ready. Come aboard."

"Very good. And who shall carry my trunk onboard?"

Gregor looked back at the young man dressed like he was to attend a formal dinner. "Did ye pay fer a servant to travel with ye?"

"Well, no..." Osmund replied.

"Well then, 'ppears ye'll be carryin' it yeself."

Osmund looked back to the driver and footman who were pulling away in the carriage, then back to the trunk with obvious concern. He took hold of the handle and lifted — he couldn't lift even one end off the ground. He attempted to push it, but it wouldn't budge. Kailem couldn't help but laugh. There was a strange satisfaction in seeing a high-born struggle. There was justice in it, though he couldn't say why. Technically, he too had been high born, once.

"Let go a me, ye sarding rat! Unhand me!" a young woman screamed from below deck. Kailem turned to see Lars forcibly escorting the stowaway above deck. When they marched past him, his eyes met hers. Kailem moved to intervene, but then paused. What could he do that might actually improve her situation, he wondered? Anything he did was more likely to result in his own dismissal as well. He watched with regret as Lars forced the girl down the gangway.

"What in Iria are you doing with this woman?" Osmund demanded to know.

"She's a sarding stowaway," Lars said with contempt. "She's lucky thrown off is all she's gettin'. I ought to hand her over to the City Watch, see what they have to say." The young woman continued to struggle against him.

An idea alit in the young nobleman's face.

"I demand you unhand her at once," Osmund said in his most authoritative voice.

Lars and Gregor were both taken aback. Lars protested, "who are ye ta tell us how ta—"

Osmund cut him off. "This is no stowaway; this is my traveling assistant. I instructed her to arrive before me and see that my quarters were in order. Now, I demand you unhand her immediately, or it will be *you* who is delivered to the City Watch."

The stowaway stood silent. Unsure of what was happening, she didn't want to contradict the one person defending her.

Lars was speechless. No one could believe this dirty, ill-tempered young woman was in the service of such a lavish nobleman. Lars clearly wanted to call out the lie, but the repercussions of falsely accusing a nobleman gave him pause. He looked to Gregor to know what to do.

"Ye said ye didn't pay fer a servant ta travel wit ye," Gregor said.

"She's not my servant, she's my 'traveling assistant'," Osmund said, over-enunciating her title. "And besides, I'm sure a strong man like yourself would not allow a young lady to do his heavy lifting."

Kailem chuckled at the last part.

"Ye didn't pay fer no 'traveling assistant' neither," Gregor said, mocking Osmund's enunciation.

"Is that so? Well, let us remedy that forthwith." Osmund took out three silver coins and placed them in Gregor's hand. The young woman's eyes bulged at the wealth he so casually handed over.

"I believe three silver florins should be sufficient," Osmund said. "Now, if you will kindly take your hands *off* the lady."

Lars still had the woman's arm pinned behind her back. He was dumbfounded, and Gregor now looked confused as well.

"You heard the man, Lars!" Kailem called from the deck. "Release the lady."

Lars looked up to him in surprise. His nostrils flared, but he held his tongue. He released the stowaway's arm, and the two sailors stomped back up the gangway.

Kailem cleared his throat and held his hand out as Gregor passed. "I'll make sure those find their way to the ship's coffer, Gregor." Gregor reluctantly put the three silver florins in Kailem's hand.

"I s'pose I ought ta be thankin' ye," the young lady said in a thick Donnelin accent. She had a delicate button nose, the greenest eyes Osmund had ever seen, and a most unpleasant odor about her.

"My pleasure, miss. I am Lord Osmund Baylor," he replied. He bowed, careful to keep his nose as far from her as possible. "And you are?"

She returned a feeble handshake. "Emerald," she said. "So, why'd ye do it, then?"

"It's simple, really. I needed a servant. Now, if you'll kindly carry my trunk on board."

Emerald stepped backward. "Steady on, now. I be no man's servant. If that be what yer after, ye can go and shove it, then."

"Well then, if you'd prefer to deal with the City Watch." Osmund looked at the two guards patrolling the docks nearby. Emerald took an instinctive step to her left, placing Osmund between the guards and herself.

"I suspected as much. I shall see you onboard, Miss Emerald. I expect it will be a pleasant voyage. Don't forget the trunk." Osmund climbed the gangway with smug satisfaction.

"My room?" he asked Kailem.

Kailem motioned with a nod of his head. "Below deck and to the right."

"Thank you," Osmund replied.

Kailem looked back at the young woman. She struggled with the trunk just as Osmund had. He again took pity on her and descended the gangway.

"Let me help you out with that," he said. He hefted the trunk in a single fluid movement and placed it on his shoulder. Emerald followed him up the gangway.

"Show off."

***

It was three days into their journey, and Osmund Baylor still vomited over the railing as much as he had on the first day. Apparently, it was still possible to vomit after not eating for three days. His voyage was already proving educational.

Three days. That's how long the sailors had told him it would take to adjust to life at sea. As Osmund had never been on a ship before, he was obliged to take them at their word, although it was becoming apparent that their estimates were excessively modest.

Such was the nature of experimentation, he supposed. You could never perfectly predict the outcome. He vomited again over the side of the ship, ejecting nothing but bile and acid. He slumped to the deck with his back against the railing, his face turning a pale gray.

The voyage had also taught him the discount for booking passage on a merchant ship with a spare cabin was not worth the inferior living arrangements that came with it. On his next voyage, should such ever occur, he would be sure to book passage on an actual passenger ship with proper accommodations.

He would also be sure to bring a proper traveling assistant. The stowaway he had rescued from a certain prison sentence had been less than useful. She constantly ate in front of him, even while he ejected his stomach contents, and once she started talking, he could sooner sail to both moons than silence her. She spoke with a thick Donnelish accent, full of soft vowels and rolling r's, and little regard for proper Cavandish grammar.

On their second day at sea, they had spotted several forest dragons flying above the forest canopy and over the coastline. They were like green vipers with two sets of wings, a larger forward set and a smaller rear set. Each pair of wings flapped opposite the other so that the dragon appeared to slither vertically through the air.

The slender winged serpents could fly so high they nearly disappeared unless you knew where to look. Then they would dive, as straight as an arrow, descending faster than a stone in freefall, and somehow enter the water with a splash the size one would expect from a mere pebble. It would take a full minute for them to resurface, usually chomping on a fish when they did.

On their third day at sea, a pod of dolphins appeared off the port side. They swam alongside the ship, occasionally leaping so high they could have landed on the deck had they so desired. It was a dazzling spectacle, but Osmund was too sick to enjoy it, and the sailors were too familiar with the sight to have any reaction. Emerald, however, watched their performance with a child-like wonder, even clapping her hands when a dolphin flipped or spun in the air.

The dolphins enjoyed having a spectator, too. They swam and performed off the port side for nearly thirty minutes before swimming away. Poor Emerald waited a full hour at the railing, hoping they would return.

"Oi, eat this," Emerald said.

Osmund looked up to see a piece of bread held before him. The mere sight of it left him nauseated. Emerald sat down next to him with her own back against the railing. Osmund's vest was unbuttoned, and his hair was disheveled, yet somehow he was still more presentable than she was.

"Ugh. Can't eat. Too sick," he muttered. He raised a weak hand and pushed the bread away from him.

"Ye know, bless me stars, I did notice that on me own. This'll help. Soak up all the sick in yer stomach, it will. So come, eat."

"That is not the way a servant speaks to her master."

"Nay? Can't rightly say, meself. N'er been a servant. But tis right the way a false 'travelin' assistant speaks to her false employer when ain't nobody can hear 'em."

Osmund looked around at all the sailors working near them.

"Oh, don't be worryin' nothin' 'bout them, they ain't listenin'," the raggedy young woman assured him. The sailors sang one of their sea shanties, which Emerald had become particularly fond of listening to. She took a bite of the torn loaf of bread. Osmund watched her chew, then begrudgingly snatched the bread from her hand.

"There's a good lad," she said, rubbing his back. Osmund was amazed at the liberties she took with a nobleman. "Say, why be there so much rope on a ship? There be rope everywhere, there be almost more rope than wood. Be the ship held together with rope? I would ha' thought twas held with nails or the like."

The ship crested a swell and crashed back down, sending ocean spray through the railing. Osmund held his stomach and groaned.

Emerald patted his thigh. "There, there, Oz. Ye be almost through the worst of it."

Osmund paused. "Did you just call me 'Oz'?" he asked.

"Ay, I did, so. 'Osmund' sounds too uppity. Don't suit you nothin'."

The day they had met, Emerald had kept her distance from him. She answered questions with one-word answers and sat by herself whenever she could. He wasn't sure what had changed, but two days later she was an entirely new person, while he was still just as seasick.

"And do you always speak to noblemen this way?" he asked. He could feel the bread settle in his stomach.

Emerald thought for a moment. "N'er spoken ta noblemen before," she confessed. "Always try ta 'void yer kind."

Osmund swallowed another piece of bread. "Then why do you speak to me this way?"

"Dunno. You seem different. Soft. And safe."

Osmund frowned. "That is not the compliment you think it is."

"Nary an insult nor a compliment, 'tis just the way it be. Feelin' better, then, are ye?"

"Not remotely," Osmund claimed. The truth was, he did feel a degree of improvement after eating the bread, but Iria could rot before he would ever tell her that. He'd never hear the end of it.

"First time on a ship, then, I'm guessin'?" she asked.

Osmund nodded and rested his head against the railing. "Yours?" he asked.

"Well now, definitely be me first time not stowin' away and the like. First time bein' on the main deck rather than down at the arse-end of a storage hole, first time seein' the sailors work and feelin' the ocean spray. But as for simply bein' on a ship, nay, tis ain't me first time."

Did she just say 'arse-end of a storage hole? Osmund thought. Out loud, he asked, "do you stow away often?"

"Only when I have to."

"And why do you have so frequent a need to travel by ship? I cannot imagine you have pressing business in faraway cities to attend to." Osmund realized only after he had spoken how sharp his words had sounded. It appeared his nausea had dulled his manners. Emerald didn't seem to mind.

"Tis not the city I go *to* that's pressin', tis the city I *leave*, innit? See, ye work a city too long, people get the wiser of you. And if ye don't leave in a jiff, eventually they come a lookin' fer ye, wantin' back their jewelry and coin pouches and the like. So, when ye hafta leave, ye don't want ta leave on foot. Tis too slow, they always catch you. And I seen what happens when ye nick a horse. They chase ye somethin' awful if ye nick a horse, ain't no chance of escapin' then. Hiding in a caravan *can* work, but tis tricky, and they ask too many questions. Stealin' passage on a ship be far simpler. Tis best to pick a ship that has a short voyage, though. Livin' as a stowaway, well, you fancy folk might say 'tis less than pleasant."

What an odd and fascinating woman, Osmund thought. He imagined her life as one adventure after another taking her to far-off places with colorful characters.

"Quite a thrilling life you lead. A part of me envies you," Osmund admitted.

Emerald scoffed. "Aye, me life be so charmin' now, innit? Always sleepin' in the streets and lookin' over me shoulder."

"Perhaps your thieving skills are lacking," Osmund said, again forgetting his manners.

Emerald sat tall and faced him. "Oy, I be better than any pickpocket in the city," she said, sticking her thumb into her chest. "If I be wantin' to, I could steal more in a day than most merchants make in a month. But then what do I do with it all?"

"Well, stop sleeping in the street, for one," Osmund said.

"Aye, I could spend a night in a nice bed if I want. But the more we steal, the more you rich folks come a lookin' for us. Steal too much too often and soon we be havin' every bounty hunter in the county on our tail."

"So do one big job a month and live on it until the next one," Osmund suggested.

Emerald rolled her eyes at him. "And what am I supposed to do with all them coins fer a whole month, then? Carry that much coin and someone'll gladly kill you fer it."

Osmund thought for a second. "You could always buy a home. Get a safe to put your coins in?"

Emerald shook her head. "Nay, we thieves need to be on the move, ye see. If ye stay in one place, people start askin' questions, wantin' to know where yer from and how ye came by them coins, and yer enemies will always know how to find ye. Yer best bet be to join a thieving crew, but theys ain't exactly the friendly sort."

As Osmund searched for a response, the ship heaved and sprayed a mist of sea water over the railing. He gripped his stomach and groaned.

Nearby, a sailor stumbled as he passed. His arms and legs were discolored, cracked, and covered in lesions, and he gave off a putrid odor.

"What is that?" Emerald whispered with her face pinched.

Osmund's eyes had been closed when the man passed, but he quickly found the sailor in question. "Ah," he said, raising the back of his hand to his mouth. He thought back to his medical texts. "Based on the symptoms, I would imagine that is a case of pellagra, a common malady among sailors. I have never seen it myself, of course, but I have read about it. They say it is an awfully painful lot, to be sure. Often deadly, with no cure."

Emerald grimaced and looked away, her hand covering her mouth.

"Nauseated?" Osmund asked.

"What?"

"Do you feel you might vomit? Throw up?" he clarified.

Emerald nodded.

"Here, this should help." He handed her what remained of his bread, which she knocked out of his hand, much to his amusement.

The Quartermaster called for a change of shift, excusing sailors and barking out assignments to the ones emerging from below deck. Osmund found it odd the Quartermaster should be the lone Mariner onboard. The young man didn't quite fit in with the rest of the crew. His hair was longer, down to his jawline, and he was clean-shaven. The rest of the crew had short hair, some shorn down to the scalp, and many wore unkempt beards. But there was something else about him, something about his build and the way he carried himself. Disciplined and self-assured, a warrior among sea dogs. Osmund found the anomaly intriguing.

Every evening, sailors prepared a table for their high-born passenger and his traveling assistant on the main deck next to the stairs that led to the quarterdeck and brought them plates from the galley. Osmund had expected Captain Gilroy to offer his honored guest a seat at his table. Instead, he stuck to the antiquated notion that the Captain's quarters were exclusively the province of the ship's officers.

The sun was setting when food and drink were placed before the passengers that night. Clouds of apricot, peach, raspberry, and lavender marbled the light blue sky. The whole display was breathtaking. And the most beautiful part of it was his seasickness was fading. Three days, right on schedule.

"Beautiful, there sunset, innit?" Emerald said. "All them purples and oranges."

Osmund nodded in agreement.

"Oi, I got ye somethin'," Emerald said. She took out a silver pocket watch on a silver chain. "For savin' me on the docks that day. Now we're even."

Osmund held up the pocket watch and examined its craftsmanship. This was an elegant timepiece, and from the heft of it was genuine silver. The honorable gesture from one so unrefined as Emerald surprised him.

"Where did you get this?" Osmund asked.

"I've me sources," she said coyly.

Osmund rolled his eyes and slid the watch into his pocket. "Thank you."

The Quartermaster arrived on the main deck with a plate of food. "Might I eat with you?"

The surprise delighted him. "By all means," he replied.

The Quartermaster set down his plate and tankard and rolled over a barrel as a makeshift seat.

"Not eating with the Captain, tonight?" Osmund asked.

"I made an appearance, but I realized I haven't formally met the two of you yet," Kailem explained. "I'm Kailem Roka, from the Marin Islands."

"It is a pleasure to meet you, Kailem. You're the first Mariner I have ever had the good fortune of meeting. I am Osmund Baylor of Devona, and this is Emerald of Donnelin."

Emerald leaned over and whispered, "I n'er told ye I were from Donnelin."

"Your accent, dear. It was a dead giveaway," Osmund whispered back.

"Aye," she replied, and then added, "don't be callin' me 'dear'."

"So, what takes you both to Barrowfort," Kailem asked.

"Well now, you might say I'm a scholar, of sorts," Osmund explained. "I have an idea for a comparative analysis of esoteric practices, so I am traveling to the great libraries collecting information."

"Esoteric?" Kailem repeated with a frown. "I'm not familiar with the term."

Osmund put down his knife and fork and sat up straight, a smile beaming from his face. Emerald huffed and leaned on the table, her cheek resting on her fist. She had no desire to hear this a third time.

"Some refer to it as the occult," Osmund began. "It refers to any practice with mythical qualities. Some practices are more widely accepted, such as the alchemical arts, others are lesser known, like sagecraft, sorcery, or divination. My analysis will compare the different treatises on the various subjects and discuss what the practices have in common, where they differ, and where they directly contradict each other. I want my analysis to track how the different theories developed over time and branched out from one another into their current state."

"I'm afraid I know little of all that, but it sounds fascinating," Kailem replied.

"It *is* fascinating; I wholeheartedly agree with you," Osmund said. "I am collecting as many esoteric texts as I can. I believe it could be influential for many generations of future scholars."

Emerald's eyes had glazed over, lost in her own thoughts.

"Indeed, I believe it will be," Kailem agreed politely. "How many of these libraries have you been to?"

Osmund lowered his head slightly, almost imperceptibly. "So far, just one," he admitted. "This was my first time in Rhinegard, first time outside of Devona, if I'm being honest. I've never been farther from home than the University of Terendor in Devona. Until now, of course."

Emerald looked at Osmund with surprise.

"I imagine you have traveled all over," Osmund continued.

"Not as much as you'd think. *The Flying Manta* only sails between Barrowfort and Rhinegard. I've been to a few other small towns near the Marin Islands, but that's it."

"Well, that makes me feel a little better about myself. Less of a hermit." Osmund took another bite of beans.

"Are you also a scholar?" Kailem asked Emerald.

The question jolted her from her private thoughts. "Who, me? I should think not, cannae even read," Emerald said.

"Didn't I see you chased through the streets by the City Watch a few days ago?" Kailem asked. Osmund turned to her with eyebrows raised.

Emerald shrugged. "How would I know what ye saw, then?" She stared at her food and took another bite.

"Why were they chasing you?" Kailem asked. Osmund was keen for an answer as well.

"A false accusation," she said with a straight face. "They thought I stole some fancy lord's coin pouch." She didn't know either of these men well enough to tell them the truth.

"Falsely accused, uh?" Kailem said.

"Tis what I said," she replied, her eyes still on her food.

"So, what takes you to Barrowfort, then?" Kailem asked.

"What then? A girl cannae travel if she be wantin'?" She took a large bite of salted pork and chewed slowly, making it clear she would say nothing more on the matter.

Osmund found Kailem too composed and well-spoken to be a common sailor. "Are you, by chance, from a noble house in Marin?" Osmund asked him.

Kailem's shoulders slumped and his tone dropped when he answered, "no."

"I beg your pardon if my question was—"

"No, no, you are perfectly fine. I *was* raised in a noble house, but my parents were... killed. Recently, in fact, and our house is no more. Speaking of my house is unpleasant for me."

"How dreadful," Osmund said with a somber tone. A moment of silence passed between them.

"Me parents be dead too," Emerald said. It was the first unsolicited comment she had made since Kailem sat down.

"I'm sorry to hear that. How long ago?" Kailem asked.

"Years. Taken by the blue fever. I was a little girl. Can't even remember their faces."

Kailem looked to his plate. "How long until the pain goes away?" he asked.

"Completely?" She paused for a moment. "Never."

Kailem nodded. Osmund suddenly felt a deep appreciation for his own parents.

"Has anyone seen my pocket watch?" a sailor called out from the stairs to the quarterdeck. It was Lars, the man who had nearly thrown Emerald off the ship. Lars looked to Emerald, who just shook her head. Kailem and Osmund did likewise.

Lars kept talking, mostly to himself, as he walked away. "It was me father's watch. I just had it here in me pocket, I know I did."

Osmund scowled at Emerald.

"What? Tis like I told ye. Now we be even."

CHAPTER SIX

PERIL IN THE BORDERLANDS

35TH DAY OF SPRING, 897 G.C.

Prince Aedon loved the sound of metal striking metal. That cacophony of tings and clanks that reverberates through your bones. Not the rhythmic hammering of a blacksmith, of course. That depressing sound reminded Aedon of criminals on their long march to the gallows. No, the sound he loved was the chaotic clash of weaponry. Sword against sword. Ax against shield. Mace against chain mail. Hammer against helmet. It was the sound of glory and conquest. To Aedon, there was nothing sweeter.

The castle bailey should never be without this glorious sound, he thought. Once he was King, he would decree that his soldiers train every day in the bailey. But today, no decree was needed. Sparring knights from every corner of Cavandel and beyond filled the castle bailey, all hoping to claim the top prize at the tournament. The Arena was filled with commoners practicing as well, as only men of noble birth and their servants were permitted in the castle.

More than a thousand years prior, the Palace of Rhinegard had been built around and over an existing castle. The origins of the castle itself had long been lost to history, but the Palace of Rhinegard was the envy of every monarch. Aedon walked along the parapets, examining the fighters below.

"Are those Shinda warriors, Dugald?" Aedon asked his servant.

"I dare say, Your Grace," Dugald said. "They arrived yesterday by caravan."

"I don't believe I've ever seen a Shinda warrior fight. How fascinating." He observed them for several moments. "They don't appear all that formidable."

"I believe that is called a Kumata, Your Grace. It's a choreographed training exercise, not true combat."

Aedon gave his servant a sideways glance. "And how do *you* know so much about the Shinda, Dugald?"

"I was squire to a sword master for a time, Your Grace. He practiced many styles."

"A sword master's squire to the personal servant of the crown prince. Sounds like you have a marvelous story, Dugald. You must tell it to me sometime."

"Whenever you wish it, Your Grace," the servant replied.

"Dugald. Your tone is depressing today. Even more so than usual," Aedon complained. The clang of metal on metal continued.

"A thousand apologies, Your Grace."

"Well, out with it. What is the matter with you?"

"It is a tragic day for all the servant staff, I am afraid. A young girl named Kris was found to have leaped from the West Tower. They found her dead in the courtyard this morning."

"Kris, Kris. Did I know her?"

"You did, Your Grace. She was fifteen years old, with curly blonde hair and freckles. The staff were all quite fond of her; she was a joy to be around. It is a terrible loss."

"She doesn't sound familiar." Aedon winced as a knight took a particularly hard blow to the helmet from a war hammer and collapsed.

"I would remind Your Grace that your first council meeting will be starting soon."

"Indeed, it is. Thank you, Dugald. Have I given you any tasks today?" Aedon asked.

"You have not, Your Grace," Dugald replied.

"Very well. Stay here and watch the fighters train. Tell me who looks the most promising."

"Very good, Your Grace." Dugald bowed as the Prince turned to descend the stairs.

Aedon left the old castle and passed through the courtyard. He walked with the impeccable posture expected of a monarch. Everywhere he went, noblemen and commoners alike stepped aside and bowed while he passed. He hardly noticed it anymore. He passed the fountains that separated the courtyard from the southern gardens and strode up the portico to the palace doors.

Inside the Grand Foyer, a new face caught his eye. He knew every young lady in court, but he'd never seen this one before. Had she been at the betrothal feast last month, he wondered?

The lady stepped aside and curtsied as he passed, just as all the women did, but when she stood straight again, she was startled to see him still standing there. His eyes moved over her, inspecting her. She was no more than seventeen, fair-skinned with Cavandish braids in her chocolate-colored hair. By the look of her dress, she had a wealthy father. How did he not know this girl?

The young lady avoided looking directly at the Prince. She tucked her hair behind her ears, then crossed her hands by her waist. Aedon stepped towards her and extended his hand. She paused, then delicately placed her hand in his.

"I do not believe we have met. I am Aedon, Crown Prince of Cavandel."

He held her gaze as he bent down and kissed her hand, letting his lips linger on her skin. She ought to have replied with her own name, but the Prince's charm left her mute. *Poor young thing*, Aedon thought, *this must be her first time in Court.* Her cheeks grew hot and flushed, and she bit her lip to suppress a nervous giggle. Aedon grinned before going on his way.

While passing through the Grand Corridor, Aedon saw Kyra speaking with the usual ladies of the Court. She stepped away from her circle and linked arms with the Prince.

"And where is my handsome fiancé off to this morning?" Kyra asked.

Aedon smiled. More of a smirk, really. He had shared his morning agenda with Kyra several times. *Women are such simple creatures*, he thought. "My first council meeting is this morning," he said.

"That's right! How exciting! So, tell me, have you heard about the servant girl?"

"Oh yes, Dugald informed me about her just a moment ago. Why do you ask?"

"He told you she jumped from the tower?" Kyra asked. Aedon nodded. "Well, the talk around Court is that she didn't jump, she was thrown."

As they walked with arms linked, they left the Grand Corridor and moved down a narrow hallway toward the Council Room. Servants now pressed their backs against the wall as they passed.

"Thrown? As in murdered?" Aedon asked. Kyra nodded with her eyebrows near her hairline. "Why would anyone bother to murder a servant girl?"

"Oh, Aedon," Kyra said, "you must know. The servants know everything. Most nobles don't think to watch their tongue when a servant is in the room, and servants have keen ears. Then in their after hours, they have nothing else in their lives to talk about, so they talk about us. Martina always hears the best gossip before I do."

"And you reckon this servant girl was killed because of some gossip she was told?"

"Told... or overheard. That's the rumor, at least. Who can say?"

"Killed over gossip. Such a pity." Aedon thought for a pace. "If she did overhear something important, I suppose killing her would make sense. The only way to bury a secret is to bury all who know it."

"Well said, dearest." Kyra sounded genuinely impressed. But then she was always genuine; the girl had no talent for subterfuge. The quote that impressed her wasn't Aedon's; he couldn't remember where he had read it, but it had stuck with him. He saw nothing wrong in accepting credit, however.

"Well, here we are," Kyra said when they reached the council room doors. Two guards stood at attention in front of the ten-foot double doors of solid oak reinforced with shields bearing the Braise Family Crest. Standing casually to the side was the Arturri's personal guard, Daron. The man had the sweetness and compassion of a saltwater crocodile. Just looking at him set Aedon on edge.

"Enjoy your first council meeting, my love. You'll be great." She kissed him on the cheek and walked away with a slight skip in her step.

Prince Aedon squared his shoulders and nodded to the guards, intentionally not looking in Daron's direction. The guards swung open the chamber doors, a labor given the doors' considerable weight. Aedon advanced into the council chamber with the stiffness of a soldier to find five councilors waiting for him.

The council chamber was elegantly adorned even by Rhinegard standards. Banners bearing the royal seal were staggered between the floor-to-ceiling windows on either side of the room. On the far side, a hundred Cavander soldiers stood brilliantly painted on a distant battlefield. At their feet laid a thousand fallen Àramen lying in their own gore, their weapons useless at their sides. On either side of the painting stood two attacking griffins carved out of solid marble, their wings unfurled.

His entrance triggered a Flurry of motion as councilmen moved to greet their new colleague, no doubt hoping to sow seeds of influence with the future king.

Aedon needed to show them that despite his inexperience, he was not their equal. He fixed his eyes on his target and strode towards him, ignoring all others.

"Lord Menden, I'm surprised to see you," Aedon said. "I thought your days of languishing in these prosaic meetings were behind you. You should be off enjoying your retirement, old friend." He gave the aged former First Officer a hearty smile and handshake. Hopefully, his denigration of the council, as well as the bald reminder of his authority to force someone like Lord Menden into retirement would put the rest of the councilors in their place. Aedon's eyes remained on Lord Menden, but he could hear the other councilors return to their seats. Aedon grinned in triumph.

"Hardly, Your Grace," Lord Menden said. "Not until your champion takes my place. And you have yet to replace my seat on the council as well."

"Yes, well, I pity the man who has to fill your shoes, Lord Menden."

Flattery had no effect on the old soldier, even when the flattery came from the crown prince.

Aedon took his seat on the right hand of the King's chair. He wasn't sure who sat in his seat before him, but the fact the previous occupant hadn't tried to retain his seat was a good sign. The scribe sitting at the corner desk wrote down the record of attendance, his quill scratching ink on parchment.

Directly in front of Aedon sat the only foreigner on the council, and the only other man who didn't leap from his seat on Aedon's entrance. Lord Leonin Arturri's position was highly controversial, but Devona had been a protectorate of Cavandel for so long they might as well have been part of the kingdom. The monarch of Devona had even abandoned the title of 'King' generations prior, opting for the more appropriate title of 'Viceroy' instead. Leonin simply gave his future son-in-law a nod, a gesture of respect between peers. Aedon couldn't keep his smile from widening.

Aedon imagined most people would find the chamber ostentatious, even excessively so — he disagreed. The décor matched the chamber's lofty function. He could feel the weight of the decisions that had been made here over the past millennia. The war plans, the peace treaties, the economic alliances. This was the room where the fate of Iria was decided.

The chamber doors again swung open. This time the King entered wearing his usual fur cape. All stood and remained standing until he took his seat between the marble griffins.

"Right to business, then, shall we? No need to spend more time in this garish room than necessary. First, let us recognize the presence of our newest member, my son, Prince Aedon."

The council gave modest applause. Aedon had thought his father might ask him to say a few words. He did not.

"Lord Menden, let's start with you," Byron said. He went around the table one by one, hearing his councilor's concerns and giving his word on the matter. At times, a servant would enter to refill their wine goblets. The scratching of the scribe's quill was a constant sound as he took the minutes of the meeting.

For Aedon, this was his chance to learn why his father was so beloved by nobles and commoners alike. He studied the king the way a fighter studies a superior rival in a tournament. Byron opened each issue for discussion from the group, but he never participated. He listened intently, absently stroking his ducktail beard as his councilors debated. He digested the opinions of the group, then gave his final word on the matter.

Aedon couldn't help but feel impressed. His father was controlled and confident, with a profound understanding of kingdom affairs. But there was also something in his voice that was genuine. His concern was for more than mere order and prosperity; he cared for his people the way a father cared for his children. People spoke frequently of the King's love for his people, but this was the first time Aedon understood why.

"And we've come to you, old friend. What do you have for me?" King Byron asked Leonin.

"As for internal affairs, Your Majesty, I see nothing amiss. I imagine future scholars will study your reign as a paragon of administrative efficiency."

King Byron rubbed his left eye, waiting for Leonin to reach his point.

"What concerns me, Your Majesty, is the distressing reports our spies have returned from the borderlands. Talk of armies amassing and encroaching on our border villages. The Marcônish to the south have been seen patrolling through Donnelin, and there are reports of the Àramen and the Shinda doing the same in the west. I believe they are testing our resolve. Your resolve, Your Majesty. And worse, I believe that only a show of force will keep them at bay."

"I've received no such reports from my scouts in the area," Byron said.

"The spies I refer to are not with the military," Leonin explained.

The King exhaled sharply through his nose. "Then who?"

"We have eyes and ears within the servant class..."

"Ha!" the King guffawed. He rolled his eyes away from Leonin.

"My sources may not be impressive, Your Majesty, but their reports are reliable."

Byron took a deep breath and exhaled. "Be that as it may, Lord Arturri, we will wait until I receive confirmation from our scouts before we react."

"I'm afraid that may be too late, Your Majesty. The Borderlands are all at least a month's march away. If they were to launch an attack, the amount of time it would take for reports to reach us, to amass a counteroffensive, and march our soldiers to the battle, well, we would have already lost half the kingdom."

Aedon's father wasn't moved. Perhaps his love of the people was blinding him to reason, or perhaps it prevented him from making the hard decisions. Whatever the cause, before his father could reply to Leonin, Aedon interjected. "I agree, father. We would be wise not to ignore the reports of the servant class. They are often privy to conversations that even our spies cannot infiltrate."

"Son, I..." the King began, but Aedon continued.

"Take this council, for example. I am the Crown Prince of Cavandel and even I had never heard a single word uttered in this chamber before today, but four times in the past hour this servant has circled our table refilling our wine goblets and not once did we halt our conversation until he had left. Our kingdom's most sensitive secrets declared openly for a man of the lowest birth to freely hear."

The servant looked like a puppy caught sneaking bacon from the butcher's shop. He looked to the King without making a sound, and a nod from the King dismissed him from the room.

"I have heard all your concerns on the matter. I will give my word, and that will be the end of it." The King let his words hang in the air before continuing. "War is never worth the cost, and never justified unless it is thrust upon us. Our sacred duty is to protect our citizens. *Every* citizen, from the highest noble down to the lowest commoner, and I will not send a single man to die on a sword until I have exhausted each and every alternative."

Silence held the table. Even the scribe in the corner had stopped scribbling, not willing to break the silence.

"That being said," the King continued, "your reports are most certainly troubling. I will send diplomats to speak with the elders of the border villages. If they can confirm these rumors, then, and *only* then, will we discuss a military response. Understood?"

A muttering consensus sounded from the table.

"Very good, then. Meeting adjourned." The King stood from the table and his advisors jumped to their feet in deference to him. With the King out of the council room, the councilors were free to mingle amongst themselves.

"I'm impressed with you, young Aedon," Lord Arturri said. "Most councilors are too timid to speak at their first meeting unless called upon. And you spoke against the King, no less. Very well done, indeed."

"You are too kind, Lord Arturri," Aedon said. Together they meandered towards the doors of the council room.

"We are colleagues now, Aedon, and you're engaged to my only daughter. I believe it's time you start calling me 'Leonin'."

"Well, thank you again, Leonin. What more can you tell me about these attacks on the borderlands?"

"We've received reports from villages in the Roserock Basin, the Valley of Oxmere, and even down into the Pavian Grasslands. Reports are mixed. Some claim they are formal regiment from Shinda and Marcôna, others say they are just raids from foreign villagers. Nothing we can't fend off or quickly recover from, but without an aggressive response from the Crown, problems are sure to escalate."

"Any attacks from the north?" Aedon asked.

"No reports yet. But we can be sure if we don't answer these encroachments from the south, the north won't hesitate."

Aedon nodded his agreement. "What do you need from me?"

Leonin stopped a few steps from the double doors and placed his hand on Aedon's shoulder. "What Cavandel needs, son, is your voice. More of what you showed here today. A voice of reason, wisdom, and strength."

Aedon stood tall and squared his shoulders, then looked Leonin in the eye. "You can count on me."

Chapter Seven

A Southern Storm

46th Day of Spring, 897 G.C.

After their dinner on the main deck, Kailem spent increasingly more of his free time with Osmund and Emerald. He had little time to spare during the daylight hours, but at night, they would drink their rations of ale together while they played cards and swapped stories with the other sailors by lamplight. After two weeks, Osmund had finally found his sea legs. He could now walk the length of the ship without stumbling, an accomplishment of which he was quite proud.

"So, there we was, sailin' through chucks of ice in the North Sea the size of woolly mammoths," Horace said in his best troubadour voice. "More than a hundred miles from the Norvian coast, we was, huntin' a pod of minke whales with no land in sight."

Horace was the ship's cook and the oldest man onboard by a decade. He leaned low to the table, the dance of the lantern's firelight flickering on his face, his hands out wide as he spoke. The old man had missed his calling on the stage.

"There I were on the bow, harpoon in hand, ready to spear the first whale o' the day, when out a nowhere, three giant *tentacles* shot into the air. They wrapped that whale tighter than a lute string, they did. Ready to pull that whale down into the salty depths. Well, I weren't about to let no prize slip through me fingers without a fight, see? So, I *thrust* my harpoon into the nearest tentacle, a direct hit. Inky blood, black as night it was, came a gushin' out. Those tentacles went all a quiver, so they did, and the beast released its hold on me whale."

"I thought a squid's blood was blue, not black," Osmund said with arms folded across his chest. Emerald, on the other hand, had forgotten to blink.

"Ay, so it is, lad, that be true. But you see, this weren't no ordinary squid, boy. Nay, this here were a *kraken*."

Several sailors smothered a laugh.

"'Tis true, I tell ye! As true as all youse be sittin' here. I saw the kraken with me own eyes, I did. That beast let go of the whale and turned its salty hate on us, it did. Six giant tentacles shot up in the air and wrapped clean around the deck. Why, if we weren't so quick with our swords and axes, the beast would a swallowed us whole. But we hacked, and we slashed, and we cut, while its black blood like tar sprayed all o'er the deck. We severed four whole tentacles before the beast left us be."

"So, you were once a whale hunter and kraken slayer, and now you're a cook?" Osmund asked.

Horace sat tall and crossed his arms. "That I was, lad, and that I am. And what of it?"

"Quartermaster," Gregor called from the top of the stairs. "Cap'n wants ta see ya. Says is urgent."

Kailem excused himself from the table, an uncommon gesture among sailors. Kailem heard Osmund looking for holes in the old man's story as he climbed to the main deck. He found Captain Gilroy on the quarterdeck standing beside the helm. Gregor stood next to him fiddling with the jasper stone around his neck.

"You asked to see me, Captain?" Kailem asked.

"Aye. Looks like a storm is a brewin' for us," Captain Gilroy replied.

The sun had set, but its afterglow remained on the horizon. Kailem looked to the east and saw nothing but clear skies.

"Not to the east, lad. To the south. Dead ahead. Look." The Captain handed him the spyglass and Kailem saw dark clouds forming on the horizon.

"A southern storm," Kailem remarked. "Very rare, especially this far north."

The Captain grunted in agreement. "I've sailed through but a few southern storms in my time, but all were back when I was just a lad. I imagine you've seen your share?"

Kailem nodded. "A southern storm moves fast. We don't want to be caught in open water when it hits. How far are we from shore?"

Captain Gilroy walked him to the table and showed him a map of the Devona coast.

"Thirty minutes if we sail directly west, but shelter will be in short supply. Nothin' but shallow water and a sandbar to drop anchor. But there is a cove another ten miles down the coast. It will shelter us right proper, but we'll be sailin' against the wind. May take over an hour to reach it."

Kailem took another look through the spyglass. "Well, that storm will be on us within the hour, but only the outermost edge, nothing harmful. We can make the cove before the real danger is upon us. But if we make for the beach, eventually the eye of the storm will hit us, and then we'll wish we had gone for the cove."

"My thoughts as well. We'll make for the cove, then. Call all hands. I want this ship tied down and moving at top speed before the rain hits."

"Aye, Captain."

Kailem rang the bell, calling all hands. As men ran from below deck, Kailem bellowed out assignments. They unfurled every sail on each mast, and *The Flying Manta* jerked forward at maximum speed. Sailors raced back and forth, securing lines and hauling equipment below deck. It wasn't long before the glow on the horizon disappeared. Osmund and Emerald emerged from below like lost children.

"What's going on?" Osmund asked. His voice strained to compete with the increasing winds.

"A storm's approaching, we're making for a cove to ride it out," Kailem said.

Osmund peered over the starboard rail. "I do not see any land."

Kailem had the same concern. Even with the angle of their heading, they should have seen land by now. They must not be going as fast as they thought.

"You and Emerald go below deck. You'll be fine; just stay out of the way." The two passengers promptly obeyed.

The night sky lacked its usual blanket of stars and moonlight. Lightning flashed intermittently, illuminating the ship for but a moment before darkness reclaimed it. The sky and the sea were the same shade of black, and the wind whistled angrily as it whipped past Kailem's ear. The rolling swells made the deck rock back and forth, and even the most experienced sailors failed to keep their feet.

The Flying Manta creaked and moaned as if crying in pain, making sounds the men had never heard. The storm grew angrier still and yet no land appeared. Kailem continued to shout orders to his men, and the men clung to his every word. Gone were the subtle rebellions and biting offenses. Now his confident voice was their figurative anchor in the literal storm.

Kailem toppled to the deck, hurled by a gust of wind that ripped across the ship. A loose barrel rolled his way, and he brought his arms to his head just in time to deflect the blow. The barrel then hit a man behind him, sending the sailor over the rails and into the water. It had been too dark to make out the man's face.

A break in the wind quieted the storm just enough for Kailem to make out a faint cry for help coming from above. He looked up to see a sailor hanging upside down, his foot caught in the shroud. It was clear from the way it twisted behind him that the leg was broken.

Kailem climbed the rain-soaked rope ladder as fast as he could, but progress was slow amid the gusts of wind and rain. The ship listed to the port side, further complicating the climb. He soon recognized the sailor in distress. It was Lars. His eyes were squeezed shut, and he howled in pain.

"Lars!" Kailem cried out. "LARS!"

It was no use. Amid the wind, the thunderclaps, and his own screaming, Lars might as well have been on the other side of Iria. The ship righted itself for but a moment, then plunged again to the port side. Lars and Kailem gripped the rigging as the mast whipped them through the sky.

The ship righted itself again and the sudden change threw both Kailem and Lars to the deck. Kailem landed at the edge near the railing, earning a bruised hip for his efforts. Lars, however, landed with his ribcage on the railing, his feet out to sea. His body bounced off the ship like a limp rag doll and splashed into the black ocean. He never resurfaced.

Men no longer raced back and forth to keep the ship in order. Anyone still on deck cleaved to whatever was tied down, hoping to live a few moments longer. More than one cried out for his mother.

The Flying Manta thrashed about like a lass afraid of drowning. Something wasn't right. Kailem looked up to the quarterdeck; no one stood behind the helm. He fell only once as he raced up the stairs to take control of the ship.

The ship sailed through a dark abyss. The Cerulean Sea was as black as the night sky, the horizon lost between them. Flashes of lightning gave him split seconds to adjust their course as he maneuvered the ship through the swells, sculling the waves to minimize the impact. He gripped the helm with steel fists while the storm did its best to cast him overboard. More than once, waves like boulders crashed over the side and threw him to the deck, and he clung to the helm until he could return his feet underneath him.

A flash of lightning illuminated the shore to his right. For that split second, he saw the cove he had gambled their lives on. He crested another wave, then spun the helm, hoping to make a mad dash for the cove.

Soon the ship was within a thousand yards of the shore. If he could hold on just a little longer, they would make it to the cove. Everyone still onboard would live. He could save them.

Without warning, a flash brighter than the noonday sun seared Kailem's eyes while a deafening boom rattled his skull. His body sailed backward and collided against the back railing. Kailem forgot where he was; his senses were too overwhelmed to think. He fumbled about the quarterdeck on his hands and knees, disoriented.

Then he saw it.

The main mast had been struck by lightning. Cracks splintered up the side of it. The mast slowly tilted forward and came to rest on the crossbeam of the foremast with a heavy thump.

Kailem abandoned the helm and raced down to the main deck, where he met Osmund coming up from below. Emerald appeared behind him, her forearm raised to protect her face from the wind. They all held some part of the ship to stay upright.

"You can't be up here," Kailem yelled over the howling wind and rain.

"The lower decks are flooding," Osmund yelled back.

That explained the ship listing to the left. Kailem agonized over what to do next. His ability to maintain a brave face neared its breaking point. Should he call to abandon ship, he wondered? And where was the Captain?

As they ascended the next swell, the sound of cracking wood reverberated through the ship. An unnatural movement overhead caught Kailem's eye. He watched helplessly as, to his horror, the main mast tilted off the crossbeam of the foremast and fell back towards them. The mighty beam of solid oak crashed into the quarterdeck, sending splinters of wood in all directions. Kailem, Osmund, and Emerald were thrown headlong into the sea.

Kailem was underwater before he could take a breath. The dark water tossed him over and under, robbing him of his orientation. He kicked and stroked, but the turbulent ocean denied him any propulsion, and even if it had been in his power to swim, he knew not in which direction was the surface. He was desperate for air. Panic did its best to drown him, but years of ocean training told him to relax and conserve his energy.

After several moments of chaos, he caught his bearings. He swam toward the surface, his lungs pleading with him to suck in seawater before he reached it.

His head finally broke into the dark night. He gasped for air just as another wave broke on his head, sending him back into the deep. The ocean again did its best to drown him.

When he surfaced the second time, after spitting out seawater and sucking in the night air, he searched his surroundings. There was no one to be found, only waves and broken ship fragments. Then Emerald surfaced some fifteen feet to his left. She was panicking, delirious and disoriented, and barely managed to keep her head above water. He swam to her, held her from behind, and side-stroked to a nearby barrel.

"Hold on tight, I'm going to look for Osmund!" Kailem shouted. The rain pelted their skin as if they were standing under a waterfall. He didn't know if she could hear him, but when he let go of her, she immediately reached out for the barrel. She clung to it like a frightened child holds her mother and squeezed her eyes shut.

Kailem scanned the water, looking for any sign of Osmund. The ocean surface rose and fell a dozen feet with each passing swell, obscuring what little visibility remained in the stormy night. He screamed Osmund's name but could barely hear his own voice; it was impossible for Osmund to hear him. Another wave crashed over his head.

Near to him was a fallen sail still clinging to its crossbeam, and Kailem thought he detected an unnatural movement under the floating canvas. He took a deep breath and swam underneath. The water was darker than coal, but he found his way by feeling the sail.

To his infinite relief, his hand brushed Osmund's leg. The poor boy kicked with manic urgency to stay afloat while breathing frantically into a small pocket of air. Kailem tried speaking to Osmund, but it was no use. He tried pulling Osmund underwater, but Osmund fought against him like a feral animal. There would be no moving him.

Kailem felt for his dagger, Malua, in the sheath attached to his right side. He used it to puncture a hole through the sail. Malua's blade cut the hole longer and longer until he could climb through it. He heaved Osmund onto the mast and Osmund clung to it, panting and coughing. Kailem slid Malua back in its sheath.

Kailem wasn't sure how much time had passed, but eventually, the worst of the storm was behind them. The waves still caused them to rise and fall several feet, and it made holding on to the mast an exhausting chore. Water splashed in their faces and down their throats. The salty taste of seawater coated their tongues.

The clouds parted to reveal the moons overhead; half the silver moon was shining, and the gilded moon was nearly full. The moonlight displayed the destruction on the ocean surface before them. Fragments of the ship littered the water. They watched as the last of the ship's hull was pulled beneath. Emerald, still clinging to her barrel, kicked her way to Kailem and Osmund.

"Ought we swim ta shore?" Emerald asked. Kailem saw a few sailors had survived and were swimming towards the coast, but it was nearly a mile through choppy water.

"No, we should just stay here. Go along with the current," Kailem said.

"But land be right there. We can make it," Emerald insisted. There was an understandable panic in her voice; Kailem had to be the one to stay level-headed. Osmund said nothing; he was too focused on breathing.

"There's a shoreline current here that pulls out to sea when it reaches the cove," Kailem explained. He had to pause between breaths and splashes of water. "That's why we didn't make it to the cove in time. If we try to swim for shore, we'll be kicking against the current and we'll exhaust ourselves before we even come close. But if we ride the current, it sweeps back towards the shore in about a mile or so, and we'll swim for the beach then."

Emerald nodded.

"Climb on here with us. You'll keep more of your body out of the water."

Emerald hesitantly reached out with one hand and let Kailem pull her onto the mast, her feet dangling on the sail the same as theirs.

Hours passed.

The shore was no longer in sight and the clouds had once again covered the moons and stars. The debris spread itself farther and farther apart. Their bodies shivered and their fingers struggled to grip the mast.

Emerald and Osmund eventually fell asleep. Kailem kept an eye out for other sailors in the water, but no one appeared. He also kept an eye out for signs of sharks and, fortunately, saw none of those either.

Why haven't we found land yet? he asked himself. He was losing faith in his plan to follow the current. He also regretted sailing for the cove. It had been a foolish gamble, he now realized, especially for one as familiar with southern storms as he was. They should have sailed directly to shore and taken refuge on land. How many had died because he made the wrong call, he wondered?

His mouth was painfully parched, and the salt was sticking to his eyebrows. The wind cut like razors as it swept over his body. Every muscle was sore, and the salt water stung his many lacerations. There was nothing to do but lie on the mast, alone with his thoughts, as the ocean did with them as it pleased.

The hours continued to pass. The only sounds were the slapping of paltry waves against the mast and the chattering of teeth. He looked in all directions but saw no sign of land. He'd even lost track of which direction was west.

After another hour, the first signs of sunrise emerged over the horizon. That meant it was east. He looked the opposite direction and there, just on the edge of the opposite horizon, so faint it could easily be missed if he hadn't been looking for it, was land. He stared at it for a moment, wondering if his mind was playing tricks on him. But the more light that spilled over the horizon behind him, the clearer the land became.

He shook his companions awake.

"We made it," he said.

"What?" Emerald asked, delirious with exhaustion.

"Oh, thank Iria," Osmund said. He squinted, unable to see after losing his spectacles to the storm. "How do we reach it?"

Kailem left the mast and found them each a new piece of driftwood to make for easier swimming. Then the three of them began kicking their way toward shore. Their progress was painfully slow.

"Is it moving away from us?" Osmund complained.

"I havnae much left in me," Emerald warned, gasping for breath.

"Just keep kicking, we're almost there," Kailem assured. Osmund took umbrage with his use of the word "almost" but was too exhausted to complain.

The sun continued to rise behind them, shining light on their destination. Little by little, kick by kick, they made their way to land.

When the water became shallow enough to stand, they abandoned their driftwood and trudged forward. They had found a rare stretch of beach along a coast that was almost exclusively populated by rocky cliffs and forests that crept up to the shoreline. With the land so close, a surge of energy shot through them, and they raced through the water. One by one they collapsed on the dry sand, unconscious.

Chapter Eight

Tin Armor

46th Day of Spring, 897 G.C.

"How much longer?" Mokain asked as he paced Mr. Marshall's blacksmith shop. It was the morning of the Grand Tournament, and the opening ceremony would be starting any minute.

"Your armor will be ready in time, Master Roka, I assure you. Only a few minutes more," the blacksmith said. "I wish you had come to me sooner."

"Had I known I needed to, I would have," Mokain said. He sat on a stool against the wall and tapped his foot against the ground. He needed a distraction, so he removed his sword, Koa, from its sheath and graced his thumb over the now-blunted edge. Crowds of commoners were on the street, eagerly making their way towards the King's Arena.

"I take it this is not the way of things in Marin?" Mr. Marshall asked.

"No, sir. We fight with dull blades as well, but no armor save a helmet. The fight ends when someone draws blood or disarms their opponent. Or their opponent yields, of course." He stood from the stool and returned to his pacing.

"I see," Mr. Marshall said. "Still sounds dangerous. I like our way better, I should think."

Regardless of whose tournament style was superior, Mokain wouldn't have known theirs at all if he hadn't overheard those contestants in the tavern. It was the phrase 'tin suit of armor' that had caught his attention. After a short inquiry, he had learned a full suit of armor was required to fight in the tournament.

Mokain had gone straight to an armorer that afternoon. There had not been enough time to make him a full suit of armor from scratch, nor would Mokain have been able to afford one even if there had been, but Mr. Marshall was able to refit a used suit of armor to Mokain's measurements.

The hardest part was having to blunt his culmination blades, Tao and Koa. It felt like betraying a friend, but he would resharpen them after the tournament. A Mariner's culmination blade was the pinnacle of function and beauty, most refused to even take them into battle. For Mokain, however, turning his blades into a wall decoration was even more offensive than blunting their edges.

"Here we are," the tired blacksmith said. "Not my best work. In fact, I'd prefer you not tell anyone I made it, should one inquire. But it'll do in a pinch."

"You have my sincerest gratitude, sir," Mokain said. He took the armor without inspecting it and placed it in a large cloth sack.

"I'm no 'sir', lad," Mr. Marshall corrected. "I'd rather have the silver than your gratitude."

Mokain took out three silver florins, less than half the price of a new, custom designed suit, and placed them in the blacksmith's hand. Then he left the shop with the sack over his shoulder and ran through the slow-moving crowd to the King's Arena atop Meager Hill.

***

The Grand Tournament had injected new life into the city. Banners bearing the burgundy and gold colors of the Cavandel flag lined the roads leading to the King's Arena. Jugglers performed and minstrels played, all paid for by the Crown. Vendors roamed the streets selling all kinds of meats, wines, and pastries. Children ran alongside Mokain, waving burgundy and gold streamers above their heads.

In the days leading to the tournament, the City Watch had moved through Meager Hill removing the beggars and vagrants to the city's northern districts. This gave Meager Hill a false air of prosperity, a convincing lie to anyone unfamiliar with the area.

Every great warrior in all of Iria, it seemed, had come to claim the royal prize. Contestants marched up Meager Hill with their entourage in tow, strutting in their armor like peacocks in mating season. Mokain was the last to ascend the hill, and he did so without so much as a squire to carry his armor, but the crowds cheered for him all the same. No one knew any of the contestants' names they celebrated, but it made no difference. These were their warriors.

Kyra traveled to the King's Arena in a palanquin carried by four royal guards. All around her were the sounds of a city abuzz with life. Curiosity overcoming her, she parted the curtain to see they were in the Central Square, roughly the halfway point between the palace and the arena. The Central Square was a pride of the city, crowned with the Rhinegard Hall of Justice on the north end and bordered by other lofty administrative buildings on the other three, but Kyra had never been fond of it. Her discomfort was due entirely to the stories her governess had told her of the many public executions they used to perform there.

Next to her palanquin strolled a flock of noblewomen surrounded by armed escorts of their own. Several ladies of the Court wore dresses that mimicked her betrothal gown, but Kyra remained a step ahead. Today, her dress was burgundy and gold chiffon with a plunging V-neck that was sure to cause a scandal. The folds of fabric were asymmetrical across her chest and ruffled down her abdomen, and the short sleeves were made entirely of lace.

Once they passed through the arena gates, Kyra descended from her palanquin and followed her escort to the royal pavilion reserved for the King and his privileged associates. Her mother met her at the base of the ramp wearing a plastered smile.

"We need to talk, child. It's urgent. But keep your voice low and continue smiling." Lady Avalina demonstrated the face Kyra was to imitate.

"What is it, mother?" Kyra asked through stretched lips.

"The King is proving even more obstinate than expected. Even with Aedon's support, your father couldn't convince him to go to war," Avalina explained.

"And why is that so urgent?" Kyra asked.

Avalina nodded to a noblewoman who passed them on her way down the ramp and waited for her to be out of earshot before continuing. "The plan cannot be delayed, child. Too many pieces are in motion. If the King cannot be swayed, more extreme measures will need to be taken."

Kyra rotated her hand indicating for her mother to continue.

"The King will need to be removed."

"A coup?!" Kyra replied more loudly than she intended.

"Sssh," Avalina scolded. She looked around to ensure no one had heard, then pulled Kyra in close by the elbow. "Keep your voice down, foolish child. A coup is out of the question; his death needs to appear natural."

"You mean to kill the King?" Kyra whispered so quietly she almost couldn't hear herself.

"Not us, child. You."

Kyra suddenly forgot to breathe.

"The Prince has shown himself quite amenable to your father," Avalina continued. "We need Aedon to take the throne as soon as possible."

Despite their leisurely pace, they had arrived at their seats.

"We'll speak more on the matter later," Avalina whispered. Then, turning to Prince Aedon, she said in her normal voice, "Your Grace, you are a vision of resplendence, as always."

The Prince wore a full-sleeved doublet of black suede with a paisley pattern of deep purple that was so faint Kyra didn't notice it until they drew near.

"You are too kind, milady," Aedon said with a formal bow. "And Kyra, you are the very essence of a beauty, as you ever have been." His eyes moved over the length of her body, admiring her dress, then held her chin and kissed her lips. "As are you, Lady Arturri," he then added as an afterthought."

"And you are too kind," Avalina said. She returned a formal curtesy and excused herself to sit with her husband on the far side of the pavilion. Aedon held Kyra's hand as she lowered herself into the overly cushioned chair set next to his.

The royal pavilion was on the second level of the three-tiered stadium, and it extended over the ground level to provide an unparalleled view of the arena. Kyra was especially grateful for the ceramic furnaces placed strategically about the pavilion to keep them warm.

The arena stands were packed with noblemen and commoners alike, each in their designated areas, of course. The stands buzzed with anticipation despite that the arena floor was still vacant.

"Is everything alright?" Aedon asked.

Kyra realized her anxiety was written across her face, and she forced out a congenial one to replace it.

"Of course, my love. This is all just so overwhelming to me. We don't have many tournaments in Devona, and certainly none so grand."

"Well, you shall have to acclimate to this level of grandeur if you are to be queen," Aedon jested.

Kyra's serene demeanor quite nearly became genuine. "I'm sure I will adjust quite nicely."

The heavy stomp of boots ascended the ramp as the King arrived with two guards in tow. The royal pavilion all stood for his arrival, and he waved them all to sit just as quickly. He stepped to the edge of the pavilion to gaze at the assembly of spectators. The crowd erupted in cheers and the King waved back, smiling through his salt-and-pepper beard.

"They really love him, don't they?" Aedon asked. His voice was a mixture of admiration and jealousy.

"They do, and they'll love you as King even more so," Kyra said, stroking his arm. Aedon's face softened.

"Are you familiar with the rules?" he asked.

She leaned toward him and wrapped her arm around his. "Enlighten me," she replied.

"It is a single-elimination tournament, which means you must win your fight to advance to the next round. Each contestant will fight once in each round. They all wear full-body armor made of only a layer of tin over a leather lining, and they fight with blunted weapons."

Kyra nodded, and Aedon continued.

"The object is to penetrate the layer of tin anywhere above the knees. A dent is not enough. They must actually crack the armor."

"And why are the weapons blunted?"

"It makes it more difficult to crack the tin. It also makes the tournament safer, although mishaps still occur, on occasion."

"I see," Kyra replied, taking it all in. "And why is the arena sand divided into those sections?"

"Well, there are sixty-four contestants today, and some fights may last ten minutes or longer. If they only fought one at a time, we'd still be here after dark, waiting for the first round to end."

"So, we'll have four fights to watch at once, then?"

Aedon nodded. "See those first two contestants against the gate of the staging area? You can tell the one on the left is Norvian. They are the only ones who use a battle-ax in combat."

"He's a giant!" Kyra remarked with a laugh. The Norvian had the look of a man who had known nothing but combat all his life, with blonde hair and a face that resembled cheese left too long in the sun.

"They do grow them quite large up there, to be sure," Aedon said. "But my gold is on the man to his right. That is a Shinda warrior."

"How can you tell? He looks like all the others." She slid her hand into his and gave a gentle squeeze.

"Well, you would know him instantly if he took his helmet off. Their skin is a shade darker than ours, though not as dark as the Àramen. But even with his helmet on, you can tell he's Shinda by the style of his armor and the curve of his blade. The Shinda are renowned throughout all of Iria. Dugald told me they were the most impressive of all the warriors training in the castle bailey this week."

"But not more renowned than a Cavander warrior, I'm sure."

"Well, of course not," Aedon said with a grin. "But that should go without saying."

***

Mokain joined the other sixty-three contestants, corralled in a small staging area and donned his armor. There was a piece to cover every inch of him from his ankles to the crown of his head, and the helmet covered his entire face save for a vertical slit up the center and a horizontal slit across the eyes, making a T-shaped space to see and breathe through.

He wasn't used to fighting in this much metal. In fact, no warrior in Marin fought in a *full* suit unless he was a mounted knight atop a massive war horse; the metal was just too heavy. Fortunately, the tin was thinner than parchment, so it was not as heavy as it first appeared. As he donned his armor, he looked around the group, wondering who he'd be fighting. A handful of men towered over him; he wasn't used to feeling this small.

The King had wisely ordered soldiers — with blades freshly sharpened — to stand guard over the contestants. More than half of the contestants were Cavander; the remainder were mostly Norvian and Devonian. There were a small number of Shinda and Marcônish as well. No Àramen had come, which was expected given the tension between their kingdoms, and no Lanians either, which was unsurprising given the quality of their fighters. No other Mariners seemed to be present. With his armor in place, Mokain maneuvered through the crowd of restless fighters for a better look.

The King's Arena was oval-shaped and made of stone three stories tall. The center fighting area was more than a hundred yards across and covered in sand.

Never had Mokain seen so many people together in one place. There must have been thousands, even tens of thousands of commoners packed into the structure. All of Suvara could have fit inside. The roar of the cheering crowd caused the arena's stone frame to vibrate. Mokain was far out of his depth.

Trumpets rang out over the clamor of the crowd. A small man dressed in velvet garb emerged onto the arena sand and bowed before the King, then began reading names off a scroll. As he did, men exited the staging area and made their way to their appointed fighting area.

"Mokain Roka!" the Herald called. The Mariner grabbed his helmet and left through the side door to the arena.

The arena sand was divided into four fighting areas by wooden barriers. Another aspect of a Cavander tournament Mokain wasn't aware of. At first, he didn't know where he was supposed to go, then he noticed only one area was missing a fighter. The contestant was staring at him impatiently.

Mokain jogged to the fighting area, using the time to size up his opponent. He was a Cavander, a short, slender man who shifted his weight back and forth. His face plate was still raised and his expression was confident, arrogantly so, and he carried a naval cutlass of all weapons.

The naval cutlass was an odd choice. He likely chose it to throw off his competitors, and the blade had a good six inches over Mokain's twin leaf blades. Unfortunately for the Cavander, the naval cutlass, while rare everywhere else in Iria, happened to be a Mariner specialty.

Three seconds. That's all it took for Mokain to cut through the tin armor covering the Cavander's right shoulder. The Cavander could scarcely believe it. He stood there staring at his shoulder, the reality of defeat slowly sinking in. Mokain was already halfway back to the staging area.

He sat on a bench and waited for the next round. Even he was surprised by how little resistance his opponent had raised, and he resisted the hope that every fight would be so facile. Looking at the other men in the staging area, he knew that would not be the case. These were hardened men full of battle experience, and one does not survive years of battle without significant skill with a blade.

Suddenly, the arena went quiet. Unnaturally quiet. Mokain did his best to see what had happened, but couldn't see through the mass of fighters huddled against the gate.

***

Kyra leaned against the Prince's shoulder as they observed the tournament. Each fighting quarter had two entry points, and the fight began as soon as both fighters stepped inside. The fighters in three of the four areas danced around each other, making half-hearted jabs and exaggerated parries to measure their opponent before committing to the fight. It reminded Kyra of new lovers meeting each other for the first time.

In the fourth fighting area, the Norvian engaged in no such dance. He was paired against a Cavander nearly half his size. The Cavander was the first to step into the fighting area, swinging his side-sword casually about. When the Norvian stepped in, he did so with his battle axe already above his head. The sound of clanging metal rang throughout the Arena.

Even Kyra could tell the Cavander was outmatched. The Norvian attacked with vicious swings of his battle-ax. The Cavander lifted his side-sword to block, but the force of the blow knocked the sword from his hands. The Norvian lifted the battle-ax again, and the Cavander had no option but to use his forearm to block the strike. The ax cracked through the tin armor and pushed the arm down, ending with a second crack to the Cavander's helmet.

Kyra screamed. She wrapped her arms around Aedon's bicep and buried her face in his shoulder. "Is it over?" she whined, her eyes squeezed tight.

"Decidedly so," Aedon said, casually flexing the arm Kyra held. "All you need is one crack in the armor."

She looked back at the arena. "But it was so fast! The little man didn't even swing at him."

Aedon smiled. "I should scarcely think he would appreciate the moniker 'little man.' And worry not, he was hardly our best fighter."

The small Cavander man took off his helmet to a trickle of blood leaking down his forehead.

"Is he bleeding? But he was wearing a helmet," Kyra said.

"Tin offers precious little protection, I'm afraid," Aedon said. "And that was a hard blow he took. Besides, it looks like his arm got the worst of it."

The Cavander gingerly removed the armor from off his forearm. There was an unnatural dent in the arm, a V-shape where the bone should be straight. Kyra buried her face in Aedon's shoulder once again.

"He'll be fine," Aedon assured. "Just a broken bone."

The Herald announced the winner and called out the two next contestants. The day continued in this manner with hours of endless brutality. Aedon explained to Kyra the different combat styles and maneuvers. Several of the contestants he knew personally from the Royal Guard.

Krya leaned over to watch her father laughing and joking with the King. Had she misheard her mother? It wasn't hard to believe her parents could order someone assassinated, but not a friend and certainly not the King. A knot twisted repeatedly in her stomach.

The sound of footsteps came ascending the ramp behind them. Aedon turned to see Lord Menden walking across the dais.

"Good afternoon, my lord," Aedon called. "For a minute, I thought you were going to miss the tournament entirely."

"And miss the chance to see my replacement in action? Hardly," Lord Menden replied. He snapped his fingers for a servant to bring him a goblet of wine. "Do we have a favorite?"

"Most of the Cavanders are advancing; you've trained your men well."

Lord Menden wasn't surprised.

Kyra's eyes fixed on the fight nearest her. Two Cavanders tested each other with half-hearted strikes, but what caught her eye was their difference in size. The smaller of the two was by no means a small man; in fact, he was probably taller than average. But his opponent was a Cavander nearly large enough to pass as a Norvian.

Kyra noticed Lord Menden had taken a keen interest in their fight as well.

"Do you know those two?" she asked.

Lord Menden nodded. "Quite well, in fact. They're two of our best. Shame they should meet in the first round. I should have liked to see them both advance." Lord Menden paused to take a drink. "But such is the nature of the draw, I suppose. The larger one is Rayne Dorman, and his opponent is Willian Wyke. I expect this should be quite the display."

The fight began in expert form. Both Cavanders wielded two-handed broadswords that looked like they weighed more than Kyra did. Their sequence of attacks and perries looked almost choreographed.

"It's clear they both had the same teacher," Aedon commented.

Lord Menden agreed. "They're each other's sparring partners as well. They can practically read each other's mind at this point."

The Cavanders' fight had lasted over twenty minutes, and the effects of fatigue started to show. Each was slower to raise their blade after an attack, and frequently they took steps back to catch their breath before reengaging.

As Rayne Dorman attacked, Willian Wyke misjudged one of his strikes. Perhaps the sun shined in his eyes, or perhaps the fatigue made him lose focus for a moment. Whatever the reason, Willian failed to block the attack. Rayne's broadsword connected with Willian's helm just below the jawbone. The blow cracked the tin inward, forcing the metal shard to bend beneath the leather and slice Willian's neck. Blood quickly followed.

Willian dropped his sword and fell to his side. He rose on his knees and left hand, desperate to stop the bleeding with his right, but the force of the blow had bent the helmet in a way that it could not be removed without causing more damage. His neck was a ripped wine skin spilling blood onto the sand.

Rayne Dorman ripped off his own helmet and tried to pinch the severed artery in his friend's neck, but it was no use. He looked around frantically, not knowing what to do. Willian was quickly bleeding out on the Arena sand.

A short, portly baron cried out from the stands and jumped down the wall separating the spectators from the combatants. He landed feet first, but collapsed to his backside upon impact. He was up again in a moment and raced to his son's side. The jagged tin still penetrated the young man's neck.

The Herald called for the blacksmith. When he arrived, he began cutting away the helm with metal shears, but by that point, Willian Wyke had stopped moving. The crowd stood on their feet, aghast.

Kyra couldn't speak. Her heart broke and her stomach churned. The young man couldn't have been more than three years her senior, almost the same age as her fiancé, and the open wound on his neck was more grotesque and morbid than her worst nightmares. But the worst parts of it all were the sounds. The sound of a man realizing he had killed his friend. The sound of a father weeping for a son dying in his arms. The sound of the son gargling as he drowned in his own blood. Aedon held her close.

***

The tournament carried long into the day; the shadows cast by the arena towers were now opposite where they had been at the start. For his second fight, Mokain was paired against another Cavander. This one was larger than the first, but still shorter than Mokain, and he was armed with a standard Cavander side-sword. His visor was already closed.

Just before Mokain stepped into the fighting area, he noticed a pool of blood soaking into the sand. He guessed that must have been what caused the arena to go quiet earlier.

The two competitors took several moments circling each other, then Mokain struck first with an overhead slash with his right blade, Koa. The Cavander parried the blow and retaliated with a direct thrust to the chest, which Mokain easily countered with his left blade, Tao. He logged the fighter's response in his mind.

The Cavander came on aggressively with diagonal slashes from either side, then spun as he made a horizontal strike. The strikes were strong and technically sound, but the footwork was sloppy, and it left his back exposed too long.

Mokain attacked the Cavander with diagonal slashes of his own, once with Tao and then with Koa. He hoped that by mimicking his opponent's attack-style, the Cavander would become overconfident. The tactic paid off. After parrying Mokain's attacks, the Cavander responded with another direct thrust to the chest. Mokain dodged the thrust and struck low, hoping to provoke an overhead response. The Cavander took the bait, and with both hands on the side-sword struck down with everything he had.

Mokain crossed his twin blades over his head to block the sword, and in one fluid motion, rotated the tip of the side-sword down into the dirt. With the Cavander's abdomen now exposed and his side-sword pinned down with Tao, Mokain thrust the tip of Koa through the tin armor at the Cavander's stomach.

The Cavander yelped, dropped the side-sword, and fell to his knees. Mokain's blade must have pierced the leather as well as the tin. The armor made a horrible wrenching sound as he pulled his blade free. The Cavander fell to his side, ripping off his helmet and clutching his stomach. Mokain inspected his blade, only a single droplet of blood at the tip. The Cavander would be fine.

The crowd was on its feet, cheering.

Mokain could see the Cavander's face for the first time. It was round and innocent, with rosy cheeks like a child's face. Mokain offered his hand. The injured man looked at Mokain's hand for a moment, distrusting, but he took the offer and rose to his feet.

"You over-committed on your overhead strike," he explained to the Cavander. His years as a lieutenant in the Mariner Army took over. "When fighting an enemy with two weapons, after your overhead strike, return to your neutral stance so you can parry his counterattack."

Mokain demonstrated the overhead strike and quick return to neutral. The Cavander did the same, wincing as he did.

"Excellent form, soldier. Keep it at." Mokain patted the Cavander on the back. A hint of a smile appeared on the Cavander's face as he ambled out of the arena.

***

"Lord Menden, pay particular attention to this Mariner here," Aedon said as the second-round fight against the Cavander began. "He had the fastest win of any fight in the first round."

Aedon explained that the Mariner's twin blades should have put him at a disadvantage, given how short they were, but it was clear even to Kyra that he was controlling the fight. When the Cavander attacked with an overhead strike, the Mariner deflected the Cavander's sword into the sand and skewered the armor around the abdomen. The crowd cheered; Kyra felt sick.

"Now that was quite the display," Lord Menden said, taking a sip of wine. "Tactically, I would say that was perfect."

"Indeed," Aedon agreed. "I know the reputation of the Mariners, but I'd never seen one fight until today."

"For good reason, I should say. The Mariners are content with their islands," Lord Menden explained. "They don't fight to expand their territory or start quarrels without a just cause, and certainly no one ever picks a fight with them. Now you've seen why."

"Indeed," Aedon said again. They watched as the Mariner helped his defeated opponent to his feet and demonstrated a maneuver to him. "Is he teaching our man what he did wrong now? How peculiar."

"I don't believe I've ever seen that either," Lord Menden agreed. "That is Conroy Wyndell, recently promoted to sergeant. His father is a baron, I believe. No one of consequence. But a nicer boy than Conroy you're not likely to meet."

Kyra couldn't believe what she was hearing. A man had just died in front of them. Not just any man, Willian Wyke, A Cavander, a compatriot and a friend. They had known him since he was a boy, had trained with him and fought with him. And now they had just watched him die. How could they continue the tournament after that? How could any of them enjoy the fighting after witnessing such a scene? She wanted to condemn this entire display, wanted to stand up and scream and flee the arena and never look back. But she couldn't let herself appear weak, so she said nothing, concealing the ache inside her.

Chapter Nine

CASTAWAY

47th Day of Spring, 897 G.C.

Emerald awoke to the rising tide rushing against the soles of her feet. Her left cheek was caked in dried sand while her right cheek baked under the blistering sun. Her head still felt the movement of the sea, and her eyes took several moments to find their focus. The sun was far too bright. Everything hurt. She saw two young men still unconscious on the beach beside her, and on instinct she crawled away from them.

With a safe distance between them, she surveyed the beach. Slowly, the memory of the shipwreck returned to her. Memories of mountainous waves and black water made her shiver. She gripped a handful of dry sand to remind herself she was safe on land. Her stomach rumbled and her muscles pulsed with soreness. Her eyes scanned the water, but she saw no other survivors, only scattered driftwood and broken barrels. She looked for the sun; it was still a few degrees from being overhead.

Kailem coughed. The sudden sound startled her, and she pulled her knees against her chest. Kailem pushed up on his hands and sat back on his knees with all the grace of a newborn fawn taking its first steps. There he rested while taking stock of his surroundings.

Emerald saw for the first time how violent the storm had been for him. His tunic was torn in several places and there was a line of crusted blood on his forehead. Bruises covered his arms from his wrists to elbows, and dried salt, sand, and debris saturated his hair.

"Well, at least we're alive," Kailem croaked. His throat was hoarse from dehydration and swallowing sea water.

Emerald nodded.

"Is it just us?" Kailem asked.

Emerald shrugged.

Kailem leaned over and shook Osmund. The young nobleman groaned and rolled away from him. Kailem let him rest.

"Have you seen any trails around here? Or food?" Kailem asked. Emerald shook her head.

Kailem looked her up and down with obvious concern. "How are you feeling?"

She simply shrugged. In truth, every muscle ached, and nearly every inch of skin had scrapes that stung like lemons in a knife wound. Her mouth was dry and felt like tree bark in the dead of summer. Her head throbbed and her mind raced with all the different ways she could die.

Kailem winced as he rose to his feet. Once standing, he brushed off the sand from his hair and body. At first, his posture was limp and lazy, but he forced himself into a strong stance. His framed blocked Emerald from the hot sun while he took in his surroundings.

"This is a short stretch of beach. Looks like the trees go all the way to the water on both sides of us. I'll walk the tree line and see if we can find any trails through the forest."

Emerald summoned the courage to speak. "Ought we stay here and wait fer another ship ta find us?"

Kailem shook his head. "No, we're not likely to see one for a while. Most ships prefer to sail farther out to sea to escape the currents along the shore. Plus, if a ship does stop, there's no guarantee they'll be the friendly sort."

Emerald was finding it increasingly difficult not to panic. If she were honest with herself, she had been panicking since she awoke, but she refused to admit it. She moved next to Osmund while Kailem left to explore the beach.

The ocean was so calm and gentle, making the shards of their broken ship horridly out of place. The water rushed up the sand and made a breathy, hissing sound as it pulled back to the sea, endlessly repeating itself. She couldn't escape the feeling she would never leave this beach alive. She looked out at the ocean water, both hoping and dreading that a ship would pass by.

After several minutes of silence, Osmund stirred awake. He popped his head up and looked around, squinting as if using his eyes for the first time.

"Am I dead?" he asked, his voice just as hoarse as Kailem's had been.

"Aye, Oz, ye are," she replied.

Osmund jerked his head toward her, reading her expression. "Well, I am glad to see our impending death has not dampened your sense of humor," he said, masking his fears with an aristocratic indifference.

Osmund sat upright and patted his hips and torso. "Well, everything seems to be intact. How fortunate. So, where is our Mariner friend? Kailem."

"Off lookin' fer a trail. Says it be better to wander forest like than to wait fer rescue."

"Well, I guess he would know."

He settled in with his arms resting on his knees. For a moment, they sat in silence, watching the water and listening to the waves scratch up and down the beach. Osmund smacked his lips every few minutes.

"I would not mind a glass of Marcônish Red right about now," he said to no one in particular. He was trying to appear calm and dignified, but the rapid tapping of his thumb against his shin told Emerald he was just as afraid as she was.

Kailem walked the tree line, scanning for signs of a trail. His mind fluttered between memories of his survival training and a paralyzing panic. It would be one thing if he were alone; he had a good chance of surviving if he were alone. But he wasn't alone. Emerald and Osmund were with him, and they had virtually no chance without him. Their fate now rested squarely on his shoulders.

The tree line met a rocky outcrop where the beach ended; there was no sign of a trail. He bent down to wash his face in a tide pool, the saltwater stinging his forehead as he did so. He took a deep breath, then another, then a third, exhaling slowly through pursed lips.

Hadn't he already been through enough, he complained to himself? After everything that had happened with his parents, and just as life began to look up, Iria knocked him down again. The owners of the shipping company would never make him captain after this, so what was he to do with himself? But he couldn't think about that now; he had to focus on surviving.

Fresh water. That was his first concern. Plus, a river would likely lead to a village or a farm. And they needed to escape the sun to prevent dehydration. Above all, he needed to stay optimistic. If the others saw him worried, they would also worry, and panic is the last thing they needed.

He gripped his hands together to keep them from shaking.

***

Osmund felt for the silver pocket watch Emerald had given him. It had fallen from his vest pocket, but it still dangled from the end of the chain still fastened to his vest. He held it up and a steady stream of briny sea water trickled out. He put it to his ear; it wasn't ticking.

"I know someone who can fix it," he said. "That is, if we survive all this, of course." He placed the pocket watch back in his vest pocket.

Kailem approached from behind with his tunic in his hands and sat beside them. In the tunic, he carried an assortment of fruits and berries.

"I found a fig tree and a blackberry bush. They're ripe enough, I reckon. The bad news is I couldn't find a trail. Looks like we'll have to blaze one of our own."

Osmund and Emerald nodded, then each reached forward to take a piece of fruit. No one spoke as they ate.

"Well, we should be on our way," Kailem said once the fruit was gone. "We'll want to find some fresh water before nightfall."

"And do you know how to find fresh water?" Osmund asked.

"Of course, we'll walk west until we find either a road or stream, either one will lead us to a village."

"That's it?" Osmund scoffed and shook his head. "I am going to die out here." His breathing quickened, his air of aristocratic indifference dissolving.

"We're not going to—!" Kailem cut his outburst short. He took a deep breath before he continued. "We're not going to die. Before long, you'll be back in your usual lap of luxury, I promise."

Osmund rolled his eyes, then tried taking deeper breaths to calm himself. It didn't work.

Emerald stood and brushed away the sand. "Well, then. If ye're right certain the forest be the way, best we be on wit it."

Kailem looked up at her and nodded, grateful someone else was being strong. "The sooner we start, the sooner we'll finish," he added.

"Exactly," she replied.

Emerald picked up Kailem's tunic, shook off the sand, and returned it. The three survivors left the beach and began trudging west through the dense forest. They walked in a single file through the trees, avoiding the brush and thickets as best they could. Kailem kept his hand gripped around his dagger, Malua, as he marched.

Trekking through the forest produces a peculiar meditative effect. The rhythmic fall of footsteps can distort one's perception of time, and such was the case with the three survivors. But the effect of the march is different for every person. For Kailem, hours passed in minutes. Reading the land and searching for food and water became second nature, and his thoughts would drift to memories of his parents or wondering what Mokain was doing at that moment. He became so ingrained in his thoughts that any sense of time was lost.

Emerald felt her mind clear of any thoughts the longer they marched. That calmness surprised her. These were the direst circumstances in which she'd ever found herself, and given her past, that was saying something. Yet somehow, she had stopped worrying about where her next meal would come from or who might be after her. She had stopped worrying that her old gang leader, Jacken, would track her down and make good on his promise to kill her in her sleep. The repetitive footfalls wiped her mind of any thoughts at all. It was a peace she hadn't known for a long time, and it was the peace itself that made her worry.

In Emerald's experience, peace and calm made you drop your guard, and it is when you drop your guard that pain finds you. Stress and distrust were assets that kept her sharp. It was safer to worry than to relax. So, she tried to focus on the danger, looking for any angle it might come at her. But try as she did, she couldn't hold on to it for long. The rhythmic footsteps continually pushed her fears out of her mind, forcing a calmness on her she wanted no part of.

As far as Osmund was concerned, their trek slowed time to nearly a standstill. He was certain they had been walking for days and yet somehow the sun hadn't moved. His thoughts were a steady stream of complaints. *Why did the sun have to be so hot?* He murmured to himself. *Why aren't there more branches to shade us? And why must the forest have so many pestering insects?*

With each ridge they climbed, Osmund yearned with all his heart to see a river or a road, and with each disappointment, his frustrations magnified. He wanted to scream, to kick something, even throw himself to the ground in a fit.

But he refused to complain aloud. Such behavior was not becoming of a gentleman. There was no prohibition about complaining in one's mind, however, and his inner monologue quickly turned poetically petulant.

The rhythmic footsteps continued.

Every hour or so, Kailem would spot something edible and they would stop to eat. There were more fig trees and berry bushes. Kailem had to swat poisonous berries out of Osmund's hand more than once when he strayed to the wrong bush. There were also the petals of the beach rose, which Osmund couldn't bring himself to try. They also munched on passion vines, buckthorn, greenbrier, and sumac. They had something to chew almost constantly, and yet their hunger only grew with each passing hour.

The sun dipped low in the sky and the air cooled along with it.

"Curse of Iria!" Osmund yelled.

Kailem and Emerald turned to see Osmund hopping on one foot with his hand against a tree for balance.

"What'd ye do, Oz?" Emerald asked, suppressing a laugh.

"I twisted my ankle on this cursed tree root," Osmund explained. "What is a root doing above ground, anyway?"

Kailem examined the injured ankle. He put pressure on the muscles, but Osmund didn't wince. "You'll be fine."

Osmund didn't seem convinced. He put his foot down, slowly shifting his weight to test it. It turned out Kailem was right; he hadn't twisted it. From then on, he placed his feet directly in Kailem's footsteps.

That lasted only a few minutes until he walked into a spider web that Kailem and Emerald had each ducked under. They both stopped to watch Osmund curse and swat at what appeared to be nothing but air. For Emerald, it was the highlight of her day.

Their lips were like cracked leather. Yesterday, water had nearly killed them; today, they would gladly surrender a limb for a single cup of it. They walked down a small knoll where Kailem hoped to find at least a small stream, but all they found was a dried-up creek bed. No one said anything; they simply trudged out of the creek bed and returned to their marching.

The long trek continued.

Eventually, Osmund stopped and leaned against a tree. "Look, you two, I am quite certain I've not another step in me," he said. Kailem and Emerald paused as well. "I'm knackered, my feet are killing me, I cannot catch my breath, I am covered in dirt and sweat, I can't see properly without my spectacles, and those berries have not taken a liking to me, if you catch my meaning. Shouldn't we have at least found water by now?"

Kailem looked to the sky. He couldn't see the sun, but the orange and purples hues in the clouds meant it was already below the horizon. Nightfall was fast approaching.

"I guess this is as good of a place as any. I'll go find some firewood."

Kailem walked away while Osmund and Emerald collapsed to the ground. Emerald put her back against a tree; Osmund laid on his back with his arms and legs flung out in all directions.

"I haven't walked that far in... ever," Osmund said between breaths. "I would not have thought myself capable of walking such a distance. How far do you say that was? One hundred miles? Two hundred?"

"Not fifteen," Emerald returned.

"That's it?! Ugh." He moaned like he was about to cry.

Emerald removed her shoes and rubbed her feet, so Osmund began unlacing his boots as well. While sliding off his left boot, a rush of blood entered his foot. The painful sensation of pins and needles seized the full length of his sole. The same sensation attacked the right foot, and a horrible smell escaped when he removed his socks.

"Uck! How repulsive," he complained. "What is that?"

Small yellow bubbles had formed around the ball and heel of both of his feet. They were unsightly and tender to the touch.

"What is wrong with my feet? Are those boils?" He inspected his feet more closely. "Emerald, I believe I may have contracted smallpox."

"Them be blisters, Oz," she replied. "Ye've truly never had a blister before?"

"I most certainly would remember if I had. And I must say, I do not much care for them. Are they fatal?" Osmund knew they were not, but in their current plight, any reassurance was welcome.

Emerald let out her first genuine chuckle since the shipwreck. "Nay, Oz, tis not fatal. Ye'll be fine."

Kailem returned as Osmund complained about his feet. He set his pile of dried sticks, pine needles, and birch bark on the ground.

"Can ye start a fire with that?" Emerald asked.

"I believe so." Kailem tore apart the birch bark and made a pile of tinder.

"How do ye do it?" Emerald asked. Osmund shimmied towards them as well. The fading light had nearly vanished, and the forest was disappearing in the darkness.

"Well, first we put together some tinder, which is anything that lights easily, then we add progressively larger pieces until we have a roaring fire."

"But how do you make the first spark?" Osmund asked.

Kailem took out a palm-sized stone, dark gray and glossy like a shard of glass. Then he unsheathed Malua.

"This is a type of rock called 'flint'. I found it just now. It should spark when I strike it with the edge of my dagger."

Kailem struck the flint. Then again. Then a third time. No sparks came. He continued striking the rock, alternating his angle and force with no luck.

"Ye sure that be flint?" Emerald asked.

Kailem inspected the stone. "I think so."

"You *think* so?" Osmund asked. "You *have* done this before, have you not?"

"Of course!" Kailem returned. "Once. Three years ago. It was part of our survival training."

Osmund groaned.

"What? I am not in the habit of losing myself in the woods with no supplies."

Emerald found a flat section of ground near the fire pit and brushed aside the twigs and pebbles, then laid back with her hands behind her head. Osmund as followed her lead while Kailem worked at the fire. The night turned the forest into a black abyss; they could scarcely see the trees nearest them. A chill settled in the air, promising a frosty night to come.

***

Elwin of Andil ran swiftly through Glendown Forest, lithe and delicate, staff in hand, careful to let as little of his weight impact the ground as possible. The subtle trail left by the band of thieves he was tracking was still fresh. As best he could tell, he was, at most, half a day behind them, but it had been over a week since he last saw another person.

The forest darkened. Absent any signs of people nearby, Elwin was safe to use his abilities openly. From the top of the next ridge, he leapt into the air, sailing forty yards across the ravine in the moonlight. The wind ruffled through his hair and coat. No number of lifetimes could make this sensation any less exhilarating. He neared the other side of the ravine and landed without a sound. It felt good to be himself for a change. He bounded through the forest again like a leaping deer.

Elwin paused.

Something rustled nearby, something beyond the usual critters and birds. Something was out of place.

There were thoughts on the wind. Thoughts too far away to hear them clearly, but close enough to recognize they were there. They were human thoughts. He moved in their direction, keeping close to the ground.

The thoughts grew louder. He still could not make out the words, but the tone was innocuous; far from that of a hardened criminal. They were likely the thoughts of an underling, perhaps even a new recruit. Whoever it was wouldn't know much, but questioning them could still be useful. He followed the thoughts through the forest.

Elwin came to a stop behind a thicket of bushes and laid his staff on the ground. The young man's thoughts were clear to him now. He was gathering firewood, but his thoughts were not on his task. He was overflowing with concern, not concern for his own safety but for his traveling companions. He felt responsible for them, and he was doubting his ability to lead them.

This was not one of the outlaws Elwin had been tracking. He turned to leave, but something inside him said to stay. He hearkened to that inner voice and followed the young man back to his camp, then observed the three companions from afar.

Elwin couldn't see much, but he could hear every word, those spoken aloud as well as those thought in silence. Such a curious group, Elwin thought. He could scarcely imagine three people less likely to form a traveling party than these three.

The young man he had followed here was berating himself for not being able to start a fire for them. The other male in the group thought only of his feet, for some reason. The young female, however, was afraid her companions would discover her secret. Elwin listened to her with particular attention. Her thoughts quickly changed to frustration that someone in her gang of thieves had managed to frame her.

These were certainly not the outlaws he was tracking. The poor children couldn't even start a fire, so how in Iria had they survived in these woods, Elwin wondered? And where had they come from? One fact was certain: if he left them here, they would not survive. The bandits were surely near, and if the bandits didn't find them, the forest would claim them.

Chapter Ten

The Royal Gardens

47th Day of Spring, 897 G.C.

"**A**re you sure you won't be too cold in this, my lady?" Martina asked. "It's a frosty one tonight."

Kyra assessed her outfit. The night was indeed cold, so common sense would dictate a thick gown with long sleeves. But Iria curse her. Beauty was worth a little chill.

"I'm sure, Martina," Kyra said. "But why don't you fetch my woolen shawl and the linen gloves, just to be safe."

"Very good, my lady."

Kyra stared at herself in the full-length mirror. Her gown was more traditional than the ones she had worn recently, but part of curating one's image was controlling the public's expectations. She couldn't wear a new design every night lest it become expected and therefore no longer noteworthy. And besides, she was only seeing Prince Aedon tonight, and he had no eye for a woman's fashion.

She had first chosen the red dress to match the roses in the garden, but as she looked at herself in the mirror, the color had reminded her of Willian Wyke. The memory of the poor lad bleeding to death on the arena sand invaded her mind.

She saw the sand absorbing the blood as it pulsed from his neck. The memory reached into her chest and squeezed.

So, she changed into the blue dress. It may not match the roses, but it was beautiful, nonetheless. More importantly, it allowed the image of poor Willian to fade.

As Martina retrieved the woolen shawl and linen gloves, Kyra looked out the balcony. The height reminded her of the servant girl, Kris, and how her father's attack dog, Daron, had thrown the poor girl over a balcony of similar height, although everyone believed she had jumped. Why hadn't the servant girl's death affected Kyra the way Willian's death had, she wondered? Perhaps it was because Willian's death had been a waste, serving no greater purpose, whereas Kris's death was necessary to maintain their secrecy. Or perhaps the loss of a young nobleman's life was simply more tragic than some nosy kitchen maid.

These were, of course, all lies. And Kyra could tell herself a thousand lies, but she'd always know the true reason the servant girl's death hadn't affected her. That reason was distance. Kyra played no active role in killing Kris, hadn't seen the girl's body crack open when it hit the stones below, hadn't seen her friends and loved ones weep over her loss. The servant's death hadn't been real. She might as well have been a faceless name in a fairy tale, and in fairy tales, only the main character matters. But with Willian, that had been no fairy tale. There had been no distance at all. She shuddered, recalling every ghastly, intimate detail, and cinched her shawl tight around her shoulders.

There was a knock at the door. Martina opened it to Prince Aedon in a black, knee-length fur coat, double-breasted with silver buttons descending either side of his torso. He stepped in without a word to Martina.

"Beautiful dress, my dear," he said. "You never cease to amaze."

"You've seen this dress before, Aedon," Kyra scolded in jest.

"And I stand by my statement, nonetheless. Shall we?" Aedon held out his elbow to her.

"With pleasure," she replied. She hooked her arm around his and let him lead her out of the room.

They took their time walking through the palace. Kyra loved how everyone would step aside and lower their heads as they passed. Ember trotted dutifully behind them as if she were a member of the Royal Guard. They descended the grand staircase and passed through the palace doors to the southern portico. It was a dark night, and few people still walked in the courtyard, but two palace guardsmen joined them all the same. When they arrived at the gardens, Aedon instructed the guards to wait at the entrance.

Nothing in Devona could rival the King's Garden. The oil lamps cast a warm glow over the foliage and flowers bloomed in every imaginable size, shape, and color. The pathways weaved in and out of the towering hedges the way Norvian women tied their hair in braids. In seconds, they were lost in their own private paradise. She gave Ember permission to run and play.

"Everything is so beautiful here," Kyra said. She squeezed the arm linked with hers.

"I'm glad you think so. A queen should appreciate her kingdom," Aedon said. Kyra shivered and Aedon unbuttoned his coat. "You must be freezing, love." He placed his fur coat over her shoulders. The bottom brushed against her ankles.

"Mmm, thank you, Aedon. I had not expected so cold a night. Devona is graced with warmer springs."

They passed the rose bushes, and she was again reminded of William Wyke. It appeared her favorite flower was now spoiled.

"Let's walk by the hydrangeas," she said with a hop in her step. "They're my new favorite."

"The flowers match your dress," Aedon said as they passed the blue blossoms. He removed his knife and selected the bluest hydrangea blossom in the bunch. "Now technically," he said with a serious tone, "it's a crime for anyone to cut a flower from the King's Gardens. But as the Crown Prince, I'm allowed certain special privileges." He placed one hand behind his back and made a show out of bowing to offer her the flower.

It was, for Kyra, a silent, perfect moment. She raised on her toes and kissed him, letting her lips linger on his.

She twirled the hydrangeas in her fingers. "I bet you've made that move with all the ladies here," she said.

"No, not as many as you'd think."

She playfully elbowed him, and he responded with a kiss on top of her head.

Behind Aedon was the gazebo where Kyra had luncheoned with her parents only days prior. The sight reminded her of her task, and the magic of the moment vanished. Her jaw clenched. She couldn't see how starting a war with other kingdoms helped their family; none of it made sense to her.

Even if it did make sense, how in Iria did her parents expect her to do this, she wondered? She couldn't just walk up to a person, let alone her fiancé, and say,

I think we should murder your father, sounds lovely, does it not? No, this would require some finesse.

"Did you have a favorite fighter in the tournament today?" Aedon asked.

The question pulled her back into the moment. "Oh, I know too little of combat to have a favorite. Who impressed you the most?" Kyra asked. They were past the hydrangeas now and entering the marigolds.

"I was quite taken by the Mariner fellow. He moved with such grace and efficiency, and he struck like a viper, but only when the moment was right. I am eager to see how he performs tomorrow."

"You *are* quite taken by him," Kyra remarked.

Aedon's cheeks flushed. "I appreciate seeing a master at his craft, is all."

Kyra recalled how the Mariner fought. "And why can't our men learn to fight as that Mariner did?" she asked.

"All Mariners train in combat when they are young. Even the girls, I am told. It begins with hand-to-hand combat, sailing, and physical stamina from the time they are barely old enough to speak. At ten years of age, they begin weapons training in everything from the sword to the spear, the javelin, and even the trident. If the Marin Islands ever go to war, every citizen may be called upon to fight. At the age of fifteen, the child chooses a particular weapon to master. When you go to battle against the Mariners, even the lowest soldier is a deadly warrior. If we were to match their skill, we would need to train our men the same way. Instead, we just overwhelm our enemies with our numbers." His voice was mournful as he spoke.

"Well, why don't you train your men the same way?" Kyra asked.

"Father would never allow such a drastic mandate. He is so focused on keeping the peace that he forgets you need strength to maintain that peace."

"My dear, your wisdom astounds me," Kyra said. "You will make a wonderful king. A strong king."

Aedon nodded but said nothing.

Kyra continued. "I look forward to the day you wear the crown, with the Fang of Rhinegard secured at your hip. You will be a king for the history books, spoken alongside the great Cavan Kohel." Her words were playful, even coquettish.

Aedon rolled his eyes and scoffed. Who could compare to the man who nearly conquered all of Iria? Still, he stood a little taller as she spoke, imagining himself as king and conqueror.

"It's just such a shame," she continued.

"What is?" he asked with a frown. Ember was heard nearby, racing through the garden hedges without a care in the world.

"Well, if your father is reluctant to do what is needed, as you say he is," Kyra began, "then Cavandel will have to wait many years before it has the strong leader it needs. Is it not so?"

"I suppose you are right," Aedon conceded.

"And who can say what calamities may befall our people before that day comes?"

"That is my fear, as well."

Kyra's stomach churned. All she wanted was to enjoy a pleasant evening walk with her betrothed. She wished with all her heart not to do this. The words of her mother echoed in her mind, telling her how all her hopes for the future hung in the balance. She took a deep breath and continued.

"So, to avoid such calamities, would it not be best for Cavandel to have a strong King this very moment?" Kyra asked.

"It most certainly would," Aedon said. "But my father is a stubborn man. He'll never change."

"Perhaps... oh, never mind," Kyra said.

"What is it?"

"Tis too dark a thought, I'm afraid. And I've already cast enough appall over our lovely evening with all this melancholy."

"We're alone, my love. You may always speak freely when it's the two of us."

Kyra hid it well, but she struggled to find her words. What she would say next would cross a line, one that could never be uncrossed. And if Aedon didn't respond how she needed him to... she forced the thought from her mind.

"Well, please know that I would never wish such a tragedy as this. You know I love your father like he was my own, and if he were to... pass away... in the coming weeks, well, everyone at Court would mourn his loss deeply. But the people would have a new king, a strong king. The king they deserve. So, speaking only in theory, it would be a blessing to the people if your father soon died and left you the throne, would it not?"

Kyra's heart was a pounding war drum while Aedon considered her words. She was certain he saw right through her, that she had been too transparent. Aedon was silent for a lifetime, and she held her breath for those few eternal seconds. At last, he spoke.

"You speak of dark things, Kyra." He exhaled before continuing. "But in theory, you are not wrong. All the scholars of ethics agree on this point: the good of the whole matters more than the good of its parts. I suppose that is true even if the part in question is the King."

Kyra finally exhaled and nodded her head. "But this is all just theory and hypothetical," she assured him. "Your father is in excellent health. He will yet live for many years to come."

"Yes, yes, he will." Aedon's voice faded as he spoke, his mind lost in faraway thoughts. Kyra rested her head on his shoulder.

CHAPTER ELEVEN

A STRANGER IN THE WILDERNESS

47TH DAY OF SPRING, 897 G.C.

Malua sent a few more sparks into the air, but no fire came of it. Kailem wished Mokain was with them. He'd have had no problem starting a fire. After several more attempts, Kailem threw his stone down and stuck his dagger into the dirt. Goosebumps spread across his arms and a throbbing chill crept up his spine. This was sure to be a miserable night.

Their hearts sank when they saw Kailem throw down the stone. Their situation continued to worsen. They had no food, no water, and now it seemed they would have no heat either. What else would Iria throw at them? Emerald was certain it would rain any second, or perhaps a bear would wander by. The three exchanged looks, not knowing what to do next.

A rustling came from behind a nearby thicket, the clear sound of footsteps moving in their direction. Kailem sprang to his feet with Malua in hand, primed to attack whatever came close. Osmund and Emerald hurried behind him. Emerald armed herself with the first rock she could find.

"Who is that?" Kailem shouted. The sound of footsteps drew nearer, and there was a third sound beside them, like the sound of a gavel hammering in time with the footsteps.

A figure emerged from the darkness, but Kailem could not make out any details. His steps were neither hurried nor hesitant, a casual stroll out in the middle of nowhere. He carried a walking staff of Àramen Rosewood that stood taller than he did.

"Just a fellow traveler," the man called out. "No one you need fear, I assure you. I am unarmed."

"Well, we are not unarmed, so identify yourself," Kailem commanded. He held his dagger with the tip pointed at the man.

The stranger wore a dark cloak, the color of an oak tree. Under the cloak, he wore a sand-colored linen shirt and wool trousers, and had a satchel slung over his shoulder. His clothing was simple, without embroidery, but was quality fabric and well-tailored. It was impossible to tell by his appearance alone whether he was a nobleman or a commoner.

"My name is Elwin of Andil. I am simply passing through the forest," the man declared.

Elwin was now close enough for them to make out his features. He appeared to be in his thirties, although a more specific age was difficult to discern. His hair was a medium length and wavy, the angles of his face were strong without being sharp, and there was a combination of confidence and joviality in his demeanor. He was like the kindly lion who would prefer to play with you, but could also take your head off just as easily.

Osmund frowned at the mention of Andil. He tried to picture it on a map, but he had never heard of it. Nor could easily determine Elwin's ethnicity. His skin was too dark to be from the eastern kingdoms, but it also wasn't nearly as dark as the Mariners or the Âramen. Osmund decided the man's ethnicity was hardly the most pressing issue at the moment.

"And who do I have the pleasure of meeting on such a fine night as this?" Elwin asked. He leaned on his walking stick with both hands in a genial, nonthreatening manner.

The three survivors relaxed a measure and spread out from their defensive formation. Kailem reached forward with his hand. "Kailem Roka," he said, as they shook hands. "And this is Osmund Baylor, and Emerald... I actually never learned your surname."

"Just Emerald," she said.

"Charmed, all of you," Elwin said. "Looks like you're having some trouble with your fire; might I lend a hand?"

Elwin sat and retrieved the flint from the ground.

"We ain't 'tirely sure that be flint," Emerald said, taking a seat beside him. Her usual mistrusting disposition had inexplicably dissipated.

"Oh, it is flint. A fine piece, in fact," Elwin said. "It should work perfectly. But as I said before, I am unarmed. Might I use your dagger?"

Kailem realized he was still holding Malua defensively. He reluctantly handed the dagger to the stranger.

"This is a fine blade," Elwin said, feeling the weight of the dagger. "Clearly Mariner steel from the pattern in the metal here. Your Culmination Blade?"

Kailem was taken aback. How had he known that, he wondered? The man must be well-traveled.

Elwin raised the dagger, inspecting it. "I've never known someone to choose a dagger as his Culmination Blade. Interesting choice. What did you name it?"

"Malua," Kailem replied.

"Ah, the Old Marin word for 'peace'," the stranger said, turning the dagger over in his hand. "I should say that is a perfect name for a weapon."

Kailem narrowed his eyes on the man. How could he know all that? Old Marin was a dead language. Mariners hadn't used it since the days of Cavan Kohel's Conquest of Iria. Since then, Cavandish had replaced Old Marin as the common tongue. Even Kailem hadn't known the Old Marin word for peace until he researched it.

The stranger made a single strike of the dagger against the flint, and several bright sparks flew out. The tinder ignited immediately. Osmund was sure he saw a curious ring of frost crystallizing around their fire pit, but it melted away just as quickly. Less than a minute later, a full fire was ablaze.

Kailem and Osmund sat down in the remaining space around the fire. Osmund walked on the sides of his feet and winced as he lowered himself to the ground.

"What happened to you, my young friend?" Elwin asked.

"I've been stricken with a case of blisters," Osmund said. "An awful plight, I might add. I would not recommend them."

Elwin hid an amused smile. "Nor would I. You would do well to place marigold leaves over the wound, or cover them with honey if you haven't any marigolds."

A small line appeared between Osmund's eyebrows. "Those are used to prevent skin corruption and blood poisoning."

"Very good, my young friend. You have some knowledge of medicine, I see."

"I have read a few texts on the subject. I hadn't realized blisters could be so serious. Are we likely to find marigolds or honey in the forest?"

"I confess, the odds would not be in your favor. Speaking of which, you do not seem to be well supplied for your journey."

"You wouldn't say this was a planned excursion," Kailem explained. "We were shipwrecked yesterday while sailing to Barrowfort. We're trying to find the nearest town."

The fire cast a glow around them, a protective cocoon that kept the looming darkness at bay. A silver ring on Elwin's hand glinted with firelight.

"Survived a shipwreck, you say? That is quite the tale. If you're looking for a town, the nearest you'll find is Ombermill, but that's still another twenty miles east of here. There's a road only eight miles to the north. From there you'll probably be able to catch a ride on a wagon if you're lucky."

Osmund came alive at the news. "Ombermill? That's my father's town. He's governor of the county. The Road to Ombermill goes right past our estate."

"I believe you have your bearings then," Elwin said. Osmund let out a sigh of relief.

Kailem hadn't found any dry sticks thicker than Emerald's forearm, so the wood was quickly consumed by the flames. Neither was the wood as dry as he would have liked, and it made a hissing sound as the new branches ignited. But the scantness of the wood notwithstanding, the warmth of the fire was invigorating. The three survivors kept their hands close and ignored the cold encroaching from behind.

"You must be hungry," Elwin said. He removed his satchel and opened it before them. "I haven't much, but here is some dried meat and cashews. I also have a waterskin, if you're thirsty."

Emerald and Osmund leapt for the waterskin, but Emerald was closer. She squeezed a long stream into her mouth and gulped it down. Osmund yanked at the waterskin and did the same.

"I can't thank you enough," Kailem told Elwin, placing another stick on the fire. "I don't know what we would have done if you hadn't come along."

"Well, I'm glad I came along when I did," Elwin said. "It appears providence has taken a liking to you." Kailem managed not to scoff at that.

As they sat around the fire enjoying Elwin's provisions, a pair of squirrels scampered in from the shadows. They each propped their front legs on Elwin's knee, who was sitting cross-legged on the ground. Elwin rubbed each of the animals' heads affectionately, as if they were pets. Kailem found the exchange curious. Small animals were afraid of humans, and even more so of fire, but these two were drawn to the man. He gave them each a cashew from his bag and the two retreated into the night, carrying their prize in their mouths. Elwin turned his gaze back to the fire.

"So, you've heard why we are out here. Now your turn," Kailem said.

"I've been tracking a group of outlaws that has been traveling south through these woods," Elwin explained.

Kailem looked him over. "You don't look like a military man. Are you a bounty hunter? Or is this personal?"

"You could say it is personal. I advise you avail yourself of that water skin while you still can."

Emerald and Osmund were suddenly ashamed of how they had guzzled back the water, and Osmund handed the waterskin to Kailem.

"What do you all plan to do once you make it to town?" Elwin asked, placing another stick on the fire.

Kailem's immediate thought was vengeance for his parents. He saw himself back home in the streets of Suvara standing over the lifeless body of Lord Vanua. He banished the thought as quickly as it arose, recalling Mokain's advice to go live and be happy.

Osmund was the first to respond. "I plan to help with the affairs of our estate," He paused to chew his cashews. "I have lost my affinity for traveling entirely, which I am sure would surprise no one."

"Are you not studying to be a surgeon?" Elwin asked.

Osmund frowned, then remembered his comment about medicinal herbs. "I fancy myself a student of all subjects, I should say. But no, I have no intention of becoming a surgeon." He rubbed his hands, then held out his palms to the fire. "My ambition is to become a scholar, in fact. Before our unfortunate episode on the Cerulean Sea, I was preparing to conduct a comparative analysis of the many esoteric practices of Iria."

Elwin dipped his head.

"I take it you are not a believer of the mythical arts, then?" Osmund asked, taking another bite of cashews.

"I confess, I have not found them to be of any use. Am I to assume that you are a believer?" Elwin asked.

Osmund sat back and rubbed the cashew dust from his hands while he considered his response. "I maintain an open mind. I neither believe nor disbelieve any proposition until I have sufficient reason to do so. However, a scholar need not accept the truth of a subject in order to study it. Do you not agree?"

"Very well said, my young friend. I believe we find ourselves in agreement."

Osmund sat taller in the firelight.

"Where did you study?" Elwin asked. His question presumed Osmund's education consisted of more than merely a private tutor as most noblemen provided their children, a presumption Osmund found flattering.

"Two years at the University of Terendor," Osmund said proudly.

Elwin tilted his head. "Only two?"

"My father felt any more time would be a waste."

"Well, a mind that thirsts for knowledge cannot be kept from learning, no matter where it is." Osmund smiled while the stranger continued. "And you, young Master Roka? What are your intentions once you find your way?"

Kailem swallowed the last of the waterskin. Why this stranger was so interested in their affairs, he wondered? What business was it of his to know their plans? And yet, despite his instinct to protect his privacy, he found himself doing just the opposite.

"I intend to travel back to Barrowfort," Kailem explained. "I need to find the patrons of our ship and tell them what happened. They'll likely put me on another ship, maybe even give me a commission."

Kailem was lying. Cato & Sons would never give him a commission after losing the ship and all its cargo. He felt Elwin eye him suspiciously. If the stranger knew it had been a lie, he let it pass.

"And you, miss Emerald," Elwin asked. "What is on your horizon?"

"Survive, as always." Emerald stared into the fire, the crackling flames reflecting off her face. She held her arms around her waist.

Elwin nodded, and several minutes passed without a word between them. Emerald laid down and nestled into a soft spot of ground close to the fire.

"I dare say I will turn in for the night as well," Osmund declared. He rolled around for several minutes, trying to find a comfortable position.

"Tell me, what personal reasons bring a man out into the wilderness alone, unarmed, looking for a group of outlaws?" Kailem asked.

"You don't trust easily, do you, Kailem?" Elwin asked. He twisted the silver ring around his finger.

"I'd like to say I trust appropriately," Kailem replied.

Elwin nodded. "Why I am out in the wilderness alone, unarmed, looking for a group of outlaws. I'd say that is a rather long story for another time. But to put your anxieties at ease, allow me to say I have reason to believe that these outlaws have a malignant plan afoot, and I find myself uniquely positioned to stop them."

Kailem frowned. "That raises far more questions than it answers."

Elwin chuckled like a grandfather. "Yes, yes, I suppose it does. And I apologize, I cannot be more forthcoming. But might I venture an observation?"

Kailem extended his hand.

"You're a young man far from home, full of potential, and it is clear your heart is not invested in sailing."

Kailem scoffed. "You could tell all that in the space of an hour?"

"Am I wrong?" Elwin asked.

Kailem said nothing.

Elwin nodded. "I expected as much."

Osmund rolled about, still looking for a comfortable position. Emerald was fast asleep. Kailem pondered a life he would love, but the thought only brought him back to the Marin Islands, to Mokain and his parents, and his home. His heart sank even lower.

"You've been through a difficult time, haven't you, Kailem?" Elwin asked. "And not just because of the shipwreck."

The image of his parents' execution flashed in his mind, and he thought of his months as a drunken vagabond before becoming a sailor. He looked at Elwin and nodded.

"Allow it time, Kailem. Your life is poised to turn for the better. I promise."

Kailem had no reason to believe the stranger, but he believed him all the same, although, for the life of him, he could not say why. There was comfort and security in his words, or perhaps it was his tone, but whatever the cause, he felt peace settle over him.

"Well, I believe I have rambled on quite enough for one night," Elwin said. "Rest now. I will stay awake a little longer and maintain the fire."

Kailem did as the stranger bid. The ground was frigid and lumpy, but his muscles ached with exhaustion. And for the first time in the past twenty-four hours, he felt safe. Within moments, he was fast asleep.

***

Something tickled Emerald's cheek. Her eyes were still closed as she lingered in the space between sleep and awake. The tickle moved from her cheek to her nose, as if it were crawling across her face.

Emerald shot up from the ground like she had been doused in cold water. She swatted her face and neck in a frenzy and continued long after the insect had fled the scene.

After taking a moment to calm herself, and assuring no other insects accosted her, she looked around their campsite. The morning dew coated the grass and dirt. Osmund was still asleep. The stranger was gone.

"Hungry?" Kailem walked into camp with his tunic full of berries.

Emerald nodded her head, stretched her arms above her head, and yawned.

Kailem tapped Osmund with his foot.

"I'm awake," Osmund said without moving.

Osmund sat up, his hair a disheveled mess. Kailem sat between them and spread out his tunic. Around his neck was a thin leather strap with a large silver pearl fastened at the bottom. Emerald wondered how she hadn't noticed that before. He didn't seem like the type to wear jewelry.

"That was, without exception, the absolute worst night's sleep I have ever had," Osmund said. He winced as he stretched his neck back and forth.

Emerald paused before putting another berry in her mouth. "What 'appened to yer cut," she said to Kailem.

"Oh yes, I forgot about it. Why? What is wrong with it?"

"Tis gone, nary a scar," Emerald said.

"Truly?" Kailem touched his forehead and felt nothing.

"And I say, my blisters are gone as well. Is that normal?" Osmund asked, inspecting his feet. The three of them exchanged bewildered expressions.

"Where be our new friend?" Emerald asked.

Kailem shook his head. "I awoke at sunrise; he was already gone. He left his waterskin, though. It's empty, but maybe we'll find a stream."

"Who was he?" she asked.

Kailem shrugged and kept eating.

After breakfast, the trio continued on their journey, following the course described by the stranger. Kailem knew well the soreness of extreme exertion; the pain was always worse the day after. He waited for Osmund and Emerald to complain about stiff, aching muscles that throbbed with each step, but the two seemed stronger than ever. It was a curious development, to be sure, but far too much had gone wrong for him to start worrying about the few things that went right.

With greater distance from the coast, the forest grew taller and thicker. Soon, they were back to the same rhythmic march as the day before.

Their second day was decidedly easier than the first. Gone was their sense of dread, replaced by a reason to hope for survival. Wooden giants towered around them, stretching their leafy arms in all directions. Scattered beams of light pierced the forest canopy, casting erratic shadows at their feet as they lighted through patches of grass and beds of clover.

Few words passed between them. In their silence, they appreciated the many subtle sounds of the forest: the rustling of wind through the leaves, the jovial melody of songbirds, the scratching of squirrels as they scurried along the branches overhead. They hadn't appreciated the forest the day before, when they had been certain they would soon die in it, but now they could see just how beautiful it was.

After an hour, Osmund broke the silence. "Did something seem off to you two about that man from last night?" Kailem and Emerald turned back to look at him as they marched.

"How'd ye mean?" Emerald asked.

Kailem knew exactly what Osmund meant. He couldn't put it into words, but there was something different about the man. He couldn't say whether that something was good or bad, but Kailem knew he'd never met anyone like him, and it gnawed at him that he couldn't explain why.

"Well," Osmund began, "he appears in the middle of nowhere, gives us food and water, starts a fire for us, then in the morning he is gone, and all our wounds have healed."

"And left us the waterskin," Emerald added.

"Exactly. I have never been lost in the woods, but I would venture that this sort of thing is not common."

"Nor would I," Kailem added.

"So... who was he?" Osmund asked. No one could offer a theory.

As they thought about Elwin, the sound of a flowing stream called to them from over the southern hill like a chorus of trumpets beckoning weary travelers. The three castaways lost all thought of anything else. They raced over and down the hill, stumbling as they ran, and threw themselves onto the riverbank. They gulped down handfuls of the crisp, life-giving water like it was the first time they had ever tasted it.

It took several minutes to drink their fill. Kailem then filled the waterskin left by the stranger. The boulders that straddled the riverbank had formed a small pool. Emerald let herself fall headfirst into the waist-deep water. She rolled to her back and floated with her limbs spread out like a starfish. Kailem smiled at her. When he finished with the waterskin, he collapsed into the stream and did the same. Osmund stayed on the bank and used the water to wash his face and fix his hair.

For the moment, they had all but forgotten the severity of their plight. After the past two days, water had become the height of luxury, and in that moment, they were royalty. Kailem and Emerald floated with the gently swirling pool and gazed at the forest canopy above them. The stray beams of sunlight that broke through trees were brighter than they had been the day before.

They drifted until their heads collided.

"Oi, watch it," Emerald said. She smacked the surface with the back of her hand, splashing Kailem in the face. Kailem responded in kind, igniting a splashing war between them.

"Hey now, enough of that," Osmund said when their splashing hit him.

Kailem and Emerald exchanged a look, then each stepped forward and grabbed one of Osmund's arms.

"No, no, wait, please—" he cried.

His objections fell on deaf ears. His two companions pulled him forward and heaved him into the shallow water. The cold pierced his body like a thousand tiny needles. Immediately, he burst from the frigid water and sucked the whole sky into his lungs in a single gasp. His look of shock and disbelief inspired a duet of laughter from his assailants.

"Yes, yes, all fun and games, then, isn't it," Osmund grumbled. He tramped out of the stream, shook the water out of hair, then laid out his vest to dry. His companions laughed harder than they had in years.

With Kailem floating next to her and Osmund, now sopping wet, laying out to dry on a rock with his feet in the water, Emerald realized she felt safe with these men. And that was cause for concern. Safety was an illusion, and the moment you feel safe is the moment you are in the greatest danger. She so badly wanted this to be the exception.

Kailem stretched his arms and suspired. "Well, shall we continue?"

Emerald and Osmund took the suggestion as an order from their de facto leader and fell in behind him. Their wet socks sloshed as they hiked back over the hill. The waterskin passed frequently between them, and that made for a much easier trek this time around.

Several hours passed.

"I don't think we'll ever get there," Osmund eventually said. "This is just my life now. Walking through the forest for eternity."

Kailem laughed and shook his head.

"We've a sayin' in Donnelin," Emerald began. "It says, 'Longer be a journey's last mile than all the miles that came before it."

Osmund thought on the saying for a few steps. "That doesn't make me feel any better," he finally said.

Emerald looked to Kailem. "Eh, I tried."

Finally, the road came into view. Osmund rushed past the group towards it, eager for the smallest piece of civilization.

"Oh, thank Iria," Osmund said between breaths. "We're alive, we made it, we're going to live, oh thank you, thank you, thank you."

Emerald and Kailem arrived behind him. It wasn't a large road, barely wide enough for a single cart to pass, and it did not appear well-maintained, but wheel marks were fresh in the dirt, and that was encouraging.

"Which way do we go?" Emerald asked.

"In my estimation," Osmund said, "the wisest course would be to stay here and await a passing carriage." He was already sitting with his back against a large rock, footsore and tired. "Someone will be along soon, and I cannot walk even one step farther."

Emerald looked to Kailem. "Works for me," he said.

Kailem sat down with his back against a tree. Emerald meandered up and down the road.

"So, you're going to go into the family business, you said?" Kailem asked. Osmund had removed his boots and was massaging his feet.

"Yeah, it's probably for the best," he said.

"I thought you wanted to be a scholar, travel the world visiting the best libraries?" Kailem asked.

Osmund's shoulders slumped. "That was the dream. But the way I see it, there is zero chance of being shipwrecked in the family business."

"And what does your family do?" Kailem asked.

"Landholdings, mostly. We own most of the county and pay families to work the land. Some farm, some raise cattle and sheep. We also own a flour mill."

"Impressive. You know how to do all that?" Kailem asked.

"Oh goodness, no, that is why we hire people. No, my job will be to ensure that all of our holdings are profitable. Running numbers, securing trade deals, and the like."

"I see. And you know how to do all that?"

Osmund scratched the back of his head. "Well, no, I can't do that either. It always seemed rather boring, to be honest. But I can learn." He put on a brave face.

"What about you?" Osmund asked. "Back to Barrowfort to find another ship?"

Kailem exhaled, his head resting against the tree behind him.

"I honestly don't know. It seems like as good a plan as any."

"You don't love being a sailor?" Osmund asked.

"I'm good at it. And I love the ocean. But no, I don't love being a sailor. At least, I wouldn't say it's what I want to do with my life. But of course, the next question is 'what *do* I want to do with my life?'"

"You don't know?"

"Not in the slightest," Kailem said.

Osmund wondered if he was weak for abandoning his dreams so easily.

"If you wanted, Kailem, you could come home with me," Osmund offered. "Stay for a time while you sort it out, if you want."

Kailem considered it. "You wouldn't mind?"

Osmund sat up straight. "Not at all! Well, I mean, just because you said you don't want to go on to Barrowfort and you don't know what you want to do. You could rest with us while you get it sorted. Not to mention, I am certain my parents will not believe I truly survived a shipwrecked unless I bring home an eyewitness."

Kailem realized he hadn't had a comfortable bed and a formal dinner since his parents' death. And he liked Osmund, truth be told, and he wasn't eager to surrender his company quite yet. "You know, I think I'll take you up on that."

"Really?!" Osmund said. "Brilliant! You will love it, I assure you."

Emerald continued pacing. Kailem looked to Osmund and motioned toward her with his head. Osmund gave him a confused look. Kailem motioned again, this time with wide eyes and an exaggerated nod. Osmund looked to Emerald, then back at Kailem, and pointed to Emerald with his brow furrowed. Kailem nodded.

"You could come too, Emerald, if you wanted," Osmund called out.

"Nay, I think not," she said without looking at them. She continued pacing and hadn't noticed she was biting her fingernails.

"No?" Kailem asked. "Why not?"

Emerald shook her head. "It's just not for me, lads." She kept her eyes looking down the road; Kailem couldn't tell if she was eager or worried someone might appear around the bend.

"Do you have someplace you need to be? Have a better offer than a soft bed and hot food for several days? For free?"

She rolled her eyes and kept pacing.

"You know, his family probably has lots of expensive things you could steal," Kailem said. Emerald paused and considered.

"Okay, well I'll thank you to please not steal anything," Osmund said, "but I would surely love for you to come. We survived a shipwreck together. Let us all make it home together."

The sound of a horse and cart came from down the road.

Emerald chewed her lip as she considered the offer. Her chief concern was avoiding any scouts Jacken surely had looking for her. A wealthy nobleman's estate would certainly be the last place they would think of looking. And if she were honest with herself, she actually did want to go with them. For some reason, she had grown fond of these boys, but being fond of someone was even more dangerous than feeling safe with them.

The cart came to a stop and Osmund negotiated with the driver, a scraggly man with a coarse beard and straw hat. Emerald couldn't hear what they said, but she knew they'd reached an agreement when they shook hands.

"Are you sure you don't want to come?" Osmund asked. There was a pleading in his voice, almost like a whine. She found it both pathetic and adorable.

Kailem leaned in close. "You know, if you come and don't like it, you can always leave. Do you really have someplace better to be?"

Emerald didn't have anywhere to be. No one in Iria was waiting for her, at least no one friendly. She had only these two young men, one of whom had saved her life and another who offered free food and lodging. "Aye, I yield," she conceded. "Here, help me up."

"Yes!" Osmund cheered as Kailem helped her into the cart. "You both will love it. Trust me, this will be splendid."

They found a place to sit in the few open spaces between crates of freshly picked apples. Kailem knocked twice on the side of the cart and the driver whipped the horse forward.

Osmund helped himself to one of the apples. "Don't worry, I'll add it to the bill," he said, just as the driver was about to object. Kailem and Emerald helped themselves to an apple as well.

"I do say," Osmund mused as the cart jostled back and forth on the bumpy road. "This is the way man was meant to travel. I hope I never have to walk anywhere ever again."

CHAPTER TWELVE

THE FINAL EIGHT

48TH DAY OF SPRING, 897 G.C.

O n the second and final day of the tournament, there was enough room in the staging area for every contestant to lay down on a bench of their own with their feet up, and they would have had tensions not been so high. The contestant field had begun with sixty-four fighters; now only eight remained.

The only remaining Shinda practiced his Kumata in the center of the room. His eyes were closed, his movements slow and deliberate. The two Norvians sat on opposite sides of the room, brooding silently. There were four Cavanders. They huddled together, laughing and boasting about their triumphs from the previous day.

Mokain sat and observed, collecting information on each of them. His old sword master had taught him that a man's fighting style permeated into every facet of his life; how he behaved when he wasn't fighting could reveal much about his combat style. His posture, his laugh, his gait, how he spoke, how much he spoke, even how he shifted his weight from one foot to the other gave away another clue, and Mokain logged each one in his mind.

"Tell me again, from the beginning," Avalina said.

Kyra and her mother sat alone on the royal platform, waiting for the King to arrive. In the King's absence, a pair of jesters performed a juggling act on the arena sand for the crowd.

Kyra sighed before repeating her story for the third time. "It was night, we were alone in the garden, I said in theory, it would be better for the people if the King died, because that meant they would have him as king that much sooner, and he said I was not wrong."

"And why did you say he would be a better king?" Avalina asked.

"Because he would be a stronger king and the people need strength to keep the peace," Kyra explained.

"And the Prince was receptive to this?"

"Yes mother, his exact words were 'you are not wrong.'"

"But it was just theoretical?"

"I said it was theoretical, but the look in his eyes said he was considering it."

Avalina shook her head. "We'll need more than just your interpretation of the look in his eyes. Now, on your feet, I hear them coming."

The King stepped onto the royal platform with the Prince, Lord Aturri, and Lord Menden in tow. Aedon sat next to Kyra and stared through the floor.

"Is all well, my love?" Kyra asked. She hooked her arm around Aedon's.

Aedon was slow to respond. "Hmm? Oh yes, our council meeting ran a little long is all." His gaze was off in the distance. Kyra caressed his arm, and it brought him back from his thoughts.

"Today should be a thrilling conclusion," he said, wanting to change the subject.

"As long as no one else dies. That was dreadful," Kyra said with a pout.

"I'm afraid a few accidents are inevitable when the game is combat."

His answer gave her little comfort.

"Most of the remaining contestants are Cavanders, as we expected would be the case," Aedon continued. "Our men have the best armor. There shouldn't be any more casualties today."

Kyra rested her head on Aedon's shoulder.

The Herald walked out to the center of the arena. "For the first fight of the third round, Pall Sigmar of Norvia against Mokain Roka of the Marin Islands."

Applause erupted from every corner of the Arena.

"This should be a good one," Lord Menden said as he settled into his seat. Lord Menden had such an imposing physique, and were it not for his grey hair and the weathered skin wrinkled around his eyes, he could have easily passed for a soldier in his thirties. He wore a grey beard trimmed so short it looked like stubble.

"Seems the crowd agrees with you," Aedon replied. "Ten gold florins on the Mariner."

"Against the giant? I accept," Lord Menden said.

***

Mokain heard his name and stood. On the far side room, one of the Norvians also stood. The man truly was a giant, a full head higher than Mokain, and his battle axe weighed as much as a sledgehammer.

The sand was no longer divided into sections, allowing the fighters to face each other in the center of the arena. The Norvian's face was cold. Mokain was used to being the largest man in the room, but this Norvian was a gorilla; Mokain had never felt smaller than he did in that moment. He wondered how anyone could defeat a man this size. Then he thought back to his sword master's training in Suvara. *Every fighter has a weakness*, the old Mariner would say. Mokain knew he could expect an aggressive fighting style from the giant, all brute force and no finesse. A plan formed in his mind.

As soon as the Herald dropped the flag, the Norvian swung his axe like he was chopping firewood. Mokain sidestepped the strike and attacked the Norvian's flank, but the Norvian had his axe raised with impossible speed. He blocked Mokain's strike with the haft of his axe, then drove the axe head into Mokain's face mask.

The blow knocked Mokain backward, disoriented. He would have fallen to his back had he not caught his fall with the tip of his sword. He landed on his knee. The Norvian came back with another overhead swing. Mokain rolled away from it then sprang to his feet.

The Norvian was unrelenting. There was no dancing about, no side-stepping each other while the fighters caught their breath. He marched at Mokain like a bear hungry to devour a wounded deer, but the Mariner refused to be his prey.

His thoughts were narrowed on the Norvian's every move, but somewhere deep in the back of Mokain's mind was the knowledge that if he lost, he had nothing to fall back on. He had secured a position as a guard by surviving the second round, but how long would a Mariner last as a tenderfoot in the Cavander

Royal Guard? All his hopes for the future were contingent upon defeating this Norvian, and all who came after him.

Mokain had no chance of matching strength, and it was clear he would not be able to beat him on stamina either. He had to wait for the Norvian to make a mistake.

The Norvian must have come to the same conclusion, because no mistakes were made. Although he put all his strength into every swing of his axe, he always managed to raise the axe in time to block any counterattacks. Mokain's strength waned. His breathing was heavy and sweat dripped into his eyes. If the Norvian was even slightly fatigued, he didn't let it show.

As the Norvian's axe hit the sand, Mokain swung with both blades at the Norvian's chest. Before he could land the strike, the Norvian's fist hit Mokain's face plate with the force of a blacksmith's hammer, sending him flailing onto his back. He dropped both his blades in the fall, disoriented.

The Norvian again brought down his axe. Mokain rolled to his left as the axe's edge scraped against his back plate. Mokain rolled again, this time to the right, and threw his shoulder over the axe head. He wrapped his arm around the haft, and before the Norvian could pull the axe free, Mokain kicked out both his knees. It was the first time the Norvian had fallen since the tournament began. The crowd erupted.

Mokain grabbed the axe and rolled just out of the Norvian's reach. The giant pounded his fist into the sand, then jumped to his feet and sprinted at Mokain. With a trenchant roar fueled by raw grit and fury, Mokain heaved the battle axe from the ground, calling upon every fiber of strength left in his body, and bashed the edge into the Norvian's breastplate. The charging Norvian crashed into Mokain with the force of an avalanche and sent both fighters tumbling to the sand.

Mokain struggled to focus his eyes. He was on his back with no weapon in his hand, fearing he had lost. He tried to feel for cracks in his armor, but his strength was spent. It took everything he had to simply rotate his head. He saw the spectators; they were on their feet shouting, but he couldn't make out what they were saying. It was impossible to hear anything over that horrible ringing in his head. He looked to his right and saw the Norvian on his back, the massive breastplate cracked open, revealing the leather lining underneath. And that's when he heard it.

The crowd. They were screaming his name.

***

Lord Menden counted out ten gold coins from his pouch. "That was worth the gold just to witness it," Lord Menden said. "I should not have thought anyone capable of defeating a Norvian of that size, at least not in single combat, anyway."

"He looked like a monster," Kyra said.

"Well, that makes my Mariner a monster slayer," Prince Aedon said. He shook the gold coins in his hand, making a clanking sound before placing them in his pocket.

Every other match of round three featured at least one Cavander. The fights were an exhibition of fighting styles, each lasting longer than they had the day prior. Aedon absorbed every moment of the tournament, explaining to Kyra every maneuver and mistake.

Kyra tapped the arm of her chair and stared at the clouds. The fights all looked the same to her, and she could only feign interest for so long. At least no one had been killed today. The high point was when the servants prepared a luncheon table: croissant sandwiches, lemon and berry tarts, and a whole array of cheeses. She had a servant bring her an assortment of everything.

The Herald walked out to the center of the arena and announced the next fight, the Mariner against Rayne Dorman, a Cavander.

"Ten gold florins on Rayne, Your Grace?" Lord Menden asked.

"Not this time, I'm afraid," Aedon said. He selected a cube of hard cheese from an attendant's serving tray. "It would be in poor taste for the crown prince to bet against one of his own, and to bet against the Mariner would just be foolish."

***

When the fourth round ended, all the contestants remaining in the staging area waited in silence for the herald to announce the next fight.

"For the first fight of the fifth round, Mokain Roka of the Marin Islands against Rayne Dorman of Cavander!" the herald called out.

A Cavander stood from a nearby bench and moved toward the gate. He was larger than the average Cavander, but small compared to the Norvian Mokain had just fought. Mokain put on his helmet and followed him out to the arena.

So, this is Rayne Dorman, Mokain thought. His name had become famous overnight as the man who had killed his opponent. Mokain had heard stories about him in the tavern. Some said he was cold and ruthless and had killed his countryman on purpose, others said he wept like a baby when his dearest friend died. As with most things, the truth was certainly somewhere in the middle.

Rayne stood in the center of the arena and swung a two-handed broadsword while waiting for the flag to drop. Mokain merely rolled his shoulders. Every muscle in his body ached. The fight with the Norvian had taken its toll. The pain reminded him of his training as a boy, his commander forcing him to fight through injury and exhaustion. *Pain is not your enemy*, Mokain recalled him saying. *Pain is simply a messenger; greet it as you would an old friend, then dismiss it.* Mokain exhaled a long breath and forced himself to stand tall.

The Herald dropped the flag, and Rayne began circling. He was preparing for a long, drawn-out fight. In his current state, an extended fight put Mokain at a perilous disadvantage. He recalled Rayne's earlier fights; each was by the book. No creativity, no improvisation. Mokain could make this a quick fight.

As they circled each other, preparing to make their first strikes, Mokain held Tao pointed directly at Rayne. Rayne stared at it, waiting for the attack to come.

Mokain sprinted forward.

Rayne thrust his broadsword for the Mariner's chest. Mokain slid on his knees, deflecting the broadsword over his head with Koa, and once he was behind his opponent, stabbed Tao through the tin on the back of Rayne's armor.

The crowd cheered. Rayne was shocked. He hadn't even felt the puncture, and he looked to the Herald for confirmation. Mokain was already walking back to the staging area.

He removed his helmet and laid back on a bench. He was alone. The two remaining contestants fought in the arena, and they sounded a league away. He should be watching the fight, studying his future opponent, but first, he needed to regain his strength.

***

"Walk with me, dearest," Avalina whispered in Kyra's ear.

Kyra stood and followed her mother without complaint. Aedon barely noticed; he was locked in a fierce debate with Lord Menden about something having to do with combat. Kyra had trouble following it.

Avalina and her daughter walked under the stadium seats of the arena, their voices drowned out by the roar of the crowd.

"If you are certain the Prince is amenable, then we need to plan our next steps." Avalina spoke in hushed tones, despite the noise from the crowd above. Kyra only nodded.

"King Byron is well-beloved by his people, commoner and noble alike. If there is but a whiff of malfeasance in his death, there will be inquisitions for years to come. We cannot allow this. The natural cause of the King's death must be beyond question."

"So, what is your plan?" Kyra asked.

"Jimson weed. It's a bitter herb, so we'll have to brew it into a tea. Be sure to make it with enough honey and chamomile to drown out the taste."

"*I* have to make it?" Kyra asked.

"And serve it to him."

Kyra's heart galloped. She swallowed any words of protest and instead asked, "when is it going to happen?"

"Suspicions will be aroused if he dies too quickly. We need to poison him by degrees if it is to appear natural. We'll arrange for you and Aedon to have regular afternoon tea with the King. We can't risk involving any servants, so we'll have the tea already prepared when the King arrives."

"But if I'm drinking out of a different teapot, won't he become suspicious?"

"That's why you're going to drink it too," Avalina said.

Kyra paused. Did her mother just ask her to sacrifice her life?

Avalina took a vial from a hidden pocket in her dress and gave it to Kyra, who inspected the dark brown slurry inside.

"It's a mixture of ground lanaver beans, epan root, and charcoal," Avalina said. "It will counteract the effects of the Jimson weed as long as you take within an hour. We'll give you a dose for the Prince as well."

Kyra tucked the vial into one of the folds of her dress.

"Remember," Avalina said, "all of this depends on the participation of the Prince. He must be a knowing accomplice. Do you understand?"

Kyra nodded.

"For the final contest," the Herald bellowed, "Mokain Roka of the Marin Islands against Kaiga Saido of Shinda!"

The Shinda was already on the arena sand having just defeated the last remaining Cavander. Mokain had studied the final minutes of their fight, and the Shinda's skill would cause any fighter to panic. His defensive style relied on quick counterstrikes and exhausting his opponent, but he countered with all the speed and venom of a cobra. The defeated Cavander limped from the arena, his armor peppered with dents.

Mokain left the staging area with his helmet on, his swords unsheathed. He leaned forward like he might break out into a sprint at any moment, but his pace was calm as he approached his opponent.

The Herald lowered his flag, and the Shinda raised his sword. He was armed with a scimitar, the customary blade of the Shinda. Mokain spun his twin leaf blades a few times to loosen his wrists.

The fight began as Mokain predicted. The Shinda waited for Mokain to attack, defied each strike with expert form, and countered with a vicious strike of his own. The scimitar was a thin blade and its lightweight made for agile attacks, but the lack of girth and dull edge made it difficult to penetrate Mokain's armor.

In the beginning, Mokain took several dents to his armor, but no cracks. As Mokain adapted to his fighting style, the Shinda's counterstrikes became increasingly ineffective, but he stuck to his defensive style.

Although Mokain proved adept at parrying the Shinda's counterstrikes, he had yet to find a weakness that would allow him to land a strike of his own. However, the Shinda's defensive style allowed Mokain to control the tempo of the fight and catch his breath when needed.

"They seemed to be evenly matched, wouldn't you say?" Lord Menden asked.

"Indeed, each is as formidable as the other," the Prince returned. "But which would make the better First Officer?"

The Mariner ducked under the Shinda's scimitar and the crowd cheered.

"It's difficult to say," Lord Menden said. "Although I must confess, I do not relish the thought of a foreigner as First Officer."

"Nor do I. I was certain a Cavander would at least make it to the final."

The crowd cheered again when the Mariner landed a kick to the Shinda's breastplate.

"Nothing can be done about that now, I'm afraid," Lord Menden said.

"On the contrary, Lord Menden. I only promised the victor could hold the position; I never promised for how long."

Lord Menden turned his eyes from the fight. "That would be quite the disgrace, Your Grace. I doubt your father would permit it."

Aedon said nothing in response.

Twenty minutes passed and Mokain had still not found a weakness in the Shinda's form. How could he defeat a man who never made a mistake? He made several dents in his opponent's armor, but the Shinda managed to block every strike with significant power behind it. It was brilliant. If the weaker strikes couldn't pierce the armor, then they weren't worth the energy to block them. Mokain would eventually exhaust himself and the Shinda would have his victory.

Mokain changed strategies. He came at the Shinda with everything he had. Every strike carried the full force of his considerable strength. He attacked high and low, direct thrusts and side swings, attacking randomly so the Shinda could not anticipate his next move. When the Shinda retreated to slow the fight's tempo, Mokain came even harder, sprinting when the distance between them became too great.

Mokain's strength waned, but the Shinda's waned faster. Each of them heaved audible breaths, moving at these speeds would soon become an inhuman feat.

The Shinda abandoned his counterstrikes and devoted all his strength to defending against the vicious onslaught. Mokain fought close enough to see the Shinda's eyes. They were stained with fear.

Mokain's breath was trapped under his helmet, hot and heavy. Without considering the risk to his life, he ripped off the helmet and let it fall to the sand.

When his body wanted to quit, Mokain pictured Lord Vanua under the Shinda's armor. Hate and fury swelled within him, and he swung his swords with the unbridled violence of a mad man. With every strike, he screamed. The sound of his swords striking the Shinda's blade was like the sound of multiple blacksmiths working an anvil in unison, and he possessed a rage he had not displayed the entire tournament.

The spectators, who only minutes ago had been cheering in revelry, were now silent and still. None had seen such passionate vehemence in a fighter. The Mariner's screaming sent a chill down their spine that left them speechless.

Mokain was relentless. His battle cry was like the roar of a lion. The muscles in the Shinda's hands grew tired and weak. Mokain struck the Shinda's scimitar just above the handle and the sword fell from his opponent's hand.

This was his moment.

Mokain spun with Koa and cracked open the right side of the Shinda's helmet across the cheek. The Shinda twisted on limp feet and collapsed to the ground, a puff of dust releasing from the sand around him.

Sound erupted. Never had the Arena crowd been louder than it was at that moment. Mokain gasped for air. His vision blurred, and he nearly collapsed. He lowered to one knee and leaned on his swords. Steam rose from his head in the chill Cavander air.

The Herald stood close to him and addressed the crowd, but Mokain couldn't make what he said out over the sounds of the crowd and his own breathing. He didn't care. He stared at the ground, letting his emotions settle. Beads of sweat flowed down his cheeks and forehead into the sand below.

"That was perhaps the most impressive fighting I have ever seen, Mariner," someone said. Mokain ignored him.

"Might you grant me the privilege of assisting you to your feet?" the man asked.

Mokain didn't recognize the voice, but he knew the tone. The words, the cadence, the confidence behind them. That wasn't the voice of a commoner, or even your average noblemen. That was the voice of a highborn, the voice of royalty. Mokain looked up to see the Crown Prince of Cavandel standing over him, his hand extended.

Mokain slid Tao into its sheath and with his freehand accepted the Prince's help to his feet.

Prince Aedon spoke to the crowd. "My good people of Cavandel, I present to you: Mokain Roka of the Marin Islands, your *champion*!" Prince Aedon grabbed Mokain's wrist and held it high in the air. The roar of the crowd continued.

A servant brought out the victor's purse and a waterskin. He handed Mokain the bag of 100 gold florins. It was even heavier than his swords. He dropped the bag, not caring that a few coins fell into the sand, and ripped the waterskin from the servant's hand.

CHAPTER THIRTEEN

THE HOUSE OF BAYLOR

48TH DAY OF SPRING, 897 G.C.

T he cart followed a winding path through dense, untamed forest, and its occupants said little as they rode. When they made their final turn, the forest blossomed into a vast and vibrant meadow. Dead leaves and pine needles became perennial ryegrass and curated flower beds. The dirt road became a manicured gravel path that passed under an archway of bronze and stone. The entrance to the estate was large enough for a woolly mammoth to pass through. Atop the archway was emblazoned the Baylor Family Crest, a traditional shield divided with stocks of wheat on one side and a quiver of arrows on the other.

At the end of the road was Baylor Mansion, a structure so large and regal it looked plucked from the center of Rhinegard itself. Kailem and Emerald were left speechless before such grandeur. Kailem was sure the mansion could easily have fit two ships the size of *The Flying Manta* within its walls and still had room to spare. Emerald tried to count the number of windows visible from the road but quickly lost track.

A man in a servant's livery with gray hair and impeccable posture exited the mansion's front doors as the cart came to a stop. When Osmund stepped down from the cart, the servant stuttered.

"Good Iria, Master Osmund... What... I..."

"Steady on, Godfrey. I am quite alright, I assure you," Osmund said as he neared his butler.

"But... your clothes, sir... and your hair... you look positively ghastly, if you'll excuse my saying so, my lord. And whatever are you doing home so soon? Had I known, I would have..."

"Yes, yes," Osmund cut him off. "Things have not gone quite to plan, I am afraid. And I'll have a proper adventure to share with you all. But for now, I desire a bath and a rest."

"Certainly, sir. Very good. I shall send someone to retrieve your effects." Godfrey snapped his fingers and two nearby servants hurried to attention. Osmund raised his hand, slowing them to a halt.

"That will not be necessary, Godfrey. I am afraid none of my effects survived the journey. However, I have two friends that will be staying with us for a time. They will need to have rooms prepared. Also, I am afraid my coin pouch did not survive the journey either, and I agreed with this driver for twelve copper pennies for the ride home."

The driver cleared his throat.

"Oh, yes," Osmund added. "And another penny for the apples we ate. Send someone to see that he is paid, would you?"

Godfrey redirected the servants.

Osmund stepped closer and in a low voice asked, "How do mother and father seem today, Godfrey? Will they be angry that I am home?"

"I am sure the Duke and Duchess will be thrilled to have you home, my lord. Shall I inform them of your arrival?"

Osmund paused, then nodded.

Emerald nudged Kailem gently with her elbow.

"Kailem," she began, "I... I wanted to thank ye, ye know, for savin' us and all. In the water and the forest. Ye got us through it; we'd all be dead without ye."

All Kailem could think was how he had failed them. As an officer of the ship, keeping them safe had been his responsibility. He didn't deserve any gratitude. He should have been able to keep the ship from sinking. He should have been able to find a faster way out of the forest. He should have been able to start a fire for them. Words abandoned him, so he forced out a smile, his lips pressed together, and nodded.

A small team of gardeners labored nearby. Kailem noticed two slave brands on the gardener working with a rake, a Norvian by the look of him. Slavery was illegal in the Marin Islands, but he was familiar enough with the custom.

In those times, when a man or woman became a slave — usually as punishment for a crime or for a debt he could not pay — the purchasing lord would brand the slave's left wrist with the seal of the lord's house. Then, if the lord ever sold the slave, the new lord would brand his own seal in the space above the original, which rendered the original brand void. Thus, the series of brands could serve as a record of who had owned the slave. The two brands on the Norvian gardener said that Lord Baylor was only his second owner.

Osmund returned to the cart with a skip in his step.

"My friends, allow me to welcome you to the Baylor Estate," he swept his hand out like a master of ceremonies on his stage. "It has been in our family for six generations. On the south side are the stables, to the north are the gardens, and, let me think, well, the best things are all inside. Follow me."

The mansion's double doors were two stories tall; a servant stood by whose sole apparent duty was to open and shut the massive oaken planks. The floors were polished granite, and their shoes echoed down the halls as they walked. The walls were covered with master works of art: paintings, vases, and busts of Baylor ancestors carved out of marble. Everything was surely priceless. Kailem was hesitant to touch any of it; Emerald, however, mused over which items were most expensive and easy to slip away with.

"Osmund, you're here!" someone squealed.

A young girl on the cusp of womanhood ran to Osmund and threw her arms around him. She wore a sky-blue gown and had blonde curls that bobbed as she ran. "And oh my, you smell terrible!" she said with a laugh.

"Sylvie, what are you doing here?" Osmund asked.

"Oh, mother didn't take kindly to a boy I fancied, so she exiled me to stay with your parents for a time. I was so sad when I heard you would be gone for months. But you're here now! And Godfrey tells me you have some remarkable story to tell us all. Perhaps that will explain why you appear to have been dragged through a sewer."

"I do have such a tale, but I believe I had better make myself more presentable first," Osmund said, looking himself over.

"Yes, I should say that would be wise," Sylvie said. Her eyes met Kailem's. "Cousin, wherever are you manners? I believe we are in want of introductions." She rose onto the balls of her feet and rested back down on her heels.

"Oh yes, forgive me. Sylvie, these are my good friends, Kailem and Emerald."

"Delighted to meet you," Sylvie said with a curtsey. Emerald was visibly confused by the gesture.

Osmund continued. "In fact, I could use your assistance, Sylvie. Would you be so kind as to take Emerald here and see that she is seen to? A bath, and something to wear for dinner?"

"It would be my pleasure," Sylvie said. She stepped forward and hooked her arm inside Emerald's. "Oof, my dear. Somehow, you smell even worse than Osmund does. Don't you worry, we'll take care of that. If you'll excuse us, boys."

Sylvie practically dragged Emerald by the arm down the hall. Emerald looked back at Kailem and Osmund, dumbfounded as she was led hostage around a corner and out of sight.

Sylvie led Emerald into a stone room, spacious by Emerald's standards but miniscule compared to the rooms they had passed on the way there. In the center was a circular porcelain bath, about eight feet wide and four feet deep. It was half-full of lukewarm water, and on the far wall was a furnace and basin of boiling water.

"Very well then. 'Emerald', was it? Such a peculiar name. Remove your clothing and I'll prepare the water." Sylvie nodded to a maid who filled a bucket from the boiling basin and poured it into the porcelain bath.

"What is this place?" Emerald asked.

Sylvie looked up at her. "Why, it's a bath, silly. Bless me, have you really never bathed?" The maid poured another bucket of boiling water into the bath.

Emerald shook her head.

"Well, you are going to love it. Now come on, off with those clothes."

Emerald hesitated, then pulled her shirt over her head. While she undressed, Sylvie had the maid pour a concoction of soap, salt, and flower petals into the water. Emerald lowered her breeches and covered herself with her hands and arms.

"This was truly all you were wearing?" Sylvie asked. "Not even an undergarment? My, my." She pinched Emerald's clothing like it might bite her and tossed it in the furnace.

"Oy!" Emerald shouted, still covering herself.

"Trust me, dear. They were past saving. Now, in you go." Sylvie clapped twice.

Seeing she didn't have much of a choice in the matter, Emerald descended the bath steps. A soothing sensation immediately penetrated her skin and flowed through her entire being. She leaned her back against the bath wall and closed her eyes. The steam filled her lungs with each inhalation, and she breathed more deeply than she thought she ever had before. The tension in every muscle melted into a joyful puddle of relaxation.

She let herself sink further until even her ears were underwater and only her mouth and nose remained above the surface. She could feel her hair untangle and fan out behind her head. Her limbs went limp and swayed in the water.

Emerald could have stayed in that bath for the rest of her life. The combination of scents and warmth and buoyancy were beyond anything she had ever experienced. She combed through her limited vocabulary, looking for the right word to describe it, but couldn't find one. Then she no longer cared about describing it. She no longer cared about anything. She just wanted to experience every second of this. Sylvie was saying something, but with her eyes closed and her ears below water, Emerald couldn't make out what it was. And to be honest, Emerald was fine with that.

Sylvie must have been asking about the water temperature, because a surge of fresh heat flowed into the bath. She took in a deep, steam-filled breath and let her entire body sink underwater.

Kailem hadn't taken a hot bath since his exile. He'd forgotten how invigorating it could be. He left the bathing room with a towel around his waist and used a second towel to dry his hair. Osmund, who had bathed first, was already dressed in semi-formal attire: a deep green silk shirt with an extended collar and ruffled wrists under a gray vest of crushed velvet.

"I had Godfrey bring some of my brother Edric's clothing," Osmund said. "I believe you two are about the same size."

Several layers of clothing were laid out on the bed. It was essentially the same outfit Osmund was wearing, but the linen shirt was a dark blue and the vest a light tan. Kailem felt ridiculous. He took particular issue with the ruffles on his wrists; not even the women in Marin wore ruffles. If Mokain could see him now, Kailem would never hear the end of it.

Kailem had a warrior's body, olive skin stretched over toned muscle, with several prominent scars on his back and shoulders. As Kailem changed into Edric's clothing, Osmund found himself suddenly aware of his own flabby physique. He wanted to ask Kailem why he wore that pearl around his neck, but felt it would be rude to pry.

"This is quite the room," Kailem said as he buttoned the silk shirt. Osmund's room might as well as have been a scholar's private study. Every inch of the walls that wasn't claimed by desks and windows was covered in bookshelves from the floor to the ceiling. The writing desk held a stack of paper, an abacus, and a quill and inkwell. Above the writing desk was an oversized map of Iria. Gadgets Kailem had never seen filled the tables. There were contraptions using mirrors and prisms, some using scales and weights, glass cylinders with unknown liquids inside. Kailem's eyes were drawn to a long cylinder attached to what looked like a bar stool. The end of the cylinder was pointed to the top of the nearby window.

"What is this?" Kailem asked, walking over to the device.

"It's called a telescope. You could say it is a more complex version of the spyglass you use on a ship. You can use it to look at the stars at night."

"Fascinating. Your invention?" Kailem asked as he finished buttoning his vest.

"No, no, another scholar invented it. I got a hold of the description and had the blacksmith and glassblower in town make the parts for me."

Kailem walked to the adjacent desk and investigated a small pile of granulated powder. He took a pinch of the powder and moved it between his fingers.

"Careful!" Osmund warned.

Kailem dropped the powder back into the pile and wiped the dust from his fingers. "What is it?" he asked.

"It's a solution invented by an alchemist in Cavandel. A combination of charcoal, saltpeter, and sulfur. He calls it black powder."

"What does it do?"

"Here, I'll show you." Osmund used a teaspoon to scoop a small amount from the pile and spread it on a tea saucer. Then he took a nearby candle and held the flame close. The powder crackled, then produced a small flame and grey smoke. This was no ordinary smoke; it had a pungent stench that stung the nostrils.

Kailem stepped back and waved the smoke from his face. "That's incredible," he said, coughing. Osmund wore a look of smug satisfaction.

"What do you use it for?" Kailem asked.

"He isn't sure yet. In our most recent communication, he was still testing to find the most potent combination of ingredients."

Kailem looked around at the rest of the many devices on the desks and shelves. "Which one of these did you invent?"

Osmund's shoulders sank. "I'm... still trying to find my big idea."

Kailem nodded. "Well, I'm sure you'll find it. Do you mind if I use your writing desk? I want to write to my brother in Rhinegard to let him know what happened."

Osmund approved, and Kailem sat down to write. After a few minutes, there was a knock at the door. Godfrey stepped in with his usual impeccable posture.

"Dinner is served, Master Osmund," Godfrey said. He bowed and stepped back from the room.

Osmund led Kailem through the hallways and staircases of the Baylor Mansion to the dining hall. Seeing all the servants in Osmund's home reminded Kailem of what it was like to have servants of his own. It was only three months ago that he was a young Lord living on a nobleman's estate. But that had been another life, and the Roka Estate had been a pauper's home compared to this.

The young men were the first to arrive. Osmund had Kailem stand behind the chair next to his, the seat that was customarily his brother Edric's, and they waited for his father to arrive.

After a moment, Sylvie walked in with Emerald a few steps behind her.

Osmund's jaw went limp.

Emerald wore a gown of forest green, the straps nearly off the shoulder, with a diamond necklace around her neck. Her hair graced her back like silk, and two thin braids on either side held the hair back from her face. Before the bath, her hair had been a dark chestnut color; now it was a golden copper glowing like embers in a fire. She looked like a genuine lady of the aristocracy.

Osmund was awestruck. Kailem, meanwhile, tried not to consider just how dirty her hair must have been before the bath.

Sylvie broke the awkward silence. "Well, cousin? Doesn't she look beautiful?"

"What? Oh, yeah, uh yes, yes she does," Osmund said. Emerald smiled, a mixture of charm and embarrassment.

The two ladies walked around the table and waited behind their seats.

I look like a parrot, Emerald mouthed to Kailem. Kailem simply held up his wrist and pointed to the ruffled cuffs on his sleeve, and Emerald suppressed a laugh. She looked back to a still slack-jawed Osmund. He tried to look like he wasn't staring, but did a rather poor job of it. Emerald noticed, and her cheeks flushed.

***

Lord Reginald Baylor allowed his servant to slide his dinner jacket over his shoulders and tie his cravat around his neck. His wife, Lady Boudica Baylor, sat in front of her vanity, allowing her servant to finish styling her hair.

"It will not be anything surprising, Boudica," Reginald said. "There will be some reason he had to abandon his work and it will not be his fault and he will go back to holding up in his room buried in one of his 'research projects'. Just you wait, soon he'll be asking to waste more time at that University."

"Well, let's not rush to judgment until we've heard him out," Boudica said. She studied the necklace she paired with her dress.

"Boudica, be serious. You really believe Osmund, *our* Osmund, has some incredible tale of adventure to share."

"Of course, I don't, Reginald. All I'm saying is you should keep an open mind. He may well surprise you." Lord Baylor scoffed.

There was a knock at the door, and Godfrey stepped through the threshold.

"Dinner is ready, my Lord," Godfrey said.

Lord Baylor approved of his cravat in the mirror. "Very good, Godfrey. We'll be down in a moment."

"And who are these strangers he's brought into our home?" Lord Baylor asked as they descended the grand staircase. "It's like he's bringing wounded animals into the house again. He's fortunate I even agreed to this dinner."

"Take it as a good sign," Lady Baylor said. "Our Osmund has never had a friend call on him. I'm not sure he's ever *had* a friend before. I've certainly never met one. Have you?"

"No, I suppose you may be right."

"You *suppose* I'm right?" she asked in her beguiling voice. Her husband gave a distinguished smile and said nothing.

Osmund and Sylvie, along with the two strangers, were all standing behind their chairs when they arrived at the dining room. Lord Baylor took his seat at the head of the table and his wife sat at his left hand. He then motioned for the rest of them to sit. He said nothing while he positioned his napkin on his lap and inspected the foreigner sitting in his eldest son and heir's chair and wearing his clothes.

Servants entered with the first course and placed them before each of the diners, beginning with Lord Baylor.

"Osmund, why don't you introduce us to our two guests here?" Lady Baylor said.

"Yes, mother. This is Emerald and Kailem."

Lady Baylor waited to hear a proper introduction that included their surnames and kingdoms, but Osmund said nothing further. "A pleasure to meet you both," she finally said. "And I assume you introduced our guests to your cousin?"

"I have, mother."

"Very good. We are Lord Reginald Baylor and Lady Boudica Baylor. Now, with introductions out of the way, I have been told you have some... noteworthy account of your travels to share with us?"

"Yes, son," Lord Baylor's voice was booming without being loud, and it caused both Osmund and Emerald to jump in their seats. "Enough with the suspense. Tell us why you are home so soon."

"We were shipwrecked, Sir," Osmund said with his head down and his hands in his lap.

"What does that mean, you were shipwrecked?" his father asked with annoyance. Kailem was stunned by the Lord's response to the news, not a hint of concern for his son's wellbeing.

Osmund kept his eyes on the table. "I chartered a vessel to take me to Barrowfort, and it sank in the Cerulean Sea. Kailem was one of the sailors, and Emerald was a fellow passenger. As best we can say, we are the only ones who survived. We washed ashore along Glendown Forest and traveled two days through the forest before we found the road."

Lord Baylor inspected his son with the same skepticism as one might a traveling salesman.

"What caused the ship to sink?"

"It was a rare storm from the south, sir."

"Sunk in a storm? Sounds like poor seamanship." Lord Baylor's eyes shifted from Osmund to Kailem as he cut into his pheasant. Kailem gritted his teeth but said nothing.

"Lightning struck the main mast," Osmund explained. "There was nothing the crew could do."

"And how did you find your way to shore when you can't swim?" his father asked before chewing his poultry.

"I held onto a broken piece of the ship and drifted with the ocean current until we could kick our way to shore, sir."

"I see. And then you walked two days through Glendown Forest just like that? No food or water or provisions of any kind?" Lord Baylor spoke with his hands, and the effect was amplified by the cutlery he held.

"I would not have made it were it not for Kailem. He has some skill in wilderness survival."

"Now *that* I can believe." The Lord cut another slice of meat from the bone.

There was a moment of uncomfortable silence, no one daring to interrupt the Lordship's interrogation. It took every fiber of control Kailem could muster to not put Lord Baylor in his place.

It was Lady Baylor who finally spoke.

"Well, it seems we owe you a debt of gratitude for saving our son." Lady Baylor's courteous voice eased some of the tension at the table, but not all. "I don't believe we've ever hosted a Mariner at our table before."

Kailem had to swallow before answering. "I don't believe I've ever had a Devonian host before. It's an honor to be here, your ladyship."

"Are you the eldest in your family, Kailem?" Lord Baylor asked.

"No, my Lord. I have an older brother."

"Osmund is a second son, as well. My first born, Edric, is off managing some of our holdings. That's his chair and clothing you're in."

Kailem looked Lord Baylor in the eye. "It's a very kind gesture, my Lord. I'm honored."

Lord Baylor was still appraising the foreigner at his table, his face showing some degree of hesitant approval. Kailem thought back to all his mother's lessons in courtly etiquette.

"I must say, my Lord, while I have not had the pleasure of meeting your heir, I have been genuinely impressed by your son Osmund. He's a wellspring of knowledge, a testament to his heritage and breeding."

Lord Baylor scoffed. "A wellspring indeed. I eagerly await the day he puts all those facts to good use. Surely, it will be any day now."

Osmund stared at his plate and said nothing.

What a repulsive man, Kailem thought. Seeing who Osmund grew up with made him respect his own father all the more. He remembered him fondly, and the ache in his heart blossomed anew. The remainder of the meal passed with meaningless small talk and occasional silence.

After dinner, Osmund and his two guests retired to his quarters. A serving cart was waiting for them, with pastries and a decanter of brandy. Osmund walked past it and collapsed face first onto his bed.

"Is your father always so charming?" Kailem asked. He poured himself a glass of brandy and sat down at the writing desk in front of the map of Iria.

"Tonight was average," Osmund said, his mouth partially muffled by the goose feather comforter on his bed. "Edric... casts a large shadow."

There was a darkness in Osmund's voice. Not an evil darkness, but one of emptiness, like all his light had been sucked into an abyss.

"And I thought it was hard being Mokain's younger brother," Kailem said, as he leaned back in his chair and sipped his brandy.

Osmund rolled to his side and put a pillow under his head. "Edric would do anything to please Father. He's the perfect son. Anything Father even remotely approved of, Edric would go and master it."

Emerald inspected the pastries on the serving cart like they were precious gems in a vault. She piled as many as she could possibly fit onto a single small serving plate, then walked about the room, taking stock of its many trinkets and gadgets.

"Too bad your father doesn't appreciate all this?" Kailem asked.

"All of what?" Osmund asked.

Kailem gestured to everything in the room. "All your studying. This is an impressive collection."

Osmund continued to stare at nothing. "Father believes it is a waste of time. But thank you for trying to defend me down there. I always dreamed about becoming a renowned scholar, joining a university, speaking in crowded lecture halls, debating with esteemed colleagues. It didn't matter the subject, I wanted to learn it all. Father said that wasn't practical."

"So, what makes someone a 'renowned scholar'?" Kailem asked. He took another sip of his brandy.

Osmund sat up on the bed. "There are two ways a scholar becomes renowned. The first is to discover something completely new that no one has ever studied or written about. The other way is to take something another scholar has already written and reinterpret it in a novel way. So far, I have proven incapable of either."

"What about your idea about... what did you call it? Magical arts?" Kailem asked.

"Mystical arts. And let's be frank. It was not very interesting. No one would have taken it seriously. It would have been just a summary of what other scholars had written, nothing new or noteworthy."

"Not to worry, Oz. Ye'll find yer big idea," Emerald said. Her reassurance eased his embarrassment.

Lord Baylor's conduct at dinner had left a vile taste in Kailem's mouth. He found himself eager to leave the wretched man as quickly as possible, and take Osmund and Emerald with him. But where would they go? The invitation to stay with Osmund for a time had been a pleasant distraction, but the reality of his situation was again settling in. He had no money, no home, no prospects, no title of nobility, and his sole surviving family was hundreds of miles away in Rhinegard. He forced the thought from his mind.

Emerald perused the bookshelves, inspecting the collection.

"Anything look interesting?" Osmund asked.

"Hmm? Oh, nay, can't even read," Emerald returned. "What be this one, then? The one with the twistin' circles. I like it." She moved her finger over the debossed symbol on the book's spine.

"That is one of the rarest books in my collection, actually. It is called the "Codex Andala". It is a history of the Sages, one of the last surviving studies that treats them as fact rather than myth. The first edition was written over 500 years ago; that particular copy is 80 years old."

He hoped that would have impressed her, but Emerald showed no reaction.

"You *have* heard of the Sages, haven't you?" Osmund asked.

Emerald shook her head. Osmund looked to Kailem who did likewise.

"By Iria!" Osmund exclaimed. He leaped off the bed and pulled the Codex Andala from the shelf. "I can't believe this! The Sages are the most fascinating legends ever told."

Emerald sat beside him on the bed and took another bite of a raspberry tart. Her hip pressed against his, and she rested her cheek on his shoulder so she could look over him to the open book on his lap. Osmund's heartbeat quickened.

He opened the Codex Andala to an illustration of a man in a robe. The man had his hands out perpendicular to his body with his palms up, and in the air around him were rocks and sundry items.

"Why is it raining rocks?" Emerald asked.

"It's not *raining* rocks," Osmund explained. "The man is making them float. He's a sage."

Their conversation piqued Kailem's curiosity. He set down his brandy and took a seat on the side of Osmund opposite Emerald.

"So, a sage be a man who floats things"?" Emerald asked.

"More than just float, they had tremendous powers. Unfortunately, there's no consensus on exactly what abilities they had. They were rumored to be as strong as oxen and as fast as stallions, that they could fly and control you with their minds. Some people said they could see through walls, or morph into animals, or even turn invisible, and some rumors even believed they were immortal. Which is false, of course, because they went extinct over a thousand years ago. Most information about them has been lost. This book goes over the leading theories about them. I have read it several times."

"Were they just people, like us?" Kailem asked.

"Some say they were. The Human Theory says they were either born with special abilities or they took a secret elixir that gave them power. Others say they only looked human but were, in fact, other creatures entirely, like the way a wolf looks similar to a dog. No one can say for sure."

"What happened to them?" Emerald asked.

Osmund exhaled. "Again, no one knows for sure. They were always small in number, but they used to live out in the open. They used their abilities to protect people and preserve the peace. Then one day they were just gone."

Osmund aimlessly flipped the pages of the Codex Andala. Most were full of dense passages of text, but others had beautiful illustrations and embellishments along the edges. Emerald couldn't read the text, but she fancied the brilliant colors and the sound the pages made as they turned over.

"What's that?" Kailem asked.

Osmund stopped on a page with a thick illustrated border of green and gold intersecting lines. In the center were two verses of a poem.

Osmund sat taller. "The Sages had a secret city where they lived. It was called 'Andalaya'. It was impossible for anyone other than a sage to find, so they left several poems with clues on how to find it. This is the only poem that survived."

"Where be it?" Emerald asked.

Osmund shook his head. "No one knows. A lot of critics who say the Sages weren't real use that as proof. If the Sages were real, they say, then we would have found Andalaya by now."

Emerald bit into a peach tart. "What's it says, then?" she asked, while chewing. It was a subtle reminder that a commoner in an evening gown was still a commoner. Her etiquette was appalling, and yet, somehow endearing as well.

Kailem read the poem aloud:

> *From southern winds, the babe will come,*
> *To find the object of her eye.*
> *On fertile shores, her feet doth land,*
> *To seek the eagle in the sky.*
> *From thence, the babe doth travel on,*
> *With feet on snakes, below she climbs.*

To meet her mark, horizon's end
Sacred circles, twelve she finds.

"Be all gibberish ta me. What's it mean, then?" Emerald asked.

Osmund shrugged. "If I knew, I would be a renowned scholar by now," he said. His smile dripped with melancholy.

Kailem repeated the words of the poem in his mind.

"What be all these other... things... ye have in here?" Emerald asked. She motioned to all the gadgets in Osmund's room.

"Here, let me show you," Osmund said. He set the Codex Andala down on the bed and led her to the telescope.

Kailem took the book and leaned back against the headboard. Keeping his finger to mark the location of the poem, he flipped through the book's pages. There were more illustrations of sages using their abilities, accounts of them fighting in wars and helping during times of plague and famine. Kailem was drawn into the book, momentarily forgetting all that was around him. Something about the Sages felt right to him, although precisely why they appealed to him, he couldn't say.

Emerald gasped. "So close, and bright!"

Kailem looked up from the poem and saw her looking into the telescope pointed at the starry night sky through the window. Osmund's hand was on the dial that focused the lenses. A proud smile stretched from ear to ear.

Kailem grinned and turned back to the poem. There was something so familiar about an "eagle in the sky," but he couldn't place it.

He flipped through more pages; the illustrations captivating his imagination. His mind played with the possibility of their reality. If they had been real, who were they? How could they do such feats, and what had become of them?

There was a sudden *pop* followed by a hissing sound. Kailem looked up and saw black smoke in the corner of the room. Emerald laughed and clapped while Osmund opened a window to let out the smoke. He must have shown her the black powder.

Kailem read the poem again. An idea occurred to him, and he carried the Codex Andala to the writing desk.

"Oz," he called. "I think I have something?"

"What do you mean?" Osmund demonstrated how his model trebuchet worked.

"I think I know what it means. The poem. Or the first part of it, at least."

"Have you, indeed?" Osmund's voice was equal parts skeptical and amused. He walked to the writing desk with Emerald close behind.

"I figure if you need a poem to serve as a set of directions, you need a starting point. The poem begins with 'from southern winds', so we start in the south." Kailem placed his finger on the bottom of the map.

"'On fertile shores her feet doth land,' that implies she came up from the south by ship," he continued. "The most fertile farming land in the entire southern coast is here." Kailem moved his finger up through the Sea of Beydal and stopped several inches above the coast.

"It's the Valleys of Veydala, right on the border between Marcôna and Lanâu. They call it a valley, but in truth, it is a whole system of small hills and valleys throughout the lowlands. The two kingdoms fight over that land constantly. At the northern end of the valley is a small mountain range, and at the top of one of the peaks is a rock formation that resembles a bird. My brother and I saw it on our way to Barrowfort. The locals call it the 'Balderlyn Falcon', after the town at the base of the mountain."

"Falcon? Thems the same as eagles?" Emerald asked.

"Well, no. But it's a rock formation. It looks like any large bird."

"And innit s'posed to be up in the sky?" she pointed out.

"I don't think it's being literal. What do you think, Oz?"

Osmund thought for a moment. He looked from the poem to the map, then back again. "I suppose it could work. As good as any other theory I've heard."

Kailem pounded the desk with the base of his fist. A plan formed in mind, a plan to redeem himself for letting his friends down on the ship and in the forest, to find some purpose in his life.

"So, Kailem solved what none o' ye smart ones could, then?" Emerald asked, both dubious and amused.

"Well, to be fair, no serious scholar has worked on this in almost a hundred years," Osmund explained. "And I am not fully convinced he is right, but... it *is* possible."

"Let's go find it," Kailem said.

"What do you mean?"

"Let's go to Balderlyn and find the falcon, or eagle, what have you. Maybe once we arrive, we can decipher the remaining clues to that place you spoke of."

"Andalaya?"

"Yes, Andalaya! Imagine it, finding thousand-year-old ruins that most people didn't even believe existed. You could write all about what we find and become a famous scholar. 'The man who found Andalaya'."

Osmund lost himself in the fantasy for several seconds before returning to reality. "No, no, no, I've done enough traveling for a lifetime. I am staying right here."

"We'll go by land, then. Absolutely no chance of another shipwreck."

"To the Valleys of Veydala? Kailem, that's almost a thousand miles from here." Osmund squinted at the map. "In fact, I dare say it's *more* than a thousand. We can't walk that far, and I am *not* boarding another ship."

Emerald chewed her lip while she examined the map the boys were looking at. She had never really looked at a map before and hadn't realized so much existed beyond the bounds of their kingdom. Iria was more massive than she had ever imagined.

"We don't need to take a ship; we can ride horses the whole way," Kailem said.

Osmund paced his room. "I don't know, Kailem. I... I'm a scholar. My place is in libraries, reading, where its safe."

"But that's not what you'll do if you stay here, is it?" Kailem asked. "You're going to take on the family business. Work all day, every day at your father's side."

Osmund stopped pacing and let his shoulders slump.

"Oz, no great discoveries are made reading about what other people have seen and done. They're made out there, in the wild, chasing down clues and experiencing the world for yourself. There's nothing for either of us here, so let's go have an adventure!"

Osmund shook his head. "I'm just... I'm not..." he stuttered, and his words trailed off.

"I'll be right there with you. I have all the combat and survival training we need to stay safe. You have all the book knowledge, and, to be candid, the finances. We'll make the perfect team."

Osmund's hands fidgeted at his sides. His mind flashed with memories of being trapped under a canvas sail in a black ocean, desperate to fill his lungs with air. "I am sorry, Kailem. Truly I am," he said. "But I cannot do it. I simply cannot."

"Well, I'm in," Emerald said.

Both Osmund and Kailem turned to her, wide-eyed and speechless. They had barely convinced her to come to Osmund's estate with them, Kailem never would have dreamed she would agree to go on a thousand-mile journey together. oi

"What?" she said. "It's not like I can stay here after ye both leave, then, can I? And I've had a taste of the finer things now. Hot baths, full meals, soft beds, sweets." She lifted her pastry plate as an example. "Not quite ready to give all that up yet."

"A taste of the finer things? You've been here one day," Kailem said with a laugh he later hoped hadn't sounded condescending.

"Ay, like I said, a taste, and I say it suits me."

Kailem could see her true reason for wanting to join them, but decided to say nothing. Plus, he didn't have the heart to tell her they would have no such comforts while traveling. He turned back to Osmund. "Well, Oz, how about it? The three of us on a hunt to find the Sages?"

Osmund considered the alternative: working with his father every day, enduring an endless barrage of disappointment, constantly living under Edric's shadow. That sounded even worse than another shipwreck.

He rubbed his face and released a sigh. "Somehow, I just know I am going to regret this." He let his hands fall to his sides. "Alright, let's go find Andalaya."

PART TWO

Narrator's First Interlude

I f there is one thing that my study of history has taught me, it is that the fate of every generation pivots on a precious handful of decisions made by a select number of individuals. Most decisions have ramifications that scarcely ripple beyond our immediate vicinity, but every now and again, there exists a single choice that will redirect the entire course of human events. There are occasions when the import of these decisions is known at the time they are made, such as when a King decides whether to go to war or when a governor decides whether to quarantine the carrier of a plague. But other such decisions seem genuinely innocuous in the moment, and it is not for years to come that the true weight of their impact becomes evident.

Such was the decision made by Kailem, Emerald, and Osmund on their first night in the Baylor Estate. If future generations knew all that had hung in the balance of that simple choice, they would exalt the day of our trio's decision to seek Andalaya with jubilance and gratitude. It would be a day that all of Iria commemorated annually with unparalleled feasts and festivity; minstrels would sing the trio's songs, children would listen to their elders tell the trio's stories, and statues would be constructed in their honor in every town and village.

And yet, despite the benefit of their deeds having endured for centuries, their story has passed largely unknown among the people of Iria. This was, in part, by design, as they never sought recognition or glory. Even I, who was fortunate enough to be raised by parents who knew their story, had heard only of their virtues and accomplishments. Such is the nature of legends, I suppose; they increase in grandeur with each retelling. But I believe their feats inspire even greater awe when their struggles and defects are considered. They did not begin life the exemplary men and women described in their songs. No, this is a story of becoming.

On that fateful day in the year 897 G.C., our three young heroes had no way of knowing how drastic the changes for good their journey would have on every kingdom and people in Iria. They could never have known the profound effect their journey would have on their own lives, nor could they have known the hardship and the joys, the suffering and the wonders that lay before them. For our three young heroes, this was simply an expedition in search of a few fabled ruins in the south of Iria.

Chapter Fourteen

The Departure

51st Day of Spring, 897 G.C.

"Are you *sure* I can't talk you out of this?" Sylvie whined. She trailed after Osmund as he lugged a sack of traveling supplies out to the stables.

"Yes, Sylvie. I am quite sure," Osmund replied. He set the bags down to rest for a moment, then continued.

"But you only just arrived," she continued.

"Well, I was never supposed to return in the first place, remember?"

"Yes, but then you did. So, you should stay." She lifted the hem of her dress to keep from soiling it on the cobbled path.

When they reached the stables, they found Raymon, the stable master, instructing Kailem on riding horseback. Emerald stood by the fence, enjoying the entertainment.

"Emerald, will you *please* talk some sense into him," Sylvie pleaded.

Emerald wrinkled her brow.

"Well, surely you don't want to go on this foolish expedition," Sylvie said. "You'll be on dirty roads having to smell the horses all day. There will be bugs and dirt and you'll sleep on the ground every night. You'll be positively miserable!"

"Actually, sounds I'll be right at home, then," Emerald replied. "Other than riding them horses, a course. Never done that before."

Sylvie huffed, realizing she had failed to account for the young woman's breeding. Clearly, one could not turn a commoner into a lady with nothing but a bath and a gown.

"Pull the reins!" shouted Raymon, the stable master. "The reins, man! Show the beast who's boss!"

Kailem's horse, a smoke-colored quarter horse named Echo, trotted about the horse pen in erratic lines. Kailem pulled at the reins with little effect, looking as comfortable as a cat swimming in a river. Emerald laughed and clapped at the man she had assumed had been an expert at just about everything. Even Sylvie put her hand to her mouth to suppress her amusement.

Osmund secured his bags to Summit, the obsidian draught horse that would carry their gear on the journey. He then walked to the horse pen and leaned his elbows on the railing. Beneath his calm exterior was a tempest of anxiety. A thousand-mile expedition was something that Edric did, not him. The first time he'd ventured off on his own had frightened him to his very core, yet this fear was far worse. If his first journey was supposed to involve only the nicest and safest parts of Iria, and somehow ended with a near fatal shipwreck, just what could he expect this time, he wondered?

In the three days since he'd agreed to this journey, Osmund had backed out twice. Each time, Kailem and Emerald were able to rouse his sense of adventure again, aided in no small measure by his father's thinly veiled disappointment in everything he did.

While resisting Kailem's every pull on the reins, Echo noticed Osmund and trotted directly to him. He pressed his forehead against Osmund's and nickered.

"I know, I know. I've missed you as well, old friend." Osmund rubbed the bridge of the horse's nose. "I need you to be a good horse for my friend Kailem here. Can you do that for me?" The horse nickered a reply.

"You've truly never ridden a horse before?" He asked Kailem. Echo stood still, enjoying Osmund's attention.

Kailem shook his head. "Only the military uses them. Moka learned to ride, I didn't."

Osmund turned at the sound of Raymon by the fence, helping Emerald into her saddle. She sat on an undersized palomino walking horse named Willow. The horse stood at ease with her new rider.

"Now, make the clicking sound I taught you," Raymon instructed.

Emerald clicked her tongue, and the horse sauntered forward.

"Use the reins to guide her to the left!" Raymon called out.

Emerald pulled the reins, and the animal followed.

"That's good," he said. "Now circle about again, but this time, give her a gentle kick with your heels."

Emerald kicked, and Willow sped to a trot. She pulled on the reins, guiding the horse in zig-zag patterns about the horse pen, and Willow obeyed as if Emerald were the only rider she'd ever known. She kicked again, slightly harder this time, and the horse sped into a swift canter.

"Very good!" Raymon called out, clapping. "Straight back, shoulders still. The hips! Remember your hips! Move *with* the horse!"

Emerald and the horse moved as one about the enclosure. Raymon walked to Osmund and Kailem, still watching her.

"She's a natural, ain't she?" Raymon said.

"She's perfect," Osmund said. He didn't realize he had said that aloud.

"A bit of show off, too," Sylvie murmured.

Emerald brought her horse to a stop next to the group, watching her. She beamed as the men clapped for her.

"I still don't understand why *you* have to go," Sylvie complained to Emerald. Proper lady or not, Emerald was better than no company at all. "You could stay here with me; we'd be like sisters."

Emerald looked like Sylvie had just asked her to eat a dead cricket. "Nay, I think I'll be on the adventure, thank ye," she said, rubbing Willow's neck.

Sylvie puffed with disappointment.

Lady Baylor arrived with a servant close in tow.

"Osmund, dear. I had the chef bake you some fresh brioche loaves and honey butter for the road. Are you all packed? You are sure you haven't forgotten anything?"

"I believe we are ready," Osmund said. "Raymon helped us prepare."

"That was very kind of you, Raymon."

The stable master bowed his head.

"Your father wished to see you off, but some pressing business required his attention. He asked me to tell you he is quite proud of you and wishes you well on your expedition."

Osmund had never heard a more blatant lie, but said nothing. He took the basket of bread and butter from the servant and secured it to Summit's pack. The black horse huffed at the lack of attention he received, and Osmund rubbed his muzzle.

Raymon led Osmund's horse, a chestnut-colored thoroughbred named Jasper, out of the stables. Osmund tied a line between Jasper and Summit, then climbed into Jasper's saddle.

"Take care, my son," Lady Baylor said. "Write to me every time you stop in a town."

Raymon opened the gate to the horse pen and Emerald and Kailem rode the horses out.

"And once you come to your senses and realize this whole ramble is foolhardy, do hurry home," Sylvie added as they passed. Emerald rolled her eyes, and Sylvie huffed again.

With that, the trio followed the road to Ombermill as Osmund's home disappeared behind the trees.

Ombermill was a twenty-minute trot from the Baylor Estate. It was a quaint little town, barely larger than a village. The three travelers caught several glances trotting down the main road as townsfolk recognized the son of their Lord casually passing through.

"Let's stop here for a minute," Kailem suggested. He pulled the reins to the right, but Echo jerked against him. Kailem pulled again, not harshly but firmly, just as Raymon had taught him, yet Echo still refused to be moved. *Daft animal,* he thought.

"What for? We're fully stocked." Osmund said as he swung from his saddle.

"A rest'll be dandy," Emerald said, hopping off her horse.

The three climbed the steps of a tailor's shop. Osmund had given Kailem and Emerald each their own money pouch full of silver and copper coins after Raymon said it would be unwise to keep all of their traveling money in the same pouch.

"My Lord Baylor," the tailor said as they entered. "You honor me with your visit, good sir. In what manner might I be of assistance?"

"I'm not entirely sure," Osmund said, turning to Kailem.

"We need new outfits," Kailem stated. "Nothing fancy. In fact, the plainest looking outfits you have."

"What? Why? What's wrong with this?" Osmund asked, observing himself in a mirror on the wall.

Osmund and Kailem were dressed in formal equestrian attire. Emerald wore a traditional riding habit, a pair of tight-fitting trousers and a coat with a long skirt that spread out to appear like a formal gown while on horseback. Emerald found it a huge improvement over what she had worn to dinner, which was what she assumed female jesters wear, but she was still glad at the prospect of wearing normal clothing again.

"These outfits are not well suited for a long journey," Kailem replied.

Osmund looked himself over. "I should say we look rather dashing," he said, striking a pose in the mirror.

"And I would have to agree with you, my Lord," the tailor said with the kind of exaggerated smile all too common among merchants.

"We look *too* nice," Kailem explained. "And that's the problem. It makes us a target."

"That is a wise point, my Lord," the tailor agreed, not wanting to lose a sale.

Osmund exhaled, still appraising himself in the mirror. "Very well. Show us what you have."

The tailor gave a servant's bow. "With pleasure, my Lord. Our plain clothing is in the..." the tailor cut off as someone entered the store. He was a rugged, gruff sort of man with a face that had a permanently furrowed brow. "If you'll excuse me just one moment, my Lord."

Osmund frowned. He'd never before been set aside for a commoner and didn't much care for it. The tailor scurried into the back room with more haste than he'd shown when the trio had entered. He emerged a moment later with a package wrapped in brown paper and twine. He handed the package to the man without any exchange of payment. As the man reached forward to accept the package, Kailem noticed a tattoo of a small bird on the man's wrist. The man and the tailor nodded to each other, and the man left without having spoken a word.

"My sincerest apologies, my Lord," the tailor said when he returned. "If you'll kindly follow me, I keep our plainest clothing in the back corner here."

The tailor selected outfits for each of them. Osmund groaned, examining them.

"Might we use your backroom to try them on?" Kailem asked.

"But of course, my Lord."

Kailem was the first to finish changing. He approved of the new clothing in the mirror and paid for them just as Osmund emerged from the back room looking like a commoner. The young nobleman inspected himself in the same mirror and winced. He struck several different poses for himself, but his frown only deepened. Emerald finished last and leaned against the counter, looking natural in her new drab shirt and trousers.

"Might I venture a suggestion, my Lord? Something to show your style without betraying your affluence?" The tailor presented a vest made of coarse linen. Osmund slid it over his shoulders and fastened the buttons.

"If my father could see me now," he muttered to himself. "I suppose this will do. And perhaps some headwear. Let me see a collection of flat caps."

Kailem and Emerald rolled their eyes and left Osmund to finish constructing his poor man's ensemble.

Across the street from the tailor's shop, Kailem saw a father and mother walking down the street. Each held the hand of a young son walking between them. They played a game as they walked, lifting him high into the air by the hands and setting him back down between strides. The boy laughed with glee, and the parents basked in their son's joy.

Kailem's thoughts turned to his own parents. In a breath, he was back in the palace square, fighting desperately to save them, watching the horrors again for the thousandth time.

Emerald stowed her riding dress in her saddlebag and turned to stroke Willow's shoulder. As she did, her eyes met those of a man passing by. He was a lean, elfin man with narrow eyes and blonde hair greased back. Emerald knew him instantly.

"Emerald?!" the man said with wide eyes. He changed course toward her.

Gobshite, she cursed. She backed herself against Willow's saddle, feeling trapped. "How'd ye find me, Sirus?"

"Oh, Em, Jacken has eyes everywhere for ye," Sirus said.

"I didn't do nothin', Sirus. Ye hafta know twasn't me."

"Then why'd ye run?" Sirus asked, moving closer. Osmund exited the tailor shop wearing his vest and flat cap, then paused, watching the exchange.

"Ye know how Jacken be. Reckon he'd believe a word I say?"

Sirus shrugged. "Still shouldn't a run, Em. We'll let Jacken decide what to do with ye." Sirus took hold of Emerald's elbow and turned to leave.

Emerald whipped her arm free. "I shan't be goin' nowhere, ye can go and shove it, then. I be done with all that."

"Ye're coming with me now." Sirus gripped Emerald's upper arm so tightly his fingers dug into her skin. Osmund stood dumbfounded, unsure how to respond. He looked to Kailem, who was staring intently at a young family across the dirt road.

"Oi! Unhand me, rottin' sard!" Emerald cried out. She scratched and hit the man, even tried to go limp so he would drop her, but it was no use.

Kailem turned away from the young family just in time to see Sirus march her away from their horses. She looked panicked and helpless. Osmund looked frozen stiff.

Kailem ran to them, bursting with the pain of his parents' memory, and grabbed the back of Sirus's collar. The shock caused Sirus to release his hold on Emerald's arm. Kailem leveraged his momentum to twist the man over his hip, sending him to the dirt. Sirus floundered in the street, unsure of who or what had attacked him. Before he could react, the Mariner was on top of him.

Kailem drove his fist into the man's face, breaking the nose on the first punch. Sirus lifted his hands, so Kailem struck the man's face from the side again and again. Sirus managed to block one of Kailem's strikes and attempted to grapple with him. Kailem grabbed the man's arm and twisted it, then drove his palm into the man's elbow. There was a loud crack as the arm bent unnaturally. The man cried out in unbridled agony.

Kailem pinned down the man's one working arm and resumed ramming his fist into the man's face. After a few more blows, the man went limp. Blood splattered after each strike. Teeth were knocked loose. Both eyes swelled shut.

He ignored the ache and bruising in his own fist and pommeled the man's face with increasing speed. This was vengeance, and in that moment, it mattered little who was on the receiving end of it.

After nearly a dozen more blows, someone pulled at Kailem's shirt, and he turned, ready to deal out further punishment. Instead, he found Osmund scrambling back from him. Only then did he realize a crowd had gathered around them.

"I... I called your name," Osmund said, "but you couldn't hear me. I... I think he's had enough."

Kailem drew heaving breaths. He looked back at Sirus. The man lay unconscious on his back. His face swelled beyond recognition, and blood pooled in the dirt underneath him. Kailem wiped the blood from his knuckles on the man's shirt.

"Call your constable," Kailem told an onlooker. "This man should be arrested for assaulting a young lady." After looking back at him, he added, "I recommend fetching a surgeon as well."

Kailem offered a hand to Emerald. "Are you hurt?"

Emerald was speechless, as was the surrounding crowd. It took a moment for his question to register. Then she shook her head and took his help to her feet.

Kailem climbed into his saddle. Emerald and Osmund did likewise.

An awkward silence passed between them as they made their way out of the village. Once Kailem's fury subsided, it was replaced by fear of what his companions thought of him. He had shown the worst side of himself. Would they be afraid of him? Would they still welcome his company on their journey? The silence ate at him.

"I will say this," Osmund said, finally breaking the silence. "I am genuinely glad you are on our side."

Emerald attempted to smother a laugh and a piggish snort came out instead. "Thank ye for rescuing me," she said with hands clasped together, imitating a proper lady in distress. Her voice was an admirable impression of Sylvie. "Oh, how I pity the next man that crosses me."

Kailem laughed, and with that, the tension between them dissolved. Kailem's outburst had completely overshadowed Emerald's conversation with Sirus, and she thanked Iria no one thought to mention it again.

Osmund had not exaggerated when he said Ombermill Road was not well-traveled. In the four hours they had ridden south, Kailem had counted only three other caravans traveling north. One could gallop from sunrise to sunset and still not encounter a single village. It made sleeping on the road inevitable.

Kailem didn't say much; learning to move with the horse, so as to avoid the pain to his thighs and backside, required most of his attention. Fortunately, Echo was content to just follow the horses in front of him. The few times Kailem tried to steer the horse or adjust his pace, Echo simply snorted and shook his head. *Rotting horse*, Kailem cursed.

At the front of their small caravan, Osmund was explaining to Emerald just about everything that popped into head. He explained the history of the area, about the different kinds of trees and wildlife they saw, and especially about the sages. Surprisingly, Emerald seemed fascinated by it all. From the little Kailem knew about her, she wasn't the type to feign interest just to be polite; her interest must have been genuine.

The sun sank beneath the trees, and the traveling party pulled off the road to camp for the night. The Ombermill Road closely followed the path of a modest river nearby. They found a small field where the horses could graze and prepared camp. This time they started a fire with ease, thanks to Raymon's fire-starting kit, and boiled vegetables for their stew. They each ate a brioche loaf with honey butter, and they had a wineskin to pass between them. Supper was spent discussing everything from the stars overhead to their excitement at the journey to come.

After she finished her supper, Emerald excused herself for the night.

Once she was in her tent, Osmund shifted on the rock he sat on. "What do you think that was all about? Back in the village, I mean."

Kailem glanced at his swollen knuckles. "I don't know. I guess I just lost control. I saw him attacking Emerald, and—"

"No, not that. Did you hear what that man was saying, before you... subdued him?"

Kailem shook his head.

"They spoke of someone named Jacken. According to the man, Emerald was a fugitive of some kind. He wanted to return her to this Jacken to answer for something she did."

"Hmm. What do you think she did?"

"That's just it. This is our Emerald we're talking about. I'm not sure if I believe him. I know we haven't known her that long, but can you honestly imagine her doing anything... egregious?"

Kailem considered it a moment. "Well, when we met her, she was being arrested for stowing away."

Osmund sat back on his rock. "True," he admitted. "And she did steal that pocket watch, so we know she's not overly concerned with the law."

After a time, Kailem shook his head. "She was a homeless orphan, Oz. Who knows what she had to do to survive? But to answer your question, no, I can't imagine her doing anything egregious, just what she needed to stay alive."

Osmund nodded. "That was my assessment as well."

They passed a quiet moment, staring at the crackling fire.

"Simply wonderful, is it not?" Osmund said. "Being out here under the stars, just the three of us. Completely free."

"It is," Kailem replied. "Not a bad way to live, I dare say."

"Can you imagine if we actually found Andalaya?" Osmund said.

Kailem tried to picture the city in his mind, but had little to go on. "What do you think it looks like?"

Osmund jumped to his feet and ran to his pack, returning with the Codex Andala in hand.

"You brought the book?" Kailem asked.

"Of course!" Osmund flipped to a page that described the city. Kailem supposed there was no reason to be stingy on what they packed if the mighty Summit was carrying it all.

"According to this," Osmund explained, "Andalaya was full of massive stone buildings that could each house hundreds of people. They had unimaginable technology not seen anywhere else in all of Iria. The streets were lined with flowers and fruit trees, and they had a series of canals that diverted a river into small streams all throughout the city."

The illustrations left Kailem breathless.

Osmund continued, "this was all a thousand years ago, so it's decayed and in ruins by now, but still. It will be amazing to see. If we find it, that is."

"I think we will," Kailem said. Osmund eyed him curiously. "Call it blind optimism, but I have a good feeling."

"I do too," Osmund said.

The river trickled nearby, and a critter moved in the shadow of the trees around them. Kailem was silent, his eyes fixed on the fire, while he summoned the courage to ask his next question. "Oz, what do Easterners believe happens when you die?"

The question took him aback. "Well," he started, "it is generally accepted that you don't just cease to exist, that you continue in some form or another, but what that form is, no one can say. We call it the 'Great Unknown'."

Kailem nodded. "And why do you believe you continue on?"

"Because it defies our deepest intuition that we just cease to exist. It's the same as the basic tenets of logic or ethics. Some truths can't be proven, but neither can we bring ourselves to reject them."

"Do you believe that?" Kailem asked. His eyes remained on the flames, the firelight reflecting off the angles of his face.

Osmund had never given the subject much thought, mainly because there was such universal agreement on the matter. Now that he was asked, he needn't think long. "Yes, I do," he replied. "What do the Mariners believe?"

"The same," Kailem replied.

Osmund suspected as much. It was his understanding that all of Iria agreed on this point.

"You ask because of your parents?"

Kailem nodded.

Osmund wanted to ask how they died, but felt it would not be proper to pry. Instead, he simply said, "I can't imagine how horrible that must have been." After a moment, he added, "What were they like?"

Against all odds, a hint of a smile crept onto Kailem's face, and he started sharing favorite memories of his home and family. The two talked long into the night, eventually falling asleep next to the fire.

Chapter Fifteen

Special Assignment

63rd Day of Spring, 897 G.C.

M okain walked down a hallway in the Palace of Rhinegard looking for the Grand Corridor, but trying not to look like he was looking for it. If he could just find the Grand Corridor, he knew he could find the path that led to the palace barracks. He couldn't fathom why any palace needed to be so large, it might as well have been its own city. Being entirely walled off from the outside world, it very nearly was.

As he passed by one of the guards under his command, he resisted the urge to ask him for directions. The guard acknowledged him with a nod, but otherwise remained unmoved at his post. The guard wore the same encumbering uniform and armor that Mokain was now forced to wear, a steel breastplate over chain mail, padded woolen trousers bearing the gold and mahogany colors of the King's house, and a helmet without a face covering. Even in the same uniform, however, Mokain still stood out like a lion in a wolf pack. Everywhere he went, people could not help but stare and whisper about him.

Mokain recognized the guard he had posted in the hallway adjacent to the Grand Corridor and made a beeline for him. Sure enough, around the next corner was the Grand Corridor he sought. He picked up the pace as he walked through the massive open space, not because he was short on time, but because it was a relief to finally know how to get where he was going.

He passed by the prince's fiancé, Kyra Arturri, talking animatedly while surrounded by several ladies of the court. She was so engaged in whatever she was saying that she was one of the few people in the Grand Corridor not staring conspicuously at him.. Mokain knew very little about fashion, but even he could see Kyra's gown was by far the most elegant, which was a certain feat among the Cavanders. Unlike the Marin Islands, where even the gaudiest of noblewomen limited their ornamentation to subtle embroidery around the hem of the dress, the women in Cavandel dressed as if it were a contest of life and death to see which could devise the most complicated assortment of fabrics that could be used to make a dress.

Leaving the Grand Corridor for the path to the barracks, Mokain found Astor Menden standing with his shoulder against a granite column.

"Might I join you?" Lord Menden asked as Mokain passed by. From the way he fell into step at Mokain's side, it wasn't really a request. "I trust you are settling into the palace nicely?"

"I believe I am, Lord Menden. Is there some way I may be of assistance?" Mokain asked.

"Can't one lord walk with another on a such a fine Cavander day as this?"

Mokain raised an eyebrow at him. The sky was overcast, as it was nearly every day in Rhinegard, and there was a faint breeze that carried a chill everywhere it went.

"I suppose not," Lord Menden said. "I'll be frank with you, Lord Roka. These are my men you have been given charge over, and I have no mind to leave them until I know the sort of man they've been given to."

Mokain didn't know if he should be offended by the remark. It carried a certain biting connotation, but Mokain felt he would certainly do the same were he in a similar situation.

"Is your concern that I will abuse your men, or allow them to become lazy derelicts?"

"If that were my concern, I would simply have a word with the King and you'd be cast from the Palace. No, Lord Roka, my interest in you comes from the rumors I have heard. It seems you have already earned the men's respect. Word is they've even named you the 'Lion of Marin'."

Mokain scoffed. Although uncommon in their time, such a moniker called back to the days of old when descriptive names were common, the days of venerated warriors like Harold the Fearless or Iain the Bloody. Mokain hadn't actually heard the new moniker, but he'd have to put a stop to it before it took root.

"Well, by all means, Lord Menden. I welcome the company, even if for nothing more than finding my bearings in this massive, garish place." The remark earned a single chuckle from the aged warrior.

Mokain finally entered the palace barracks with his arms crossed behind his lower back. He would have preferred to live in the barracks with his men, as he had in the Marin Islands, but the prince insisted his First Officer have a room and office closer to the royal residence. Lord Menden followed closely in tow.

The men jumped to attention when their commander entered the barracks. Most of the royal guards were out on their various assignments; those who remained were preparing for the night shift. Mokain walked the rows, speaking with each of them, calling them by name and asking about their families.

"You already know all their names?" Lord Menden asked, with eyebrows raised.

Mokain nodded with nonchalance before addressing his next guard.

A lanky young boy dressed in a servant's livery with light eyes and trimmed brown hair came scampering into the barracks. Then he remembered his decorum and straightened his back, walking as a dignified servant should. He stopped in front of Mokain and gave a servant's bow, hips nearly reaching a right angle.

"Dugald told me to find you here, Lord Roka," the young boy said. "I am at your service."

Mokain frowned at him. "And who is Dugald?" he asked.

Lord Menden leaned forward. "Dugald is Prince Aedon's personal servant. He is also in charge of the servant staff in the palace."

"I see, and who are you?" he asked the boy.

The young boy, who Mokain guessed was no more than fifteen, looked confused by the question. "My name is Vivek, milord. I am your new personal servant. I apologize. I understood you were expecting me. Oh, and this is for you, Lord Menden."

Vivek handed Lord Menden a rolled note with a wax seal. Mokain did remember some discussion about a personal servant, but there had been so much to learn this past week that it must have slipped his mind.

"Ah, yes," Mokain said while Lord Menden read his note. "Well, I have nothing for you to do at the moment, so I suppose just follow me about for now."

Mokain looked to Lord Menden for confirmation he had given an acceptable command, and Lord Menden returned a subtle nod. Mokain finished distributing assignments and dismissed his men.

"Very well, Lord Roka," Lord Menden said. "You seem to have your post in control. The King has called an emergency council meeting today, so I must depart."

"Is all well?" Mokain asked.

"Alas, it is not. There are reports of hostility and unrest throughout the kingdom, especially near the borders. The reason is currently unknown to us, but it is a cause for genuine concern. I will leave you to your duties. Good day."

Lord Menden departed, leaving Mokain with his new servant. Vivek stood there silently, awkwardly, waiting to be told what to do.

Mokain took a breath. "I'm going to the blacksmith shop. Would you like to come along?"

Vivek furrowed his brow. A nearby guardsman looked puzzled as well.

Mokain looked from Vivek to the guardsman and back. "I mean, we're going to the blacksmith shop, Vivek. Come along."

"Might I ask, mi'lord, why we're going to a blacksmith shop, sir?" Vivek asked as he followed him out of the palace.

"My swords need sharpening," Mokain said. Tao and Koa were still blunted from the tournament and his new duties had kept him too busy to sharpen them.

"Well, I can do that for you, milord," Vivek said. He reached for the hilt of the sword on Mokain's belt.

Mokain grabbed the young servant's wrist and twisted, causing him to wince and drop to his knees.

"Never reach for another man's sword without his leave," Mokain said. When he released the hand, Vivek held it like it had been pulled from boiling water.

"Of course, milord. A thousand apologies," Vivek said with his head down. They had drawn the attention of some passersby.

Mokain regretted the harsh response and helped Vivek to his feet.

"Not to worry, Vivek. We're still becoming acquainted. It will take a while for you to learn how I do things. No harm done."

"Thank you, milord," Vivek said with his head still down.

"Oh, come now, Vivek. Cheer up," Mokain said in a buoyant tone. He put his arm around the servant and led him by his side toward the blacksmith shop. "No need to be so sullen. I think you and I will get along perfectly."

Vivek looked curiously at the massive arm around his shoulder. His new master was not at all what Dugald had prepared him for.

Together they moved through the horde of Cavanders on the King's Ascent.

"And I'll tell you something else," Mokain continued, "when we are in private, you can dispense with all the 'milords' and other formality nonsense. Just call me 'Mokain'. Agreed?"

Vivek, bewildered, looked up and nodded.

Mokain clarified, "but only in private. Maintain appearances when we are in public."

"Very good, milord," Vivek replied as they walked down the busy market streets. Mokain grinned.

The blacksmith shop hit them with waves of heat, the smell of burning coal, and the sound of a beating hammer. It was the same blacksmith shop where Mokain had procured his tournament armor. Mr. Marshall ceased hammering when they entered his shop.

"Lord Roka?" he said in surprise. "The Lion of Marin back in my shop! What can I do for you?"

Great, the name is already spreading, Mokain thought. Stopping the name would be impossible now.

"I wonder if I might trouble you for a turn at your grindstone, good sir. I'm afraid my blades need sharpening."

"I was there that day you won the tournament," Mr. Marshall said. "Quite the display, it was. I tell everyone who comes in I made the armor you wore that day. Be those the blades you were using, then?"

"They are indeed," Mokain said. He unsheathed Koa and displayed it for the blacksmith. "Forged them myself, actually."

"Impressive craftsmanship. I wish my son were here to meet you, but I sent him to the iron mill not an hour ago." Mr. Marshall returned the blade. "Forgive me, Lord Roka, but you now live in the palace, do you not? Why not have the royal blacksmith sharpen them?"

"I did ask, and he offered to sharpen them for me, but apparently, he is as strict with who handles his tools as I am with my swords. I would just prefer to sharpen them myself if it's all the same."

"Be my guest," the blacksmith said with his hand out towards the grindstone. "I will tell everyone my grindstone sharpened the Lion of Marin's own blades."

Mokain sat on the stool, wet the grindstone from a nearby water bucket, and pressed the pedal to rotate the stone. He graced Tao's edge over the stone; the steel hissing a low pitch as he worked. Vivek wandered around, inspecting the shop and its contents while his master worked.

Working in a blacksmith's shop brought Mokain back to the days he helped Kailem forge his Culmination Blade, Malua. Their father had been away on business, so the two of them spent several weeks in the blacksmith shop together. Most people had gawked when they heard Kailem had chosen to forge a dagger. And it was a strange choice by all accounts, but anyone who knew Kailem knew a dagger suited him perfectly. Kailem had a natural talent for combat, but no taste for it. Mokain returned Tao to its scabbard and put Koa to the grindstone.

Thinking back on those days brought a smile to Mokain's face, and it reminded him just how much he missed his brother. It felt like ages since they had all been together as a family. There was a sting of guilt in his chest. He wondered what Kailem was doing now, if he was safe and happy.

With a lethal edge restored to both blades, Mokain paid Mr. Marshall a silver shilling for use of the stone, against the blacksmith's objections. Mokain not only had a lucrative income now, but living in the palace meant he had virtually no expenses on which to spend the coins.

As they returned to the palace, a conversation between merchants caught Mokain's ear.

"I swear to you, that is the last time I ship anything with Cato & Sons," one merchant said to the other. "Not two months ago, I lost a shipment of sugar when they dropped it from the gangway, and now I receive word that *The Flying Manta* has sunk off the Devona coast. Unacceptable, I tell you, entirely unacceptable."

Mokain froze at the name of his former employer. It took a moment for his mind to process, and then he turned to the merchants. Vivek walked for another six paces before he realized his master had stopped, then hurried back to Mokain's side.

"I'm sorry, sirs, I hate to interrupt," Mokain said, "but did I hear you say *The Flying Manta* sank off the Devona coast?"

"You did indeed, sir." The plump merchant turned his full attention to the new audience. "Awful business, really. This will set my profits back by two months. I don't know how we'll recover."

"Yes, but were there any survivors?" Mokain asked.

"Did I mention this is the second time Cato & Sons has lost my cargo? I will tell everyone I meet never to do business with tha—"

"Please, sir! I need to know. Were there any survivors?" There was panic and urgency in his voice.

"I'm afraid there were not," the merchant said solemnly. "I just received word this morning. When the ship did not arrive on schedule, another ship was sent to look for it. They found the wreckage on a wild stretch of coast. There were bodies on shore, but no survivors."

The air fled from Mokain's lungs. The world faded into the distance, and he put a hand out to Vivek's shoulder to steady himself.

"My Lord, what it is?" his servant asked with grave concern.

"I'm fine, I'm fine. Thank you, Vivek, I'm fine," Mokain insisted.

He leaned on Vivek for another few seconds while he found his feet, then turned and ambled away down the market streets toward the palace. One man bumped into him as they walked by, then another, then another. Mokain didn't care, in fact, he didn't even seem to notice them.

Kailem was dead.

The rush of emotions was disorienting. His exterior was a walking corpse, but inside was the need to scream and weep, to break anything within reach and collapse to the floor. He berated himself for staying in Rhinegard. He knew it had been wrong to leave his brother. All they had after their exile was each other. They should have stayed together no matter what came their way. Now Kailem was gone, and Mokain had no one. If he had been there, maybe he could have kept the ship from sinking. Or maybe he could have rescued Kailem and helped him to shore. Or maybe...

'Maybe' meant nothing anymore. It didn't matter what he could have done or what he should have done. What mattered was he hadn't done it. He had failed his brother, and now his entire family was dead.

Somehow, they were back in Mokain's palace quarters, on the floor just below the royal residence. He didn't remember entering the palace, nor did he remember climbing the staircases. Vivek was still with him. He must have led them here. But how did Vivek know which quarters were his? It didn't matter. Kailem was dead.

Mokain laid back on his bed and Vivek removed his boots for him. Mokain hated to have someone else dress and undress him, but he said nothing. Kailem was dead. He would have to perform the Mariner funeral rites. But he didn't have the body, so what would he place on the pyre?

Mokain was nearly catatonic when Prince Aedon walked into the room. Vivek jumped to his feet and bowed before the Prince. Mokain didn't move. Aedon opened his mouth to speak, then paused, puzzled by Mokain's unusual lack of deference.

"Your Majesty, please forgive my Lord Roka. I am afraid he is not well at the moment."

"Clearly, and you are?" the Prince asked.

The servant bowed again. "I am Vivek, Your Majesty. Lord Roka's new personal servant."

"New indeed," the Prince replied. "In the presence of royalty, a servant remains silent unless instructed otherwise. And if you are told to speak, the formal address 'Your Majesty' is used exclusively for the King. You will refer to me as 'Your Grace', and any other members of the royal family as 'Your Highness'."

The boy winced but said nothing further. Dugald would surely hear of this.

Mokain sat up to see who Vivek was speaking to. When he saw the Prince in his quarters, he slowly ambled to his feet.

"A little early in the day to be so heavy with drink, wouldn't you say?" the Prince asked.

"A thousand apologies, Your Grace. It is not the drink that has me so heavy," Mokain said.

"No, I should say not," Aedon said, inspecting him. "I don't smell a drop of it. Tell me, what has brought my fiercest warrior so low?"

Mokain tried to explain, but his mouth refused to form the words. "With your permission, your grace, I'd rather not say. How may I assist you?"

Aedon motioned for Mokain to sit on the bed and sat himself in the desk chair. Vivek took several steps back and remained at attention, as Dugald had taught him.

"This should lighten your spirits, Mariner. I have a special assignment for you. We have been receiving reports of raids in the borderlands. We need you to lead a unit of soldiers to investigate."

Mokain tilted his head. "Isn't that a job for the military, Your Grace? I only command the palace guard."

"No, you are my First Officer, and you serve at my pleasure, do you not?"

"Of course I do, Your Grace. I only meant…"

Aedon waved off any further comment. "I know good and well what you meant, and there was no offense in it. And you are correct, normally this would be a matter for the military, but they answer only to my father, and well, the King isn't taking the matter as seriously as he should. That is why I am sending you. I am also sending you with some soldiers, to protect you, of course. You'll have a full battalion at your side. Do you understand what I'm telling you?"

A battalion was a unit of five hundred soldiers, second in size to a legion, a unit of two thousand. Although the battalion's official orders would be to protect Mokain, in reality, he would be their commanding officer.

"I understand, Your Grace."

"I knew you would. See, don't you feel better already?"

Mokain felt nothing, but he managed a nod for the Prince's sake.

"When do we leave?" Mokain asked.

"On the morrow. I've selected the Fifth Battalion of the 1st Legion for you to lead. I'm sorry, to protect you on your journey, and the lieutenants are preparing their men as we speak. I imagine you'll want to introduce yourself to your new... protectors."

The Prince grinned at what he mistook for cleverness and stood to leave. Mokain remained seated. Aedon waited for him to stand in respect, and when the Mariner did not, he considered a rebuke, but instead placed his hand on the Mariner's shoulder.

"Feel better, my friend." The Prince looked to Vivek, who bowed nearly to the ground, then he showed himself out.

That night, Mokain and Vivek traveled beyond the city wall to the northern coast. They rode a horse-drawn cart full of construction timber, and for nearly an hour, they assembled a pyre and doused it in whale oil. Neither of them spoke a word. Vivek, bless him, was able to deduce the next steps in their construction without breaking the reverent silence between them.

It was the Mariner tradition to burn a pyre, even for those lost at sea whose bodies were never recovered. In place of a body, Mariners would place objects on the pyre that had belonged to the deceased. Mokain had none of Kailem's possessions to place on the pyre. Instead, he placed a full basket of oysters on top in memory of their time spent oyster diving together. He also placed an oyster knife, a coil of sailor's rope, and a mango, Kailem's favorite fruit. He put his torch to the pyre. It was quickly engulfed in flames.

Mokain stood in a soldier's stance, the firelight reflecting in his eyes. His face was hard as stone, save for a rebellious tear that escaped down his cheek.

Vivek had no knowledge of Mariner funeral customs, and he wondered if he was supposed to say something. Even if words were expected, they surely were not expected from a servant. But his master was clearly in great pain. It seemed wrong to stand there doing nothing. He lifted a comforting hand to place on Mokain's shoulder, then thought better of it. He lowered his hand, but somehow that felt even worse. He raised the hand again, pausing just above Mokain's shoulder, then placed it down gently.

Mokain looked at the hand for a moment, then turned to Vivek. His new servant's face shone with empathy. Mokain nodded gratefully, then looked back to the fire. The two men remained for hours, not a word spoken between them, as the pyre reduced to ashes.

CHAPTER SIXTEEN

THE CEREN RIVER

75TH DAY OF SPRING, 897 G.C.

For three weeks, they rode south, passing through Glendown Forest and into Monkwood Forest on their quest to find the mythical Andalaya. The trio had fully adjusted to life in the wild. Even Osmund had ceased complaining about his lack of usual comforts. He estimated they were ten days from reaching the northern edge of the Pavian Grasslands.

They made camp in a small clearing near the Ceren River and sat around their fire, eating half rations of salted meat and stale bread. Though they were following a map, they had missed the village where they had planned to purchase supplies; they had been nearly out of rations for two days now. Osmund insisted it was the map that was wrong and not his reading of it, and he swore that this time they were only half a day's ride from a village.

"Really? Foxes?" Kailem asked.

"Of course, everyone in Devona keeps foxes," Osmund said, poking the fire with a stick for no apparent reason. "And that is far from the strangest pet in Iria. The Shinda keep bobcats and the Norvians even keep bears."

"Pet bears? How are they not mauled by them?"

Osmund shrugged and drank from his wineskin. Insects chirped over the sound of the crackling fire.

"We keep jackals in Donnelin," Emerald said. "Never had one meself, o' course, but I did play wit' one once. Dandy little critters, they be, ears just as long as their snouts. Ye truly keep no pets on the islands?"

"Not many," Kailem replied. "A few people kept dogs, no one I knew personally. Although, I did have a seal once."

"A seal?" Emerald laughed. "How do ye keep a pet seal?"

"Well, he wasn't exactly a pet. He was a wild seal that would frequent the cove by our home. He was this awfully curious little thing, far more than a seal should be. He swam close to me after I had been spearfishing from the rocks and I fed him a fish. We formed a bond that day."

"O' course, ye made friends wit' a seal," Emerald teased.

Kailem was unaware a smile had split his face. "We'd swim about in the cove and then lay out on the rocks under the sun. He'd rest his chin on my knee and would snore when he fell asleep. I'd say he was my best friend that summer, except for Mokain, of course."

"What happened to him?" Emerald asked. "The seal, not yer brother."

"I don't know. One day he just stopped coming around."

Osmund thought for a moment. "He was probably eaten."

"Oz!" Emerald scolded. He raised his palms, not understanding what he did wrong. Kailem seemed fine with the comment. She still shook her head at him.

Osmund needed a change of topic. "Do either of you have a favorite food?" It was the first thing he could think of.

"White fish," Kailem answered. He removed Malua from its scabbard and glided a whetstone over the edge, sharpening it. "Like wahoo or mahi, blackened and smothered in mango glaze." He thought back to the last meal his mother had cooked for him. He missed her.

"Well, mine's Beef Wellington," Osmund said. "Not every chef can make it correctly. Too many will undercook the mushrooms or not wrap the crepes tightly enough, but if you have the right chef, mmm, simply delicious. It pairs splendidly with a nice Marcônish Red, something dry and medium-bodied, preferably with strong notes of plum and cedar. And strawberry marzipan for dessert. Emerald?"

She paused. "What'd we eat that night wit' ye parents?"

Osmund reluctantly thought back to their first dinner together. "The main course was roasted pheasant."

"Well, that be me favorite. Twas the best meal I ever had, as far as the cookin' be concernin'. Didn't right know food could taste just so."

Osmund had hated that dinner, and not only because the pheasant had been somewhat dry. The way his father had humiliated him that evening had not been a new experience, but to be so berated in front of his new friends made it particularly painful. Osmund didn't want to think about it.

Emerald poured herself another bowl of stew while Kailem continued sharpening his blade.

"You seem quite fond of that dagger," Osmund observed.

Kailem looked up from sharpening with a gleam in his eye. "All Mariners are fond of their Culmination Blade. I suppose it's just our way."

Osmund frowned as he looked at the dagger more closely. "What are there those wavy lines in the steel?"

Kailem raised the blade so that the firelight reflected off the polished steel. "We have a unique forging process in the Islands," he explained. "We use several different classes of steel to make a single blade. Each class has a different amount of charcoal in the iron and therefore is a slightly different color. When we forge and hammer them together, these patterns emerge."

"Fascinating," Osmund said, inching closer to him. "And is that technically considered a dagger or stiletto?"

"Malua here is a dagger. It's a 10-inch blade, which is longer than the average dagger, closer to a stiletto, but stilettos have a very thin, needle-like blade, whereas Malua here is three fingers wide at the blade."

One eyebrow rose on Emerald's forehead. "Ye measure blades in fingers?"

"Of course. Well, to measure thickness, at least. For example, in the eastern tradition, a standard side-sword is 2-3 feet long and 3-4 fingers wide. A broadsword is about a foot longer than a side-sword and 5-6 fingers wide, and a longsword is anything longer than 4 feet, usually 4-5 fingers wide. And outside the eastern tradition, there is also the cutlass, the scimitar, the saber, the tachi, and then all manner of polearms, like the short spear, the javelin, the pike, the lance–"

Emerald snored obnoxiously, silencing Kailem and drawing a laugh from Osmund. Kailem tore off a piece of flatbread and threw it at her.

The trio slept soundly that night. It was warm, at least by Devonian standards, and they lay under the stars close to their slowly dying fire. It was the same as they had done most nights since they left. Their time together meant more than any of them would openly admit. Kailem no longer felt alone in the world, and his nightmares came only once a week. Osmund felt alive and free for the first time in his life, and for the first time had made a true friend, and two of them at that.

Emerald, in spite of her best efforts to the contrary, felt safe around the young men. She felt wanted, and not because of what she could contribute to a gang of thieves. She felt wanted for just being herself, which wasn't something she had thought possible a month ago. She no longer needed an escape plan everywhere she went, no longer needed to keep one eye open when she slept. Around Kailem and Osmund, she felt a part of something approaching a family. She was just being silly, of course, and she dismissed the thought every time it occurred to her.

Emerald was the first to rise the next morning. Osmund was snoring next to her. The morning dew had settled on their thick woolen blankets, which Kailem had managed to throw off himself during the night.

Emerald yawned and stretched, rolled her blanket and sleeping mat, then went searching for firewood to cook their breakfast. She looked for the driest wood around, like Kailem had taught her. Then she remembered they had no food left to cook. She sighed and dropped her pile. She was accustomed to going a day or two without food, but the last few weeks had spoiled her.

Kailem stirred awake when she returned to camp. As usual, Osmund was the last to awake. The first thing he saw when he opened his eyes was Emerald's face as she fitted her saddle onto Willow. She was humming some melody he didn't recognize, bobbing her head back and forth to the rhythm. She was horribly tone deaf, but that made it all the more endearing somehow.

The village Osmund had promised was just where he said it would be.

With their provisions fully restocked, they set out again, following the Ceren River south. They passed a few clearings of farmland, but mostly, they rode through a forest so dense they couldn't see the sky above them. At night, they gathered around the fire while Osmund read to them stories about the sages out of the Codex Andala.

On the third day since the village, a forest dragon swooped from the trees and landed on a low branch, watching their caravan as they continued on down the road. Emerald turned in her saddle to keep her eyes on the dragon. The beast was as long as a man was tall and as thin as a man's leg, but the wingspan made it an imposing figure.

That night they sat around their fire waiting for their stew to simmer. Only a sliver of the gilded moon shined overhead. They had run out of jokes to tell and stories to share, but they were comfortable enough that they could sit in silence and enjoy the sounds of the forest. The light of the fire reflected in their eyes and danced on their faces, and the call of forest dragons echoed through the trees.

They were so relaxed that none of them noticed when a stray ember floated down into a patch of dead grass near a thicket. They didn't notice when a thin feather of smoke rose from the grass, nor did they notice when a flame formed in its place.

The horses, however, did notice. Echo was the first, as he was the closest, and the other three were not far behind. They reared on their hind legs, their front hooves fighting invisible foes, and they struggled to flee. The entire patch of grass had caught fire before the three travelers noticed it. The horses fought against the straps that tied them to nearby trees, but only the mighty Summit was strong enough to burst free.

All three of them jumped to their feet, knocking over their pot of soup as they raced to the burning grass.

"You two put out the fire!" Kailem yelled as he sprinted after Summit. The black horse galloped away from the flames, the partly filled packsaddle still strapped to his back, unknowingly heading straight for the Ceren River. It was so dark and the horse was so scared that he galloped headlong into the water and was swept away by the current.

Kailem dove headfirst into the dark torrent. Frigid water seized his body, and he abandoned his streamlined form to scramble to the surface. He gasped for air. The current was swift and angry, but Kailem forced himself downstream after the panicking horse. Summit's black hide all but disappeared amid the black water, and Kailem could scarcely hear the frightened horse over the roar of the frothing rapids. Summit squealed and kicked but barely managed to keep his head above water.

Kailem swam downstream through the dark until he unwittingly crashed into Summit. The current swept him around the massive horse and threatened to pull him under, but Kailem reached out and grabbed the first thing his hand touched. It was the branch of a fallen tree, the same set of branches that Summit had become entangled in. Kailem couldn't see anything, but he felt about the branches, careful to stay clear of the horse's violent hooves.

It wasn't the horse that had become entangled, but the packsaddle they had forgotten to take off. Kailem pulled and tugged at the branches and at the pack-saddle, but he was powerless in the dark. River water splashed down his throat and the branch cut into his hand. He had to find a solution, and fast.

He reached for Malua and cut the strap. It took four strokes to sever the leather, then Summit broke free, swept away downriver. Kailem stuck the dagger back in its sheath and let go of the branch, drifting along the same path as the horse.

Summit soon managed to plant his hooves on a sandy bank and climbed towards dry land. Kailem grabbed hold of his tail as he floated by and let the horse tow him until he found his own footing. Summit was still panicking when he made it out of the water, but by that point he knew Kailem well enough that the Mariner's voice calmed him. Kailem guided the horse the half-mile upriver back to their campsite.

When he returned to camp, Osmund and Emerald had put out the fire and managed to calm the other three horses. They had even managed to salvage a bit of the stew that hadn't spilled from their pot. When they saw Kailem and Summit enter the camp, Emerald ran and threw her arms around Kailem, holding him tightly. Summit trotted to Osmund for comfort.

"What happened?" Osmund asked.

Kailem ran his hands through his wet hair. "Summit ran straight into the river and was swept away. Then his packsaddle got stuck in some tree branches, so I had to cut it loose to free him."

Osmund's face drained of color. "Well, did you keep the packsaddle?" he asked.

Kailem frowned at the question. "No, we were caught in the river. I was pre-occupied with not drowning. I did save your horse's life, though. You're welcome for that, by the way." Kailem wrapped a blanket around his shoulders.

"Kailem, without that packsaddle, we have no way of packing our gear."

"Our plight is worse than that, I'm afraid. We forgot to unpack Summit before we cooked our supper. Most of our new provisions were still on the packsaddle."

Osmund threw his hands in the air and began pacing.

"All the food, then?" Emerald asked.

"Oh, not just food," Osmund said. He began counting on his fingers. "We've lost our frying pan, our tents, our change of clothes, our maps, our, our... what are we going to do?!"

"It's okay, Oz," Kailem said. "We'll figure this out."

"What is there to figure out? We're going to starve out here!" Osmund kicked a stone into the fire, sending bits of ember into the air. "Why would you cut the packsaddle? Had you taken leave of your senses, or did you not have any to begin with?"

"Excuse me?" Kailem said, letting his blanket fall to the ground.

"You heard me," Osmund said. "You might have just killed us all. We're out here in the middle of nowhere. We *just* refilled our supplies after days of going hungry... that food was supposed to last two weeks, and you go and lose it all on the third night!"

"*I* lost it?" Kailem shot back. "I'm the only reason we've even made it this far, you pathetic craven."

Emerald made herself small. "Come on, you two," she whimpered, "this ain't—"

Osmund didn't wait for her to finish. "*You're* the reason I'm not safe at home! I never should have come on this... this... imbecilic journey with you. Why would I listen to some ignorant, low-born islander in this first place?"

No sooner had the words passed Osmund's lips than he regretted them. Kailem's fists clenched and his nostrils flared, and Osmund knew he had gone too far. Kailem's eyes narrowed on him, and he took a step forward, his shoulders tense. He was soaked from head to toe, and the firelight lit his face from below. Osmund's eyes went wide. He clumsily took a step backward, nearly tripping over himself. The image of Kailem pummeling the stranger in Ombermill replayed in his mind.

"I'm sorry, Kailem. I didn't mean that, I take it back," Osmund stammered.

The fear in Osmund's eyes shook Kailem from his rage. The Mariner turned away and took a deep breath, then another.

Several moments passed in miserable silence. No one looked at each other. Their fire had nearly died.

Emerald sat apart from the men with her knees pulled into her chest. "What do we do now?" she whispered.

"We still have all our coin pouches," Osmund said. "If we make it back to town, we can just replace what we lost. But I don't see how we make it several days with no provisions." Then he gestured to Kailem. "You're our wilderness survival expert. I will defer to your judgment in this matter."

He hoped the gesture of respect might dispel some of the tension between them. If it worked, Kailem didn't show it.

The Mariner took a moment to think. "We should eat whatever soup you were able to save while it's still good. Fortunately, we did unpack some of our blankets, not all of them, but enough. Let's build an extra-large fire tonight, so we stay warm until morning."

Osmund and Emerald agreed, and they spread out to find more firewood. They piled the wood on the smoldering coals and sat close to eat their soup.

Kailem shivered and nearly placed his hands into the flames.

No one said anything for the rest of the night.

When Osmund awoke the next morning, Kailem was gone. Emerald sat with her knees to her chest, her arms wrapped around her shins.

"He left," was all she said.

Osmund twisted to see around the campsite. "He just left? Where did he go? Is he coming back?"

Emerald didn't move.

Osmund threw off his single blanket and went to the horses. At least Kailem hadn't stolen one. They still had the few provisions that hadn't been lost in the night's debacle. They might last a day, maybe two. After that, he didn't know what they would do. Would Emerald stay with him without Kailem there, he wondered?

"We ought ta go back," Emerald said. It was like she read his thoughts.

Osmund sat next to her. "We find ourselves in agreement." At length, he added, "I can't believe he left us."

A tear trickled down Emerald's cheek, and her hand leapt to wipe it away. Osmund pretended not to see it.

A rustling came from behind the nearby thicket. Both their heads whipped to the right at the sound. Kailem approached with a forest dragon laying limp over his shoulder. The head hung near his waist and its tail brushed the ground behind him. Its wings were partially unfurled and covered in oblong scales, their texture between snake scales and feathers.

This time, Emerald didn't leap to her feet. She pulled her knees even tighter against her chest and looked at him with distrusting eyes.

Osmund was a confusing mix of emotions. His first reaction was relief Kailem hadn't abandoned them, but was he still angry? Was he going to stay? He stood and brushed off his trousers but didn't approach the Mariner. Kailem dropped the dead forest dragon next to the fire.

For a few moments no one said anything, but not for want of anything to say. Osmund yearned to apologize for insulting him and casting the blame on him, to admit he was actually grateful he'd saved Summit. Kailem wanted to apologize as well, to say he hadn't meant to scare him and he never would have actually hurt him. Emotions were ready to burst from them, but neither could find the words.

"I beg your pardon," Osmund finally managed to say. His words were timid, almost unintentional, and, most importantly, genuine.

"Me too," Kailem replied. He looked at the ground when he said it, not meeting Osmund's eyes.

Osmund held his hand out to Kailem. After a second of looking at the hand, Kailem took it and pulled Osmund close, wrapping his other arm around him. The gesture surprised Osmund. Something melted inside him, and he reciprocated the affection.

Their one-armed embrace lasted but a moment. When they let go, they wore a smile that said the issue was behind them.

Emerald watched the exchange in disbelief. *That was all it took to be friends again,* she thought? *Lads are daft, the whole lot o' 'em.* She stood and faced them.

"I thought ye'd left us," she said. She looked in his direction but would not meet his eye.

Kailem winced at the comment. "I would never just leave you two," he said. *You two are all I have,* he added in his mind.

Emerald finally looked up at him. She studied his face. Then she stepped forward and put her arms around him, burying the side of her face in his chest. Kailem held her for a long moment.

"Is that a dead dragon?" she asked.

"Oh, that's breakfast," Kailem said as she stepped away.

"What?" Osmund and Emerald said in unison.

"Yeah, I couldn't sleep last night. Then I heard the dragon nearby. So, I figured since we lost our provisions...."

"How did you kill it?" Osmund asked.

"Sharpened a long stick, then waited by its nest until it came close." He mimicked stabbing with an invisible spear.

No way I be eatin' dragon, Emerald thought. She didn't like the idea of eating anything that had been alive, but especially not after seeing those majestic creatures in flight.

"I have never dined on dragon meat," Osmund said, surprised it was even an option. "What does it taste like?" His face was like someone had asked him to eat pig slop.

"It's fairly tough, but flavorful," Kailem explained. "It has a sort of smokiness to it."

Neither Osmund nor Emerald could watch as Kailem skinned and gutted the animal, then stuck a long stick through the torso for a spit. He set the neck and tail aside to cook later.

The thin creature cooked quickly over their campfire. Kailem was the first to take a bite, then handed it to Osmund.

"I cannot believe I am doing this," he said. He slowly, timidly sunk his teeth into the flesh, cringing as he did. Then his eyes brightened, and his lips spread into a grin. He passed the stick to Emerald, still savoring the bite.

Emerald pulled her head as far back from the dead animal as her neck would allow.

"Seem ta lost me hunger," she said, handing the stick back to Osmund. The two men laughed and finished the roasted dragon between them. Emerald had to look away each time they took a bite.

The return trip to the village took two days. All they had for food was the leftover dragon meat, but Kailem found enough berries to keep Emerald's hunger pangs at bay. Once in the village, they replaced the items they had lost to the river, and Osmund tried not to think about whether they would have enough coins for the return trip.

CHAPTER SEVENTEEN

A MISTY FIELD

1ST DAY OF SUMMER, 897 G.C.

Kyra found herself in an unfamiliar field. Both moons were full overhead in the night sky, a rare phenomenon not due to occur for several seasons. The ground was covered in a thick fog that obscured everything below her knees as far away as the tree line. She was barefoot, wearing only a white nightgown, and wet mud under her feet sloshed between her toes when she moved.

When she thought about it, she realized she had no memory of how she had arrived in that field or why. That should have frightened her, but for some inexplicable reason it seemed perfectly natural that she should be alone in a field at night wearing only her nightgown, which she could see now had been recently laundered. She stuck her arms out as she walked to keep from falling, and her feet made a slurping suction sound every time she took a step out of the mud.

Her foot caught on something cold and metallic, and it sent her tumbling to the ground. Mud splashed all around her, soiling her clean nightgown. She wiped her face with the back of her hand, then shook the mud off her hand, cursing to herself. Against the white fabric, she saw red in the mud. Not the red mud of clay, but swirls of red mixed into ordinary mud.

Still sitting in the filth, she looked around for an explanation. The cold metallic object she had tripped over was within reach, but it proved too heavy to turn over with one hand. She rose to her knees and used both hands to roll the object over, and when she did, she discovered it was the breastplate of a slain soldier who had been left face down in the mud.

Her breath caught in her chest. With the hem of her nightgown, she reverently wiped the mud from the dead man's face and recognized him immediately. It was Willian Wyke.

She scrambled away from the corpse, and the fog swirled around her, concealing the body once again. *This isn't possible*, she told herself. That couldn't have been Willian. It made no sense. There she remained for several minutes, not caring she had mud on her face and in her hair.

A light breeze arose from the south. How she knew it was from the south, she couldn't say, but she knew it, nonetheless. She climbed to her feet as the fog was blown away, revealing a vast field of dead bodies in cold, metallic armor. They surrounded her in every direction, and each of them bore the face of Willian Wyke.

She had to get away. She ran for the tree line, jumping and dodging corpses as she went, but no matter how long or fast she ran, the tree line never came any closer. The more she ran, the more she panicked, driving her to run even faster still. The tree line never moved.

As she ran, one of the bodies caught her eye, one that was unlike the rest. This one's armor was made of black steel elegantly emblazoned, and strapped to its side was the Fang of Rhinegard.

"It can't be," she said to herself. Her worst fear crept to the front of her mind, but she had to know. She stooped next to the body and rolled it over, revealing the face of Aedon Braise.

"No, Aedon, no!" she cried out. A pain unlike anything she'd ever known exploded in her chest, and she began to weep harder than she ever had before. Her hands shook as she held them out to him, not knowing what she should do.

With considerable effort, she pulled his dead body close to hers and wrapped her arms around him, tucking his face into the crook of her neck. She held his body close to hers, rocking back and forth and weeping uncontrollably.

"Please no, Aedon, no!" she repeated again and again, completely unaware of anything else around her.

Suddenly Kyra was in her bed in the royal palace with Martina shaking her shoulder.

"Milady! Milady, wake up!" the handmaid insisted.

Kyra waved her away and sat up in bed disoriented, trying to remember what day it was.

"It is only a nightmare, milady," Martina said.

Kyra looked up at her, slowly accepting the truth of her statement, and nodded.

"You were shouting the prince's name, milady," Martina said. "Did you dream he was attacking you?"

Kyra gave her a look that said not to say such stupid things. Had it really been just a nightmare, she wondered? It had felt so real, as real as any waking moment she'd ever had. Looking back on the impossible scenario, it should have been obvious it was just a dream, but her dreams always seemed real in the moment, no matter how preposterous the scene.

"Shall I assist your dressing, milady?" Martina asked. "Your mother insists you come to the Great Hall to plan your wedding day."

Kyra exhaled her tension, then nodded. "Very well, Martina. I will wear the new green dress today."

Kyra's wedding day was but a season away, and Avalina had taken control of the Great Hall to plan for it. The King had thought it absurd when she requested to take it over; surely, so much space would be excessive, he thought. It turned out to not be space enough. Florists, tailors, bakers, artists, musicians, and even historians — present to ensure the event followed proper Cavander traditions — all crammed into the Great Hall and pressed for Avalina's attention. The table space was an explosion of fabric, flowers, and food of every form and variety.

Kyra had looked forward to this day since before she could remember, just as did every young woman of the aristocracy. Her mother had filled her head with dreams of the fine young prince she was to marry, the palace in which she would live, and the sons and daughters she would bear him. It would be a glorious event, the standard by which all future celebrations would be measured. Every dignitary and nobleman in Iria would be there to celebrate her. The very thought of it had been deliciously sweet.

Now it was vinegar.

This pestilence of artisans and their attendants felt like a swarm of field ants crawling over her skin, and she fought the urge to swat at anyone that approached her. Fortunately, Avalina was both content and capable of handling them all on her own. Unfortunately, Avalina had not missed the abrupt change in Kyra's behavior.

Kyra knew perfectly well the reason for her sullen demeanor; the answer was as obvious as a bull in one's bedchamber. That said, she felt powerless to change it. No matter what she did, her thoughts betrayed her, retreating back to that misty field where Aedon laid dead in the mud. His pale face, blue lips, and lifeless stare haunted her mind whenever she closed her eyes.

The few times she had been able to avert her thoughts, they found their way to the death of Willian Wyke. She could see in her mind's eye the awful gash in his neck, the way the blood spurted and oozed from the wound, the ghastly gurgling sound he made as the blood pooled in his lungs and throat, the way his skin turned pale, the way his body fell still and the light slipped from his eyes, the way his father had screamed and wailed as he watched his only son die in his arms.

And the way everyone had returned to the tournament as if it were nothing.

That alone would have been enough to sour her enthusiasm for wedding planning, but the orders to arrange the death of the King amplified her melancholy several times over. Murder the King. It didn't seem real. The man was her fiancé's father. Her own soon-to-be father-in-law. A man who had been kind to her since the day they met.

The means of killing the King would be entirely different than it had been for Willian, but the end result would be the same. The poison would spread through the King's body, slowly eating away at his insides. First, his strength would fail, leaving him feeble and helpless. Then his mind would go, leaving him delirious and incompetent. Before long, the once-proud king would be incapable of putting on his own trousers in the morning. Then his body would fail. He would vomit and shiver, his joints would ache like they were made of shattered glass, his skin would go pale, and his hair would fall from his head, his organs would cease to function, and then just like young Willian, the light would leave his eyes. The King's death would be far worse than Willian's had been.

And this time, it would be entirely her fault.

She sat silently at a bench table in the Great Hall, rubbing her right palm with her left thumb, inspecting the hands that would kill the King.

Avalina was busy comparing fabrics for the wedding gown. "Kyra,' she called, "come tell us which of these you fancy most? The dress is, after all, for you." She somehow made the polite invitation sound condescending.

Kyra exhaled. "Just pick whichever one you'd like, mother."

Avalina dropped her hands and scowled, then turned to address the hall. "Attention. Everyone out. My daughter and I need the room." She clapped twice as a signal to quicken their pace.

She could have just as easily pulled her daughter out into the corridor. Two people leaving the Great Hall would have been far easier than five dozen, but such was not Avalina's way. Seconds later, she and her daughter were alone.

"There, now out with it, child. What in Iria is the matter with you?

"I'm fine, mother."

"This is fine? Today was supposed to be a happy occasion. Now here you are moping like we were planning your funeral instead of your wedding."

It wasn't her own funeral that concerned her.

"I'm not sure about all of this," Kyra said, still rubbing her palm.

Avalina sat down and placed her arm around her daughter. "My dear, a little trepidation before one's wedding is perfectly natural. We all have it to some degree or another. But Prince Aedon is the best pick for a husband in all of Iria. And you're going to be Queen of Cavandel soon."

"Mother, that's not—"

"Is it the wedding night that frightens you? Don't worry, dear, we Arturri women know how to command the bedchamber. A few days before the First of Autumn, you and I will sit down, and I will ..."

"Mother, stop!"

Avalina huffed. "Well then what, Kyra?"

Kyra couldn't help but consider betraying her parents to the King. It was her civic duty, after all, and it would relieve her of having to take anyone's life. But it would also guarantee her parents would be executed, and that felt just as wrong. But more importantly, revealing their plan would certainly end her engagement; the crown prince could never marry the daughter of traitors.

The bride-to-be stood from the table and summoned her courage.

"I'm not sure about our plan with the King," Kyra said.

"Ssssh!" Avalina hissed. She grabbed Kyra by the elbow and sat her back down on the bench. "Not so loud, you daft girl. How many times must I tell you?"

Kyra's head sank.

"What's wrong with the plan?" Avalina whispered. "Has something happened?"

"I'm not sure I can go through it. I can't kill anyone, mother. I just... I can't. It doesn't feel right."

Avalina inhaled through her nose. "Child, listen to me. Your father and I have worked on this plan for years. It is perfect. Once it is complete, we'll bring about an end to all war, to all hunger and poverty. All suffering in Iria will be but a distant memory. We're going to create a perfect world for you and your children to live in. Now isn't that all that worth the life of the one man who stands in the way of it?"

Kyra shook her head, then mumbled, "I suppose so."

Kyra had no desire to debate ethics with her mother. Not only was she not in the mood, but there was no winning a debate with Avalina. As for the plan, she had no idea how they would accomplish all that. She hadn't been privy to most elements of the plan. In fact, before that moment, she hadn't even known their end goal. They had only told her the parts that directly concerned her.

She still could not understand why they had to kill the King to accomplish that. The King was a good man; Kyra was certain that Byron was unaware he stood in the way of progress. They should be laboring to persuade him, not kill him.

She wanted to share all these thoughts and more, but instead she asked, "Why do you need me to do it? Didn't you say you had 'operatives' working for you? Why can't you have one of them do it?"

"My dear, certain tasks are too delicate a matter to trust to anyone but family," came the reply. Kyra searched her mind for a counterargument. She found nothing.

"I don't know, mother," she finally said. "It just doesn't feel right. There has to be another way."

"No, Kyra. There isn't one," she said curtly. "Now, it's time for you to grow up and face the reality. You're not a child anymore. You live in the height of comfort and luxury, and you're about to become Queen of the most powerful kingdom in Iria, which means you're going to have to play your part and do a few things you find unpleasant. If you can't do that, then you're not fit to be Queen, nor are you fit to be our daughter."

Kyra's breath caught in her throat.

"Now," Avalina continued, "can I count on you to put this foolishness behind you? To be an adult and do what is expected of you?"

Kyra nodded. Everything she loved, her hopes and dreams and future, were all trapped under an executioner's blade, and with one misstep, that blade would fall. She wiped away a tear before it escaped down her cheek. She wondered if her parents could really disown her? Or worse, sabotage her engagement to Aedon. Deep down, she knew they wouldn't hesitate.

"Good. Now take a moment to compose yourself. I'm going to go let everyone back in the hall, and you are going to start planning the most extravagant wedding Iria has ever seen. Agreed?"

Kyra straightened her back, raised her head, and pulled her shoulders back. She took a deep breath and then forced on a smile.

"That's my girl."

CHAPTER EIGHTEEN

THE PAVIAN GRASSLANDS

35TH DAY OF SUMMER, 897 G.C.

The trio followed the Ceren River south for many days as the forest grew thin. The space between trees increased and more sunlight penetrated the canopy of leaves overhead, but their surroundings were otherwise the same. Then, over the course of a single day, the hilly terrain and forest gave way to sprawling plains of knee-high grass. Suddenly, they could see for miles in every direction. Echo knickered and stepped in place, itching to gallop full speed through the grass, wild and free, but Kailem managed to calm him. He and the willful horse had reached an understanding during their time together.

A breeze swept over them, carrying the scent of wildflowers and the citric scent of Pavian grass. Clouds rolled above their heads like the sky was a steady, flowing river. Beams of sunlight burst through the sky, shifting in concert with the rolling clouds. This was Emerald's first time in the grasslands. When she considered it, this was the farthest south she'd ever been. She marveled openly at the sight, and her gleeful wonder infected the others.

They camped that night on a small rise that could scarcely be called a hill. The first thing they did was completely unpack the horses. The four beasts found the quality of grazing far superior in the grasslands. As they prepared camp, Osmund explained that the plains were roughly the halfway point on their journey, and they would need to look out for the junction in the road that would take them southwest to Balderlyn.

Kailem started a fire to make their usual vegetable stew. Emerald and Osmund rolled two stones next to each other to use as seats.

"Now, before we move on to consonants, let's make sure you have all of the vowels," Osmund said.

He had been teaching Emerald to read at night by drawing letters in the dirt with a stick. It was a slow process, but by their first night in the grasslands, she had nearly mastered all eleven vowels.

"What sound is this?" Osmund asked, drawing the first of the vowels in a random order. He swatted away a mosquito that landed on his arm.

"Oo," Emerald said. That was the letter she knew best.

"Good, and this?" Osmund erased the letter with his foot and drew a second one.

Emerald thought for a second. Too many of the vowels sounded similar to her. "Ay?" she answered, unsure of herself.

"Yes! Very good," Osmund said, impressed by his own teaching ability.

They went through each of the eleven vowels. She answered only two incorrectly, but each time she corrected herself before Osmund had a chance to. Then Osmund gave her the stick and told her which vowels to draw. Her characters were sloppy and undisciplined, but clear enough to identify.

"Perfect, I dare say you are ready to move on the consonants," Osmund said.

"How many constant-ants are there?" she asked.

"They are pronounced 'con-son-ants'," he replied, enunciating each syllable. "And there are twenty-three."

Emerald rolled her eyes, threw her head back, and groaned.

"Dinner's ready," Kailem called. He smacked at a mosquito on his neck.

Emerald helped herself to a bowl of vegetable stew. Osmund surprised his companions, and himself, by devouring the dragon meat like a ravenous boar. He noticed them staring and chuckled as he wiped some dragon meat juice off his chin.

From their little hilltop, they could see for miles in all directions. Both moons were nearly full that night, and they could see hints of Monkwood Forest in the distance.

"Do you hear that?" Osmund asked.

Kailem and Emerald turned toward the source of the sound. It was like a storm whispering close by, but the night sky was full of stars overhead. They all put down their food and walked to the edge of the hilltop for a better look.

"What are those?!" Emerald exclaimed.

Galloping through the grass near their hill was a herd of wild horses. Emerald looked closer. These weren't a typical breed. They were slenderer, and yet they ran with impossible speed. The entire herd moved as one, reminding Kailem of the schools of fish he would see in the cove that moved as if they were of a single mind. Each horse's coat was a solid color without a single spot. Some were the purest white, others silverish blue, steel gray, and obsidian black. Each coat had an almost imperceptible sheen to it, like recently polished silver, that could only be seen under the reflection of moonlight.

"I think those are wind horses," Kailem said. "I've never seen one before."

"Nor have I," Osmund said. "But I've read about them. They are exceptionally rare."

The herd slowed to a stop and began to graze among the grass near their hill.

"I actually thought they were a myth," Kailem said.

"There are not many good studies about them," Osmund explained. "They are surprisingly intelligent, far more than a regular horse. Some scholars believe they may be as intelligent as humans. They're nearly impossible to catch, and even if you do catch one, a wind horse will never break like a regular horse will, no matter how long it's kept in captivity. They cannot be trained or used for labor or for riding. They will not breed in captivity either, so horse breeders can't raise them."

"Why are they called wind horses?" Emerald asked.

"Because of how fast they run," Osmund explained. "Some illustrations even show them having wings, which is clearly erroneous. They are said to run so fast that they ride the wind and carry good fortune with them everywhere they go."

The wind horses meandered toward the base of their small hill.

"Be they dangerous, then? Could I... could I pet one?" Emerald asked.

"Any wild animal can be dangerous," Kailem said.

"Actually, I read that a wind horse can sense whether you are friend or foe. If they sense you are a foe, they will simply run away and you'll never catch it, but if you are a friend, they'll let you approach. That's why some say it's a good omen to see one."

Without hesitation, Emerald marched down the hill.

"Emerald!" Kailem called in a hushed tone.

She ignored him and made her way to the nearest wind horse. The animal raised his head when she came near and stared at her. She stopped, meeting his eye. Its silver blue coat was even more majestic up close, and he examined her with a knowing eye. When neither moved, she took a few more steps forward.

I'm yer friend, I'm yer friend, she thought as loud as she could. *Don't be scared, now. I be just a lass who wants ta pet ye.*

The wind horse stepped forward, closing the gap between them. Emerald couldn't believe it. Up close, she could see the shimmer in each strand of hair in its mane and coat.

"Hey there," she said, stroking the wind horse's neck. "How beautiful ye be."

The wind horse huffed as if it understood, and Emerald put her arms around its neck. The horse ran its nose over her head, sniffing her strawberry hair. She giggled like a child.

Osmund would not be left behind. He ran down the hill towards her, but slowed as he approached the herd. One by one, the wind horses came to investigate the new strangers. They nuzzled against Osmund and Emerald, inspecting their hair and their clothes. Some were satisfied and went back to their grazing. Others pranced about the humans and nudged them with their noses. They possessed a level of awareness and curiosity Osmund had never seen in a regular horse. He and Emerald shared a glance that wondered if this was real. Osmund knew this was an experience few would ever have; he would have to write about it when he returned home.

Kailem remained at the top of the hill, next to their four regular horses. He sat down and took out his mother's pearl from under his tunic. He watched his friends engaged with the mythical horses, wishing he could join them. But Osmund had said a wind horse could sense if he was a friend or foe; what would they sense in him, he wondered? How would they judge him? Would they think him untrustworthy? Dangerous? Would they flee when he approached, spoiling the moment for everyone?

Kailem didn't want to know the answer.

The problem with the Pavian Grasslands was that each mile looked the same as the last. At least in Glendown and Monkwood there had been hills and valleys, lakes and meadows, cliffs and ravines. Passing all those landmarks helped a traveler gauge their journey, gave them a sense of forward progression. But in the grasslands, there was scarcely a hill more than half a dozen feet high. One could travel for days, even weeks, without any change in scenery. A fortnight in the grasslands was almost enough to relieve the three travelers of their sanity.

The sole source of variety in the region was the farms that appeared every fifty miles or so. Farmers working in their fields watched the motley group of travelers with a curious eye. A young Devonian man, a young Donnelish woman, and a young Mariner, all dressed in common drab, yet riding purebred horses, was not a common sight.

Kailem rode in the rear of their company. Their road weaved through a wheat farmer's field, the first flecks of pale-yellow grain appearing among the green stalks. At the edge of the farmer's land, the wheat returned to Pavian grass, and on they rode.

It was early evening; the sun dipping below the horizon, and the air had become still and cool, at least by Pavian standards, so it puzzled Kailem that sweat dripped from his every pore.

A bend in the river seemed as good a place as any to camp for the night. Kailem swung his leg over the saddle and lowered to the ground, then leaned against the horse for a moment.

Emerald glanced at Osmund, struggling to unpack his gear. "Oz? Ye well?"

"Oh yes, just tired," he said between labored breaths. "I'm... I'm fine."

Then Osmund collapsed to the dirt.

Emerald rushed to his side. His skin was pallid, and his clothes were as damp as if it had been raining.

"Kailem! Come quick!" Emerald yelled.

The Mariner fumbled towards them, then fell to his knees next to Osmund.

"He be a torch," she said, with her hand on his forehead. "What do we do?"

"I... I don't..."

Kailem collapsed next to Osmund.

Emerald stood in a panic. Her eyes darted between them. Neither moved. She looked around in all directions, running her hands over her matted red hair; there was nothing but Pavian grass and the night sky as far as the horizon. What was she supposed to do now, she thought?

She knelt next to Oz and felt his brow again. It was warm to the touch and slick with sweat. Was it blue fever? Her thoughts briefly returned to her parents.

Osmund moaned.

"Oz? Oz, tell me what ta do." She needed some instruction while he was still conscious.

"My... lips... what color?" he asked between breaths.

Emerald looked him over, then shrugged. "They be normal."

Osmund held up his hand. "Fingers... what color?"

Emerald inspected his fingers. "Same. Normal."

"No discoloration... not blue fever."

Emerald sighed audibly and sat back on her feet. It was like Osmund had read her fears and put them to rest.

"Fever. Sweats. Chills. Fast onset... of symptoms. It's congestive fever. What color... are my eyes?"

"Blue," Emerald said.

Osmund shook his head. "The whites. Around the edges. Yellow?"

Emerald looked closely. "Nay. They be white."

Osmund nodded. That must be a good sign.

"Build a fire, keep us warm. And fetch water."

Osmund closed his eyes while Emerald hurried about her task. She was grateful beyond words to have something to do, to feel like she was helping in some way. After starting the fire and refilling their water skins, she covered them each with a blanket and placed a rolled blanket under each of their heads. When she was done, she put her hand near each of their mouths to be sure they were breathing. Blessedly, they both were, thank Iria.

Something metallic caught her eye from the dirt near Osmund's chest. She bent down and found the pocket watch she had given him during their days on the *Flying Manta*. It must have slipped from his vest pocket when he fell. She opened the cover to look at the clock face. The hands were still motionless; so, why did he carry it, she wondered? She looked down at Osmund asleep on his cot and brushed a lock of hair off his brow.

The horses had shown some concern for their riders' illness, at least at first. Echo had gone so far as to bend down and sniff the boys as they were asleep. Now all four horses were asleep themselves. Osmund had explained to her that horses had special knees that allowed them to sleep while standing; he was always sharing interesting little facts like that.

Emerald stayed awake all night by her boys' side, continually checking their temperature and breathing and keeping the fire replenished. The boys reeked of sweat and disease, and they turned in their sleep, mumbling incoherently. Kailem called out for his parents and made threats against someone named Vanua, and frequently asked Mokain what he should do. Osmund said nothing but apologies to his parents.

Near sunrise, Osmund opened his eyes to see Emerald sitting at his side, his left hand clasped between hers.

"Now, there's a sight for sore eyes," he said with a feeble voice. Emerald dabbed away some sweat from his forehead and helped him drink from the waterskin.

"I say, if I didn't know any better, I'd say you've been worried about me."

"Nay," she said. "Barely noticed ye were sick."

"Is that so? Because... I do believe I can feel myself... slipping away..."

"Oh, hush," she scolded.

Osmund grinned, and moments later was asleep again.

CHAPTER NINETEEN

SPARRING PARTNERS

23RD DAY OF SUMMER, 897 G.C.

Mokain walked the avenues of his battalion's camp with mud sloshing up his boots as he went. It was the first week of their march west to the borderlands. With each cluster of tents, he met looks of disdain and derision from the men. Soldiers were supposed to stop and salute as he walked by. For Mokain, at best, they gave sloppy, half-hearted salutes as he passed; others simply ignored him. It was a stark contrast to the treatment from the royal guard back in the capital. Those had been good, obedient soldiers who respected him instantly. These men, however, were cut from an entirely different cloth.

Mokain ignored their insubordination for now and searched for a particular lieutenant. Although he had met the man before, he couldn't recall his face, but lieutenants were easy enough to identify. They were the only soldiers who wore brigandine armor: a thick woolen coat with segmented metal plates riveted to the inside.

He found his man sitting around a campfire with six other soldiers. They all laughed at crude jokes through mouths full of bread and stew. The laughter ceased on their leader's arrival.

Mokain masked his anger poorly. "Lieutenant Dorman, you were not at the officers' meeting this morning. Explain yourself."

Lieutenant Rayne Dorman sat tall and met his eye but did not rise to his feet. The other six soldiers stared at the ground or at their food, anywhere but at Mokain. None of the soldiers took well to the Mariner leading their battalion, if for no other reason than he was a foreigner with no history in the Cavander army, but Rayne also had personal reasons to despise the newcomer. Rayne had been a favorite to win the Prince's tournament until Mokain defeated him in the penultimate round. Were that not enough, Mokain's presence recalled to Rayne's mind the tournament and, by extension, the memory of that fatal, unintentional strike to Willian Wyke's neck.

"I beg pardon, *Lord* Roka," Rayne said. "I was busy seeing to the needs of my men. I must have lost track of time."

Rayne over-enunciated the title "Lord", not so exaggerated as to be insolent, but just enough to remind Mokain of his place. If Mokain had been a military officer, leading a battalion would have made him a colonel, surpassed in rank by only the generals and the King himself. But as Mokain's official position was First Officer of the Royal Guard, he was technically not a member of the military, and it certainly did not help that the Royal Guard's armor was so distinct from military armor. Dorman's use of the title "Lord" was an unsubtle reminder of that fact. The message was clear: "you are not one of us."

"I need your report of the Fourth Regiment," Mokain said.

"You've interrupted a meeting with my sergeants. You'll have my report as soon as I am finished, *Lord* Roka."

One of the soldiers snickered but quickly silenced himself. They all continued to avert their eyes. Mokain glared at each of them before continuing.

"Deliver it today," he commanded. "The soonest you can manage."

Mokain marched away with tense shoulders and clenched fists. He had taken no more than three strides before the soldiers resumed their laughter. The other lieutenants had given him similar problems, and not one had come to the officer's meeting.

Lieutenant Lowin, commander of the Fifth Regiment, was the last officer Mokain had left to confront. He knew the general location of the Fifth Regiment's section of the camp, but had no interest in searching out the lieutenant.

"You there," Mokain said. "You are with the Fifth Regiment, are you not?" He addressed a soldier with a sergeant's armor: thick strips of woven leather with metal plates spaced apart and studded to the outside. He was a short man, but had the brawn of a seasoned warrior, and his trimmed beard accentuated a prominent scar across his chin.

"That is correct, Lord Roka." The man stood at attention. "Sergeant Shaw, at your service."

It was a respectful response, coupled with a pejorative title that left Mokain puzzled, but he had more pressing issues to address at the moment. "Show me to your lieutenant."

"Right away, sir." Sergeant Shaw led Mokain through the grid of tents to one in particular, and stood at attention near the opening. Inside, Mokain found Lieutenant Lowin on a stool, running a whetstone over the edge of his side sword.

Lieutenant Lowin sprung to his feet so abruptly that the sword and whetstone fell at his feet. He bent to retrieve them, then paused at the midpoint, torn between his duties of caring for his weapon and standing at attention for a superior officer. After a heartbeat, he decided to leave the sword and remain at attention.

Well, at least this one stood for me, Mokain thought.

"You were not at the officer's meeting this morning," he said.

Lieutenant Lowin was a lanky man without a single imposing attribute to speak of. Mokain couldn't see how this spindly soldier had ever been promoted to lieutenant.

"A thou– thousand apologies, Lor– Lord Roka. Sir. It won't happen again."

Mokain stood directly in front of him. "Disobeying a direct order requires more than an apology, lieutenant. Explain yourself."

Lieutenant Lowin searched for words, but no suitable response came to mind.

"And I will know if you are lying," Mokain added, "so the first explanation better be the honest one."

Lieutenant Lowin's eyes dropped for only a moment, then he stared forward as he spoke. "I ignored your order at the behest of the other lieutenants, sir. There was an agreement not to attend your meeting."

Mokain grit his teeth. "I see. And who was the architect of your little rebellion?"

The lieutenant winced at the word *rebellion*, and his voice quivered as he explained. "I was approached by Lieutenants Dorman and Balfour, sir. I don't know which of the two had the idea first. I'm terribly sorry, sir."

Mokain vacated the lieutenant's tent without another word. He should have guessed it was Dorman and Balfour. His highest-ranking officers engaged in organized insubordination; he could have them publicly horsewhipped and thrown in a stockade for this. Had they been on a ship, the captain could have them thrown into the sea with chains around their ankles for mutiny. Mokain considered having them caned to set an example, but that would only cause the battalion to despise him all the more.

He marched back through camp with as much composure as he could maintain. Soldiers fled from his path as they would a boulder rolling down a hill. A sentry stood at the opening of the command tent; he didn't salute as Mokain stormed past. Once inside, his composure expired. He kicked the map table with such force it toppled to its side, scattering papers, ledgers, and an ink well across the dirt.

"Pleasant chat, I take it?" asked Lord Menden. He sat in a padded chair in the corner of the tent, sipping his wine and reading a history on the borderlands.

Young Vivek set immediately to righting the table and cleaning Mokain's mess. His master knelt beside him as well.

"I can clean this for you, milor... Mokain. Sir." Vivek doubted he would ever be at ease calling his master by his given name. What would Dugald say of such impropriety?

"I clean my own messes, Vivek," Mokain chided.

Vivek stopped helping and lowered his head; if he had possessed a tail, it would have been tucked between his legs. Mokain took a breath and placed a hand on Vivek's shoulder. "But I do appreciate the gesture. Now help me lift the table."

The two men heaved the oaken table back on its four legs. Mokain plopped into the padded chair next to Lord Menden with all the grace of a walrus, while Vivek fetched him a goblet of mulberry wine. Lord Menden had relinquished all his duties to Mokain and was officially retired, but he accompanied Mokain on his own initiative to offer his experience and counsel.

"The men don't respect me, Menden," Mokain said. He rubbed the bridge of his nose. "They see me as a foreigner with no business leading them."

"Well, of course, they don't," Lord Menden said. "You *are* a foreigner, and you *don't* have any business leading them. You're not a military officer. But you were appointed by their crown prince, so they must respect you anyway."

"Would you mind telling them that?"

Lord Menden chuckled. "Respect cannot be forced, my boy. It can be feigned, but never forced."

"The Royal Guard took to me almost instantly," Mokain said. He let his head fall back to stare at the tent ceiling.

"Well, that was different. *They* saw you fight. They saw you defeat the best warriors in all of Cavandel. In all of Iria, for that matter. You cost me ten gold florins in that tournament, by the way."

Mokain lifted his head to give him a mirthless glare.

Lord Menden continued, "But most of these men here were not given leave to watch the tournament. To them, you are not the Lion of Marin, you're just a foreigner they've been suddenly forced to take orders from. They've been given no reason to respect you."

"So, you're saying I should go find the best warriors in the battalion and beat them within a breath of their lives?" Mokain said. He leaned forward to take another drink of his wine.

Lord Menden scoffed. "That was hardly the conclusion I was guiding you towards." He swirled the remaining wine in his goblet.

"I know, I know." Mokain sat back in his chair and ran his hands through his wavy black hair.

They sat in silence for a moment. Vivek looked around for some way to make himself useful, as Dugald had taught him, but nothing came to mind. He decided to sit and wait for an instruction. But wait, should he be sitting? He stood and waited patiently, mimicking a soldier at attention. Then he remembered Mokain telling him it was okay to sit, three times in the past week, in fact. He sat back in the chair.

"Lord Roka," the sentry said from the tent opening.

"Yes, what is it?" Mokain asked with his fingers pinching the bridge of his nose.

The sentry stepped into the tent. "Sergeant Conroy Wyndell is requesting an audience."

"Who?" Mokain asked.

"Lord Mason Wyndell's son. Good lad," Lord Menden said, without lifting his eyes from his book.

"Let him in," Mokain told the sentry.

A young man in his mid-twenties with an average build and a child's face entered the command tent. He walked to Mokain and stood at attention.

"At ease, Sergeant," Mokain commanded. Conroy moved into a relaxed position. There was something familiar about the lad, but Mokain couldn't place him. "What can I do for you?" he asked.

The moment he was allowed to speak, all decorum was forgotten. "Sir, I mean, my Lord, uh, Commander Roka," he said, deciding on an informal title that could apply both in and out of the military, "I needed to introduce myself again and thank you for what you taught me. I've been practicing every day."

Mokain frowned at the Sergeant.

Conroy continued, "I also want to welcome you personally to the battalion and tell you if you ever have a special assignment or need someone you can trust, I'm your man, sir.. I mean, Commander."

It finally occurred to Mokain how he knew the young man. He leaned forward in his chair. "You're the one I fought in the tournament! The one who over-committed on his overhead attack. Second round, if I'm not mistaken."

"I am, indeed, Commander," Conroy said, standing as tall as his average frame would allow.

"It is a pleasure to see you again," Mokain said. He stood from his chair and shook the Sergeant's hand. "So, you've been practicing the move I taught you?"

"I have, sir, and my sparring has certainly improved. I'm not overextending myself anymore and I'm faster at defending counterstrikes."

"That's excellent to hear. Keep at it. No matter how good you are, you can always improve. Have you taught the maneuver to your squadron?"

"I have, Commander, and they are coming along as well. And if you ever have time to show me any new maneuvers, I would be a grateful student."

Lord Menden snickered. *How easily star struck the young become.*

Mokain looked out the tent opening, an idea forming. "How does right now sound?"

Conroy's face instantly brightened.

At Mokain's command, Vivek hastened from the command tent to retrieve two blunted sparring swords from the armory. Mokain and Conroy followed behind him and stood opposite each other in the space outside the tent's opening. Lord Menden set down his book and watched with curiosity.

"From what I remember, your striking form was sound, but you lacked the ability to combine your strikes into a natural rhythm. You see, certain strikes naturally lead to specific counterstrikes. When your opponent uses one of these strikes, you can be almost certain he will use the corresponding attack next. Knowing how your opponent will strike next can help you prepare your own counterattacks in advance, leading to faster swordplay."

"But what if he doesn't use the strike I'm expecting?" Conroy asked.

"If your opponent uses a different attack, it will be a slower one. That will give you time to adjust accordingly. Understood?"

Conroy nodded, and Mokain proceeded to show him three different strikes, as well as those most likely to follow them. They moved through the maneuvers slowly, with Mokain correcting his stance and arm position as they went. Conroy proved an adept student. He made mistake after mistake, but never the same one twice.

Once Mokain saw no other mistakes needing correction, they gradually increased the tempo. Little by little, the speed of his attacks reached combat levels. The sound of the clashing swords caught the attention of nearby soldiers.

Before long, at least a fifth of the camp had come to watch the display. They formed a ring around the fighters, careful to leave them enough space for their complex footwork. Some even cheered, always for Sergeant Wyndell, of course. He and Mokain exchanged blows at lightning speed.

The bout ended with Mokain halting the tip of his sword just as it touched Sergeant Wyndell's chest. Conroy hadn't been fast enough to parry the attack. He was breathing heavily after the bout, whereas his commander appeared unfazed by it.

Rather than feeling defeated, Conroy beamed at how long he had lasted against the Lion of Marin. He had never fought better.

The spectating soldiers gave a hesitant round of applause, their faces a mix of stale disdain and budding admiration. There was still no love lost for their new leader, but none could deny his skill with the blade, and he clearly knew how to teach the sword as well. Mokain spotted Sergeant Shaw and Lieutenant Lowin in the crowd. He didn't see Lieutenants Dorman and Balfour.

Mokain placed a hand Conroy's shoulder. "I'll make you an offer, sergeant. Tomorrow we're continuing our march to the Westham Plains. Meet me in front of my tent every evening an hour before sundown and we'll continue your lessons."

Conroy's smile shined like the sun.

"And that goes for anyone else looking to improve their skill," Mokain announced. "My tent, an hour before sundown." He spoke loudly for all the soldiers to hear. They were already dispersing to their various tents, but enough of them turned their heads at the offer.

Mokain returned to the command tent.

"Lessons in swordplay. That is how you plan to win them over?" Lord Menden asked.

"It was the best idea I had," Mokain said. "Have anything better for me?"

Lord Menden shook his head. "I suppose we will see what happens."

Mokain watched from atop the hill as the sun dipped toward the forest canopy. It had been a month since his invitation to train the battalion. Sundown was less than an hour away. No one had come.

Sergeant Conroy Wyndell stood alone in front of Mokain's tent, practicing his forms while he waited for their next training session to begin. Mokain let out a heavy sigh and stepped forward with his training sword.

"On guard, Wyndell," Mokain called. Conroy jumped in place, then fell into his stance.

"Today, I'm going to show you how to recognize an opponent's weakness and turn it to your advantage," he continued. Conroy forced a stern face to hide his boyish excitement. "As we spar, I'm going to make certain mistakes, either with the blade or my footwork. I want you to stop me when you reckon you've spotted the error, and then we'll discuss how to turn it into an advantage."

Conroy nodded and shook his shoulders, both to loosen his muscles and to shake off his nerves.

Training Conroy reminded Mokain of the days he spent sparring on the beach with Kailem. His younger brother never had much interest in combat training, but he would jump at any excuse to compete against his older brother. It didn't matter if it was a foot race, a wrestle, or just seeing who could hold their breath the longest; if it was a competition, Kailem was ready and willing. And he proved a fierce competitor. By the time of their exile, swordplay had been about the only challenge wherein he hadn't beaten Mokain at least once.

Mokain's heart ached.

"We'll start off at half speed," Mokain said.

The two exchanged strikes and parries in front of Mokain's tent. If Conroy missed a mistake, Mokain would stop and point it out to him, then explain how that kind of mistake could be turned into an advantage. He would do the same for any mistakes Conroy made, albeit Conroy's mistakes were never intentional.

Mokain couldn't imagine a better student. Conroy hungered for every morsel of expertise Mokain could give him. He never complained, never asked for a break, and never let his attention waver. He absorbed every word his commander said. Unlike Kailem, who had just wanted to beat his older brother, Conroy sought to master every aspect of the sword.

"Good. Now I want to show you what to do if you ever lose your weapon in battle," Mokain said. Conroy looked down at the sword in his hand. He had never considered what he'd do in that situation.

"Do you carry a knife or a dagger on you?" Mokain asked.

"No, Commander, only my side-sword." Conroy said. He slid his blade back in its scabbard at his side.

Mokain unsheathed his dagger. "You can use mine for now, but should carry one of your own."

Watching Conroy test the weight and the balance of the dagger reminded Mokain of how Kailem would use his Coronation Blade for everything from shucking oysters to cutting his meat at dinner. Conroy noticed the sore smile on his commander's face.

"If you lose your weapon, immediately close the gap between you and your attacker," Mokain explained.

"Shouldn't I keep my distance?"

"That will be your impulse, but it's motivated by fear, not strategy, so don't listen to it. The sword is designed to kill someone at just over an arm's length away. But if you fight in close range, even a side-sword is too long to be used effectively."

Conroy nodded.

"Now, as I come at you with an overhead strike, I want you to close the distance between us and stop my attack by catching my wrist in your hand. Ready?"

Conroy nodded again. They moved at half speed, and Conroy moved forward and caught Mokain's wrist just as his overhead strike was coming down.

"Good, now grip my wrist tight so I can't pull away. Like that, perfect. Now, with your other hand, take the dagger and move like you're going to ram it under my chin."

During the first attempt, Conroy fumbled while retrieving the dagger, and the second time he was so focused on retrieving the dagger correctly that he didn't catch Mokain's wrist. The third attempt he caught the wrist and retrieved the dagger but didn't grip the wrist tightly enough and Mokain broke free too soon. But the fourth time was a success. Conroy stopped the dagger just below Mokain's jaw.

"Perfect," Mokain said as they stepped back.

Conroy cocked his head at him. "Is everything alright, sir?"

Mokain frowned at him.

"Forgive me if I am out of line, Commander. But your smile, it looks sad, somehow."

Mokain hadn't realized he had been smiling. "You're fine, Sergeant. It's just, you remind me of my younger brother, Kailem. We used to spar out on the beach in front of our home. I taught him this very move on that beach. You learned it almost as fast as he did."

"I take that as a compliment," Conroy said. "I can't wait to meet him."

Mokain took back his dagger, looking like an empty wineskin. "We'll end it there for the night."

Although no one else joined their training sessions, several had come near to watch. They would observe from afar or pretend to be engaged in some other task, but their interest was obvious to anyone paying attention.

The next week, they arrived at the village of Tarwick. The battalion was almost the population of the whole village, so they prepared camp on the outskirts of town. Using Tarwick as a base camp, Mokain assigned a number of sergeants to take their squadrons of twenty men to nearby villages and return with a report.

"Write down any accounts of raids or attacks that you hear, but I want more than just the word of the villagers," he instructed. "Take note of evidence, anything that can substantiate their claims."

"Like what, exactly?" asked Lieutenant Balfour with his arms folded.

"Look for damaged buildings, discarded arrows, wounded villagers, signs of that nature," Mokain explained. The sergeants nodded as he spoke. "I want every squadron back here within two weeks ready to send their report to the king. Dismissed."

With squadrons embarking in all directions, Mokain went into Tarwick village. Lord Menden and Vivek accompanied him, along with Sergeant Wyndell and several soldiers from his squadron.

The citizens of Tarwick recoiled at the soldiers' presence. Those who were able retreated indoors, while others scowled or turned their backs.

"Not the warmest welcome, is it?" Conroy said.

"Not very warm at all," Lord Menden agreed.

If a village had a raiding problem, would they not welcome a soldier's presence? Mokain reasoned.

When they reached the village square, a large group of men, women, and children had gathered around a man dressed in black. The man was standing on a small barrel, speaking to the people.

"The people do not need some monarch in a faraway palace, who knows nothing about them and their way of life, telling them what they can and cannot do," the man on the barrel said. There were murmurs of agreement from the crowd. "And they certainly do not need some monarch in a faraway palace taking a portion of their goods and crops every year!"

The crowd heartily agreed.

The man on the barrel saw the soldiers but did not miss a beat.

"The truth is, you good people need no one to govern you. You are perfectly capable of governing yourselves. You should choose your own leaders, from among your own members, for who could know the needs of your village and how best to meet those needs than one of your own?"

Lord Menden turned to Mokain. "We should put a stop to this. What he's saying is treason. It could lead to an insurrection."

Mokain thought about Lord Menden's counsel. "I hardly think an insurrection from a couple of villagers over a thousand miles from Rhinegard is a threat. What does concern me is their cooperation, and if we walk in with a show of force on our first day, arresting a man who clearly has the people's favor, we'd doom our investigation from the start."

Lord Menden nodded, surprised by the young leader's wisdom.

"And besides," Mokain added, "I happen to agree with the man."

CHAPTER TWENTY

BALDERLYN

35TH DAY OF SUMMER, 897 G.C.

The final leg of their journey was blessedly devoid of incident. It had been nearly a month since their fever, and nearly two months since the night with the wind horses. They hadn't seen the herd again.

The grass was increasingly brown and brittle the farther south they traveled. Patches of bright green shrubbery burst from the ground every dozen yards or so. Farmhands harvested fields under the punishing sun from dawn to dusk. Gone was the citric scent of the Pavian Grasslands, replaced by the arid, earthy scent of Veydala.

The morning they would arrive in Balderlyn, they woke early and packed camp before sunrise, estimating they were less than twenty miles from the village. Kailem was now a competent horse rider, and Emerald had become a veritable expert. They rode at a steady canter until they reached the main road into town.

At the market, Kailem jumped from his horse and raced to a fruit vendor. It was the first time he'd seen mangos for sale since his exile. They were a copper penny each, and he purchased five of them.

Like most villages between major cities, Balderlyn had only a single inn and tavern. They found it near the end of the main road under a sign that read: The Autumn Sun. They tied their horses to a post out in front.

Across from the inn, a woman in a black blouse and black trousers stood on a small barrel, speaking to a crowd that had gathered around her. She had a figure that flirted the line between slender and buxom and spoke with a distinctly Norvian accent, long vowels and a raised tone at the end of her sentences. Her voice was melodious and alluring. She could have drawn in a crowd regardless of what she was saying. It beckoned the three travelers as well.

"And this is not a new injustice, you all know it as well as I," the Norvian woman said. "We commoners have always taken care of ourselves. What has the monarchy ever done for you, sir? Or you, my good man, what has your lord ever done for you?"

"Nothing!" the man called back.

The speaker pointed to the man emphatically. "'Nothing!' he says. Nothing at all. He speaks the truth, does he not? Indeed, truer words ne'r a man has spoken! Our overlords offer us nothing but oppression and starvation!"

The crowd murmured in agreement.

"What is this?" Kailem asked one of the onlookers standing in the back of the crowd. He had one of his mangos in hand as he peeled back the skin with his dagger.

"She be one of them Blackbirds," the old man returned. "Theys been goin' town to town tryin' to recruit us all to their... cult or whate'er they be."

"They're called the 'Blackbirds'?" Kailem said with a chuckle. He cut off a slice of mango and savored it.

The old man chuckled in kind. "Ain't a name to strike fear in the heart, now innit?"

"Unlike the aristocracy, we Blackbirds keep our promises," the speaker continued. She waved her arms as she spoke, often pounding her fist into her hand. "We promise every man their independence, power, and prosperity. We will not abandon you like the aristocracy has. We take care of our own, and..."

The trio left the crowd and crossed the street to the Autumn Sun. The Norvian woman's passionate speech faded as the door closed behind them.

"We require a room, my good man," Osmund told a man wiping down a table. Kailem found a rubbish bin to dispose of his mango pit and wiped the juice from his hands on his trousers.

The man stood and sighed in annoyance. "Then you'll want to talk to her. This here's Ms. Mallory's place." The man pointed to a woman sitting behind a desk scribbling in a ledger.

Ms. Mallory wasn't short, but her rotund figure gave the illusion she was. In truth, she was average height, with streaks of white in her thin grey hair.

"One room, please," Osmund said when she finally looked up from her scribbles.

Ms. Mallory snarled as she inspected them. Their clothing was drab and dirty, and she knew the type of woman that traveled alone with young men.

"I don't tolerate rough housing, lawbreaking, or any other kind of tomfoolery in my inn. This here's a reputable establishment," she said.

"We have no interest in anything of the sort, ma'am, I assure you," Kailem said. With the clothes he had made them wear and the weeks they'd been on the road, they hardly seemed the ideal customers. "We just want a decent hot meal and a place to lay our heads."

"And a bath," Emerald added. "If ye got one."

Ms. Mallory eyed them skeptically. "It's a copper florin a night per room. Another three copper shillings if you'll be wantin' meals, and that's per person, and it don't include any drinks you'll be havin' neither. And I'll be insistin' on payment upfront."

"Very well, that's not a problem," Osmund said. He tallied the total in his head and took out three silver pennies. "This should cover us for two nights. We'll pay more if we decide to stay longer, but I will need my two copper shillings in change, please."

Ms. Mallory's eyes went wide at the sight of Osmund's coin pouch. A cheerful, accommodating hostess blossomed in her place.

"Very well, then. It will be our pleasure to host you. And to answer your question, young girl, we do offer hot baths for the cost of two... pardon me, five copper shillings."

"I'll take it," Emerald said. She looked to Osmund and waited.

All three of them had bathed regularly in the river, which had been perfectly suitable for Kailem, and while Osmund wasn't nearly as amenable to life as a traveler, five copper shillings was far more than he was willing to spend on a simple bath, not after having paid to replace nearly all the gear they lost the night of the fire. He turned to Emerald ready to object, but after seeing those green eyes against her pale, freckled skin, the objection was nowhere to be found. He reluctantly counted out three more copper shillings from his coin pouch.

Ms. Mallory's smiled spread like a hyena while she placed the coins in her lockbox. "Thand here will show you to your room." She gestured to the man wiping the tables. "And little miss, if you'll follow me, I'll prepare that hot bath for you."

"We'll need our horses seen to as well," Osmund said.

"Of course, of course.!" Ms. Mallory mused it over. "We offer stable services for—"

Kailem cut her pondering short. "I would assume that such a reputable establishment as this would have complimentary stable services."

If Ms. Mallory was surprised or angry by the interruption, she didn't let it show. "Of course we do, young sir. All I was 'bout to say is 'we offer stable services for each and every guest who stays with us.' Thand will see to the horses after he takes you to your room. Ain't that right, Thand?" Ms. Mallory's pleasant tone had suddenly vanished with her last sentence.

Thand grunted. "Follow me," he grumbled as he walked by.

Kailem noticed four slave brands along Thand's forearm. Four brands meant he was probably sold for cheap the last time he was purchased. That would explain how an innkeeper like Ms. Mallory was able to afford him.

Thand walked them up a rickety staircase and showed them to their room. There was nothing in it but two beds and a single window barely large enough for one to put their head through.

"There are only two beds," Osmund said. "There are three of us."

"We ain't got no rooms with three beds," Thand said.

Kailem reached into his own coin pouch. "Just bring us an extra pillow and a few extra blankets." He placed two copper pennies in Thand's hand.

Thand stared at the coins. Tipping a slave was against custom; in fact, most slave owners forbade their slaves from even handling money, let alone owning coins for themselves. Thand gripped the precious coins in his hand and raced off with a skip in his step.

Kailem and Osmund took some time off their feet while they waited for Emerald to finish with her bath. Then they waited some more. Thand returned with their extra blankets and pillows, and they continued waiting. Just how long does it take to bathe?

"Fancy a glass?" Osmund finally asked. "We're but miles from the Marcônish border. I find myself keen to learn what wines they carry."

"I wouldn't say no to a pint," Kailem replied.

They returned to the tavern and found Thand tending the bar.

"I'll see a list of your wines, good sir," Osmund said as he sat on a stool.

Thand frowned. "We serve lager and ale, nuttin' more."

Osmund's shoulders slumped. *A reputable establishment indeed*, he thought. He would have to find a wine merchant while they were in town. They each ordered a pale lager instead.

While Thand set the pewter tankards on the bar, the Blackbird recruiter entered and sat on the stool next to Kailem.

"Darkest ale you have, Thand," she said in her melodic Norvian accent.

Kailem spotted a tattoo of a small bird on her wrist. It was the same tattoo he had seen on the man in the tailor's shop back in Ombermill. And just like the man in the tailor's shop, this Blackbird wasn't asked to pay. Kailem realized whoever these people were, they were more than a regional operation.

"What is it, exactly, that you Blackbirds do?" Kailem asked the woman.

The Blackbird turned to him, failing to hide her excitement.

"Oh, we're simply a group of like-minded men and women, a collective you might call us, who are fed up with the status quo." She leaned close and spoke softly, forcing Kailem and Osmund to lean in as well. "We mean to change things around here. By the time we're done, all of Iria will be different. You won't even recognize it anymore."

The woman sat tall and let her words settle on her two-man audience. She whipped her blonde hair over her shoulder and drank from her ale.

"I see," said Osmund, leaning forward to see around Kailem. "And how do you mean to accomplish this change?"

The woman looked about as if to make sure no one could hear, then leaned in again. "You see, love, I can't talk about it here. Can't let the wrong sort in on our plans and all. But you're the right sort, I can tell. Are you fed up with how the nobles oppress us? How they take the work of our hands like they're entitled to it, and then make *us* pay *them* for our homes and food and expect us to act like we're grateful for it?"

"Absolutely," Kailem said, with venom on his tongue. "I have no patience for nobility. They can all go leap off a cliff for all I care." He said it with such a straight face that Osmund almost believed him.

"Well said, my good man!" the woman said. She slapped Kailem's thigh for emphasis. "I reckon we might have a place for the likes of youse."

"Well, we'd need to know more before we join anything," Kailem said.

"I understand, I understand. You're a cautious couple of lads. That's smart. Here's what I can tell you. We have a secret weapon up our sleeves. I can't tell you all the details, but I'll tell you this: it has to do with the magic of sagecraft. I know, I know. And don't ask me anymore, 'cause I shan't say another word on it."

Osmund came alive at the mention of sagecraft. "Well, as it happens, we ourselves are..."

Kailem stomped on Osmund's foot against the foot rail.

The woman narrowed her eyes at Kailem, then back to Osmund. "You yourselves are what?"

"We ourselves are... familiar with sages. From reading history books, I mean. They are somewhat of a passion subject of ours," Osmund explained. He looked to Kailem to see if he had said something wrong. He hadn't mentioned they were searching for the lost city of Andalaya or that they had a good lead on its location. Kailem's face told him nothing.

"See, I knew you were the right sort. Sharp as razors, you are," the woman finally said, nodding as she spoke. "What did you say your names were?"

Kailem answered quickly. "I'm Tag, and this here is Quinn."

The woman removed an invisible top hat from her head and gave a polite nod. "It is truly a pleasure, masters Tag and Quinn. I am Livia Yannsin. I hail from Norvia, but you may have already put that together yourselves, being the quick wits that you are."

As the Blackbird recruiter continued her sales pitch, waving her hands as she spoke for emphasis, Emerald descended the staircase to the tavern. Her hair was still wet, but she looked and felt cleaner than she had in weeks. She found her boys sitting at the bar, then stopped. A woman, the Blackbird recruiter from earlier, was seated at the bar with them. The three of them were in a lively conversation. The woman had her boys captivated, Osmund especially. Emerald clenched her teeth and made her way to the bar.

"We'll be having a meeting near here in a few days to initiate new members," Livia explained. Stay close and I'll find you when it's time, yeah?"

"Be sure you do," Osmund replied.

Livia winked at them before she stood. Osmund's eyes followed her until she was out the door, not realizing his cheeks had flushed. Kailem rolled his eyes and took a drink.

Emerald arrived at the bar just as the woman passed through the front door.

"What's that all 'bout, then?" she asked, sounding as disinterested as she could manage.

"Just a load of nonsense is all," Kailem said dismissively. "Ready for the hike?

Emerald nodded. She looked to Osmund, who had a smile on his face. Not a smile leftover from the Norvian woman's conversation, but a smile that had appeared when Emerald reached the bar, a smile that weakened her annoyance with him.

The trio followed the main road out of town. They had no map to lead them and there were no markers along the trail; their only guide was Kailem's memory. He had to stop a few times to remember how he and Mokain had climbed it before, and more than once they had to double back the way they came. They finally found a goat herder who gave them directions.

Acacia and Joshua trees covered the hillside. The shrubbery gave an earthy, herbal scent like cedar bark and rosemary leaves. The sun was unforgiving, and precious few places offered shade enough for all three of them. Squirrels climbed on the sparse branches overhead while lizards, the size of a thumb, crawled on the sandstone rocks near their feet.

They climbed for hours. Osmund's stamina was not as meager as it once was, nor his belly as soft as it once had been, but these improvements notwithstanding, he twice required them to stop and rest during the ascent. He likely would have required more rest had his excitement not added fuel to his tired legs.

The rock formation did not become visible until they reached the summit. What they saw there would have taken Osmund's breath away had he not already been out of breath.

Perched on the mountain peak was a curious sandstone formation. On either side of the feature were two dome-shaped boulders, larger than any of the others. They had a steep slope inward and were rounded on the outside in the shape of unfurled wings. In the center of the grouping was a pinnacle-shaped rock, not as tall as the side boulders, with a small outcrop at the top in the shape of a beak.

This was it, what they had traveled the past two months to see. Osmund reverently placed his hand on the bird-shaped stones, letting the moment sink in.

"From southern winds, the babe will come, to find the object of her eye," Osmund said.

"Well, it be right windy then, innit," Emerald said, struggling to keep her wild hair out of her face.

Osmund continued, "On fertile shores, her feet doth land, to seek the eagle in the sky."

From the mountain peak, they could see lush farmland ready for harvest in all directions as far as the horizon. These were certainly "fertile shores," and no one could doubt the Balderlyn Falcon could have just as easily been the Balderlyn Eagle.

"So, how be we sure this be the place, then?" Emerald asked.

"Well, if it's the right place, we should find the rest of the markers, right?" Kailem said. "What comes next?"

Osmund continued from memory. "From thence, the babe doth travel on, with feet on snakes, below she climbs. To meet her mark, horizon's end. Sacred circles, twelve she finds."

"I don't fancy snakes," Emerald said.

"I'm sure it's a metaphor of some kind. I'm just not sure what it means," Osmund said. Emerald didn't know what a metaphor was, but decided not to ask. The three meandered about, looking for clues.

"If we had come from the south," Kailem started, "that means we would have been traveling north. And if we were to "travel on", that would mean we would continue north, right? Which way is north?"

It was nearing sunset, so east was easy to find. That meant north was directly behind the eagle rock. They walked behind the boulders and looked down the mountain. It was far steeper than the path they had taken to reach the summit.

"There, do you see the path?" Kailem said. "There are switchbacks carved into the mountainside. They curve back and forth..."

"Like a snake!" Emerald cut in.

"Exactly! What do you think, Oz?" Kailem asked.

Osmund considered it. He looked around at the fertile land around them, the eagle-shaped rock formation at the top of a mountain peak, and the snake-like path down the northern face of the mountain. Each clue alone was tentative at best, but all of them together were too much to be coincidence.

"I dare say we've figured it out," Osmund said in disbelief.

Kailem turned to Osmund. "We figured it out?"

The two young men said the words again and again, growing louder and louder until they were shouting and hugging in celebration. Emerald joined in the hug as well.

"Well, Oz, was it worth a thousand miles on horseback?" Kailem asked.

Osmund ran his hands through his loose curls, now soaked in sweat. "To solve a thousand-year-old riddle? I'd go a thousand more."

"Okay, okay, so what do we do next?"

"Let's see," Osmund said. "After descending the snake, we 'meet our mark' at 'horizon's end'. Do you see anything at the edge of the horizon?"

Farms covered the land from the base of the mountain to the horizon, but a road cut through them in a mostly straight course. At the edge of the horizon was another ridge of hills, barely visible from their summit.

"I reckon if we follow that road across the valley," Osmund said, "we'll find something represented by 'twelve sacred circles' at the base of those foothills."

They gazed over the valley to the foothills on the horizon, imagining what awaited them.

"Twelve sacred circles, what do you think that means?" Kailem asked.

Osmund thought for a moment. "I haven't a clue," he finally admitted. "But I'm anxious to find out."

Kailem took in a breath. "Alright, then. First thing tomorrow?" Osmund buoyantly agreed.

Their feet were as light as freshly-picked cotton as they trotted down the mountainside, arriving at the inn not forty minutes later.

CHAPTER TWENTY-ONE

SHINDA WARRIORS

36TH DAY OF SUMMER, 897 G.C.

"More wine, Lord Roka?" Vivek asked.

Mokain held his goblet up to Vivek, keeping his eyes fixed on a report from the first squadron to return.

Fifteen squadrons had been dispatched to surrounding villages, leaving his forces diminished by half. Lieutenant Dorman had gone through the nearby village of Tarwick and returned with a stack of reports from the villagers. Each page Mokain finished, he would hand to Lord Menden to read sitting next to him.

Sergeant Conroy Wyndell gave combat instructions outside the command tent. Mokain still had yet to win over any new recruits to his evening training sessions, but he considered the fact that several soldiers were at least willing to train with Conroy to be a step in the right direction.

A commotion stirred outside the tent. It was faint at first but grew steadily louder. Through the tent door, Mokain saw a horse gallop into camp. Its rider slid from the saddle before the horse fully came to a stop and barged straight past the sentry at the tent doors. Mokain rose from his padded chair.

"Commander Roka," the scout said, breathing heavily. The scout's right shoulder bled from an arrow wound.

"Shinda," the scout managed to say. "A full regiment. Perhaps three, even four hundred of them. I was spotted before I made an accurate count."

Every officer in the tent stopped to hear the scout's report. The word 'Shinda' provoked a clamor of fearful mutterings from the small crowd.

"Silence," Mokain commanded. "Where?"

"Through the pass, less than a day's march from here," said the winded scout.

"Cavalry?"

"None that I saw, Commander."

"Will they be in position to attack before nightfall?"

"I don't believe so, sir. But they will be by morning, there can be no doubt."

Mokain nodded. "Good work, soldier. Now, see that your wound is tended."

The scout gave a rigid salute and left the tent.

Mokain ignored the fearful mutterings that again arose around him and walked to the map desk. On top was a detailed map of the Westham Plains with tokens marking the villages they had sent squadrons to. He flipped through the maps underneath, finding a map of the village of Tarwick and its surrounding topography. He slid the map out and tossed aside the tokens to lay the new map on top.

Lord Menden appeared at his side. "What is your plan?"

"I'm figuring that out now. Sergeant Wyndell!"

Conroy Wyndell had stopped teaching the moment the scout arrived and had been watching from outside the tent. At Mokain's command, he hurried inside and saluted.

"Run through the camp and gather every sergeant and lieutenant we have. I need them here immediately. Go."

While Conroy ran off, Mokain left the tent and looked to the mountain. The mouth of the pass opened to a wide field, roughly two miles of flat terrain. In his mind, he saw all the ways the battle could occur, a plan forming in his mind. He returned to the tent just as Conroy arrived with the officers filing in behind him.

Each sergeant reported how many men they currently had in camp.

"Two hundred twenty," he said to himself aloud. "Two hundred twenty against three to four hundred Shinda."

The tent was silent.

"We should retreat," Lieutenant Balfour said. Several officers agreed with him.

Mokain shook his head. "If we retreat, they'll chase us down and come upon us while we sleep. Or worse, we leave the Tarwick villagers to be slaughtered."

"How is that worse?" a sergeant muttered to himself.

Mokain whipped his head at him. "Those villagers are Cavandel citizens under our protection. They depend on us; we won't abandon them." The men scowled and scoffed, but said nothing. "If you don't care about the villagers, consider your own men. More than half our battalion will be returning over the next five days, scattered in squadrons of twenty or less, and with no idea they would be walking into a trap. Each of them would be dead before the week's end."

That seemed to resonate with the officers. They may not be willing to die for borderland villagers, many of whom didn't even consider themselves Cavanders, but none of them were quick to abandon a fellow soldier.

"It is imperative that we choose the battlefield. The mountain pass opens to a spacious field," Mokain said, pointing to the area on the map. The officers circled around the map table. "We'll wait for the Shinda there, depriving them of the high ground advantage."

"Even without a high ground advantage, they still have us outnumbered, possibly two-to-one," said Lieutenant Dorman. No one would admit it, but the Shinda would be better trained as well. They were facing a force of both superior numbers and superior skill.

"This is suicide," Dorman said under his breath.

Mokain ignored the comment. Acknowledging it would only add to the men's fear.

"How familiar are your men with a crescent formation?" Mokain asked. He was met with blank stares. "Your men do know the crescent formation?" Several officers shook their heads. He let out a frustrated sigh and looked back at the map, abandoning the plan.

"What about an oblique formation?" Mokain asked.

More blank stares.

"A pincer movement?"

No response.

Mokain's disciplined facade quickly faded. "Then what *do* you know?!"

Most officers stared at the floor.

"*We* know every maneuver there is," Dorman defended indignantly. "The issue is whether the squadrons are sufficiently trained to execute them without further practice."

"You haven't been training your men?" Mokain asked. He directed his question to the entire group, not believing what he was hearing.

"Not in battle formations," Lieutenant Balfour said. "I've never needed to."

"I just haven't gotten around to it," added Lieutenant Lowin, sheepishly.

Mokain stared at his officers, his jaw unhinged.

"We stopped training in formations because we hardly ever use them," Sergeant Wyndell explained. "Our battle strategy is always the same, no matter the foe. We form a line and give our men commands as the battle progresses. If they shoot arrows, we raise shields. If the commanding officers tell us to, we charge, or stand fast, or retreat."

"And that is the full extent of the battle maneuvers your men are prepared for?" Mokain asked.

Wyndell nodded.

It had become clear to Mokain how the mighty Cavender Army won their battles: superior weapons, superior numbers, and an intimidating reputation. None of that would help them here.

This is *suicide*, Mokain thought.

He looked at Lord Menden sitting in the corner. The old man was the only one not fidgeting. He sat in his padded chair, leaning comfortably to the side. His eyes met Mokain's. There was a look in those eyes that conveyed confidence in the new leader, confidence Mokain sorely needed. He looked back to the map.

"Then forget the field," Mokain said. "We'll have to fight them at the mouth of the pass."

"And give them the high ground?" Lieutenant Lowin asked with a slight crack in his voice.

"Yes, it will prevent them from using any of those tactics I mentioned against us. It might give them a false sense of superiority as well." Mokain nodded as the budding plan took shape in his mind. "This is what we're going to do. After sundown, thirty of our best archers and..." he paused to think, "forty of our best infantries will march up the sides of the pass. Archers will take cover among the trees here and here. The infantry will take position fifty yards higher up the pass."

Mokain paused to make sure his officers were following him. All listened intently.

"This will leave us with one hundred fifty men. I will lead the main force to the mouth of the pass. The whole plan depends on the soldiers who leave tonight, remaining undetected. You will have to take a wide course to remain unseen.

"When the Shinda signal a charge, they sound a ram's horn. That will be our signal for the archers to fire. Once the arrows are flying, the Shinda will try to neutralize our archers by sending troops up the hillside . When that happens, our infantry from higher up the pass will run down from the tree line. The Shinda won't be able to gauge how many more men are hidden in the trees, and with any luck, the uncertainty will cause them to break ranks and scatter. I'll lead the men up from below while the archers continue to fire in the middle. Understood?"

The officers all nodded or muttered approval.

"Good. Go explain the plan to your men. I doubt any of us will sleep tonight, but do your best. Dismissed." As the officers trickled out of the command tent, Lord Menden walked to the map desk. He observed the terrain and reviewed the plan in his mind, then patted Mokain on the shoulder. He then walked back to his chair, having said nothing.

As night fell, the fires of the Shinda regiment began shining down from the pass. The archers and infantry who had been selected to advance up the mountainside ate an early dinner and left after sundown. Mokain ate a silent meal with Vivek in the command tent.

That night was a sleepless one, and Mokain arose from his bed before first light. He put on his own armor and belted his twin blades around his waist. When he left his personal tent, he was surprised to see most of the men had already done the same. He asked around camp after Lord Menden and learned the aged warrior had left with the advance team.

"Old fool," he muttered.

Mokain marched his small band of one hundred and fifty soldiers through the main village road and across the field. The villagers had seen the Shinda's campfires as well, and they lined the road to watch the soldiers pass through. Most of his men carried long spears. Others were armed with swords and shields. Once they were through the village, they spread out into a line across the mouth of the pass while the Shinda were still forming ranks. Four hundred had been a modest estimate.

Mokain carried a shield in his left hand. With his right, he pulled Koa from its sheath. He looked for any sign of the archers in the tree line and found none. Either they were just exceptionally hidden, or the Shinda had discovered them during the night.

His men fidgeted. Some stared at the sky or the ground, anything to avoid the army forming ranks before them. Others stared at their enemy intently as they shifted their weight between their feet. Mokain should have said something to improve their morale, to lift their spirits and inspire them to battle, but nothing came to mind. Despite his years of training and study, competing in tournaments, standing guard, and leading patrols, this was his first moment facing actual combat. The fear was visceral, far worse than he had expected. Instead of a speech, he settled for a confident, reassuring nod to the officers on either side of him. He held onto a foolish hope that the officers would pass the assurance down the line.

The Shinda horn blew.

The enemy roared, a sound so feral it made several Cavanders jump. Then arrows flew from either side of the pass. There weren't many, but they caught the Shinda by surprise. Their feral roar turned to a frightened scream. Their carefully formed ranks shattered almost immediately.

Instead of sending men up the hillside to meet the archers, as the plan predicted, the Shinda charged downhill away from the arrows. An army outnumbering his own three-to-one was closing fast, ready to slaughter each and every one of them, and now the Cavander regiment up the hill wouldn't arrive in time to surround the enemy. There was only one response he could think of.

Mokain roared his battle cry and ran uphill to meet the Shinda head on. He couldn't be sure if the men followed his lead. For all he knew, he was leading a one-man charge to his death. He plowed into the front line of charging Shinda with his shield held in front of him, knocking down multiple enemy soldiers like empty wine bottles.

Two Shinda spearmen leapt over their fallen comrades and thrust their spears at Mokain's chest. Mokain deflected the first spear with his sword and the second with his shield, then swung Koa at the nearest Shinda's head. The sword didn't penetrate the helmet, but it knocked the soldier to the ground. The other spearman attack again.

A Cavander spear came from behind Mokain and caught the Shinda square in the chest. Mokain's men had followed, and they quickly surrounded him. Screams of death came from every direction as he deflected swords and spear tips. His training took over, his muscles remembering the thousands of hours he had practiced each swing of the sword.

He thrust his sword into the abdomen of an advancing soldier. He felt the moment the blade punctured the man's skin, felt the moment it sliced through the man's spine. A revolting sensation shot through his arm like noxious heat. When he pulled his sword free, blood gushed from the wound. No amount of training could have prepared him for this moment. The man gasped, his face twisted in agony, the fear of death in his eyes. Blood splattered from his mouth onto Mokain's armor, and he collapsed to the ground.

Mokain was in shock. The reality of war, the gore and butchery before him, was too much to comprehend amid the chaos of battle. He had just taken the life of another man. This wasn't some faceless enemy far away, not just a number on a strategy table. He thought he had been prepared for it; thought he knew what battle would feel like. How terribly wrong he had been. Some deep, primitive part of his mind took control of his body. The memory of his years of training kept him alive as his conscious mind floundered. When an enemy sword lodged itself in his shield, he abandoned it and pulled Tao from its sheath. Surrounded by Shinda, he whirled his twin blades with lethal precision.

He killed another man. Then another. He sent countless men into the Great Unknown. Men he didn't know. Men with whom he had no quarrel. Men who certainly had families and friends. Men who were just following the orders of their superiors. The Lion of Marin wanted to weep. Wanted to vomit. Wanted to throw down his swords and flee. But his body wouldn't let him. His limbs continued fighting, continued killing. To all others, he was a mighty warrior, an unstoppable force of death on the battlefield, but inside, he was collapsing.

He couldn't say how long they had been fighting. His sense of time distorted beyond recognition. He thought he heard himself scream with each strike of his blade, but he couldn't be sure. There was so much screaming around him. So much blood. So many bodies on the ground.

He was so lost in his mind that he didn't realize when the advance team cut their way through the rear of the Shinda regiment. He didn't realize his men had the Shinda surrounded. He simply swung his swords at anything that wasn't a Cavander.

When his conscious mind regained control of his body, he was standing over a man who had thrown down his weapons and knelt in surrender. The man cowered at Mokain's feet, his hands before his face, waiting to be butchered by the Mariner's blade.

Mokain surveyed the carnage surrounding him, sucking in huge lungfuls of air. Blood dripped freely from both of his swords. There was blood on his hands and his armor. He wiped his forearm across his brow and a mixture of blood and sweat streaked across it.

The fighting had stopped. More than a hundred of his men still lived, and at least forty Shinda were on their knees in surrender.

His men raised their swords and cried out in victory. One by one, they began to chant.

"Roka! Roka! Roka! Roka!"

This wasn't what battle was supposed to be. At least, it was not like he had imagined. Mokain turned and walked through the field of dead men back towards Tarwick. Soldiers clapped him on the back and shoulders as he passed, but he said nothing. The villagers cheered his return as he marched down the main road, but he didn't acknowledge them. Soon he was back in camp, and his hand began to shake.

Mokain sat in the command tent, the intensity of battle slowly draining from him. He hadn't changed his clothes or washed his face. Vivek had removed his master's armor and prepared a wash basin. It sat idly on the table next to him.

His lieutenants had taken command after his abrupt departure, securing their prisoners and marching their men back to camp. Lord Menden, who had by then washed and changed his clothes, brought Mokain a goblet of their strongest wine.

"First battle, I take it?" Lord Menden asked. He took a seat in the chair next to Mokain and drank from a goblet of his own.

Mokain nodded. His hand shook as he tried to sip the wine.

"It's never easy," Lord Menden continued, "not for anyone, but you seem to take it harder than most."

Mokain stared off into the distance. "It was horrid," he said. "Worse than any nightmare. I hated every moment of it. I feel stained by it." He looked to Lord Menden. "Is that normal?"

Lord Menden nodded. "Anyone who doesn't feel that way has no business leading men into battle. Life, especially human life, is the most valuable thing in this world, and we just ended the lives of hundreds."

"How do you manage it?" Mokain asked. He looked at his hands, suddenly becoming aware they were covered in dried blood. He scrubbed them in the water basin as if the blood would poison him, as if it would permanently stain his skin if left there another second.

"You develop a numbness to it," Lord Menden explained. "A thickness of skin, if you will. Some men, after so many years of war, they lose the ability to feel entirely. That's why I transferred to the Royal Guard, so I could focus on enforcing peace rather than waging war. But even then, that numbness stayed with me. Do you recall the young man who died during the Grand Tournament?"

Mokain nodded.

"Willian Wyke was his name. Good lad. I trained him personally. And when he died right in front of me, I felt that numbness take over. It protects you, in a way. Allows you to deal with the horror in your own time and on your own terms. But deal with it you must."

"How?" Mokain asked, inspecting his clean, wet hands.

Lord Menden set his goblet down and leaned forward. "War is vile, wretched, and even profane, but it is also inevitable. There will always be evil men who are willing to kill and oppress to achieve their ends, and there will always be a need for good men willing to stand and defend those who cannot defend themselves, such as the villagers of Tarwick you saved today." Lord Menden paused briefly before adding, "Just always make sure you are aware of which side you are on."

Mokain sat quietly, considering the advice.

The sentry entered the tent and saluted. "Sergeant Conroy Wyndell to see you, Commander."

Mokain waved with his hand, signaling for him to enter.

Conroy stepped forward and saluted. Mokain returned the salute from his chair.

"I have the casualty numbers, Commander," Conroy said.

Mokain finished his wine and braced himself.

"We lost eighty-three men, including three sergeants and one lieutenant."

Mokain nodded thoughtfully. He had expected the numbers to be much worse, but hearing any of his men had lost their lives wore heavily on him.

"I have the list of names, sir."

Mokain looked at the page in Conroy's hand. "Just place it on the table." Conroy complied while Mokain poured himself another glass to the brim and drained it dry.

"Which lieutenant was it?" he asked just as Conroy was about to leave.

"Rayne Dorman, sir, of the Fourth Regiment."

Lieutenant Dorman. The most insubordinate of all his officers. The man who had killed Willian Wyke in the tournament. Even his death was difficult to hear. Mokain walked to Conroy's side and placed a hand on his shoulder.

"I'm promoting you to Lieutenant. Congratulations." He walked back to his chair and flopped down again.

"Thank you, sir," Conroy said with a furrowed brow. He had never heard "congratulations" said in such a somber tone. He watched his commander bury his face in his hands, heavy as an ox.

Conroy stepped forward. "Sir, you should know that all the men are talking about you. In a good way. No one thought we would survive the day, and yet here we stand victorious."

Mokain scoffed at the word victorious.

Conroy continued with renewed conviction. "The men know it was because of you, sir. It was your battle plan and your leadership. None of us had ever seen a battalion leader charge at the head of his men like that — commanding officers always stay behind us and give orders from a safe distance. And I have a particular need to thank you, sir. I would not be standing here alive were it not for the skills you taught me. You're the reason we defeated a regiment of nearly four hundred Shinda."

Mokain sat back in his chair and stared off into nothing. For a long moment, no one said anything. Conroy wondered if he should excuse himself, but then Mokain spoke. "I'm not certain they were Shinda, Lieutenant."

Conroy cocked his head. "They certainly looked like Shinda. They wore Shinda uniforms and carried Shinda weapons."

"Ethnically they were Shinda. There's no doubt about that. But they did not fight like Shinda, at least not properly trained Shinda military."

Conroy frowned. "You think they were Shinda commoners posing as military? But why?"

Mokain finished his third goblet of wine. "I don't know what I think yet. I'm going to my personal tent. The Prince will be expecting my report soon. See that I am alerted when more squadrons return to camp. Otherwise, I am not to be disturbed."

"Understood, sir."

No one saw Mokain for the rest of the day.

Chapter Twenty-Two

A Night in the Autumn Sun

36th Day of Summer, 897 G.C.

The tavern of the Autumn Sun overflowed with commoners in various stages of inebriation. There were the local townsfolk who were present nearly every night, traders who rode the river barges down from the mountain country, and even the odd vagrants passing through town. Ms. Mallory waddled in and out of the kitchen carrying plates to tables while Thand worked the bar. Osmund and Emerald found an empty table in the far corner, while Kailem ordered their first round.

The Blackbird recruiter had another small crowd around her table while she pontificated on the many atrocities committed by the aristocracy. She wore an evening gown rather than the blouse and trousers she had that afternoon. The dress was still entirely black, clearly a theme with the Blackbirds. It was tight along the waist, bosom, and shoulders and flowed loose around the arms, hips, and legs. The three friends couldn't hear exactly what she said, but every few seconds, a chorus of agreement sounded from the men and women around her.

"Do you reckon she's talking about... you know what?" Osmund asked.

"I doubt it," Kailem said. "That seemed like a secret saved for the already initiated."

"But she told us about it."

Kailem leaned over and nudged him. "Well, that's because she fancies you." Osmund blushed.

"What are youse on about?" Emerald asked.

Osmund leaned in close despite that no one in the raucous tavern could have heard him. "That woman there is a recruiter for some kind of group called the Blackbird Society."

"I remember," Emerald said, scowling as she recalled the woman talking to her boys before the hike.

"Well," Osmund explained, "they mean to abolish the aristocracy somehow, or something to do with the nobility. She was not abundantly clear on that point, but she said they meant to do it using sagecraft."

Emerald raised her eyebrows. "Sagecraft? As in our sages, ye mean?"

Osmund leaned back in his chair and nodded. Emerald turned and took another look at the woman.

"Do you think she's telling the truth?" Kailem asked, taking a drink.

Osmund scoffed. "Hardly. Those secrets were lost at least a thousand years ago, if they ever existed in the first place. But they have certainly found a way to make people think they can use sagecraft. Some kind of sleight of hand or illusion, or perhaps the work of a malcontent apothecary."

Ms. Mallory set down three plates of boiled lamb cuts under brown gravy with boiled corn and stale rye bread on the side. Osmund's back was to her, so she didn't see the face he made as she set it down. She then snapped her fingers at Thand who was tending the bar.

Thand scurried over with a bottle of wine and a wineglass.

Ms. Mallory cleared her throat. "Thand here informed me you had inquired if we carry any wine, so while you were out, I procured this fine bottle of Marcônish Red, just for you, good sir. Only one silver shilling per glass."

Emerald's eyes bulged at the price, and she nearly spat out her ale.

Osmund answered immediately. "Wonderful, I'll take the bottle," he said, not bothering to negotiate in the slightest. This time, it was Ms. Mallory's eyes that bulged as she watched him count out five silver shillings and place them in her hand. Kailem heard her whisper to Thand to go buy several more bottles of it. Osmund slid his mug to Kailem and filled the wineglass.

The sun had completely set, and darkness fell over Balderlyn. Thand and Ms. Mallory went around lighting candles throughout the tavern, casting an orange glow about the room. Four minstrels entered, carrying a mandolin, two fiddles, and a flute. The tavern was soon alive with music and drunken dancing between the tables.

"I am quite certain this wine is *not* Marcônish," Osmund said, staring at the red wine as he swirled it around in his glass. He threw his head back, draining the wine down his throat, and poured the glass full again.

The three adventurers had several rounds delivered to their table. Osmund finished off his bottle of, well, whatever that wine was, and then paid another five silver shillings for a second one.

Wealthy folk, Emerald thought, shaking her head.

The minstrels began a new song, and the patrons all cheered as they recognized the tune. The tavern sang along in drunken unison, horribly off-key and not caring in the slightest.

After the chorus, a tavern patron stood on his chair and sang. He was almost through the verse when he seemed to forget the words. When he fell behind, the people yelled and threw food at him until he stepped down from his chair. Then they sang the chorus together:

> *I am a man of ill-repute,*
> *And here I sing it with this flute!*
> *I'll punch my fist square in your jaw,*
> *But please, oh please, don't tell me ma!*

Emerald looked over at Kailem and caught him singing along to the chorus.

"Ye know this song?" she asked with a grin.

"Of course!" he said proudly. "This is 'Please Don't Tell Me Ma'. It's an old sailor's tradition. Everyone knows the chorus, but the verse changes every time. Someone stands on their chair and improvises the verse on the spot, and if you fail to sing the entire verse, you lose."

Another man was on his chair singing to the verse, but he likewise could not maintain the rapid tempo. He too was derided until he sat down. The tavern sang the chorus in unison again.

"Well then, let's hear it!" Emerald said over the deafening music.

"Hear what?" Kailem asked.

"Up on yer chair wit ye!" she dared him.

Kailem hesitated. He looked to Osmund, who gestured for him to stand.

"Very well, then!" Kailem announced. He took one last pull from his mug and slammed it down, ale splashing to the table. Then he stood on his chair. Once the chorus was over, he began to sing:

> *From down below, I sailed ashore,*
> *And found a man ne'r saw before.*
> *A tiny man, his nose in books,*
> *I saw that he was not a crook.*
> *We journeyed south to victory,*
> *Beyond the hills and through the trees.*
> *We found the rock, just like a bird*
> *But now I slur my every word!*

The tavern erupted in cheers when Kailem finished his improvised verse. Instead of jeers and bread thrown at him, men surrounded him to shake his shoulder and tussle his hair as if they had known him all their lives. They dragged him to the bar to buy him drinks.

"Who knew he could sing?" Osmund said.

"I reckon the ale brings it out of him," she replied.

A young man left the dancing and extended a hand to Emerald. He was dressed in coarse wool that frayed at the edges, likely a local farmer's son. Emerald looked to Osmund in surprise, but he was just as taken aback as she was. Before Osmund could think of what to say, Emerald had timidly placed her hand in the farmer's and was flung from her seat to join the dance.

Emerald was not the most gifted dancer, far from it in fact. But once she had broken free of her timid shell, she danced like she had just struck gold, and every eye was drawn to her. She spun and swayed and jumped and twirled, her red hair shimmering in the firelight.

Osmund longed to join the dance, but hadn't a lick of rhythm to speak of. It was no matter, there were plenty of farmers' sons eager to dance with Emerald. Osmund had no problem watching her dance with them. No problem whatsoever. He drained yet another glass of wine.

After a good number of songs, Emerald sat to catch her breath. "Oi, what fun! I've not been this merry in ages!"

Osmund swayed in his chair as he watched Emerald drain the last of her pint. He suddenly took note of all the empty pints of ale around Emerald at the table, yet somehow the petite young woman was sober as a stone.

"I say, for such a tiny lady, you sure can hold your liquor," he observed.

"Can I tell ye a secret?"

Osmund leaned in, prepared to hear some salacious confession.

"This was my first pint," Emerald said.

Osmund frowned. "But..." he pointed to the empty mugs around her.

"I switch out the full mug in front of me fer an empty mug in the middle whene'er the two of youse ain't lookin'. A little sleight o' hand is all." She whirled her fingers in the air, grinning deviously.

Osmund's jaw dropped. Such a clever little thing she was. Then he realized the implications of what she had said: just how much had Kailem been drinking? Osmund looked around and found him still dancing with the townsfolk.

"Why?" Osmund asked. "You don't care for the taste?" He practically had to shout to make himself heard.

Emerald shrugged. "'Tis never wise fer a homeless orphan girl ta fall low with drink, now innit? Nary ends well."

"Emerald, my dear, you are as wise as you are beautiful," Osmund said. Then a thought occurred to him. "And you are very beautiful, of course. I realize that would not have been much of a compliment if I thought otherwise."

Emerald's cheeks flushed. "And ye, dear Oz, be frightfully drunk."

"Right again!" Osmund said, sharing a laugh with her. He found himself hopelessly enchanted by her Donnelish accent. From the mouth of anyone else, the Donnelish accent was pedestrian and vexing; one might even call it vulgar. But from Emerald, it was beautiful.

The roar of the tavern seemed to fade into the distance. For a moment, they simply smiled at each other.

Emerald was the first to break eye contact. "I be off to bed, then."

"Well, a gentleman always stands when a lady leaves the table," he replied. He leaned on the table for support as he rose on unsteady feet.

No one had ever stood when Emerald left a table before. She watched him steady himself with a grin stretching ear to ear, then she kissed him on the cheek before turning toward the staircase.

Osmund pressed his hand to his cheek. He felt so light he risked floating away with the smallest breeze. Emerald turned back to look at him once more before climbing the stairs. Osmund collapsed back into his chair smiling so hard his cheeks hurt. Kailem was still surrounded by men at the bar. Several young maidens had joined him as well looking for any excuse to close the distance between them. Kailem made it easy for the closest one when he put his arm around her and pulled her close.

Osmund shook as someone unexpectedly sat in Emerald's chair. It was the Blackbird recruiter, Livia Yannsin.

"It's you! The right sort from this morning!" Livia said. She seemed as drunk as Kailem.

"It's you! The... Blackbird lady!" Osmund returned in kind.

"Was that your lady I saw leaving the table?" she asked.

"Who, Emerald?" Osmund looked into his wine considering how to respond. "No, no, just a good friend is all," he said with a hint of sadness in his voice.

"So, you are unattached, then. Lucky me," she said. Osmund's head shot up. His cheeks turned the same shade as the wine in his glass. He looked back down and took another sip.

Livia leaned in as if to whisper, but the tavern was so loud she still had to shout at him. "Tell me, love. Have you given any thought to my invitation this morning?"

"Yes, yes I have, quite a bit, actually," Osmund said.

Livia reached forward and placed her hand on top of Osmund's. "It's so good to meet another sage enthusiast, like myself. We're a rare breed nowadays, are we not?"

"We are indeed," Osmund said, feeling both flattered and vindicated. "And I have a secret to tell a fellow enthusiast. Today we found clues to the secret city of Andalaya."

The woman's eyes went wide at the revelation, all traces of inebriation suddenly vanishing. Osmund relished her reaction.

"Impossible," Livia said. "You must tell me everything."

"And I *will* tell you everything!" He proceeded to give her a full account of everything that had transpired since the day he boarded *The Flying Manta*. Livia listened intently, absorbing every word that came out of his mouth.

Kailem, still surrounded by young maidens at the bar, saw Osmund drunkenly running his mouth to a pretty woman. *Good for him*, he thought. Then he recognized the woman Osmund was talking to. Kailem excused himself, despite the immediate rise in pouting faces from the ladies around him, and returned to Osmund.

"Come with me, Oz, I need to speak with you." He grabbed Osmund by the elbow.

"But I was just..." Osmund tried to protest, but he was already being pulled out of his chair. He turned back to Livia. "I will be but a moment."

Kailem pulled Osmund through the crowd until he was satisfied no one was listening.

"What exactly were you telling her?"

"We were talking all about the sages," Osmund said excitedly. He stood up straight, and a burp echoed up his throat.

"And what did you tell her?"

"Well, everything," he said honestly.

Kailem exhaled, grit his teeth, and shook his head. "You should not have done that."

Osmund lowered his head like a scolded pup.

Kailem thought for a moment. "We are leaving at first light, so perhaps it will not matter. But straight to bed, for both of us," he instructed.

"Yes, sir," Osmund said with a salute.

Livia eyed them as they climbed the staircase.

Back in their room, Emerald was already asleep under her covers. Osmund collapsed into the second bed and was asleep before his head settled on the pillow.

Kailem rolled out the blankets on the wooden floor and made a bed for himself. He placed his hands behind his head and closed his eyes. As tired as he was, the sounds of the tavern below kept him from immediately falling asleep.

His thoughts found their way back to the Baylor Estate, to the first time he heard about the Sages. This whole journey across Iria spawned from a poem Osmund happened to read, after Emerald happened to pick out the Codex Andala out of all the books in Osmund's room, and that poem happened to refer to a natural rock feature Kailem had happened to visit only months prior. It all seemed so improbable.

And yet, he had been right. They had found all the clues and solved a centuries old riddle. No one could convince him it was all coincidence. There had to be a reason for it all, a purpose. He couldn't say for the life of him what that purpose was, but there was comfort in the thought. That comfort lulled him to sleep despite the clamor downstairs.

Later that night, their bedroom door creaked open. Kailem didn't hear it, nor did he hear bootsteps on the timber floor as a brute crept across the room. He hadn't even stirred until someone held him by his tunic, and his eyes blinked open just as a fist collided with his forehead. Normally, one punch would not have rendered the trained Mariner unconscious, but normally he was not so drunk either.

Emerald awoke to the sound of men apprehending Kailem. She saw him with a black sack over his head and his hands being tied behind his back. She screamed, but to the tavern patrons downstairs it would have been less than a whisper amid their raucous singing. She scurried to the corner of her bed with her back against the wall, trembling.

Her screaming did manage to rouse Osmund, but there was little the young nobleman could do about it. Within moments, all three had black sacks over their heads. The intruders dragged them down the stairs, out the back door, and disappeared.

Chapter Twenty-Three

Ji-Bora

37th Day of Summer, 897 G.C.

The evening after the Battle of Tarwick, Mokain tossed and turned on the cot of his private tent while memories of the morning's battle haunted his thoughts. He could recall every man he had killed, could see the pain and fear in their eyes as they met their end. He could still feel in his hands the moment his swords punctured flesh and cut through bone, sending men to the Great Unknown.

There was no glory in war; he knew that now. He felt betrayed by the men who had trained him, by the historians who gave ancient conquerors names like "the great" and "the mighty." There was nothing great or mighty about war, nothing noble about leading a group of men to die for the vanity of their king.

While the terrors of war replayed in Mokain's mind, the sound of revelry invaded their camp. The Tarwick villagers were celebrating their battalion's victory and had even sent them sweet meats and barrels of ale to thank them. Although most of the soldiers partook in the revelry, Mokain wasn't seen the rest of the night.

It was nearly dawn when he finally abandoned the hope of falling asleep. He stepped out of his tent into the moonlight, breathing in the moist night air. All the fires in their camp had been put out, but the gilded moon was full that night and it bathed the camp in a soft glow. He meandered aimlessly through the rows of canvas tents, lost in his thoughts, the grass and dirt crunching under his feet as he walked.

He left Tao and Koa in the tent. When he didn't feel them shift on his hip as he walked, he realized this was the first time in months he had been without them. That fact bothered him.

He eventually found his way to the only men awake in camp, the guards watching over the Shinda prisoners. The prisoners were huddled in a circle, still in their bloodied and torn uniforms, with iron shackles connecting their ankles. Their wounds had been bandaged, but they sat in the cold dirt shivering in the open air. A dozen Cavander guards in warm clothing, including Sergeant Shaw, encircled them standing next to torches stuck in the ground.

Mokain recalled the doubts he had shared with Conroy about whether these men were actually Shinda. They certainly looked the part, but he couldn't escape the feeling something wasn't right.

Mokain approached Sergeant Shaw, who squinted at him from a distance, then stood tall with a salute once he recognized his commanding officer.

Mokain returned the salute. "Sergeant Shaw, you're on watch? Why didn't you assign your men to it?"

"They need the rest, sir," Shaw said.

Mokain nodded. "How long have you been on watch?"

"Less than an hour. This is the last watch before sunrise."

"And how many prisoners do we have?"

"Forty-seven."

"Do we know their names and ranks?"

"No, sir. None of them are speaking."

Mokain nodded thoughtfully. "Walk with me."

Sergeant Shaw carried the torch behind Mokain as they circled the prisoners. They walked slowly, appraising each Shinda as they went. These were bitter, callous men. Most avoided eye-contact, although a few stared back in defiance.

Mokain spotted a young Shinda huddled near the center of the group. The boy's hair was thin, his eyes were sunken, and the skin was tight over his cheekbones. He was shivering more than most, and there was fear in his eyes.

"Him," Mokain said. Sergeant Shaw unsheathed his sword and told the prisoners to move aside, then unlocked the young man from his shackles.

The Shinda prisoner was moved into Mokain's personal tent and made to wait for over an hour. When Mokain finally entered, Lord Menden and Lieutenant Wyndell were with him. Chairs were brought to them while the prisoner sat on Mokain's cot. The young man made himself as small as he could. He refused to look at them, bracing for the torture that was sure to come.

"What's your name, soldier?" Mokain asked.

The prisoner didn't move. His eyes remained fixed on the ground.

"How long have you been in the army?"

Silence.

"You don't want to say anything. I understand. I'm sure you've heard terrible things about what happens to prisoners of war. You must be terrified."

The young man's right hand shook, and he gripped it tightly with his left, his mind likely racing with all the different methods the Cavanders had for inflicting pain.

"I'm also aware that many young men join the army just so they have something to eat and a warm place to sleep."

The Shinda's eyes looked up to Mokain for just a moment, then fell back to the dirt floor.

"You must be starving after that battle, and I can't imagine you got much sleep huddled out in that field." Mokain stood and opened the tent door. A group of soldiers came in with a small table and arranged a breakfast of bacon, eggs, hot oatmeal, and a goblet of violet wine. Mokain took a bite of the eggs, then drank from the goblet. The prisoner stared as his captor chewed and swallowed.

"Feel free to eat as much as you like," Mokain said, "then sleep. We'll speak again later once you've rested."

Mokain and his associates left the tent, leaving the prisoner alone with the food. At first, the young man didn't move, but soon they could hear him eating and drinking like it was his first meal in weeks.

They re-entered the tent hours later, after the sun was high overhead. The sleeping Shinda didn't even stir when they sat down. He did, however, awake at the smell of lunch being served. Instead of the usual soldier's rations, Mokain had a meal brought in from the village: freshly baked bread, artisan meats, and cream of sweet potato soup. The prisoner sat up on the cot, confused.

"Good morning. Well, afternoon, to be technical," Mokain said. "I trust you slept well."

The prisoner's eyes fixed on the food.

"I hope by now you see you have nothing to fear from us, despite what you may have heard. We are more than willing to treat you decently, provided you are willing to provide us with some information."

The prisoner's eyes moved from the food to Mokain, then back to the food, and finally settled back down on the dirt floor.

"Of course, the alternative is we take you back to the other prisoners. You'll insist you kept your mouth shut, of course. But, given that you've been gone for more than seven hours now, and there's no sign you've been tortured in any way, I doubt they will believe you."

The prisoner thought for a moment, then moved to the edge of the cot, still avoiding eye contact.

"Why don't we start with your name?" Mokain suggested.

"Ji-Bora," the young Shinda man replied. His voice cracked as he spoke.

"Nice to meet you, Ji-Bora. My name is Mokain Roka." He moved a plate of food and a bowl of soup in front of the prisoner. "I'll make you a deal, Ji-Bora. For every question you answer, you can take a bite of food. You already told me your name, so why don't you break off a piece of bread for yourself?"

A feather of steam escaped the bread as Ji-Bora tore off a section. He put the piece in his mouth, and his eyes rolled back as chewed.

"Let's try an. Try, try the soup next."

Ji-Bora took a spoonful of soup and savored it as the warmth passed over his tongue.

"Now tell me, does your army fight in service of the King of Shinda?"

Ji-Bora's head shot up at the question. He looked from Mokain to the other two Cavanders beside him, then shook his head.

"As I suspected. Then whom do you serve?"

Ji-Bora was allowed to eat freely as he explained who the army was and for whom they fought. The more he ate, the more freely he spoke. Soon Mokain no longer needed to ask him questions. Ji-Bora had become a free-flowing fountain of information. He explained he had been recruited into a group of revolutionaries called the Blackbird Society. They posed as Shinda Warriors and attacked villages throughout the Valley of Oxmere to the south. Similar attacks were being coordinated all throughout Iria. Ji-Bora said their purpose was to start a war between the various kingdoms of Iria, although he couldn't speak to their ultimate purpose. He also told them that after their squad had attacked the village of Tarwick, they were supposed to march south to some place called the Riverkeep in the Valleys of Veydala to join the other Blackbirds, for what purpose he couldn't say.

Mokain and his associates left the tent, allowing Ji-Bora to finish his meal in peace.

"This is troubling news, indeed," Lord Menden said as they made their way back to the command tent. The sentry stood tall and saluted as they passed.

"I agree, but can the information be trusted?" Mokain asked rhetorically. "Lieutenant Wyndell, see that our friend in there is given enough coins and provisions to travel back to Shinda. Give him some non-military clothing as well."

Lieutenant Wyndell saluted and left.

"What are you going to do?" Lord Menden asked.

"First, I need to write to the Prince. Then we'll march south through Roserock Basin. If similar deceits are occurring throughout Iria, we'll probably find more reports in the Basin. If we do, then we'll investigate this Riverkeep."

Chapter Twenty-Four

KIDNAPPED

37th Day of Summer, 897 G.C.

Kailem was jostled about, in what he could not be sure, but it was certainly some kind of carriage. The more important questions were who had taken him, where were they taking him, and how could he escape?

He had only a vague memory of being kidnapped. He remembered a noise that woke him, but before he could focus his eyes, his world had gone dark. The light hadn't returned since. It took only a few moments for him to realize the darkness was, in fact, just a black sack placed over his head, but he had no reference for how long he had been unconscious. It took him longer than it should have to bring his panic under control.

With his hands tied behind his back, Kailem was forced to rub his head against the floor and pull at the sack with his teeth. After several minutes and a considerable amount of difficulty, he pulled the sack over his head.

The sunlight seared his irises, and he squinted and blinked as his eyes adjusted to the bright afternoon. Then he took stock of his surroundings. There were two other individuals with him with similar sacks over their heads, clearly Osmund and Emerald. They were in the back of a wagon with a locked cage over their heads. If he rose to his knees, his head would surely touch the top. The terrain looked similar to what they had seen the day previous; hopefully, that meant they hadn't been taken far. They traveled a road that followed the base of the foothills.

Kailem maneuvered like a worm on the wagon floor until his back was against Emerald's. She let out a scream when his hands touched hers.

"Emerald! Emerald!" he hushed. "Calm down. It's me, Kailem. I'm trying to untie your hands."

Emerald quieted, but her breathing was still labored and audible. The rope around her hands was tied better than the string had been around his neck, but not by much. Clearly, their kidnappers were not sailors. It took Kailem less than a minute to free her hands.

She immediately ripped the sack off her head, using brute force to peel it over her head rather than bother to untie the string. She blinked against the sunlight while her eyes adjusted. Then she untied Kailem's hands, and then Osmund's.

Emerald and Osmund looked at Kailem the way that frightened children look to their parents, gauging just how frightened they should be. As long as Kailem didn't look panicked, they didn't need to panic—too much.

"Is everyone okay?" Kailem asked.

They both nodded affirmatively. Osmund massaged his wrists, which were red and swollen from the rope. Emerald had moved her back into the corner with her arms wrapped around her knees, holding them close to her chest.

"Who do you suppose took us?" Osmund asked.

"I haven't seen them yet, but I have a pretty good idea." Kailem analyzed the metal bars and the lock on the cage.

"We can write to my parents; they will pay any ransom, I'm sure of it. But we're so far from home, I don't know how long it will take for the gold to arrive."

"I don't think gold is what they're after," Kailem said.

"What then?" Osmund asked.

Kailem said nothing. He reached instinctively for Malua at his side, but his dagger was gone. He looked around the wagon, but he knew he wouldn't find it. Disarming him would have been the first thing they did. He felt for the pearl tied around his neck. Fortunately, they hadn't found it. He pulled it out from under his shirt and rolled the pearl between his fingers.

Kailem crawled around the wagon, staring intently at the wooden floor. Osmund and Emerald eyed him curiously, wondering if their kidnappers had hit him a little too hard in the head. Kailem found a long sliver of wood protruding from the floor and pried it loose with his fingernails. Then he used the splinter to pick the lock.

At first, Osmund and Emerald watched intently, certain their freedom was moments away. Then seconds turned to minutes, and it became clear Kailem wasn't entirely sure what he was doing. They had all but abandoned hope when they heard a metallic *click*. Kailem removed the lock and slowly opened the cage door.

He placed a finger to his lips, telling them to be quiet. Then he motioned for them to slip out of the back of the wagon. Emerald went first, and Osmund was close behind.

"Hey!" a man's voice called out.

The wagon came to an abrupt stop.

"Run!" Kailem commanded. He jumped out of the cage door and followed after Emerald and Osmund, who were sprinting down the road. He saw out of the corner of his eye a rider on horseback who had been following alongside the wagon.

The rider swung at Kailem's back with a club. Kailem tried to dodge the blow, but he misjudged the rider's speed and was knocked to the ground. The rider did the same to Osmund, knocking the air out of his lungs. Then he rode out in front of Emerald, holding the tip of the club inches from her chest.

"Well, you are a lively bunch!" a woman said, approaching behind them. They recognized her Norvian accent immediately.

"Secure them again," Livia Yannsin said. "Don't bother with the hoods, but make sure the lock is shut tight this time."

In moments, they were back in their cage, this time with their hands tied in front of them. Emerald retreated again to her corner and wrapped her arms around her knees. There were two men taking orders from the Blackbird recruiter. One was a thin redheaded man, the other was tall and brawny with blonde hair and a blonde beard. Kailem watched the skinny redhead put together an improvised, haphazard knot around Kailem's hands.

"I guess this is as good a time for lunch as any, wouldn't you say, boys?" Livia said. Her two henchmen muttered their agreement and took out provisions of dried meat and fruit. Livia carried a large bag from the wagon and sat next to them.

"Now, you, love. The short one, what did you say your name was?" Livia asked.

"Um, Osmund?" he responded. Kailem's head darted toward him in disappointment.

"Actually, your friend here said it was Quinn, but no offense taken. I, too, would have given a fake name. Still, it is a pleasure to meet you again, Osmund. I must say, the three of you make an awfully peculiar traveling company. A Devonian nobleman, a Donnelish peasant, and a Mariner out of water. I'm surprised you didn't throw in a Vangorian sheepherder for good measure."

Livia thought herself clever, but when no one laughed with her, she continued. "I'm sure by now you've sorted out why you're here, so are you going to make things easy on yourself? Just tell us what we want to know?"

Osmund's face pinched, then his eyes searched into the distance.

"Oh dear, perhaps you haven't sorted it," Livia said. "I may have credited you with more intelligence than was deserved, love. The sages, my dear man. You told me last night you knew the way to the fabled 'Andalaya'." She spoke the name as if it were a magical incantation. "Now, you're going to take us there."

"None of us know the way to Andalaya," Kailem said. "Osmund had too much to drink last night; he spouts absurdities when he's drunk. Remember that night you went on and on about how you could turn any piece of bread into a cake?"

It was the first nonsensical thing Kailem could think of. Osmund stared at him blankly.

"Well, of course, he doesn't remember," Kailem continued. "He never remembers anything the next morning. The point is, you can't trust a word he says once there's more than a glass of wine in him."

Livia stared at them, studying their faces. Her two henchmen sat chewing their dried meat.

"I see," Livia said, "and that must have been why you rushed to pull him away from me before he could say anything more, to keep him from spouting more harmless nonsense. No, I suspect the opposite is true, love. You've heard the saying 'there is truth in wine', yes? I think your friend does know the path to Andalaya, and you know he does."

Livia stopped to take a bite of an apple.

"Do you know why I am so confident in my suspicions?" she continued. "It is in no small measure because of this." She reached into the bag at her feet and retrieved a large leather-bound book. The Codex Andala. Osmund threw himself against the iron bars.

"Hey! That's mine, give it back!"

"It *was* yours, to that extent you are correct," Livia said, flipping through the book's pages. Her minions laughed through mouths full of food. "Some fascinating information in this book. I'm sure I've never seen anything quite like it. If anyone could find Andalaya, it would probably be someone who owned a book like this. Now, I haven't had a chance to read all of it, obviously, I only just acquired it last night. Well, you were there, you remember. Anyway, while I haven't read all of it, I'd be willing to bet there are clues in here as to Andalaya's location. And I think you've already discovered those clues, so you're going to lead us to it. And before you say no, let me remind you that we have three of you, and we only need one, if you catch my meaning."

Livia let her words hang as her companions finished their lunch.

Back on the road, Livia took the horse and rode beside the wagon. The road was poorly maintained, and the three prisoners were tossed about, occasionally hitting their heads against the metal cage.

Something occurred to Osmund. "We haven't given you any directions to Andalaya, so where are you taking us?"

"To the Society, my dear boy!" Livia said. "The Blackbird Society. There are quite a few men who will be awfully eager to talk to you."

Kailem snickered.

"Is something humorous?" she asked from atop of her horse.

Kailem adjusted in the cramped cage. "I'm sorry, it's just, why the Blackbird? Why not... the eagle or the bear or... or anything but a..." he laughed again despite his efforts.

Livia showed no emotion. She had clearly been asked this before.

"True, the blackbird may not be the most menacing or imposing creature on its own, but when they need to, blackbirds come together. Just a few at first, then by the dozen, then by swarms, until there are thousands, even millions, so many that they block out the noonday sun, all flying in unison, as if they were of one mind and one purpose."

Kailem looked to Osmund for confirmation. Osmund nodded. "It is called a murmuration. I have read about them and even seen it once for myself. It is quite a sight to behold."

"That it is, my dear boy," Livia said. "And the Blackbird Society is no less impressive. None of us may have what it takes to oppose the aristocracy on our own, but banded together, we block out the sun. We have two days until we reach the camp, Love, you'll see it then. We are, as you said, quite a sight to behold."

Livia sat tall in her saddle, an arrogant smile across her face.

"Would you like to know why I joined this revolutionary society of ours?" Livia asked. The woman was far too fond of words, and her prisoners had long since tired of her prattle, but Livia was intent on making the most of a captive audience.

"I'll assume you do," she said. "Would you believe I was married once? A blushing young bride, I was, eager to have a family. My loving husband was a humble sheep farmer, and together we worked the land side by side. Our days were full of rapture and bliss. Sometimes, when I close my eyes, I still remember the smell of the fields after a light rain, the sound of the sheep bleating when we called them, or how my husband would surprise me with a romp in the hay."

Emerald recoiled at the uncouth remark, which Livia seemed to take pleasure in.

Livia continued, "But although we worked the land just as my husband's father had his whole life, and his father before him, back seven generations, we did not own the land. No, that land, for no good reason I can see, was the property of a mid-ranking nobleman, an earl I believe. And you see, the earl required that we purchase all our tools and supplies from his 'lordship', at a cost that he set himself, and we were often obliged to purchase them on credit."

"Well, one autumn night, there was an unseasonable freeze. Only lasted the one night, but that one night was all it took. We lost over half our flock before the sun returned. We begged for more time to pay the debt, but that earl, he had a better idea. He exercised his right to restitution through enslavement. Sent my beau to the copper mines and left me out in the cold, hoping I'd turn to the oldest profession for my keep, no doubt. Not two months later, I heard my husband had died in a mining collapse. We were honest, hardworking folk, but to our 'lord' we were no different from the sheep we raised. That's how noblemen see people like us."

She paused to look Osmund in the eye, and he wilted under her stare.

"In the end, the earl destroyed our lives for a bit of fun and a few extra coins. So, when the Blackbirds found me, and told me how they were going to bring down the entire aristocracy, I didn't hesitate."

The prisoners blessed the moons when she finally finished. Livia had told a sympathetic tale, to be sure, but any chance she had at converting them to her cause had disappeared the moment she had kidnapped them.

Night came. Livia told her henchmen to pull the wagon off the road to camp for the night. The Blackbirds made themselves a meal of beans and bread while they sat around the fire. Osmund's stomach rumbled audibly. The tall minion caught him staring at their food. He scooped a spoonful of beans and flung it at the wagon, prompting a laugh from his comrades.

The night drew cold. Livia practiced throwing Kailem's dagger at a nearby tree, unable to penetrate the tree trunk. The two henchmen passed a wineskin between them until they fell asleep by the fire. Livia took out a blanket and laid down by the fire between them.

Kailem waited until he was sure the three Blackbirds were asleep. He made quick work of their ropes and found another sliver of wood from the wagon floor. He refused to let Osmund and Emerald down yet again. This time, he picked the lock in seconds.

Livia stirred.

The three prisoners froze with bated breath, but the woman didn't wake.

"Make for the hills," Kailem whispered. "It will be harder for them to track us."

Osmund and Emerald nodded. Their steps were as light as the morning dew, but in the quiet of the night, the gravel screamed under their feet. The hillside was steep and there was no trail for them to follow. Kailem took the lead, with Emerald between them and Osmund at the rear. In the dark of night, with no lantern and but a sliver of moonlight overhead, each step was a struggle to know where to place their feet, but each step placed more distance between them and the sleeping Blackbirds.

Osmund let out a sudden yelp. He fell to the ground, gripping his ankle, and rolled several feet down the hill.

Kailem turned to Emerald. "Go."

Emerald sprinted up the hill. She didn't look back as the Blackbirds chased after them. She followed an erratic path, just as she had while evading the Royal Guard back in Rhinegard, and didn't slow down as the voices faded behind her.

Kailem ran back for Osmund. He wrapped Osmund's arm around his neck and lifted him to his feet. Osmund winced and favored his injured foot as he hobbled up the hillside, leaning on Kailem for support.

The sound of the Blackbirds chasing them grew louder. Osmund slipped again, this time falling to one knee. The light from the Blackbirds' torches shone through the trees. Outrunning them wasn't an option.

Kailem pulled Osmund into a nearby bush and waited for the Blackbirds to pass. Their eyes were useless in the dark. They waited in silence for the sound of footsteps. The glow of torches fingered its way through the branches that surrounded them. Dead leaves crunched nearby. Twigs cracked. Grown men huffed, out of breath. The sounds grew louder, then grew softer as their assailants made their way farther up the hill. Kailem was itching to flee. The faint glow of torchlight finally disappeared.

"Let's go," he whispered. Osmund leaned on him and together they slowly stood, squinting in the dark.

A sword unsheathed.

They turned to see the tall minion with a sword pointed at Osmund's neck.

"Down here!" the man bellowed.

Kailem cursed himself. He had been too eager to escape. He should have known better, should have waited until he was sure the coast was clear.

In seconds, Livia and the red-haired goon were back down the hill, torches in hand.

"Where's the girl?" Livia asked.

Osmund and Kailem said nothing.

"Well, I suppose it doesn't matter, loves. I did say we only needed one of you." Livia snapped her fingers, and the henchmen marched Osmund and Kailem back down the hill to their cage. Their hands were tied behind their backs, their feet bound together, and their elbows tied to the cage wall. They spent a shivering, painful night behind bars.

Chapter Twenty-Five

Royal Reprimand

40th Day of Summer, 897 G.C.

Prince Aedon sat in the royal council chamber holding a folded sheet of paper in his hands. This was the fourth meeting he had attended in the chamber, and its opulence was losing influence. The room was quickly becoming the place where his father's ineptitude was destroying the kingdom.

The double doors to the council room were pulled open and the entire council rose to its feet. King Byron entered, his face pinched with annoyance. He marched to his seat without a word.

"Be seated," he grumbled. The council members promptly obeyed. "Well, son, you called us all to this emergency session, you'd best tell us why."

Aedon stood and unfolded the paper in his hand. "Many weeks past, I sent my First Officer, Lord Roka, on an assignment to the borderlands. Some of you may question my judgment in sending him, a foreigner, to lead this expedition, but you should know that Lord Menden is attending him and providing him counsel. You all know Lord Menden, and his reputation is above reproach, so know that Lord Roka's report was made under Lord Menden's watchful eye."

Aedon was relieved to see appeasement in the council members' faces.

He continued, "Lord Roka led a battalion to the village of Tarwick in the Westham Plains. From there, squadrons were sent in all directions, collecting reports from nearly every village in the western borderlands. His report arrived today by carrier hawk. It is as we have feared. More than half of the villages reported raids occurring in their land. Some gave reports of foreign commoners leading armed raids against them, but most reported their attackers wore Shinda and Àramen military uniforms."

The council began to mutter and shift in their seats.

"What is worse, a Shinda regiment of four-hundred warriors attacked our battalion while their squadrons were abroad and their numbers depleted. Fortunately, our battalion was able to turn what was certain death into a victory, under my First Officer's leadership."

"This is, of course, only a summary report. His full report will arrive weeks hence by messenger, but we needn't wait. There can no longer be any doubt on the matter." The Prince handed the report to his father for verification, then placed both hands on the table. "Our lands are under attack. Whether we like it or not, war is upon us, and we *must* respond." He pounded his fist on the word *must*.

His words drew a murmur of agreement from several council members. He looked to Lord Arturri, who gave him a reaffirming nod.

The King finished the report and tossed it on the table to think for a moment.

Aedon grew uncomfortable in the silence. "Father, you said that if the rumors of attacks on the Borderlands could be confirmed, you would approve a military response. Well, we have proved the rumors. Now is the time to act." He enunciated each word for emphasis.

Several council members muttered their approval when Aedon sat.

"I said we would *discuss* a military response, not that I would approve one." The King's stare lingered on his son before turning to the rest of the council. "I will send emissaries to Shinda and Ârema. The King of Ârema has always been reasonable, and I consider the King of Shinda a friend, of sorts. I will send both emissaries with an entire legion of infantry as a reminder of the force we wield. If we are unable to resolve the issue diplomatically, I will authorize military action, but not until we have exhausted every other option before us."

Aedon clenched his fists. "Father, it's too late for that. It took months for us to confirm these rumors, and who knows how much that delay has cost us. Sending emissaries will take three months at least. We don't have time to..."

"Aedon, you will sit and be silent." The King's words were not loud, but they were heavy, and the Prince crumbled to his chair. King Byron looked each councilman in the eye, including his son; all but Lord Arturri shrank under his glare.

"I have given my word, and it is final," the King said. "We will say no more on the matter. Meeting adjourned."

No one moved at first. The weight of the King's tone kept them pinned to their seats. After exchanging glances, they rose from their chairs one by one and made for the doors. Aedon stood to do the same, but the King grabbed him by the crook of his arm and stood.

"While the Royal Council is convened, you will address me as 'My King' or 'Your Majesty', never as 'father'. And you will never raise your voice to me again." He let go of his son's arm without asking if he understood and dismissed him with a nod.

Aedon turned immediately so his father wouldn't see the fury on his face. He clenched his teeth as he walked away to keep from speaking his mind.

Lord Arturri met Aedon just before he left the council chamber.

"You did the right thing, Aedon; never doubt it. Integrity is honorable, even when praise is wanting."

Aedon was fuming. "He can't... I just...." The crown prince wanted to kick something, but Lord Arturri put a tender hand on his shoulder.

"I know, son, I know," Leonin said in a low voice, not quite a whisper. "Your father can be difficult, but he is the King, and heavy is the head that wears the crown. You will learn this for yourself one day, and I have reason to believe you will be the greatest king that Cavandel has seen in centuries. The next Cavan Kohel, I dare say."

Aedon looked to Lord Arturri, still fuming but regaining some semblance of control. "Thank you, my lord. I mean, Leonin." He spoke in a hushed tone similar to Leonin's.

"You needn't thank me for telling the truth, son. But I fear for the welfare of the kingdom if the raids on the borderlands are not soon addressed. The situation is more dire than most realize. I fear there may not be much of a kingdom left by the time the crown passes to you." Leonin let his warning hang in the air before continuing, "but, there is nothing you can do about it now. Go enjoy your day."

Aedon nodded and left the council chamber, feigning composure.

A moment later, King Byron arrived at Leonin's side. "What did you tell him?" the King asked.

"I told him your experience had given you wisdom and he would be wise to learn from it."

Byron scoffed. "Little chance of that. The boy is headstrong. Stubbornly so."

"As were we at his age, I'm afraid," Leonin said. "But you handle him well, Your Majesty."

Byron and Leonin walked slowly together down the crowded palace halls. Leonin's personal guard, Daron, walked just far enough behind them to give their conversation privacy.

"I don't know what caused you to finally come to my side, Leonin, but I am grateful."

"I finally saw reason, Your Majesty. My apologies it took me so long to see, but I am only as useful as my opinion is honest."

"Yes, well, it wouldn't kill you to voice your support during the council," the King said.

Leonin gripped his hands behind his lower back as he walked. "Your word is law, my king. I hardly believe my support would strengthen it. My counsel is all that has value. But as I am a foreigner, my position on your council is tenuous. I thought it unwise to offend the other council members more than my presence already has."

"I should think you ought to fear the wrath of your king more than the wrath of your king's councilors."

Leonin smiled. "Oh, you frighten me to my very core, Your Majesty; I assure you."

Kyra sat patiently while Martina combed her hair. Ember slept peacefully by the fire, snoring ever so quickly. The room was tranquil until Aedon threw open the door and entered like a storm.

"Leave us," the Prince commanded.

The abrupt command made all three of them jump. Martina dropped the brush on the vanity with an inelegant clank and hurried from the room.

Aedon grabbed a flower vase from the nearby table and threw it against the wall, shattering it. He sat on the bed with his back to Kyra and ran his hands through his hair.

Kyra walked around the bed, put her arms around Aedon's neck, and held his forehead against her chest. Aedon ran his hands up the back of her legs, then wrapped his arms around her waist.

"Whatever it is, I'm here," she said.

Aedon leaned back and searched for words. "It's my father. He makes decisions out of fear. And his incompetence is going to destroy the kingdom, but there's nothing I can do about it."

"Surely you exaggerate, my love. Your father would never destroy the kingdom." Kyra sat next to him and rubbed his back.

"He refuses to send our armies to protect the borders. By the time we convince him to act, we will have lost all the Westham Plains, maybe even the Roserock Basin as well. Our enemies could be at our gates, feasting on provisions stolen from our own lands, and still he would not act."

Kyra breathed through her nose. "Whatever happens, I take comfort knowing you will reign someday. You will be an amazing king, my love. But is there nothing we can do in the meantime?"

While Aedon searched for an answer, Ember jumped onto the bed and settled on Kyra's lap. Aedon stood and paced the room, struggling with what he had to say.

"I know of only one solution, and I am an evil man just for thinking it."

"Aedon, you could never be evil. Tell me your solution, please."

Aedon took a deep breath. "Do you recall our discussion that night we walked alone in the palace gardens? You said that if the King were to pass away, the Court would mourn him, but it would be a blessing for the kingdom if it meant a stronger king would take his place."

"I remember," she said, turning on the bed to face him. "It was a hypothetical, such as if he were to take ill or fall in battle. I believe you said, 'the good of the whole matters more than the good of any of its parts, even if the part in question was the King.'"

Aedon nodded. Then his mettle failed him. "Never mind," he said. He shook his head and turned towards the hearth.

A moment of silence passed between them. The only sound was the crackling of the fire.

"Perhaps the King needs to die," Kyra said. Her voice was doleful and soft, using the words her parents had taught her.

Aedon whipped his head toward her. His beautiful, tender-hearted fiancé had just committed treason. Even uttering those words was punishable by death. To say those words in front of him meant, she trusted him with her life. Of course, they were the very words he wanted to say, but hearing them said aloud stole his nerve.

Kyra scratched Ember's chin, pretending all was well and normal. "I will defer entirely to your judgment, Aedon. Only you can make this decision. I'll be at your side, no matter what."

Kyra had played her part beautifully, and in her mind, that was all it was. She was an actress in a theater reciting the lines her parents had written for her, because she knew if she did not act like this was all pretend, she never could have done it.

Aedon slumped down on the bed. "If we *were* to do it, hypothetically, how would we go about it?" He spoke with melancholy, as if already mourning his father.

"Well," she said thoughtfully, "I don't know. I suppose he would need to die publicly to avoid any suspicion. And it would have to look like he died of natural causes." She paused, feigning that an idea occurred to her. "I know of a poison we could administer by degrees. It's called 'Jimson Weed'. Members of the Court would see his health failing for days before his death, so no one would suspect foul play."

"And you have such a poison? Here?" Aedon asked.

"Don't be silly. What reason would I have to just keep such things lying around in my quarters?" she said with a grin. "But I can obtain it, should the need arise."

Aedon rubbed his face as if trying to wake himself from a dream. "I can't believe we are even discussing this. And how do you know of such things?"

At that moment, Kyra was grateful to her parents. They had prepared her for every question Aedon might ask. "I learned it from my governess as a girl."

"Your governess taught you how to poison people?" he asked incredulously.

"Of course not," she said, as if that should have been obvious. "She taught me about antidotes. She said the wife of a nobleman needs to be able to recognize the signs of poisoning so she can know which antidote to administer when time is of the essence. I never anticipated I'd ever use the knowledge, but it stuck with me, nonetheless."

Aedon accepted her explanation, as ridiculous as it was. He walked to her balcony to view the city below, the city that would suffer if he did not act.

"Let me think on it," he finally said. "Perhaps I can try once more to convince my father. If I do decide this course is best, I will speak to you again."

"I believe that is the wisest course, my love. You will make a fine king, indeed. And I will be honored to be your queen."

Aedon leaned down, cupped her cheek, and kissed her deeply. The kiss almost made her tell him the truth. It made her want to take it all back and run away with him. But she stayed silent. Aedon let his forehead rest against hers. Then he excused himself for the night.

Kyra sat, breathing deeply. The memory of Aedon's face dead in a misty field flashed again through Kyra's mind, and she nearly retched into her pillow. She groaned aloud and fell back on her bed, hating herself.

Chapter Twenty-Six

The Sage

37th Day of Summer, 897 G.C.

Emerald kept a safe distance from the Blackbirds. Probably too safe a distance; she was so far away she risked losing them entirely, but in her experience, there was no such thing as being too cautious.

Being kidnapped in the middle of the night had only strengthened that belief. Even though it was a veritable impossibility for the recruiter and her two henchmen to hear her, she still crept carefully along the arid hillside.

More than once she questioned why she stayed, why she risked recapture when there was virtually nothing she could do to free them. But where else would she go? In the past few months, she had come to know the feeling of safety, of friendship, of knowing where her next meal would come from, of having a purpose beyond just surviving. She couldn't go back to living on the streets, picking pockets to pay for her meals. She couldn't go back to another thieving crew surrounded by dangerous, despicable men whose company forced her to sleep with one eye open.

Emerald stood behind an acacia tree, looking around the tree trunk with one eye. The Blackbirds had stopped for lunch. Osmund and Kailem were still tied to the cage wall. As best she could tell, they hadn't been allowed to move in over twelve hours.

Leaves crunched behind her.

Emerald whipped around in a panic. She was so startled that her legs became tangled in the process, and she tumbled to the ground.

A man stood above her, looking calm and gentle. He carried a walking staff, but otherwise appeared to be unarmed. He held up his hands to show he was not a threat. It did little to set her fears at ease.

"Hello there," the man said. "You needn't be afraid, I assure you. In fact, I'm fairly certain you and I have met before."

Emerald's fear turned to confusion.

"Three months ago, I believe it was," the stranger explained, kneeling down to her level. "In Glendown Forest, you said you had just survived a shipwreck."

Emerald stared at his face, then recognized him. "Yer the man from the forest, gave us water and started the fire."

"You are correct, my lady. Elwin of Andil," he said, extending his hand.

Emerald looked at it for a moment, ultimately deciding to accept his help to her feet. She held her arms across her abdomen and kept a distance between them.

"What be ye doing here?" she asked. She looked around to see if he was alone, making sure she wasn't being surrounded.

"The band of outlaws I was tracking, they led me here. But I believe we have a more pressing issue at the moment." Elwin pointed down the hill with his staff.

Emerald looked back at her friends locked in the wagon. "Those men've swords. I don't right know what to do."

"Oh, I shouldn't expect they will prove a challenge."

Elwin walked down the hill on a leisurely stroll, neither hurried nor hesitant, while Emerald followed from a safe distance.

Elwin emerged from the hillside onto the road only a stone's throw from the wagon. The tall minion saw him first, and he tapped the recruiter on the shoulder.

"Can we help you, traveler?" Livia asked when Elwin drew close to their fire.

"Indeed, I do believe you can," Elwin said. "I should consider it most helpful if you would be so kind as to release these fine young men you have here."

"Oz, who is that?" Kailem whispered. His back was to the events unfolding in camp and his bonds prevented him from turning his head. Osmund simply shrugged his shoulders.

Livia motioned to her two henchmen, who drew their weapons. "I'm afraid I can't do that, love. Perhaps we can help you on your way instead." The Blackbirds spread out, ready to flank Elwin from either side.

"Gentlemen, I strongly advise against this," Elwin warned. When the advancing henchmen paid him no mind, he sighed.

The taller of the two charged at him. Elwin pointed his staff at him, then whipped it toward the wagon. Gravity lost its hold on the man, and he flew through the air as if falling sideways. Osmund saw the light around the minion twist and distort, like he was watching the man from underwater. The minion's body collided with the cage wall and dropped to the dirt below.

"What was that?!" Kailem yelled after the henchman's body crashed against the cart. Osmund's face was wide-eyed and speechless.

The redheaded minion turned to stone, his face carved into fear and shock. Elwin had seen this reaction a thousand times before; seeing sagecraft for the first time was difficult for anyone to process. The sage swung his staff sideways, striking the redhead across the cheek. He fell to the ground, knocking over their pot of beans as he collapsed.

"Oz, I can't see. Tell me what's happening," Kailem said. All Osmund could do was stare in disbelief.

Livia ran; this was another common reaction. She made for the foothills, hoping to find cover among the trees. Elwin extended his hand, and she was flown forward through the air, colliding with the very tree she had hoped would have offered protection. All three Blackbirds had been subdued in seconds.

Elwin walked to the cage as casually as if he were perusing a library. At his touch, the ropes loosened and fell from Kailem's wrists and elbows. He did the same to Osmund's. The two boys untied their ankles and scrambled to the far side of the cage like mice cowering in front of an overgrown house cat. Elwin walked around to the cage door and the lock clicked itself open in his hand.

"Stay back!" Kailem yelled. How in Iria was he supposed to threaten this man, he thought? Kailem looked at the three Blackbirds lying unconscious in the dirt, and not knowing what had put them there made the man all the more terrifying, if he even was a man.

Elwin took several steps back and held out his hand, inviting the boys to exit the cage. For several seconds, neither moved. They looked around, wondering what other dangers lay in wait for them.

"It's perfectly safe, I assure you," Elwin said.

Kailem hesitantly stepped down from the cart, followed by Osmund, who was careful to stay behind Kailem at all times. Emerald emerged from the tree line. She ran to the cart, throwing one arm around Kailem and the other around Osmund.

After the shock of seeing her wore off, Kailem guided Emerald behind him and faced the stranger.

"It be aright, Kailem, he be here to help," Emerald explained. "This be the man who helped us in the forest."

That only raised more questions, so many Kailem couldn't settle on just one to ask aloud.

"Pleased to see you once again, young lords," Elwin said. He paused to offer a formal bow. "You needn't worry, I assure you. You may recall at our last meeting I said I was tracking a group of outlaws? Well, these are three of them. You're lucky I came along when I did."

Kailem and Osmund relaxed only slightly, and they kept their distance while Elwin loaded the three unconscious Blackbirds into the wagon. He grabbed each one by the backs of their shirts like he was picking apples out of a barrel and tossed them inside the cage. Kailem couldn't believe his eyes; no man could possibly be that strong.

"The three of you have a choice to make," Elwin said. "Balderlyn is at least a day and a half's journey back in that direction." He pointed down the road. "Without any water or provisions, you're looking at a difficult trek, to say the least, but not an impossible one. In that direction," he said, pointing up the road, "you'll find the village of Oswyn. It's less than three hours away, and I plan on making the trip in this fine wagon here. You're more than welcome to join me."

The decision was obvious.

Osmund and Kailem retrieved their belongings from Livia's bag. Kailem wiped the dirt and grime from Malua and slid it into the sheath at his side. The wagon's driver bench only had room for three, and because Kailem was the largest, he was stuck riding the horse next to the cart. The animal proved just as obstinate as Echo had.

The first half hour of their journey passed in silence. Elwin enjoyed the quiet and the serenity of nature, while the other three struggled to find the nerve to speak. Eventually, Osmund could no longer keep his questions inside.

"You're a sage, aren't you?!" The words suddenly burst out of him.

Elwin smiled. "I wondered how long it would take you to ask me that."

"So you are, aren't you?" Osmund asked again. Elwin replied with a nod, and Osmund suddenly forgot how to speak. "What... how... I mean... ah!"

"You seem to be having trouble finding your words, my young friend," Elwin said.

"How can you be a sage? You're supposed to be extinct. How many of you are there? What abilities do you have? How do you have them? Why don't you make yourselves known? Are those men dead?" He asked his last question, looking at the unconscious bodies behind him.

"Easy, Osmund," Elwin said. "There will be time enough for your questions. For now, I have a question for you. Tell me, what did the three of you do to warrant your incarceration?"

Osmund lowered his head. An uncomfortable silence filled the air until Emerald spoke.

"Thems thought we knew the way ta that secret city o' yers. Andalaya," she confessed. "Had a mind ta force it out o' us."

"But we never would have shown them, sir. Honest," Osmund added.

"I see," Elwin said. "And how did they come to the notion you knew the way to Andalaya?"

"Because we do," Osmund said. His voice was low, as if confessing some reprehensible crime. "We sorted out the clues you left. Well, most of them, and we were confident we could solve the remaining few."

"Clues? What clues?"

"Well, in the poem, of course. The poem that reveals the way to Andalaya."

"There is no poem that reveals anything about Andalaya," Elwin insisted.

Osmund scrunched his face. "Yes, there is. That's what led us here."

"Osmund, the location of Andalaya was one of our most closely guarded secrets. No outsiders were ever permitted to see it. In fact, most of the young initiates of our Order never saw it. So, why would we have left clues that would allow just anyone to find it?"

"Well..." Osmund searched his mind for a response but found none. Kailem and Emerald were equally stunned, as if that should have been obvious all along.

"But there is a poem," Osmund insisted. "It's here, in this book."

Osmund reached beside his feet where he had stashed the Codex Andala. He flipped to the page with the poem and handed it to Elwin. Elwin gave the reins to Emerald and took the book, reading the poem in question.

"Oh yes," Elwin said, recalling a pleasant memory. "I wrote this poem, nearly," he thought for a second, "eighteen centuries ago. I wrote it for a fellow sage who was quite fond of puzzles. You see, we had monasteries throughout Iria, one of which was in the Sidian Islands. My cousin, also a sage, was leading a group of young initiates from the Sidian Islands to a monastery not far from here, a monastery with which the sage was unfamiliar, as it was quite new at the time. He was a good friend of mine, so I wrote the poem as a kind of puzzle for him to figure out the directions. I also left a set of clear directions with one of the initiates, in case the clues proved beyond him. As to how the poem managed to find its way into your book here, I am afraid I am at a loss. What is this?"

"It's a study of the Order," Osmund said flatly. He slumped in his seat, looking dejected and miserable. Elwin flipped through the book's pages.

"I have a question for you," Kailem said from atop his horse. "If you wouldn't mind."

Elwin looked over at him. After a moment, he replied, "I suppose I could indulge a question or two, if only to pass the time."

"You said you tracked these outlaws all the way from Glendown Forest. Why are you so invested in them?"

The question caught Osmund and Emerald's attention as well. Elwin returned the book to Osmund, then took the reins back from Emerald.

"This particular group of outlaws are more dangerous than at first they appear. You three narrowly escaped them in the forest that night we met. After you fell asleep, I managed to find and dispatch a few."

"Thank you for that," Kailem said.

Elwin dipped his head in a nod. "From what I've learned, this group is attempting to foster an insurrection among the kingdoms of Iria. They seek to upset the established order and seize power for themselves. They have grown considerably in numbers, due to their promises of freedom from tyranny and the aristocracy. But to others, they claim to know the mysteries of sagecraft and promise to train them in our ways."

"And you wish to prevent that?" Kailem said.

"I do."

Elwin was stunned by his own candor. The existence of Sagecraft was the very secret he had spent so long protecting. But his instincts on the matter could not be ignored. There was more to this situation than he understood, and he trusted the facts would make themselves known at the proper time.

The village of Oswyn soon came into view. They stopped by the constable's office and Elwin delivered the three Blackbirds into his custody, giving him a diluted account of what had transpired. They next made for the inn and reserved themselves two adjacent rooms. Elwin's three companions stayed silent everywhere they went, following him the way baby chicks follow their mother hen.

Elwin placed his staff in the corner of the room and sat down on the bed. Through the window, he could see dusk settling over the village. The other three sat on the bed across from him.

"I would imagine you have more than a few questions for me," Elwin said.

The trio nodded in unison.

"I assumed as much. Very well, I propose your questions wait while I give you a brief recount of our Order. I imagine many of your questions will be answered in the process. Is this agreeable?"

The three nodded again. Elwin twisted the silver ring around his finger as he began.

"Two millennia past, the Order of the Sages flourished. We had several hundred Sages and even more in training, perhaps thousands at our peak. We made it our mission to relieve suffering and prevent injustice throughout Iria. And we were exceptional at it. For centuries, we were an unstoppable force for good. Those were blessed times. But somehow, over the years, the people came to fear us. Not because of anything we did, but because of what we were capable of doing. We were an unchecked power in the world, and they feared what would happen if we turned on them. So, in their fear, they turned on us."

Elwin fell silent. Recounting his history had allowed painful memories to float to the surface, memories he didn't care to relive.

"What happened? When you they turned on you?" Osmund asked.

Elwin shook his head. "A story for another time, perhaps. Suffice it to say that by the end, our numbers fell from the thousands down to a little more than a dozen. I can't be sure of the exact number because most went their separate ways, and I never saw them again."

Emerald, Kailem, and Osmund sat motionless on the bed, wondering what force in Iria could have sent a thousand Sages to the Great Unknown.

"For the first few centuries, we would happen upon each other every decade or so. A few times we discussed reforming the order, but even after centuries had passed, the pain was still too fresh in our minds. Since that time, I have made it my purpose to suppress any knowledge of our Order and the art we practiced. That includes eradicating all written accounts of our Order, such as what you have in that book of yours. I thought I had managed to find and destroy all such literature. That must be a rare copy you have there."

Osmund gripped the book tightly against his chest.

Elwin continued, "Where eliminating all memories of the Order was not possible, I instead spread false and contradictory accounts, and over time, people ceased to believe we had ever been real. As for this band of outlaws, I don't know how much they have learned or how they learned it, but what I do know is that they are well-organized and well-funded, which means they have the support of some very important people. I need to learn how much they know and who knows it before I can plan how to deal with them."

Elwin gave them time to respond.

Kailem spoke first. "That answered all of my questions," he said. Emerald nodded as well.

"I still have a few," Osmund said softly.

"I assumed you would, Osmund. And that is an admirable trait. You have a thirst for knowledge that serves you well. But it's late, and as you can surely imagine, relating my story, as short as it may have been, has taken a rather heavy toll on me. Might I entreat your patience and answer your questions another time?"

Osmund's face might as well have been a ram's horn, bellowing his disappointment. He was eager, even desperate, to continue asking questions until the sun came up, but he reluctantly nodded in agreement.

"I cannot, with sufficient emphasis, express the importance of keeping this information private. These were events I have not spoken aloud in many centuries, and I have labored diligently to keep them secret. Can I trust in your discretion?"

Each of them said "yes" in turn.

"I believe you," Elwin said. He stood from the bed. "I bid you goodnight."

"Elwin," Osmund said, leaping to his feet. As soon as the word left his mouth, he recoiled, wondering if he'd made a mistake in speaking.

"It's fine, Osmund. Ask your question."

"Could you... I mean... before you leave, could you give us another demonstration, just once more, of sagecraft, sir?"

Elwin smiled tenderly. He reached forward, and his staff levitated from the corner, floating slowly into his hand. The light around the staff twisted and warped, the same as it had when the Blackbird was thrown against the cage. All three of their mouths gaped open.

"Goodnight," Elwin said.

Unlike the last inn, this room had three beds. The day's events had drained the travelers of every morsel of strength. They settled into bed almost immediately after Elwin left, but despite their exhaustion, sleep evaded them.

"Can you believe this?" Osmund asked.

"Barely," Kailem replied. "I'm sure I never would have believed it had I not seen it with my own eyes."

Osmund stared at the ceiling in wonder. "All our lives we lived in a world where these phenomenal abilities existed, and we had no idea." He paused, considering it. "How can we go on knowing that such powers exist but are beyond us?"

Emerald turned to him. "Aye, Oz, I cannae *imagine* livin' a world where others have all ye e'er dreamt of while yer left out in the cold."

Her sarcasm made Kailem grin.

It took Osmund a moment to understand her meaning. When it finally dawned on him, he dropped his head and sought to change the subject. "What should we do now? Our clues don't lead to Andalaya, as we assumed, just to another monastery, and I just promised not to publish anything I discover. Not much sense now in continuing. And besides, why should we bother trying to find ancient ruins when we've found an actual living sage?"

Kailem felt for the pearl around his neck. It had been weeks since he had thought about avenging his parents; perhaps that need was slipping away from him. He couldn't allow that.

"Let's figure that out in the morning," he suggested. The other two agreed and sleep quickly followed.

Chapter Twenty-Seven

Royal Tea

45th Day of Summer, 897 G.C.

Kyra sat patiently at the table under the gazebo in the Palace Gardens. Martina brought out a tea set of fine porcelain on a sterling silver tray. This was the third time Kyra had taken tea with Prince Aedon and King Byron this week, and the handmaid knew to leave immediately after setting down the tray.

Once she was alone, Kyra took the vial of brewed jimson weed from a concealed pocket in her dress and held it between her fingers. The substance was dark green, slightly more viscous than water, and had the odor of bitter herbs spoiled in the sun. She lifted the lid from the teapot and poured in the poison, only a drop at first, then a steady stream, finally tipping the vial upside down.

She replaced the lid just as Prince Aedon sat at the table with her.

"Is it ready?" Aedon asked.

Kyra held up the empty vial.

Aedon placed his hand on hers. "You seem troubled."

Of course, I am troubled. Are you not? She thought to herself. Her disdain for this task was etched in bold print across her face. She wiped it clean with false relief.

"Oh, no, I'm fine. Just my mother being my mother again," she said with a smile.

"Well, once you're Queen, she won't be able to say a word that displeases you."

Kyra's laughter was genuine, albeit morose. "Aedon, I could be the Queen of all Iria sitting on my throne and she'd *still* tell me to sit up straight and stop slouching."

The Prince laughed with her.

King Byron came hobbling down the garden path, followed by two Royal Guards on either side. He looked like death's own head upon a mop stick, even from a distance. He had lost weight, his hair was thinning, and his skin looked gray and sunken, as if he had aged twenty years in a single week. The emaciated man winced with every step.

Kyra's smile disappeared.

The King turned and waved for his guards to stand back several steps, then finished his walk to the table. Aedon, ever the dutiful son, stood to help his father as he struggled, lowering himself into his chair.

"Thank you, my boy," King Byron said as he adjusted feebly on the seat.

"Of course, father. What did the physicians say?" He held his father's hand and leaned forward.

"Oh, you know physicians, they cannot agree on anything. My surgeon suspects a disease of the thyroid. My herbalist believes the kitchen staff mistook a poisonous herb for something edible. Nightshade, pennyroyal, or the like. My apothecary believes I ate some bad mushrooms and gave me a concentrated bottle of fig brandy. Then my alchemist believes I have an imbalance of fluids. He gives me an elixir with powdered dragon bone and other such nonsense."

While the King listed his physicians' erroneous theories, Kyra poured him a cup of the true culprit.

"I figure between the three of them, one of their treatments should have me back to full health in no time." He required both of his shaky hands to lift his teacup to his lips.

The King's herbalist had come the closest to a correct diagnosis, but that was no surprise — of course, an herbalist would suspect an herb was the problem. Unfortunately for the King, none of the poisons he listed had an antidote that would counteract jimson weed.

Fortunately, or perhaps regrettably, depending on one's perspective, the King always took a great deal of sugar in his tea. This only helped to mask the bitter taste of the weed. Kyra rarely put sugar in her tea, but now she had to put in nearly as much as the King just to swallow it.

The King coughed as he set the teacup back on the saucer, and Aedon rubbed his father's back tenderly. He was so much better at this than Kyra was. She reached into her concealed dress pocket and gripped the two vials of antidote she carried, resisting the urge to slip it into the King's cup somehow.

"But enough about me," the King said. "The First of Autumn is fast approaching; how are the wedding plans progressing? I would ask your mother, Kyra, but once she starts talking, I'm afraid I have not yet learned how to stop her."

Kyra laughed, and it helped her keep back a tear that formed in her eye. "We are nearly finished, actually." She reached over and squeezed Aedon's hand. "All the arrangements have been made and the guest list has been finalized. The scribes are writing out the invitations now. We plan to send them before the next full moon."

"That is wonderful to hear," the King said. He turned to Aedon. "The day I see you marry will be one of the proudest days of my life. I wish your mother could be here to see it. During the last days of her pregnancy, she spoke fondly of witnessing those momentous occasions. First steps, first words, your wedding, your first child."

Kyra's chin quivered.

"I wish she could be here too, father," Aedon said.

"She would have been very fond of you as well, Kyra." The King added.

Kyra looked up and met his eye. "I wish I could have known her," she replied honestly.

"Ask your parents. They can tell you all about her. We were all friends when we were young, although our visits were infrequent for the distance. I'm sure they have a story or two."

"And you wanted to remarry?" she asked.

Byron shook his head. "All my advisors urged me to. Needing to sire more children and secure the royal line and all that, but I could never love another. And besides, should the worst happen to my son, he has more than enough cousins who would gladly take the throne. The dynasty is not in peril."

Kyra's eyes dropped to her lap, so she didn't have to watch Byron take another sip of his deadly tea. She heard the clink of the teacup placed again on the saucer, then the sound of the ailing monarch breathing in the crisp air of the afternoon. She wiped away a tear from her cheek as the conversation changed course.

"Perhaps you'll be pleased to hear, Son, I've chosen my emissaries to send to Shinda and Ârema. Each of the battalions is preparing for the journey."

"I am pleased, father. And again, I apologize for my behavior in the council chamber. Lord Arturri has helped me to see the wisdom in your restraint. I know I still have a lot to learn from you."

The statement was so saccharine and rehearsed that even a simpleton could have seen through it, but King Byron just patted his son on the shoulder. Perhaps it was the illness dimming his wits, or perhaps he just accepted what he wanted to hear. Either way, he then turned to Kyra.

"Your father has been an excellent influence on my son," Byron said. "We are most fortunate to have him on the council."

Kyra could do nothing but nod. She gripped the vials in her pocket so tightly she worried they might shatter.

A moment of silence passed between them. There was a slight tremble in the King as he strained to remain seated upright. His arms curled around his abdomen, an unconscious gesture from the joint pain, and his eyes struggled to keep their focus.

"Well, my children, as enjoyable as this has been, I'm afraid I must bring this pleasant social to an end," said the King. "My physicians suffer fits of hysteria should I be out of my bed for too long. But I believe these daily tea visits have been good for me. The sunshine and fresh air, the loving company."

"We've enjoyed them as well, father," Aedon said.

"Do not forget, we are having a banquet in the Great Hall tonight. Every Duke in the kingdom has traveled here for it."

"I won't forget, father." This was the third time he had reminded Aedon in two days; they had even gone together to greet some of the dukes who had arrived from distant counties. The jimson weed must be dulling his memory.

The King stood from the table but stopped short of his full height, then called for his guards to escort him back to his quarters. Before leaving, he leaned down and kissed the top of Aedon's head. "I love you, son."

When he was gone, Kyra took out the two vials and gave one to Aedon. They each drank it immediately. It was even more bitter than the poison had been.

CHAPTER TWENTY-EIGHT

THE PLACE WITHOUT SHADOWS

38TH DAY OF SUMMER, 897 G.C.

Elwin shut the door to his room and leaned against it. He sat down on the bed, his thumb tracing along the engraving of a mountain range around his ring. Why had he shared so much, he wondered? After centuries of silence regarding his past, of denying the very existence of sagecraft, to now share such personal, painful details with perfect strangers, it defied reason.

As a young man, when his age had been a mere three digits, Elwin had been a devout disciple of logic and reason. He'd even penned several tomes on the virtues of logic and debated with the wisest philosophers in Iria. Logic and reason had governed his every decision. But as the years passed, and his age grew a fourth digit, his conviction faded. Eventually, he developed the opinion that, at least from a pragmatic point of view, intuition was superior to reason. Try as he might, he could not justify rationally why intuition was superior, and the irony of that inability was not lost on him, but it had been proven true time and again.

So, he had learned to trust his instincts. They had never led him astray; however, neither had they led him to something quite so illogical as what he had done that night. He was missing something, and greater guidance was needed.

He positioned himself on the floor in the middle of his room, the curtains drawn, the candles extinguished. His legs were crossed, his eyes closed, his hands resting comfortably on his knees. He breathed deeply, allowing a deep relaxation to drift through every muscle in his body. He felt the floor beneath him, the bed and the table near him, the walls around him. Then he let go of them, allowing himself to drift away into an immaterial abyss. He watched his thoughts come and go, like watching strangers pass on the street, but he did not engage with them. His thoughts gradually slowed until they ceased entirely. Nightfall set on the street of his mind.

Elwin remained untethered in this blank state for only a moment. Soon his mind became saturated with thoughts that were not his own. When he opened his mind's eye, he was back in that place again. The place where one communes with the Aura of Iria.

This place appeared differently for every person. Some found themselves on a tranquil beach or a majestic mountain top, others said it was a royal palace court of unspeakable grandeur. He'd even heard of people finding themselves in their childhood home. For Elwin, this place was a meadow surrounded by mountain peaks. Wildflowers of every color burst from the ground under his feet. Trees of unknown varieties lined the edges of the meadow, trees that had no analog in the physical world. The colors around him were more vivid here, and even though it was as bright as noonday on a cloudless afternoon, he had never seen a sun in the sky. It was as if light originated from every point around him, as if the world itself was made of light, a place without shadow.

Elwin knew this meadow well. Every leaf and flower were familiar to him. This is where he came when he had a difficult decision to make, when the world proved too much for him. When his Order was lost, he spent almost every waking moment here trying to make sense of it. This place hadn't given him any answers then, but it had comforted his soul.

He knew immediately that today would be different. A river now cut through the center of the meadow, deep and wide, a river that had never been there before. Anomalies were the way the Aura of Iria spoke to him, and he had learned to listen.

On his side of the river, a host of forest animals emerged through the trees. He saw deer and elk, foxes and squirrels, badgers, and raccoons. Elwin walked among them, and the animals mostly ignored him. He ran his hands down the mighty elk's neck. The beast's shoulders were level with his own, and its antlers reached several feet above his head. The elk turned and looked him in the eyes.

A single blackbird flew by. It was the only winged animal he had seen thus far. Then he saw another blackbird flying beside the first. Another came flying from the nearby trees, then another. The small grouping soon became a flock, with more and more birds joining, seemingly from nowhere, as they moved as one through the sky.

They came faster and faster, flying in swirling, undulating patterns above his head. Their numbers grew so large they cast a dark shadow over the meadow despite the absence of a sun overhead.

Then the blackbirds began to swoop down and peck at the animals. The frightened creatures tried to run for cover, but none could be found. Elwin's peaceful meadow had become a place of chaos, and even he was not spared the birds' attack. He crouched amid the wildflowers and covered his head as the birds pecked at his arms and shoulders, the harsh flapping of wings in his ears.

Suddenly, they were gone. Elwin raised his head and saw that he was now on the other side of the river. From this side, he could see the murmuration of blackbirds swarming through the forest animals like locusts devouring a field of wheat. He longed to rescue them, but for the first time in centuries, he felt powerless. There he stood, safe and alone, helplessly watching others suffer.

Something rustled in the trees behind him. He turned to see a brown bear emerge from the forest. The bear was unnaturally large, its head at least ten feet above the ground even when it walked on four legs. If it rose on its hind legs, it would surely have been fifteen, even twenty feet tall.

Two more creatures emerged behind the bear. The first was a mountain lion with green eyes and fur the color of wildfire. The second was a wolf with grey fur and a peaceful wisdom behind its eyes. They too were unnaturally large, yet where Elwin should have felt danger, there was only peace.

The three animals walked to Elwin's side and looked him in the eye, then turned their gaze to the other side of the river. The swarm of blackbirds was now so large and violent he could no longer see the forest animals amongst them.

These creatures, predators who in the wild would never hunt together, now bounded across the coursing river. Once across, they leaped in the air, swatting at the birds with their giant paws and catching them in lethal mouths. The birds began dropping from the sky, twitching on the ground before laying deathly still. But there were simply too many of them. For every bird the giants killed, five others would land on their heads and backs, pecking into their thick fur.

More animals emerged from the forest on the side opposite Elwin. These new creatures were their natural size, more deer and foxes and squirrels, but unlike the previous animals, these came to join the fight. They stomped their hooves, swung their antlers, and gnashed their teeth. Even the tiny squirrels leaped in the air, grabbing birds mid-flight.

Elwin stood alone across the river, feeling useless. He could not see who was winning the fight, and that amplified his helplessness. The birds seemed to have the advantage, but the forest animals refused to relent.

Before a victor became clear, the vision went black. Elwin was back in the abyss, devoid of all thought. He opened his eyes.

He was back in his room at the inn, sitting in the middle of the floor.

***

Osmund awoke after a night of deep, uninterrupted sleep. He dreamt he was a sage flying through the clouds above a Devonian forest. He slept soundly, despite the torrent of thoughts rushing through his mind. Had the events of the previous day not left him exhausted, both physically and mentally, he might not have slept at all.

He sat up in his bed and stretched his arms high above his head. His companions were still asleep. It felt odd for him to be the first one awake for once. He left their room and crossed the corridor to Elwin's room, hoping the sage would be in a more sharing mood that morning. He found the door ajar.

The room was empty. In fact, there was no evidence anyone had slept there that night. Osmund raced down the stairs and checked the tavern. No one was there. Osmund ran out the front door. There was the usual commotion of a small village starting its day, but no sign of the sage.

Osmund ran his hands through his hair, then let them flop to his side. He had hoped to spend the day at the sage's feet, asking every question under the sun. Perhaps that had been too good to be true. He stuck his hands in his pockets and reentered the tavern, not knowing what to do with himself. For now, all he wanted was to climb into bed and pull the covers over his head.

As he made his way toward the stairs, he heard voices from within the kitchen. The kitchen staff was laughing. Osmund peeked his head in.

"Osmund! Good morrow!" Elwin greeted. The sage wore an apron, helping the kitchen staff prepare breakfast; the three ladies laughed so hard they could barely cook.

Osmund was filled with a mixture of confusion and elation that left him speechless. He hadn't known what to expect from a sage, but it certainly wouldn't have been this. Here was a man more powerful than kings, who had lived to see dynasties rise and fall, who possessed a wealth of experience and wisdom beyond description. Yet here was in the kitchen, laboring beside the servant class, wearing an apron and cracking jokes.

"Breakfast is almost ready, young Master Baylor," Elwin said as he rotated a whisk in a large bowl. "Why don't you go fetch the others?"

"Okay..." Osmund replied with a frown. He paused a moment longer before tearing himself away from the scene.

He returned moments later with Emerald and Kailem in tow, still groggy and shaking off sleep. Elwin had set a table for four with a floral centerpiece and a spread of scrambled eggs, bacon, freshly baked bread, and a carafe of cactus pear juice.

"I trust everyone slept well," Elwin said as they sat down to eat.

Emerald was the first to fill her plate.

"We did, and we appreciate the room," Kailem said. "Also, I don't think we ever properly thanked you for rescuing us yesterday. With everything that happened, I guess we forgot."

"Well, consider me properly thanked," Elwin said, lifting his glass of cactus pear juice.

"How'd ye sleep?" Emerald asked without looking up from her plate. Osmund knew her well enough now to know that was her attempt at politeness.

"Briefly, but effectively," Elwin replied. "And I have quite the experience to relate."

He proceeded to tell them of his vision the night previous in exquisite detail. Any retelling of an interaction with the Aura of Iria deserved to be told properly. As the story went on, his three listeners gradually stopped eating, even Emerald. The account earned him their reverent, undivided attention.

When Elwin finished, the three sat motionless, absorbing what they'd heard.

Osmund was the first to speak. "Well, the symbolism there is fairly obvious."

Emerald tilted her head at him.

"Indeed. The Aura of Iria wants to be understood," Elwin explained. "It does not try to speak in riddles, although sometimes that cannot be helped."

Now Emerald was thoroughly confused.

"The blackbirds clearly represent that society who kidnapped us," Osmund said. "And the green eyes and auburn fur make for an obvious allusion as well." He glanced at Emerald.

After a moment, her eyes widened. "Youse sayin' the lion were me, then?"

Elwin nodded. "The mountain lion, yes. And I believe the bear was Kailem, and the wolf was young Osmund here."

A lioness, Emerald thought. She sat a full inch taller in her seat.

"What really matters," Elwin continued, "is that it was no coincidence the three of you found each other. I believe you were brought together for a purpose, and it is clear that purpose concerns the Blackbirds in some way."

Kailem's heart seized. Why would he, of all people, be chosen for anything, he wondered? He was just the second son of a minor lord of a house that was no more; he had not been able to keep the *Flying Manta* from sinking. He had not been able to find his way out of the Southerbe Forest without Elwin; he had not kept them safe in Balderlyn, and he failed to help them escape from the Blackbird's cage. Of what use could he possibly be, he wondered. Perhaps whatever it was had found the wrong Roka, that it meant to choose Mokain and got him instead.

The three friends exchanged heavy glances, their faces echoing the same insecurity that Kailem felt.

"What are we to do?" Kailem asked.

"What indeed?" Elwin replied. "Such is the very question I have been pondering myself. After the vision last night, I went to the constable's office to chat with our friends in jail. They were careful with their words, each of which was a lie, but fortunately, they were not as careful with their thoughts."

Osmund leaned forward in his chair. "Wait, you can hear people's thoughts? Do you listen to our thoughts?"

"I confess, I did listen to your thoughts when I first met you, while I determined whether you were a threat. But since that time, I have not. And I will not from henceforth, you have my word on it. Your private thoughts are your own."

Osmund had so many questions he didn't know which to ask first. What other abilities did a sage have? How were these abilities possible? What did they use them for? Before he could settle on just one, Elwin continued.

"I learned from my unwitting informants that most Blackbirds don't know any sagecraft, they've merely used a few lesser-known apothecary tricks to convince their new recruits. However, the recruiter truly believed, in spite of this, that their highest leaders were in fact training in genuine sagecraft, and that demands further investigation."

Elwin swallowed another bite of his eggs and dabbed his mouth with a napkin. "Which is where you three come in. The recruiter sent a rider ahead advising that she was bringing in a man who claimed to know the location of Andalaya. That is our way in."

"How so?" Kailem asked.

"I suggest that you and I pose as members of the Blackbird Society. I took the liberty of relieving our incarcerated friends of their uniforms last night. We will arrive at their camp with Emerald and Osmund in tow as our captives. The Blackbirds will be expecting us. When they inquire as to Livia Yannsin's absence, we will explain she sent us ahead so she could continue recruiting in the neighboring villages."

"Well, I'm in!" Osmund said.

Kailem was visibly more hesitant. He sat in silence, letting the proposal digest a while.

"Hold on, now," Emerald said, having scraped her plate clean for the second time. "What be in it fer us, then?"

Elwin leaned back in his chair and grinned. "What would you like?"

"How much be it worth to ye?" she countered. She had learned enough about negotiation tactics from Jacken to know never to be the first one to suggest a price.

"Teach us about the Sages!" Osmund blurted out.

"Osmund," Emerald said through her teeth.

"What? It is not like we were going to ask him for money," Osmund said.

"Speak fer yerself, ye daft lad," she said muttered to herself.

"I have plenty of money. When we return home, you can have as much as you want, but when else will we be able to learn directly from a living sage?" He turned to Elwin. "I want to know everything, your history, all of your abilities, how you obtain them, what this 'Aura of Iria' is, all of it."

Elwin sat back, thoughtful. He looked at Emerald and Kailem, then back to Osmund. "I accept your terms. I'll tell you everything you want to know about us *except* how to train in sagecraft. That is where the line must be drawn."

"Wait. Wait, is sagecraft something you could teach just anybody?" Osmund asked. He hadn't even considered that. "You could teach us?"

"Everything you want to know *except* how to train in sagecraft. Do we have an agreement?"

Osmund slumped back in his chair. "Agreed."

Elwin looked at Emerald. "I s'pose," she muttered.

He looked at Kailem. The young Mariner was thoughtful and slow to respond, his concerns nearly palpable. Experience, as well as simple common sense, told him not to trust someone who came offering exactly what you wanted. Promises that were too good to be true usually were. But this man who called himself a sage had already saved their lives twice. If he meant them any harm, he could have easily done it. Rejecting him now seemed foolish.

Eventually, Kailem nodded.

"Very good," Elwin said. "There's one other matter to discuss. If Kailem and I are going to pass as Blackbirds, we'll need to have their tattoo on our wrists."

PART THREE

NARRATOR'S SECOND INTERLUDE

As I relay this account, I feel compelled to say a word on the character of our heroes. It is abhorrent to me when great men and women such as these are vilified by their inferiors, and I am ever watchful that I am not guilty of the same. But in telling their story, I am bound by oath and honor to present them just as they have been presented to me, complete with their every weakness, blemish, and vice.

Perhaps you recoil at the portrayal of Kailem Roka being overcome by his guilt and rage, as I once did. Perhaps you protest, and rightly so, at the description of Osmund Baylor consumed by his affluence, or of Lady Emerald presented as timid and unsure of herself. These are not the descriptions that have survived to our day, to meet the ears of us precious few who know their story. I scarcely would have believed such flaws existed in giants among men had I not heard these accounts directly from those who knew them best. Even with such irreproachable sources, I still wrestle with accepting it. It is my hope that all those who read these words will think less on who our heroes were and more on who they became.

And thus, we arrive in our tale at the events that propelled our heroes on their path to greatness. Condemn them not for their errors, but rejoice that, even in their weakness, they showed forth their valor when it mattered most.

Chapter Twenty-Nine

Long Live the King

52nd Day of Summer, 897 G.C.

Animals have an uncanny knack for perceiving emotion. Simple, ordinary creatures, incapable of any kind of complexity, instinctively know when someone is a friend or foe, or whether a person is content or concerned.

This is especially true when the animal has a bond with the human, so it shouldn't have surprised Kyra that her fox knew she was troubled. The soft white of Ember's chin rested just above Kyra's knee, her warm, round eyes staring up at her, while Kyra sat with her back against the padding of her tufted headboard, rotating an empty vial of jimson weed poison between her fingers.

Ember rubbed her nose against Kyra's leg, and her human absently massaged behind her ear. Unsatisfied, Ember inched her way closer, ears tucked back submissively, and whimpered until she received the undivided attention she deserved.

Kyra relented. She put down the vial and invited Ember onto her lap, who accepted the invitation eagerly.

"I'm fine, Ember, I'm fine," Kyra assured her. The fox licked Kyra's chin all the same, drawing a genuine laugh from Kyra for the first time in weeks.

The door to Kyra's chambers flew open. Prince Aedon stepped into the room, silently fuming.

Ember left Kyra's lap and crawled to the edge of the bed with her ears pinned back and her tail wagging, just as she had done to Kyra. Aedon struck the fox with the back of his hand, sending her to the floor with a yelp.

"Aedon!" Kyra yelled.

Ember found her footing and scampered under the bed.

Aedon ignored the complaint. "It's not going to work! The royal physicians. They won't allow father to come to tea anymore. They've not left his side for days. And the royal alchemists, every hour they bring him some new concoction, some new elixir, to work some new wonder for the old man."

"Calm down, my love. Tell me what has happened. Is your father dying?"

"Dying? Kyra, that would be cause for celebration. No, no, he is most certainly alive, and by all accounts, it appears he will stay that way!"

Kyra knew not what to say. Panic and relief both seized her at once.

"Did you hear what I said, Kyra? My father is going to live, and when he recovers, there will be an investigation. This is a disaster."

"Be calm, my love. We'll find a solution," Kyra finally said.

"Stop telling me to be calm! Sarding Iria! This was all your rotting idea. I never should have listened to you."

Kyra silently agreed with him.

Aedon continued pacing. "I need to finish this myself," he concluded. He nodded repeatedly, trying to convince himself. "Yes, the blade must do what the poison could not. No physician in Iria can cure a dagger to the heart."

"Aedon, I can't believe what I'm hearing!"

He turned to her, his anger ready to burst at the seams. "Is a slow death by poison so much kinder than the swift death of a blade?"

"But to kill your father by your own hand? Aedon, that is not who you are."

"And what manner of man would I be if sent another in my stead?"

Kyra looked into his eyes and saw fear turn to resolution, and she feared what she had turned him into.

"Do nothing yet," she said at length. "Let me speak to my father first. He will know what to do."

"Your father?" Aedon paused briefly. "Yes. Yes, Leonin will know what to do. Tell him of our plans. He can be trusted. And afterward come find me in my chambers."

It was a brief walk through the palace residences to Lord and Lady Arturri's quarters, and yet Kyra was accosted by more sycophants, well-wishers, and rumormongers than should have been possible over so a short distance. Kyra did her best to hide her guilt while maintaining her sadness. Appearing ambivalent to the King's declining health could be just as dangerous as looking guilty for it. It was a fine line to walk, emotionally speaking; this whole affair had left her with little strength to speak of.

She shut the door to her parents' quarters and leaned against it, relieved.

"I take it you've heard the news?" Avalina said. There was a hint of accusation in her voice as she paced their sitting room, flicking her thumbs together.

Kyra nodded.

"It was a simple task, Kyra. You had to pour a vial into a teapot. Leave it to you to bumble such an easy…"

"Come now, Avalina. We cannot be certain the fault is hers," Leonin said. Her father sat in his corner chair wearing his reading spectacles, an open book on his lap. A calm demeanor was the way a proper Devonian handled a crisis.

Avalina continued. "Did you give him the full dose? You've always lacked a spine, child. You couldn't go through with it, could you? Now you've ruined everything!"

"Avalina," Leonin repeated. This time, his voice was low and stern, and it silenced his wife without another word. She sat on a fainting couch with her head down.

He turned back to his daughter. "Did you give Byron the full dose? Every time?"

Kyra nodded.

"Then perhaps we underestimated the old man's vitality. We should have chosen something stronger."

"We couldn't risk a poison that could be identified," Avalina said. "Perhaps… perhaps if we spoke to Torin, he could—"

"Be silent," Leonin commanded. Beneath his voice was wrath barely contained, and he sent her a glare that could have boiled the sea. Avalina curled into herself.

Kyra repeated the name 'Torin' in her mind, trying to place it. She thought she knew all of her father's associates, but she couldn't remember a Torin.

Leonin removed his spectacles and the book on his lap. "How is Aedon handling it?"

"He's concerned, father. He believes I am here revealing our plan to you."

The faintest hint of a smile appeared in one corner of Leonin's mouth, but it disappeared just as quickly. "Did he say what he wishes to do?"

Kyra nodded. "He thinks he should use a dagger to finish the job."

Leonin exhaled, then set his book on the end table. "That would be foolish."

He stood from his padded chair and walked from the sitting room to the bedroom. Inside the wardrobe was a locked box. Leonin unlocked the box and took out a vial of black liquid. He returned to the sitting room and gave the vial to Kyra.

"Go now to the King's Chambers and slip this into one of the elixirs those mutton-headed alchemists keep bringing him."

Kyra's eyes went wide. "Me? Why me? I did everything right!"

"When your given a task, Kyra, it is your duty to see it through to the end, no matter the complication. Let this be a lesson to you."

She opened her mouth to protest, but then thought better of it. There was no use arguing with the man. She looked to her mother. Avalina still sat on the fainting couch like a scolded child with her head hung low, flicking her thumbs together. Leonin returned to his padded chair, put on his spectacles, and opened his book. The silence in the room was painful, and it drove Kyra out the door without a word.

The walk to the King's Chambers was considerably longer. She walked in a daze, unaware of anything happening around her. She passed through several layers of Royal Guards who stepped aside as she approached and returned to their posts after she passed.

The King's bedchamber was larger than all of her chambers and her parents' chambers combined, and more opulent as well. The canopy was open on the King's four-post bed, and the King was in his nightgown propped up on pillows. The bed was surrounded by physicians, alchemists, and advisors, each identifiable by the unique robes they wore. No one noticed when she entered the room.

How was she supposed to manage this, she wondered? As soon as she approached, she would stand out like coal in a box of gold.

"I need everyone to leave the room," she said more quietly than she had intended. No one responded.

"Excuse me," she said, only slightly louder than before. Still, no one saw her.

She stepped forward until she was close enough to touch one of them.

"Everyone, leave this chamber immediately. I would have a word with our King." This time, her voice bellowed with authority. Everyone turned to look at her, then looked at each other, wondering what to do.

Kyra said nothing further. She had given her command and had no reason to repeat it. She stood tall with her shoulders back, gripping her hands to keep them from shaking. She met the eye of each man who looked at her. Once the first man gave in, the rest trickled from the room until she was left alone with the King.

Byron's eyes were shut; he seemed to slip in and out of consciousness every few seconds. On the end table next to the King's bed were nearly a dozen glasses of elixirs of every color and consistency. Kyra didn't recognize any of them, but most were less than half full. The glass nearest the King was still nearly full, and it was a dark substance that would hide the new poison perfectly.

She uncorked the vial and held it above the glass, but stopped just before the first drop fell. Everything inside her screamed not to do it. Her hand trembled. But she knew she could not face her parents if she didn't. And what would Aedon say if he knew she had been given a way forward and didn't take it, she wondered? Her hand trembled to the point that a drop accidentally spilled from the vial. That one spill made the second drop easier, and the third was easier still. She emptied the entire vial into the glass.

"What... what has happened? Who is there?" the King asked through labored breath.

Kyra sat on the bed and took Byron's hand. "It is I, Your Majesty."

"Oh, Kyra, my darling. So good of you to visit. Your voice is the sweetest sound I've heard all week."

Kyra winced. "I would have come sooner, Your Majesty, but your physicians have not allowed visitors."

"Sarding physicians." The King coughed violently before settling back against his pillows. "They claim to know everything, but all they do is make blind guesses and fill me with their tonics until something seems to work." He coughed again. "I swear their cures are more likely to kill me than the sickness."

Kyra smiled. Even with death looking over him, Byron had his sense of humor. She took a hand towel from the end table and dabbed at the sweat on his pallid brow. She could feel the heat emanating from his forehead. His coughing fit grew worse.

"Elixir," he managed to say between coughs. He pointed to the glass nearest him.

Kyra lifted the glass of dark liquid, then paused. Her heart was pierced. She set the poisoned elixir down and gave him a glass of water instead.

Byron struggled to breathe, and when he coughed again, blood splattered from his lips. Kyra didn't know what to do.

"Stay here," she finally said, "I'll... I'll fetch help."

She hurried to the chamber door, then paused, torn in half. A part of her, the better part, was desperate to save the King no matter the consequence. The weaker part knew this was the opportunity her parents had been looking for.

The King convulsed on his bed, gasping for air. Blood sprayed with every cough. Kyra stood frozen in the center of the room.

Byron's lips turned blue. Kyra could stand it no longer.

"Come quick!" she screamed as she ran for the door. "The King is dying! Come now!"

Physicians rushed through the King's sitting room and into the bedchamber.

"I don't know what happened, he just started coughing, and..." Kyra's voice faded as she realized no one was listening to her. Physicians attended the King frantically. She stepped back farther and farther, tears streaming from her eyes, hands covering her mouth. In the end, she ran from the room like the coward she knew she was.

Chapter Thirty

A Bear Among Blackbirds

40th Day of Summer, 897 G.C.

Kailem had been scratching his wrist all morning. Tattooing the blackbird symbol hurt far worse than Kailem had expected, though he successfully concealed that pain during the process. Elwin set the ink himself, first on his own wrist and then on Kailem's. The process left Kailem's skin red and swollen until Elwin placed his hand over the area. Twenty seconds later, the redness and swelling were gone. He feared the itching, however, might be permanent.

"But if back then everyone knew about sages, why did you keep your city a secret?" Osmund asked from the wagon cage.

He and Emerald were locked away, posing as his prisoners, their hands tied in front of them. Osmund pressed himself against the front of the cage, collecting his participation fee. Emerald sat with her back against the rear of the cage, admiring the countryside. Meanwhile, Elwin and Kailem sat on the driver's bench in their borrowed Blackbird uniforms. Kailem scratched his wrist again.

"If everyone had known where we lived, we would have been overrun," Elwin explained. "There would have been people trying to discover our secrets, people wanting every little malady healed, even people just wanting a demonstration for entertainment. So, we had to separate ourselves from the commoners. Even our monasteries were strategically placed in areas that were difficult to access."

"And where does your power come from? Is it magic? Or alchemy? Are... are you actually human?"

Elwin guffawed like a jolly old grandfather, which seemed odd coming from a man who appeared in his thirties. "We are most certainly human, Master Baylor, the same as you. And I assure you, it has nothing to do with alchemy or magic. A sage uses such piffle no more than does a bird in flight. It may seem arcane, but there is nothing unnatural in it."

Osmund nodded, then thought carefully over his next question. "So then, how was sagecraft discovered? Who was the first sage?"

Elwin was amazed at himself. He couldn't remember the last time he had been this open with anyone. It was refreshing, even liberating. He hadn't shared this part of himself, his real self, in a millennium.

"Sagecraft was first theorized over three millennia ago by a man named Temen Namtilla. Back then, we didn't have individual scholars, physicians, or royal advisors. Such responsibilities were all fulfilled by a single individual, called a 'sage'. Temen Namtilla was a sage, and he theorized there was an energy created by all living things, or that gave all living things life."

He paused as the cart bounced over a poorly kept section of the dirt road. "Namtilla called this living energy 'aura'. He believed that learning to control one's aura was the key to untold strength and vitality."

"Was he right?" Osmund asked.

"Mostly," Elwin said. "His entire life he studied ways to access his aura, and he made some progress, but the truly gifted one was his daughter. Her name was Temen Saphronia. She studied under her father until the day he died. She was the first one to genuinely understand sagecraft, and she was the first one to teach it to others. After a few decades, the word 'sage' came to refer exclusively to someone who mastered their aura."

"Did ye knew her?" Emerald asked.

Osmund was startled; he hadn't heard her crawl beside him.

"I *do* know her," Elwin said. "She is my great-grandmother. And as far as I am aware, she is the only other sage still with us. When she was younger, until she was a few hundred years old, her friends and family called her 'Sophie.' But since then, she's been known simply as 'mother'."

"Why 'mother'?" Emerald asked.

"She had a large family, and one's posterity just about doubles with every generation, so when you've been alive as long as she has, well, nearly everyone in Iria today is her descendant in one way or another."

"'Mother'," Emerald repeated thoughtfully. She sat back against the cage wall, alight by the reverent way the sage spoke of Sophie.

"When did you say your Order ended?" Osmund asked.

Elwin took a deep breath. "As the years are measured now, it was 186 B.G.C., although that is not what we called it at the time."

"186 *B.G.C.* That's more than a thousand years ago. What have you been doing all that time?"

Elwin chortled. "Shall I summarize a thousand years for you? Let me think. I've served as an advisor to several kings, served as many a nobleman's personal body-guard, spent time in universities, both as professor and student. I have owned and operated inns and taverns, worked in all forms of menial labor, but mostly I wandered. I went everywhere, read everything, saw everything, tried everything. I've seen just about everything Iria has to offer. Even had a few romances. Nothing ever too serious, for obvious reasons. But it is important to always maintain a purpose, something to work towards. Many sages simply faded away because they lost a reason to continue living."

Osmund considered the words quietly.

"What about all the wars during that time?" Kailem asked.

Elwin was surprised to hear Kailem speak; the Mariner had been silent since they left the inn that morning. "At first, I fought for the side I thought was right. The Winter Wars, the War of Heirs, the Àramen Rebellion. But there was always another war; always more killing, more death. Eventually, I had to step away from it. I swore to myself centuries ago that I'd stay out of any future conflicts. See here, I believe our destination draws near," Elwin said.

The Blackbird Society was encamped at a massive, abandoned castle on the banks of the Vondal River, known as the Riverkeep. Kailem marveled at the valley's beauty. It burst alive with brilliant wildflowers and the promise of prosperity.

From a distance, the castle looked like a giant child had crammed together a series of towers,road, then placed flying buttresses between them. The towers were staggered in height, each with a conical roof. The tallest towers in the structure stood twice the height of the tallest tree in the region, and the structure as a whole could comfortably house over two hundred lords along with their families and servants, so it surprised Elwin to see encampments erected on both sides of the valley road leading to the castle. There were surely thousands of them, little tents dotting the fertile ground. Blackbirds emerged from their tents on either side of the road, curious to see who came rolling into camp.

"Act confident," Elwin whispered to Kailem. "Remember, we are one of them. We belong here. Once we're in, just follow my lead."

Kailem nodded. He pulled his shoulders back and lifted his chin, pretending he had walked this road a dozen times before.

When their wagon drew near to the castle walls, the guard recognized their uniforms and raised the portcullis. Elwin brought the wagon to a stop in the castle bailey.

"Take these two to a holding cell. We're going to have a little chat with them later," he commanded.

A man approached them just as Emerald and Osmund were taken away. From the way the man walked, he was clearly some kind of authority.

"What is this?" the man asked. He had coffee-colored skin typical of the Marcônish.

"These are the two that claim to know the location of Andalaya," Elwin said. "We brought them here for questioning."

"What happened to Livia?" the man asked. "Her letter said she would bring them in personally."

"That was her plan until we happened to meet on the road," Elwin explained. "We are Carsten and Kai, returning from our recruiting assignment in the Roserock Basin. When Livia heard we were returning to Riverkeep, she asked us to transport her prisoners so she could return to recruiting."

The man nodded. "That does sound like Livia," he admitted. "I am Galen." He gave each of them a bow of his head.

I can't believe they pulled me out of the command council for this, Elwin heard Galen think to himself.

"A pleasure to meet you, Galen," Elwin said. "Are we late for the command council?"

Galen started. "What did you say your names were?"

"I am Carsten, and this is Kai. Now, the command council?"

Galen looked them over, studying them. He noted the tattoos on their wrists.

"Did you bring any tribute?" Galen asked.

Elwin searched Galen's thoughts before speaking.

"Our only tribute is our unfailing loyalty and devotion," Elwin said, giving the passphrase known only to Blackbird leadership.

Galen turned to Kailem. "Do you agree, Kai?"

Kailem was dumbfounded. He had hoped to get through the day without being asked to speak. Talking about tribute made no sense to him at all. Maybe he should just say yes. That would be the safest course.

Before he could speak, a voice sounded in his mind. It wasn't an audible voice, more like a thought he knew wasn't his, or a memory of a voice he was now recalling. It told him to say *what greater tribute can there be than this?*

Kailem froze, unnerved by the sudden intrusion into his mind. He could scarcely comprehend the mere presence of a foreign voice in his head, let alone comprehend what the voice had said. Galen grew suspicious waiting.

This is Elwin, Kailem. You need to give him the pass phrase. "What better tribute can there be than this?" Say it now.

"What better tribute can there be than this?" Kailem finally said aloud.

Galen glared for several heartbeats, then nodded. He still didn't trust them, but what more could he do? They had the tattoo and the uniform, knew about the command council, and had given the correct pass phrase. He led them inside the castle, up several flights of a narrow spiraling stone staircase, and down the hall to the council room. Inside, seven men dressed in black sat around a table that could have easily fit fifteen. There were several empty chairs at the far end. The room fell silent when they entered.

"Captain Edric, this is Carsten and Kai, from our Roserock sector," Galen introduced them.

The man at the head of the table made a face at Galen that silently asked, *did you verify them?* Galen nodded.

"Very well. Welcome, Carsten and Kai. We are always glad to have our brothers from the Roserock Sector join us. I am Edric, Captain of the Riverkeep Sector. Why don't you have a seat?" He motioned to the empty seats at the far end of the table.

Edric. Edric. Why did that name sound so familiar? Kailem thought as he took his seat.

"We were just discussing the problems in Devona," Edric said.

"I am not familiar with any problems in Devona," Elwin said.

A grizzled man sitting to Edric's right explained. "Our recruiters in Glendown Forest keep disappearing, along with their new recruits. We've lost three units so far without a trace."

"I see," Elwin said. For the briefest moment, Kailem thought he saw the hint of a smile on Elwin's face.

"Do you have a report from Roserock to share with us?" Edric asked.

Elwin looked around the table. "Recruiting in Roserock is going even better than expected," he said.

"That's excellent news," Edric said. "When can we expect the recruits to arrive?"

They better not be longer than a month, Edric thought.

Elwin looked at Kailem, and Kailem spoke the words Elwin put into his mind. "With as many recruits as we've had, we decided to send them down in companies to avoid attention. The first of the companies should arrive no later than a month, but most will not arrive for at least two or three months."

Edric hung his head. "Very well. At least some of them will be here within the month. Lord Vanua, from our Marin Islands sector, is sending new recruits as well, but as yet, there has been no date set for their arrival."

Kailem sucked in air through his nostrils. His jaw clenched so tightly his teeth nearly shattered.

One of the other men at the table, a portly man in his forties, spoke. "I was told Lord Vanua has governed the Marin Islands since the death of their king. How, then, is he recruiting?"

"He's not recruiting personally," Edric explained. "He's giving our men special sanctions to recruit however they please. Pinning the Marin king's murder on that nobleman was one of my better strokes of genius. Now every commoner in the islands hates the nobility. Recruitment is up tenfold."

Edric sat back in his chair with smug satisfaction.

Kailem was filled with murderous rage. His heart pounded, his nostrils flared, his skin grew hot. He gripped the dagger at his side. In his mind, he saw himself bound across the table and leap at Edric, slicing his throat before anyone knew what was happening. He could take out at least three more before any security came into the room, and if the sage fought beside him, perhaps they could take out the entire Society. He prepared to make his move.

The sage's voice spoke in his mind. *Calm yourself, Kailem. Now is not the time.*

These men murdered my parents, Kailem thought back. *They framed them for killing the king and beheaded them right in front of me. They die today.*

I promise you will have justice, Kailem. But now is not the time, Elwin said.

THEY DIE TODAY! He yelled back in his mind. *ALL OF THEM!*

Beads of sweat trickled down Kailem's forehead. The skin of the hand gripping Malua stretched tight over his knuckles. His heart was ready to burst out of his chest.

He imagined stabbing Edric again and again. Imagined crushing his fist into the man's face until his skull collapsed, snapping his neck, choking him until his lips turned blue. In seconds, Edric had died a hundred different ways in Kailem's mind.

Somehow, the poisonous effects of a deep, abiding calm spread throughout Kailem's body. He clung to the hatred in his heart, desperate to retain the rage that was fueling him, but he might as well have tried to hold the sea with an open palm. The other seven continued their discussion, completely unaware of the exchange between Elwin and Kailem.

Calm yourself, Kailem, the sage repeated.

No, Kailem replied in vain. His chin quivered helplessly.

You will see justice, Kailem. I promise you. But you need to let go.

Tears welled in Kailem's eyes. He squeezed them shut.

Have faith in me, Kailem. The right time will come. Let go.

Kailem exhaled a long, enmity-filled breath from his body. The invasive calmness now fully infected every part of him.

He released his hand from his dagger.

***

Emerald and Osmund were led to the far side of the castle courtyard, where the stables had been converted into a holding cell. The Blackbirds hadn't bothered to clean the filth and hay from the stall's previous occupant. The two prisoners sat next to each other on a small section of stone they had swept clean with their boots.

"I'm starting to reckon this wasn't the best plan," Osmund said.

Emerald nodded. "Shoulda asked fer silver."

"That's not what I meant." Osmund looked around their holding cell, careful not to touch anything. "This is beneath me. Those two had best not delay."

The rope binding their wrists had been replaced with iron shackles. They were secured by a single guard sitting in a chair across from their cell. He was a small man, similar in stature to Osmund, and he had his back against the wall behind him, nearly asleep.

"So, these are the two that are going to teach us sagecraft, eh?" said a man walking by. He had an average build, slightly larger than the guard in the chair, and the unmistakable scent of ale on his breath was noticeable even from the holding cell several feet away.

The guard roused at the sound of the larger man's voice.

"No, no, you have it all wrong," the small guard said as he rubbed his eyes. "These are the two that are going to show us the way to Andalaya."

"Andalaya?" The larger man repeated.

"The secret city of the sages. Once we find it, we'll raid their libraries and teach ourselves sagecraft."

Osmund scoffed. "I highly doubt the two of you could teach yourselves to use a quill, let alone sagecraft."

The larger man turned to him. "You calling me a halfwit?"

"Of course, I am. And were you not a halfwit, that should have been obvious to you."

"Osmund!" Emerald said.

The young nobleman realized his folly. The offended guard took the key ring and unlocked the cell door.

"I'd think a smart little lad like yourself would show his betters some respect," he said with his fists clenched.

"Steady on, Ulrich," the short guard said. "We're not to harm 'em."

Osmund lifted his arms just before Ulrich's boot would have crashed into his face; the boot met his forearms instead. The force knocked Osmund to his side, and the man stomped on his rib cage. The wind fled from Osmund's lungs.

With Ulrich's back towards her, Emerald laid against the stone floor and kicked the back of the man's knee, dropping him to all fours.

Ulrich whipped his head at her. "Looks like the kitten needs to learn some respect as well." He left Osmund on the floor in the fetal position, winded and gasping for air.

The man swung the back of a hand against Emerald's cheek, sending her face down on the pile of spoiled hay. Her cheek was hot and stinging, but her eyes shot back up at her attacker, her survival instincts taking hold.

"Ulrich, enough!" the short guard shouted.

"Shut up!" Ulrich yelled. He turned to Emerald again and drew back his hand.

Emerald saw the man's eyes go wide as Osmund jumped on his back. Osmund wrapped his manacle chains around Ulrich's neck and leaned backward. Emerald's eyes bulged as much as Ulrich's did at the surprise attack.

The guard jumped from his chair and ran into the cell. Ulrich was trying to throw Osmund from his back, but Osmund had his legs wrapped around his waist with ankles locked.

While Osmund struggled to hold on to Ulrich against the guard, pulling at him, he heard a loud *thump*. Over Ulrich's shoulder, he saw the short guard collapse to the stone floor, unconscious. Emerald was standing over him, holding a shovel that had previously hung in the adjacent cell. Ulrich shoved his back into the wall, smashing Osmund between himself and the stone. Osmund dropped to the floor.

The man fell to his knees and gasped, finally able to breathe. Emerald took another swing of the shovel, putting in every ounce of anger and venom she had.

Crack!

Osmund was sure he heard the neck bones snap when the shovel hit the side of his head.

Emerald knelt beside him. "Are ye well?" she asked. Her own lip was bleeding.

Osmund winced, his hand touching his side. "I believe he bruised a rib." He looked down at the two unconscious guards. More would certainly be there soon. "What... do we do now?"

"We run," came her reply.

She dropped the shovel on the hay bed and retrieved the keys from the prison door. They unlocked each other's manacles and fled from the stables without any sense of where to go.

Near the stables was a door in the castle wall. Because the door could only be opened from the inside, it was left unguarded. Emerald and Osmund heard shouts that the prisoners had escaped just as they slammed the door shut behind them. They followed the castle wall down to the Vondal River.

"We need ta swim fer it," Emerald said.

"I can't swim!" Osmund said from behind her.

Emerald stopped and glared at him. She looked back at the river. It was at least 50 yards across, possibly more, and it was impossible to tell how deep. It had to be at least deep enough for those small ships at the dock to have sailed up the river, so wading across was out of the question.

"Sarding fussock," Emerald swore.

"Emerald! Language!" Osmund shot back.

"Come on!" she yelled.

She grabbed him by the hand and led him knee deep into the Vondal River. They walked along the river's edge with their heads down low, hoping for cover among the plants and bushes.

***

"Edric!" a man said as he burst into the command council. "The prisoners have escaped, sir," he said, out of breath.

Edric shot to his feet. "Which way did they go?"

"We don't know, sir. We found their guards in the cell. One had his neck broken."

While Edric and the man spoke, Elwin looked out the window. From his vantage, he could see Osmund and Emerald in the distance, crouched low as they made their way through the shrubbery on the river's edge.

Edric pounded his fist on the table at the mention of a fallen comrade.

"After them," he commanded. "Send the dogs with you, catch them at all costs."

"Wait," Elwin said.

Edric turned to him. "They killed one of ours. We wait for nothing."

"Hurting them won't bring our man back," Elwin explained, "but if they are killed, their secrets of Andalaya die with them."

Edric was silent for a moment, and the man at the door waited for instruction.

Elwin continued, "assemble a small group of men you can trust. The prisoners couldn't have gone east without running into the tents. They most likely went west, across the Vondal. Send some of your men across and the other half downstream. No dogs, we can't risk them mauling the prisoners. Kai and I will go upriver. Between the three parties, one of us will find them and bring them back alive."

Edric looked to the man at the door. "See to it," he commanded.

The man nodded and rushed out of the room.

Elwin stood and made for the door with Kailem close at his heels.

"We'll be taking some horses," Elwin said, a statement rather than a request. He didn't wait for a response.

Osmund and Emerald crouched in the water hidden by the brush on the riverbank. They were out of breath and shivering. The Riverkeep was still visible in the distance, like a figurine sitting on the horizon. Two horses galloped down the riverbank towards them.

"Sarding Iria, keep yer head down," Emerald said.

"We're going to have a talk about your language after this," Osmund said.

Emerald shot him a look.

The two horses drew near, and Osmund and Emerald squatted even lower in the water with only their heads above the river's surface. Shortly before the horses would gallop past, Osmund recognized the riders.

He leaped from behind the bushes, sopping wet, waving his arms and yelling their names. The horses reared to a stop and turned. Emerald emerged from the river behind Osmund.

"We haven't time, come along," Elwin said.

Osmund jumped on the back of Elwin's horse, aided by Elwin's aura, of course, and Emerald did the same on Kailem's. The poor beasts strained under the extra weight, but they marched forward at a swift canter without protest.

They abandoned the riverbank and made for the mountains nearby. The horses slowed to a steady trot as they climbed the hillside, and they soon disappeared amid the forest. Once they could no longer see the river through the trees, they dismounted and continued up the mountain. After an hour of trekking uphill without a trail, they stopped to rest at a small stream that fed into the Vondal River in the valley below.

"I didn't see anyone following us," Kailem said.

"Nor did I," Elwin said. "We'll send the horses back. With any luck, they will think us deceased and move on, although it would not be wise to count on it."

Kailem agreed. "We need somewhere safe to lie low. Do you have somewhere in mind?"

Elwin nodded. "I know just the place."

Osmund realized the mountain they were on was north of the Balderlyn Falcon.

"You are taking us to your monastery!"

"Very good, young Osmund."

"So close to the Blackbirds' camp? Why haven't they found it?" Kailem asked.

"It's a difficult mountain to traverse, and there is no road leading to it. It is nearly impossible to find unless you know exactly where to look. That's why we selected this place."

The sound of a snapping twig sounded nearby. They turned to see antlers moving behind the thicket. A bull elk emerged standing five feet tall. It looked at Elwin, then to his three companions, then back to Elwin. The elk walked to the stream near where Elwin sat and drank from the water.

Kailem, Osmund, and Emerald were aghast. The beast was as massive as it was majestic, with powerful legs that could stomp them to bits and antlers that could rip them to shreds, but the elk walked casually, even reverently. He took a step toward Elwin, and the sage reached out and rubbed his snout. He mewed a satisfied tone, then stepped through the stream on his way. The four of them watched the beast disappear among the trees.

"We should be on our way. The monastery is still a good distance away," Elwin said.

The forest was quiet. The three friends relied on Elwin's calm demeanor as evidence they needn't fear an army of Blackbirds chasing them.

As they walked, Osmund had time to contemplate the day's events. He was sure he had heard Ulrich's neck snap. Emerald had killed a man. But that wasn't what most bothered Osmund. The man likely would have killed them, or worse, if she hadn't done it. No, what bothered him was how she seemed entirely unaffected by it. Even in self-defense, how could she end another man's life and be so calm? His breath caught in his throat. Was that not her first time? His thoughts returned to the man who tried to take her back in Ombermill.

Elwin hadn't exaggerated the distance. Even with a guide, it took well over two hours at a swift pace to reach it. The trees grew denser the higher they climbed, blocking out the sun overhead.

Their route made a large arc, eventually moving back in the direction of the Riverkeep, only now they were on a mountain ridge rather than a valley floor. They came to a relatively flat area on the mountain face about three-quarters of the way to the summit. The trees there were particularly dense; Osmund didn't notice the monastery until he could have thrown a stone at it. The entire outside wall was at least fifteen feet tall and covered in lichen and green ivy, disguising the structure from potential wanderers.

Elwin walked to a section of the wall that looked no different than the rest of it. He pulled back the web of ivy to reveal a wooden door reinforced with a steel grid. The door had no handle or keyhole. Elwin moved his hand across the door and from within came the sound of metal pins and tumblers turning over. He pushed the door open and invited the others in.

"Please remove your shoes," Elwin said, closing the door behind them and locking it. The door had a locking mechanism on the inside so it could be un-locked without the use of sagecraft.

The three friends took off their shoes and placed them in a chest against the wall at Elwin's direction.

"Allow me to show you to the dormitories. I imagine we'll all want some rest."

The monastery's interior was as dignified as the exterior was provincial. Elwin led them to the residential wing. The rooms were small and modest, yet well-constructed. Each room had a spacious window with a view of the courtyard that separated the residency from the outer wall.

"There are fresh linens for your mattresses and general supplies in the trunks at the foot of your bed," Elwin explained. "You should find soap, candles, and various sundries. I'll bring you some fresh clothes in a moment."

"Have ye a bath?" Emerald asked. The boys rolled their eyes.

After showing her the washroom, Elwin retrieved fresh clothes and returned to the dormitories. He found Kailem in his room, lying on his bed, staring at the ceiling. Elwin placed the fresh clothes on a nearby dresser and sat on the bed with a cloth in his hand.

"Your wrist, if you'd be so kind," he said.

Kailem sat up and extended his arm. As Elwin rubbed his thumbs over the tattoo, Kailem felt a peculiar warming sensation, pleasant and relaxing. He thought he even saw the area glow, but it was obscured by the ink rising out of his skin. Elwin wiped the ink away with the cloth every few seconds until no trace of the tattoo remained.

"You did well today, Kailem," the sage said. "I know what you learned wasn't easy, but you showed great restraint."

Kailem knew he hadn't. Whatever the sage had done to him had kept him from attacking; had he been left to his own devices, he would probably be dead. He stared at his wrist, now devoid of a tattoo, saying nothing.

"I recommend you rest. We'll discuss our next steps in the morning."

Elwin patted him on the shoulder as he left, and Kailem laid back on the bed, replaying the day's events in his mind.

Elwin next went to Osmund's room. He found him already fast asleep.

CHAPTER THIRTY-ONE

CORONATION

54TH DAY OF SUMMER, 897 G.C.

King Byron's lifeless body lay on a stone slab in the crypt below the palace. It was a damp and musty place, lit with only the dim glow of lantern light. A glass shield encased the body, which protected mourners from the stench of death and decay as much as it protected Byron's corpse from rodents and other vermin. The former king was dressed in royal splendor, adorned in furs and silks and crushed velvet. Deeper into the crypt was an open sepulcher with the king's likeness carved on the lid, where Byron would soon be entombed.

The Prince stood before the stone slab, his arms behind his back, appearing solemn and thoughtful. "It does not feel as I imagined it would," he confessed.

The only living soul within earshot was Kyra. The crypt had been cleared of everyone save the future King and Queen so that Aedon could mourn his father privately with his fiancé by his side. Kyra's chin quivered uncontrollably as she fought to maintain composure, although several whimpers and sniffles still managed to escape.

"I had imagined my heart would be conflicted," Aedon continued, "but blessedly I am as calm as a shadow. Strange, is it not?"

Kyra said nothing. Despite her best efforts, her composure fell for but an instant. Her face wrinkled in pain and her shoulders shook, but she caught herself just as quickly. A tear had managed to fall nearly to her quivering chin before she noticed and wiped it away.

In the ancient Cavander tradition, Aedon and Kyra were dressed in black sackcloth to show the great depth of their grief. The clothing was meant to be drab and coarse, but for decades the aristocracy had taken to having their sackcloth neatly tailored and lined with the finest and softest wool, so that mourning attire had become a fashion statement all of its own.

Kyra, however, abandoned this trend. Her gown was little more than a large potato sack, dyed black with holes cut out for her arms and head. She had bathed and combed her hair, only to show respect for the occasion, but she wore no braids in her hair and no perfume on her skin. It was a stark contrast to Aedon's attire, who wore his customary style merely devoid of color.

While pondering his own curious lack of emotion, Aedon's attention turned to the signet ring on his father's left hand. The seal was an image of a griffin, the symbol of the House of Braise, sitting calmly with wings unfurled. For Aedon, that seal fully embodied the reason his conscience was so unburdened. His father had been like that griffin, sitting calmly in the face of danger, refusing to act when action was needed. Aedon despised that image and all it stood for. He lifted his own left hand to admire his own newly forged signet ring; his father's ring would be buried with him.

Unlike the Fang of Rhinegard, that passed from king to king, each new king received his own signet ring with a unique seal to represent his reign. Aedon had chosen a griffin in flight with claws and beak exposed, ready to attack. That image would epitomize his reign. He resolved to be a strong king, a king that would be remembered for ages, the kind of king they would revere and write songs about and men would aspire to emulate. A king like Cavan Kohel had been, the type of king his father should have been, the type of king that Cavandel deserved. Now was the time for strength.

Cracks were splintering up the wall that held back Kyra's emotion, and behind that wall was a tempest of shame and horror. She had actually gone through with it. She had murdered a good man, and now there was nothing she could do to bring him back.

She thought for sure he would have survived when she called for the physicians, but she had acted too late. It had been her voice that agreed to the murder, her hand that delivered the poison, and her decision to withhold the antidote. That she had been acting under orders from her parents, and under threat of losing all she had, no longer granted any reprieve. Now standing above her victim's body, seeing his face gone pale and lifeless, she silently begged for Byron's forgiveness.

Aedon noticed her shoulders had begun to shake, and she raised her hands to keep from weeping. *What a tender heart she has,* Aedon thought. So greatly had she loved his father, but she had loved him even more. She would make an excellent queen.

Kyra's emotions finally overcame her, and she turned and ran from the crypt.

Aedon let her leave. It was no matter; there were none around to witness the outburst, and the funeral services would be starting soon. They were scheduled to end in the afternoon and the coronation ceremony was to begin that evening before the feast. It seemed to Aedon that each event was significant enough to merit its own day, but such was their tradition.

After the funeral, Kyra retreated to her quarters and let Martina help her out of her funeral garb and into her coronation gown. She diligently wiped every tear from her eyes, but the redness remained, betraying the shame that all mistook for grief.

Lord and Lady Arturri entered Kyra's quarters dressed in opulent garb for the ceremony. Their personal guard, Daron, waited for them outside. Pride beamed victoriously from their faces.

"You did well, my daughter," Leonin said.

"Indeed," Avalina added. "I have never been prouder." Avalina gave her daughter a tight embrace, cheek pressed against cheek. When she stepped back, she appraised Kyra's fashion choice, a traditional light blue gown paired with matching sapphire necklace and earrings. After Avalina nodded her approval, Leonin stepped forward and gave her a kiss on the forehead.

Kyra was sure she would vomit. She wished they would condemn her, berate her, even slap her, but perhaps the pain of the compliment was exactly what she deserved.

Leonin sat in the corner armchair. "I've spoken with Aedon. Our conspiracy has bound us together, even before your nuptials are complete. Our plans are moving perfectly. He has agreed to make the war public soon."

"How soon?" Kyra asked. "Against whom?"

"The exact moment will be up to him. But the army will march against both Shinda and Ârema. Preparations will begin tomorrow morning," he said.

Kyra's father had never shared so much of their plans with her, and she thought he must trust her now that she had killed a king for him. Visions of her nightmare flashed through her mind, and her lungs filled with panic. War on so grand a scale meant devastation, meant thousands of dead men on both sides strewn about a battlefield. Men who were fathers and brothers and sons, men who had futures and dreams. Perhaps Aedon would be one of them.

If causing the death of one man had broken Kyra's heart and spirit, she feared what causing her future husband's death, to say nothing of the death of thousands more would do to her. She was sure she would not survive it. But unlike the death of King Byron, a death she could never take back and that would haunt her forever, there was still something she could do to prevent the war. What that was, she didn't know, but she had to try. She had been the one who planted those toxic seeds in Aedon's mind. She was the one who had led him down this monstrous path, so it was up to her to rescue him from it. Perhaps that night, after the coronation feast, she could find time to reason with him.

Kyra followed her parents down to the Great Hall, and they took their place on the front bench. Because she was not yet married to Aedon, she was technically still a foreigner and could not sit with Aedon and the Dukes of Cavander on the royal dais. Kyra would have a coronation ceremony of her own on the First of Autumn after the wedding.

Scores of noblemen and women entered the Great Hall, many of whom offered her their deepest condolences, but she scarcely managed to look at them. Her mind could think of nothing beyond searching for a way to change Aedon's mind and prevent the war. If she had been allowed to sit by him, she could have whispered to him immediately, at least sowing the seeds of doubt in his mind. But barred from the royal dais as she was, she was forced to wait until after the ceremony to speak with him.

In Cavandel, the new king is crowned by a duke, one chosen by vote to represent all dukes in bestowing royal authority upon the new monarch. Because Lord Arturri was a foreigner, he was excluded from consideration. The dukes had elected Lord Erastus Menden, the elder brother of Lord Astor Menden, to conduct the ceremony. No two brothers could have been less alike, and this was entirely evident by their frame and appearance. Whereas Astor had been a feared warrior well into his elder years, Erastus had been a prolific glutton and inebriate since his youth. He had a bulbous face with jowls that hung from his cheeks like broken egg yolks. The rest of his body was even less appealing.

Erastus made a short tribute to King Byron before extolling the virtues of the former king's son, Aedon, to the congregation. He spoke of the sacred trust that a kingdom places in their king, how a king is the product of all the great men who have come before him, and how in his blood is the strength to rule and the might to conquer. He predicted that King Aedon would be the greatest king Iria had known in centuries. His speech was laden in political philosophy and shameless adulation, and he repeated the same ideas again and again in the most flowery language Cavandish had to offer.

When the speech ended, much to the congregation's relief, Erastus invited Aedon to take his place on the empty throne at the center of the dais.

"The crown of King Byron has been melted," Erastus told the assembly, "in accordance with the grand tradition of Cavandel. The same gold was then used to forge this crown which will sit atop the head of our new monarch, King Aedon of the House Braise. The reuse of gold shall symbolize the progression of power between monarchs, as is the Cavander way, and the new design shall symbolize that the reign of a new king has begun, and that old rules and customs are to be laid aside at the new king's pleasure. A new era has begun."

Where King Byron's crown had been elegant, yet subtle and unassuming, the design of Aedon's newly forged crown alluded to the flames of an inferno reaching angrily for the sky. Kyra knew its significance instantly: Aedon meant for his armies to sweep across Iria the way a fire sweeps across a prairie during the dry season. The congregation marveled.

Erastus made a show of lifting the crown high above his head, walking it behind Aedon, then slowly, too slowly, lowering the crown on Aedon's head. He then walked in front of the throne and knelt before the King.

With the crowning ceremony complete, the oaths of fealty began. One by one, every duke, earl, and baron in the great hall came and knelt before the King, following an ancient, carefully scripted procedure. First, the man unsheathed his sword. The hilt always pointed towards the king, and the tip always pointed back at himself. This detail was key, as it was punishable by death to ever point a blade at a king, even in passing. Then the man descended to his right knee and placed the weapon on the ground, bowed his head and held out his hands, his palms pointed forward. This was the silent oath of fealty to the new king.

The king accepted this oath with a nod, and the man returned the blade to its sheath, always careful never to point it at the king, and walked backwards from the throne. The next subject approached until all had sworn fealty to King Aedon. It was a lengthy, silent, and reverent process. Once every nobleman had sworn the silent oath, Erastus again stood before the congregation.

"All hail King Aedon, son of King Byron of the House of Braise, Ruler of the Kingdom of Cavandel and all its protectorates," Erastus called like a herald.

"Hail King Aedon," the congregation returned in unison.

Dozens of servants entered the Great Hall bearing trays of wine goblets, the first of which was given to the King. King Aedon began the tradition of the King's First Word.

"Today is both a day of mourning and celebration," Aedon began. "We mourn the unexpected passing of a great man, my father, and none more so than I. But we also celebrate the shining future that is on the horizon for this great kingdom of Cavandel. We Cavanders are a proud people, and for good reason. We hold ourselves to be the leaders of truth and justice, of strength and innovation, for all of Iria.

"It was no secret that my father abhorred war in all its forms. But we have recently learned some shocking and terrifying truths about our neighbors to the west. We have trustworthy reports that our villages in the Borderlands are under attack from the armies of Shinda and Ârema. If they remain unchecked, those same armies will march to this very city and destroy all that we hold so dear.

"Now is the time for strength. My father was reluctant to call us to arms, but I know that had he known the information we so recently received, even he would have ordered his armies to advance on our enemies. But what my father would have done is no longer a concern, for today is a new day, and a new reign has begun. And I will not stand by while our people are attacked. I will take the Might of Cavandel and march across Iria like a fire blazing across the grasslands."

No, not now, Kyra thought. She rubbed her right palm with her left thumb, then switched hands. Aedon was preparing to declare war here and now, in front of half the aristocracy, and she hadn't had a chance to talk to him yet. If he declares war now, he will never be able to back down without looking weak. The faces of Willian Wyke and King Byron flashed through her mind, followed by the thousands of dead bodies strew across the misty field. She refused to be a coward any longer. She had to do something, and it had to be now.

Kyra rose from her front-row seat. Avalina reached for her daughter, but reacted too late. Kyra slipped out of her reach and climbed the dais steps to Aedon's side, interrupting his speech mid-sentence.

"What are you doing, Kyra?" Aedon asked through clenched teeth.

"Please don't do this, Aedon," she whispered into his ear. "Please, not war, I beg of you."

Aedon looked out to the audience, and Kyra's eyes followed his. Every face in the Great Hall was aghast. Men and women turned to each other, whispering conspicuously. The nobility loved nothing more than a good scandal, and the most delicious scandals always involved royalty. So for the King's own betrothed to demonstrate such disrespect on so grand an occasion, Aedon was certain they were all mocking him.

He took Kyra by the arm and led her to the hearth at the back of the stone dais.

"Have you gone mad?!" he said in a roaring whisper. "It is the First-Word! You've made a fool of me!"

"Don't do this," Kyra repeated. "Consider how many lives will be lost. The lives of fathers and sons, your people. It's wrong."

Aedon's face twisted into creases. "Lives of commoners, sacrificed for the greater good of the kingdom," he returned. "This was all your idea, Kyra. This is what we've worked for."

"Don't do it, Aedon. For me, for the love we share, if nothing else. Please, don't do it."

"Enough," he commanded. He put up a hand, silencing her.

Lord and Lady Arturri approached behind them.

"Kyra, what is the matter with you? A thousand apologies, my king," Leonin said.

"Take her to her seat. This outburst is over," Aedon said.

Avalina grabbed her daughter's hand and pulled her towards the steps, but Kyra twisted her wrist until she broke free.

"People of Cavander," Kyra said to the congregation, "war is not the answer. We cannot avenge the lives of a few by ending the lives of thousands. We must be better than that."

Kyra couldn't believe what she was doing; perhaps she *had* gone mad. But she couldn't think about that now. She had become fixed on a singular purpose: she had to prevent more death before it was too late, no matter the cost.

Aedon fumed. Shock and scandal screamed in the faces of the assembly. His moment of triumph had soured into humiliation, but what stung most of all was that Kyra was the culprit. This betrayal was worse than anything he thought her capable. This would be the talk of the kingdom for years to come. His entire reign would be stained, marred by this public act of rebellion by his own fiancé. His face went flush and hot.

"Kyra, I am warning you. Sit down," Aedon commanded. He gripped her by the arm. He was far stronger than her mother, but Kyra fought like a feral car until she broke free. Aedon could not contain her without publicly abandoning his decorum, but decorum was quickly losing its importance.

"You are good people," she continued. "My time in your wonderful kingdom has taught me that. I know you do not wish to shed the blood of so many innocent men. It is not what King Byron wished, and I know if you search your hearts, it is not what you wish, either."

If Aedon didn't control this now, he would lose every shred of dignity for the rest of his reign. Now was the time for strength, and in that moment, he hated her. His nostrils flared and his lips twisted like a lion bearing his fangs.

Rage took over.

Aedon grabbed the iron poker from the hearth. The tip glowed red hot from the roaring fire inside. He marched to Kyra, still addressing the congregation, and swung the iron poker.

The glowing red iron struck Kyra's face, and the force of the blow sent her stumbling to the stone floor. Flesh sizzled from her temple to her chin, instantly cauterized. The scent of burning flesh filled the hall, her screams the only sound.

Aedon stared at his once-beloved fiancé writhing at his feet. His body shook with rage, but his heart was numb. Her punishment, inflicted in front of the entire nobility on his first day as king, had sent a powerful message. He could not back down lest he appear weak before his subjects. His nostrils flared.

"She is no longer fit to be my queen," Aedon yelled to the congregation. He was unhinged and shaking with wrath.

"I will not tolerate a word of defiance to my rule," his rant continued. Saliva sprayed from his lips as he screamed. "I will treat it as sedition and punish it as such."

Aedon turned to Kyra's parents, the hot poker still in his hand, and pointed the tip in their direction.

"Lord and Lady Arturri, what do you have to say for your daughter's treason?"

The Arturris stood in shock and horror. Their daughter writhed on the ground, moaning in pain, her face permanently deformed. The congregation stared at them on the dais, waiting for their answer.

Leonin and Avalina kneeled before the King.

"She is no daughter of ours," Leonin said.

"Our loyalty is to the King and none other," Avalina followed.

Tears flowed from Kyra's eyes, stinging her wound as they trickled down her cheek. Everyone she loved, everyone she thought loved her, had just cast her aside, a mongrel dog to be put down.

Aedon threw the poker back in the fire.

"Guards, take her away," he commanded. "Cast her from the palace, never to step foot inside again."

Royal Guards stepped forward and dragged Kyra's limp body from the Great Hall.

The congregation was silent. Lord and Lady Arturri were still on their knees. Everyone waited with bated breath for what the new King would do next.

King Aedon retrieved his wine goblet from the table and lifted it high into the air.

"To war!" he yelled.

The congregation thundered back, "to war!"

***

Kyra's body was a loose ball of yarn. Her mind vacillated between searing pain and a black abyss. She was sure Aedon had cracked her skull. For some reason, the palace floor was sliding underneath her legs. No, she had it backwards — she was being dragged down a corridor.

Two royal guards held her by the arms, their hands tucked under her armpits. During her moments of consciousness, if she ignored the throbbing pain in her head, she could see the faces of noblewomen and other courtiers. Most had their hands to their mouths. This scandal would be the palace gossip for the next year, at least.

Resisting the guards was out of the question; she barely had the strength to raise her eyelids. She tried to determine where they were taking her. The holding cells? Perhaps they'd lock her in her own quarters? She thought she had heard Aedon say where they were to take her, but she couldn't remember. Even thinking was painful.

Her ankles clanked against the portico steps as the guards dragged her outside. The gravel road between the palace and the gates carved jagged grooves into her shins, but so intense was the pain in her head she hardly noticed it.

Once they passed through the palace gates, the guards simply dropped her in the street. She landed in a puddle. Had it been raining? The smell of the puddle told her otherwise. She didn't have the strength to crawl out of it. The world faded into darkness.

When she awoke, the sun had set, and both moons shined brightly above her head. The streets were never empty in Rhinegard, not completely, but there were times when it was nearly so. This was one of those times. The footprints on her dress said that people had walked over her, and on her, while she had been unconscious.

She fumbled to her feet.

There was a tavern nearby. If someone had seen her trying to stand, they undoubtedly would have thought her inebriated. She walked down the cobblestone road, unsure of where she was going.

She stopped at the reflection of her face in the tavern window. There was a gash of scorched flesh from her right temple, less than an inch from her eye, down her cheek to her chin. Part of her lip had melted. The glowing iron had cut deep into her skin; she thought she could see part of her cheekbone exposed in the wound. Yellow blisters had formed along the edges of the wound.

She stared at the reflection, wondering who that grotesque person was staring back at her. Her mind refused to accept this monster could be her. Her lower lip quivered. Tears welled in her eyes and spilled out onto her cheeks, stinging her wound. She forced herself to look away. It was all too much for her. Yesterday she was the King's fiancé, weeks away from being crowned the queen of the most powerful kingdom in Iria. Today... she couldn't finish the thought.

Goosebumps blossomed on her skin, and she shivered like a plucked harp string. A slight breeze blew past, stinging her wound again. She walked past the alleyway on the side of the tavern. Perhaps there might be some discarded fabric she could use as a blanket, or maybe even some discarded bottles with liquor still in them to help her feel warm. She hobbled down the alley and rummaged through discarded crates and piles of rubbish.

The tavern doors opened and shut. Men stumbled out together, laughing and swaying. She backed into a stack of crates, knocking one over in the process.

"Oi, someone there?" one of them asked. The three of them crept down the alley. There was nowhere for her to hide.

"What do we have here, then?" one said. He had a scruffy beard, a shaved head, and a bulging gut.

"Looks like this one's had a little too much to drink," said another man. This one was tall and dressed a shade finer than the first. Kyra could say nothing. She simply cowered against the tavern wall with arms folded, her shoulders caved in as much as the joints would allow.

"Aw, you can never have *too* much to drink, right love?" said the scruffy man. He took the bottle of whiskey in his hand and poured in on Kyra's head. The pungent liquid spilled down her cheeks and into her wound.

An entire nest of hornets stung Kyra's cheek. She let out a deafening, blood-curdling scream. Her scorched face sang with unimaginable pain, nearly as intense as the initial blow from the Prince had been, only this time it did nothing dull her consciousness. She dropped to the filth of the alley floor, holding her hands close to her face, unable to actually touch her cheek without worsening the pain.

"We've got a live one here, don't we, fellas?" said the tall man.

"Hang on a minute," said the third man, the shortest of the three. "That is a fine dress she's wearing. That would fetch us at least a dozen florins, *silver* florins. Now, where did a little thing like you find such a fine dress like that?"

"How do you know the worth of a dress?" the tall man asked, half challenging and half mocking.

"My uncle's a dressmaker. I seen it in his shop. He buys old dresses and fixes 'em up right nice for tidy profit."

"She probably stole it," said the scruffy man. "We ought to take it and give it back to its rightful owner."

"I agree," the tall man said. "It's our civic duty, innit?"

The tall man rolled Kyra onto her face and unlaced her dress. Without the help of an experienced handmaid, it took the prodding and pulling of all three men to remove the dress with the fabric mostly unripped. The pain in Kyra's cheek was so severe she barely noticed when her dress moved off her shoulders. She whimpered uncontrollably, but there was no fight left in her. The men slid off her dress until she was left lying on the ground in only her slip, leaving little of her figure to the imagination. Then they ripped away her sapphire necklace, breaking the clasp in the process, and used little finesse in removing her earrings. Kyra shivered in the cold.

"There we go. Now, let me have a look at you," the tall man said. "Well now, you are a pretty little thing."

He moved her chin to the other side, exposing her right cheek to the lamplight. He gasped and recoiled at the sight of it.

"Ah! Looks like someone punished you something awful, didn't they? Now what did you go and do to deserve a wound like that?"

Kyra avoided the man's eyes. Her only sound was her teeth chattering. He stood over her, assessing her, as if trying to decide what he would do next.

The scruffy man put his hand on the tall man's shoulder. "Come on, then. We got a dress to sell and a bottle to drink."

The tall man waited a moment longer before agreeing to be done with her. The three men left, leaving Kyra alone on the ground shivering in her slip.

CHAPTER THIRTY-TWO

AN ANCIENT ORDER

41ST DAY OF SUMMER, 897 G.C.

O smund woke to the sun already high in the sky. The sun had still been out when he crawled into bed the day prior as well. Just how long had he been asleep? he wondered.

On the dresser was a clean set of loose-fitting white linen clothes. The shirt's collar was wide and low off the neck and the sleeves ended several inches above the wrist, with the bottom of the shirt ending down by his hips.

Osmund crept out of his room with an inexplicable feeling he was trespassing, but the itch to explore the ancient monastery was too much for him to ignore. The stone tiles were cold under his bare feet, and the granite swirls of grey and white were like a gentle river frozen in time. Everything in the monastery was made with expert detail and precision. He rotated in slow circles as he walked, looking in every direction for fear of missing the most minute detail.

The wooden walls had relief carvings the entire length of the corridors. They depicted different sages, men and women using their unnatural powers in exotic, faraway places. The barrel-vaulted ceilings were painted with colorful frescos of intricate lines and patterns. And yet for all its ornate beauty, the monastery still had an air of warmth and meekness that was usually lost in aristocratic architecture.

Once he had passed through the dormitories into the main quarter, he would manage only a few feet before he found something new to stop and examine. Osmund couldn't believe where he was, and he feared he might wake up in his family's estate at any moment. There was something sacred about this place. Perhaps it was simply the result of idolizing something for so long without any hope of finding it, the way commoners idolize tournament champions but never get to meet them. Osmund never would have believed such a place as this existed — he had hoped at best to find a crumbling, dilapidated building and a library of decaying books with scarcely a legible page inside. But the sages were real. He knew one of them by name, and now he walked freely in their pristine, arcane monastery. He was certain no man had ever been so lucky as he was in that moment.

He walked down a cloister hallway where daylight spilled in from above, past a solarium with a vibrant indoor garden. Farther down the hall, he found a set of ceiling-high double doors slightly ajar. If whatever was inside was off-limits, he reasoned, surely the door would not have been left unlocked. The door was perfectly silent as he pulled it wide.

Inside the room were at least a dozen chair-sized pillows on the floor. The room was lit by several small skylights which let sunlight in through the ceiling. Painted clouds spread seamlessly from the walls onto the floor and ceiling, creating the effect that he was walking on air.

Elwin sat on one of the floor pillows in perfect stillness, breathing slowly. Osmund tiptoed in front of him, his bare feet not making a sound. Elwin's eyes were closed, his face peaceful. It seemed wrong to disturb him.

Osmund chose a nearby floor pillow, close to but not immediately beside Elwin, and tried to mimic his position and posture. He peeked open his right eye to verify he did it correctly.

Welcome to the Aether Room, Osmund, a voice spoke in his mind.

Osmund fumbled to his feet in a panic. He looked around him. Elwin was still as calm as a statue on his floor pillow, and there no one else was in the room.

You can relax, Osmund, it is I, the voice said again. Osmund instinctively took a step backwards, then, after mustering some courage, leaned forward inspecting him.

"Elwin?" he whispered.

Not aloud. We do not speak in the Aether Room, Elwin said in Osmund's mind. *This is a place for quiet contemplation. Have a seat and close your eyes.*

Osmund hesitantly lowered himself back down to his floor pillow, and he resumed Elwin's position.

Now, breathe deeply...

"No. No, no," Osmund said aloud as he jumped to his feet. "Too strange! Too strange by half." He crossed the Aether Room like the floor was made of hot coals. The hint of a smile shone through Elwin's otherwise stoic face.

Eventually, Osmund found the room he was certain would be his favorite. The library walls were covered floor to ceiling in bookshelves, with gaps in between for stained glass windows depicting peaceful pastoral scenes. The layout was astonishingly similar to his room back home, only this room was an order of magnitude larger. The walls were two stories tall, and every fifteen yards a spiral staircase led to a mezzanine that lined the upper level of the bookshelves.

Osmund let his hand grace across the wooden shelves. Each shelf had a glass casing that rotated open to access the books inside. Osmund surmised it was to keep the air out so the pages would not decay as quickly.

"Not bad," Kailem said from behind him.

The sound made Osmund jump and the book in his hands fumbled to the mezzanine floor. Kailem and Emerald stood in the doorway in similar white linen clothing. Emerald had clearly taken another bath this morning.

"By Iria, Kailem! Don't do that." Osmund bent down to pick up the book and allow his heart rate to return to normal.

"I knew we'd find ye here," Emerald said as she climbed the spiral staircase.

"Have you ever seen a more beautiful room?" he asked as he slid the book back onto the shelf.

Emerald took in the room from the mezzanine vantage. "Aye, 'tis lovely," she finally said. "I still fancy the forest better." When Osmund seemed genuinely offended by the comment, she gave him a playful nudge with her elbow.

The three friends perused the bookshelves, reading the titles out loud. Emerald mostly admired the engravings and illustrations, hoping she'd soon be able to read them. There were texts on history, natural philosophy, and a host of other topics Osmund hadn't reached. They had tales of fiction and of fables and poems, and an especially large collection of books on the history of the sages. Many of the books were in a language Osmund didn't recognize.

"Oz, come look at this," Kailem called from the mezzanine near the stained-glass window. Osmund climbed the stairs nearest him.

"I reckon these are instruction manuals on sagecraft," Kailem said.

Osmund quickened his pace across the mezzanine. Kailem was right. He held an instructional manual on the art of healing. Osmund grabbed several more volumes and carried them down to one of the leather chairs that sat in a beam of green and yellow light from the stained glass. Kailem selected a history book, and Emerald found a book of children's stories with animated depictions alongside the text.

The trio spent the next two hours buried in books. Osmund was a starving peasant in front of a king's banquet, and not even the full Might of Cavandel could pull him away from it. Just one of these books would have been a priceless treasure to him. To be surrounded by thousands of them was more than he knew what to do with.

"Oi, Oz, what's this on about?" Emerald called.

Osmund looked at her, not wanting to leave his reading. When he didn't come straightaway, she waved him over with a playful urgency. Her brilliant green eyes, fierce red hair, and roguish smile left him powerless to resist. He reluctantly left his books and sat in the reading chair beside hers.

On Emerald's lap was a book of zoology, a textbook covering all the many creatures of Iria. The book was opened to a section on winged creatures with detailed illustrations of every specimen it covered.

"This here," she said.

Osmund read the passage she pointed to. "It's discussing different species of dragons," he explained.

"I 'member this one here from the woods." She pointed to an illustration of a forest dragon. It was a shade between green and turquoise and was raised on its tail like a viper preparing to strike, its wings extended just before taking flight. "What about this one?"

Osmund read the passage aloud. "Fire dragons. Native to the Sidian Islands, so named as they nest near active plumes of flowing lava. Unlike the forest dragon, fire dragons have only one set of wings and no feathers. Their head, forearms, and hindquarters closely resemble those of a lizard, while their wings closely resemble those of a bat. Highly intelligent, can be broken and trained by a strong hand, and will remain fiercely loyal to its trainer. Its colors may be mahogany, obsidian, or ash. Its preferred sources of food are shallow water fish and birds such as the seagull and the phoenix."

"Wait, what's a phoenix?" Emerald asked in wonder.

Osmund turned to the section on birds and read aloud. "Phoenix. A seafaring bird with an average weight of nine pounds and an average wingspan of five feet. Native to the Sidian Islands, can be identified by their brightly colored feathers of crimson, ruby, and tangerine. Prefers to lay its eggs in volcanic ash abundant in Sidia."

The book's illustrations captivated them both, but Emerald especially. Together they read page after page, each more fascinating than the last. Emerald's favorite was the pixie, a small creature similar to a fruit bat, the size of a human thumb and with colorful wings like a butterfly or hummingbird. The book said they were naturally affectionate, making them easy prey, and if you ever saw one, it meant there were likely no predators nearby. One illustration depicted small birds flocking in such numbers that they filled the entire sky like ominous storm clouds; she thought of the revolutionaries assembling at the base of their mountain and shuddered.

She brightened at the page about wind horses, remembering back to their first night in the Pavian Grasslands. There was a section about krakens that lived in the northern seas and were large enough to devour a ship. It called to mind the mast of *The Flying Manta* collapsing and sending her into the deep.

"What's this?" she asked, pointing to a bear with white fur.

"You've never heard of a polar bear?"

She shook her head.

Osmund explained, "Every creature that lives in the southern lowlands has another version of itself that lives up in the mountains and the snow." He kept his finger in the section on beasts of the north and found the section on beasts of the south. "In the south, we have black bears and brown bears. In the north they have polar bears, which have white fur. In the south we have elephants, in the north they have the woolly mammoth. Here we have gorillas, there they have the yeti."

For every creature he named, Osmund would flip between sections so Emerald could see the similarities between them. She rested her head on his shoulder, just as she had when he showed her the Codex Andala. Kailem watched them from his own reading chair and grinned.

"I see you found the library," Elwin said. All three of them looked up. No one had heard him enter. Osmund saw Elwin recognize the books he had left open on the table and was relieved when the sage didn't mention it.

"I'm glad you are all here. We have certain matters to discuss," Elwin said. He extended his hand, and a nearby chair slid towards him. Osmund was sure Elwin would reprimand him for reading their training manuals.

"The Blackbirds are going to be scouring this area for weeks," Elwin said. "You'll have to remain in seclusion until it is safe to leave." Kailem's countenance darkened at the mention of the Blackbirds.

"Ye cannae fight them all, then?" Emerald asked.

"Well... I could," Elwin admitted, "but that would only draw more attention. And we avoid using sagecraft in violence whenever possible."

"What's our plan, then?" Kailem asked.

"You can stay here as long as you'd like. We have enough food and there's a well of fresh water—"

"I meant, what are we going to do about the Blackbirds?" Kailem interrupted. Elwin noticed only now the rage that was once again rising inside the young man.

"I don't believe we need to do anything. I searched their captain's thoughts and found nothing to indicate they practice sagecraft. I also learned a good deal about their leadership. The Blackbirds are led by a man named Leonin Arturri."

"Lord Arturri?" Osmund remarked in surprise.

"An acquaintance of yours?" Elwin asked.

"He's a close friend of my father's. His daughter Kyra is engaged to Prince Aedon."

"Why would the Blackbirds be led by aristocrats?" Kailem asked. "The core of their message is to dismantle the aristocracy."

"Must be lyin', then," Emerald said.

Kailem and Osmund both frowned, realizing the answer should have been obvious to them.

Elwin nodded. "I agree. Their true agenda is not being shared with their rank-and-file." He then turned to Osmund, the sage's face shadowed with reluctance. "There is something else I learned, something you will not want to hear, Osmund, but I cannot in good conscience keep it from you."

Osmund shifted in his chair, not realizing he was holding his breath.

"Lord Arturri is the leader of their society," Elwin began, "and their second in command is another prominent Lord of Devona, a duke by the name Reginald Baylor."

The blood drained from Osmund's face. That couldn't be right, Elwin must have misheard. Osmund's eyes stared out into the distance.

Elwin continued. "And the captain whose thoughts I heard, he referred to Lord Baylor as 'father'."

"Edric!" Kailem blurted out. "That's where I recognized that name."

Not until he saw the expression on Osmund's face did Kailem realize the implications of what he had said. Osmund's entire family were not only members, but leaders in the Blackbird Society. Osmund's family had his parents murdered. Osmund's family was the cause of his exile.

Osmund was silent for a moment. He wanted to scream at them, to insist they were mistaken, that it was impossible his family could be involved in something like this. But he was not so naïve, and with two witnesses against them, there was no sense in denying it.

"My whole family?" he said to no one in particular. "Why would they do this? Why would they hide it from me?"

There was silence in the library for several long, uncomfortable seconds. Emerald placed a tender hand on his forearm.

"My condolences, young Osmund. I would that the truth had been kinder to you," Elwin said.

Osmund nodded, his gaze still off in the distance. Kailem's anger, however, neared its boiling point.

"We cannot sit here and do nothing," Kailem insisted. "Sagecraft or not, the Blackbirds need to be stopped."

"I do not meddle in the affairs of common men, Kailem. No matter how worthy the cause."

Kailem squeezed his fists to keep from yelling. "This is more than a worthy cause," he seethed. He stood from his chair and began to pace. "You heard what they said in that meeting. They mean to upend order in the kingdoms, to sow chaos. If they are not stopped, thousands will die. Hundreds of thousands. Iria itself will become unrecognizable!"

"Which is tragic, to be sure. I would never suggest otherwise. But having me intervene is not a solution. I preserve the secrecy of sagecraft, nothing more. Believe me, Kailem, I know—"

"They murdered my parents!" he screamed, pounding his fist on the top rail of his chair. "They cut off their heads, Elwin! Right in front of me!"

The outburst shook Osmund out of his stupor. He hadn't known the details of their execution, and Kailem had never been keen on sharing. Emerald brought her knees up to her chest as her eyes lost focus.

Kailem was quivering. His jaw was set, his fists clenched. Self-control was slipping away from him; any second, he would become aggressive, even violent. Then he felt it again, the same calming sensation he had felt in the Riverkeep washing over him, gentle and deep. His eyes flashed at Elwin.

"You swore to stay out of our minds," he said. He took a slow step away from the Sage.

"I am not listening to your thoughts, Kailem. Only helping you remain calm."

Kailem took another step back and thumped against a bookshelf. "I neither need nor want your help," he said in a low voice that rumbled in his throat.

Elwin looked down, and Kailem felt the boiling rage return as the calming sensation abandoned him. He took a deep breath and steadied himself, looking off into the distance.

The salon stayed silent for several unsavory seconds.

"Perhaps it is time I share what destroyed the Order of the Sages," Elwin said. "It would be easiest if I showed you." Kailem refused to look at him. Elwin began his story all the same.

"I told you before that we had been a powerful force for good in the world. For centuries, the people loved and trusted us, but it was not to last. Their adoration curdled into contempt within the span of a single generation. Entire armies united against us. And although they outnumbered us nearly 100 to 1, they stood no chance. Mind you, this was all before the invention of steel swords and armor. We defended ourselves when necessary, but we took no joy in it. Eventually, the entire order retreated to our city, Andalaya, so a plan could be devised."

As he spoke, a vision materialized in his students' minds. The trio saw Elwin and others like him traveling about Iria, using their power to heal and protect. Then he saw the people's unease, the angry crowds gathering to protest the Sages' very existence, and violence erupting from the mob. For Kailem, it looked remarkably similar to the mob that had demanded his parents be executed.

Elwin continued. "There were, however, disagreements among us regarding how to handle the situation. Half of us, myself included, thought we could win back the love and trust of the people. But the other half was convinced that our only path forward was to exert our power over the people, to subjugate them and compel them to peace and prosperity through dominance. I tried to convince my opponents that if we followed such a course, we would only be confirming the very fears that had caused the people to rise against us in the first place, but it was no use.

"Disagreement devolved into contention, contention soured to animus, and animus burned into violence. There was a battle. Sage fought against sage, and we did to ourselves what all the armies of Iria never could. There had been thousands of us at the time, but when sun rose after, scarcely a dozen remained. I hope with all my heart that none of you ever know the pain of being forced to take the life of your own family, your own children, of watching your people swept away in a day."

The trio saw a mighty battle among the sages, with all the powers of sagecraft engaged against one another. The fighting spread across a valley high in the mountains occupied by palatial stone buildings of curious design. The valley was a paradise, a perfect fusion of nature and architecture not seen anywhere else in Iria. The trio's view of the great battle weaved in and out of the buildings where sage fought against sage with the impossible force of a tempest.

Although the power they saw was beyond comprehension, that display of sagecraft paled in comparison to the emotions exhibited by the survivors. The trio watched in horror as mothers and fathers held their dead children, even as the battle continued to rage around them. Some of the sages were so possessed by hate and rage that they seemed to kill whoever was near them without reason or restraint. Others stood stoically, ready to die before taking the life of a loved one. Those sages were seen holding their dead until they were forced to join them. Then there were those who, like Elwin, pleaded with their attackers to abandon the fight, waiting until the last possible moment before defending themselves.

In the end, the once idyllic valley was left desolate. Trees were upended, buildings lay in ruins, and the dead lay scattered across the ground. The loss that occurred that day would have been difficult to appreciate had the trio not seen it for themselves. Then the vision faded, and they were back in the monastery. Emerald lifted her feet onto the armchair and wrapped her arms around her knees, while Osmund lifted his spectacles to brush away a tear before it fell from his eye.

Kailem could see the pain in Elwin's eyes over the loss of his people, and he was not without sympathy for him, but neither was his anger quenched. Fury mingled with sorrow, leaving him in a confused, emotional haze. Elwin's story explained why he so adamantly refused to intervene, but it did nothing to justify that refusal. It only made him a coward. But how could Kailem say that after Elwin shared such a painful story? Kailem chose to say nothing and simply left the room instead.

In the afternoon, Osmund found Kailem on a bench in the solarium. He was leaning forward with his elbows on his knees, his fingers interlocked, his head hanging low. His heel bounced off the floor like it was vibrating.

Osmund approached him like a child about to be scolded. Kailem looked up at him with eyes that were red and swollen, but said nothing.

"May I?" Osmund asked, pointing to the empty space on the bench.

Kailem thought for a moment, then nodded silently. Osmund sat beside him.

He struggled with what to say. "I feel like I should apologize," he finally said. "On behalf of my family, I mean."

Kailem scoffed.

"I know. It is... a paltry gesture, at best. It's just, what ought a man to say in such a situation?"

Kailem didn't move.

"But I am sorry, Kailem. I know it doesn't change anything. I doubt it even makes you feel better, but still, I am sorry. Terribly so."

Kailem exhaled and looked up at him. "You're right, Oz. It doesn't make me feel better." Kailem stood from the bench and aimlessly paced the solarium.

Osmund opened his mouth, then closed it. He tried to speak a second time, then a third, but what could he say? He stood from the bench in defeat and left Kailem in the solarium without another word.

Kailem wasn't sure how long he spent pacing the solarium, fuming. Hours, at least. Pacing wasn't helping. While walking back to his dormitory, he passed by Osmund's open door. Osmund was lying on his bed, staring off into nothing. The Baylor family had murdered his parents and destroyed his life, and there was a Baylor right here before him. For the briefest of moments, a split second and no longer, Kailem thought to take his revenge.

The impulse disappeared as quickly as it arose, and an unbearable shame blossomed in its place, forcing Kailem to look away. Osmund had been a better friend than Kailem had ever known, save only for Mokain. How could Kailem think so dark a thought, no matter how short its duration? The shame was like acid dissolving his anger. He knew Osmund was hurting just as he was. Kailem had been grieving his parents' loss for almost a year now; Osmund's loss was only hours old.

Kailem entered and sat next to him on the bed. Osmund said nothing.

"Thank you," Kailem finally said. "For the apology, on behalf of your parents." He placed a grateful, comforting hand on Osmund's shoulder. After a moment, he added, "and I'm sorry about your family. That must have been terrible to hear."

"It was," Osmund said, still staring off into the distance.

Kailem straightened his back and wiped away the tear that formed in his eyes. "So, what do we do now?"

Osmund sat up and shook his head. "I can never go home again. In fact, I do not care to ever *look* at them again."

Kailem nodded. "I wish there was another sage who could help us. Or, if I'm wishing for things, I wish we could just do it ourselves."

Osmund thought for a moment. "I have an idea."

Kailem followed him back to the library. Elwin sat in a different chair than before, staring aimlessly out one of the stained-glass windows. Emerald was on the second-story mezzanine, perusing the bookshelves.

Osmund went to pull the nearest chair closer to Elwin's. It proved heavier than he expected, so he walked behind to push it. He didn't notice when Elwin gave a soft auratic push to help him move it into place, and Osmund sat while Kailem leaned against the bookshelf nearby, his arms folded across his chest.

"Something on your mind, young Osmund?"

"Yes... sir. You said your... vision with the, uh..." Osmund tried to remember the term.

"The Aura of Iria," Elwin said.

"Right, that your vision with the Aura of Iria meant that the three of us were brought together for a purpose, correct?"

The sage nodded. Emerald walked down the spiral staircase, curious to hear the conversation.

"And we know that purpose has something to do with the Blackbirds," Osmund continued. Elwin shifted in his seat as he listened. "Well, there is only one way that we could have any chance of fighting the Blackbirds." Osmund exhaled, then squared his shoulders. "I believe we are meant to become Sages."

"Osmund, we made an agreement. I would explain anything you wanted to know, but I am not going to train you."

"True, true, that was our agreement, but I am not saying you should train us because we helped you. I am saying you should train us because the Aura of Iria wants you to."

Osmund still wasn't sure what the Aura of Iria even was, but he knew Elwin trusted it.

Elwin shook his head. "I'm sorry. That is something I simply cannot do."

Osmund sat back in his chair. "Why not?"

"You must understand. I spent centuries training new sages, young men and women just like yourselves. A few of them were even my own children. And then I had to watch them kill each other until almost none were left. Some, I was even forced to kill with my own hand lest they kill me. Sometimes, I wonder if I should have let them. The grief and sorrow that has plagued me since is something I would not wish on anyone. I will not go through it again. I am sure I would not survive it a second time."

"But that won't happen with us," Osmund assured. He spoke not with rhetoric, but with eager conviction. "I believe that's why the Aura of Iria gave you that vision, to tell you that it will be different this time, that it's time to reestablish the Order."

Elwin breathed in a single deep breath and exhaled through his nose.

"I considered that myself," he said. "The problem with the theory is, I didn't see the end of the conflict. When the vision ended, the Blackbirds were winning. I didn't see if you survived. The Aura of Iria could just as well have been warning me not to let you engage with the Blackbirds lest they prove the end of you. It may have been a warning to protect you."

Osmund was running out of arguments.

"You promised me justice, Elwin," Kailem said, still leaning against the bookshelf, his arms folded. "While we were in their command council, I could have taken out several of them right then and there, perhaps all of them, but I didn't because you made me a *promise*."

Elwin shook his head. "What you're describing isn't justice, Kailem. It's vengeance."

"And do you think we'll find justice hiding away in this monastery, doing nothing?" Kailem asked.

Elwin looked to the ground. The young man couldn't be reasoned with.

"You promised," Kailem repeated.

No one said anything. Kailem gave Elwin time to respond, but when no response came, he left them again in the library.

He returned to his room and laid down on his bed. If Elwin wouldn't help him, he would find justice on his own. Perhaps he could return to Rhinegard and enlist Mokain's help. Or perhaps he could return to the Riverkeep. He still had the Blackbird's uniform, and he could explain that Osmund and Emerald had escaped and had killed Elwin, or 'Carsten', in the process. If he told them they used sagecraft to do it, they would believe him. Then he could end each one of them silently as they slept.

His thoughts became increasingly graphic and morbid. The room turned dark as the sun retired for the evening. He must have been in there for hours imagining his revenge in vivid detail.

There was a knock at the door. Kailem looked up to see Emerald standing at his doorway.

"Are ye well?" she asked.

Kailem sat up on the edge of the bed and rested his elbows on his knees. After a moment, he shook his head.

"Fig'red as much," Emerald said in a tender voice. "Elwin sent me to fetch ye. He cooked us dinner."

Kailem followed her to a dining area. Osmund sat at the table while Elwin brought out the last of the food he'd prepared. There was fresh bread, grilled vegetables, a bowl of boiled lentils, and a bottle of blackberry wine.

The four of them sat at the table and began eating.

Elwin was the first to break the silence. "I've had some time to consider. I can't be certain if the vision meant we are supposed to fight the Blackbirds or if I should reestablish the Order, but no matter what the correct interpretation is, one thing *is* certain: the three of you were meant to come together, and I was meant to find you. I cannot imagine any reason for this that doesn't include me training you in sagecraft."

Osmund dropped his spoon and looked up. Emerald and Kailem exchanged puzzled glances.

Elwin lifted his hand before they could speak. "Let me be clear, I am not re-founding the Order, and I have some conditions you must agree to before we can start."

"Anything," Osmund said.

"First, you must swear to maintain the secrecy of everything I teach you. You cannot speak of sagecraft to anyone, even those you know to be trustworthy. You cannot use this power in public unless it is absolutely necessary, and most importantly, you cannot teach these skills to anyone else."

"Agreed," Osmund said with delight.

Elwin continued, "second, you must swear to follow my every instruction with exactness. At first, some of them will not make sense. You may ask any questions you have; some I will answer, others I may not, but you must follow my instructions either way."

"I can do that," Osmund said, nodding his head.

"Third, sagecraft involves unspeakable power, more than all the armies of a mighty king, so you must swear to use sagecraft only for good, to protect the weak and defend what is right."

"Of course," Osmund said.

"And fourth, you must swear never to interfere in the affairs of the common man. We help those who cannot help themselves, but we stay out of politics and the aristocracy's struggle for power. That includes the Blackbirds. If you find them abusing the innocent, you may intervene, inconspicuously, of course, but we will not go on a crusade to defeat them."

The fourth requirement was the most difficult. Osmund and Emerald looked to Kailem, waiting for what he would say. He stared at Elwin, saying nothing.

Osmund spoke first. "I swear to all four of your requirements."

"As do I," Emerald added.

Elwin nodded his acceptance of their oaths. Then he turned to Kailem.

"And you, Kailem?" he asked.

Kailem was not quick to respond. Could he make such an oath? Could he keep it? The need to put every Blackbird in the ground still burned within him. When the opportunity came, could he hold back? But what would Elwin do if he refused the oath? Would he expel him from the monastery, shutting him out from his friends? After musing for several uncomfortable seconds, he nodded silently, then added, "I swear."

Elwin searched Kailem's eyes, looking for hints of honesty in the young man's oath. Kailem shifted slightly under his gaze, wondering if the sage was reading his thoughts. Elwin had sworn never to invade their minds again, but if he ever broke that promise, Kailem would have no way of knowing.

"Very well," Elwin finally said, hesitantly. He stood slowly from his chair. "Sleep soundly tonight. We begin in the morning."

CHAPTER THIRTY-THREE

THE ROSEROCK BASIN

54TH DAY OF SUMMER, 897 G.C.

The countryside in the Roserock Basin had little shrubbery and even fewer trees — the men often went days without seeing either — yet the landscape was still as green as any the soldiers had ever seen. The land was covered in a blanket of jade grass no more than an inch high, with stone slabs protruding in scattered patches, and even the stone was covered in lichen and green moss.

After the Battle of Tarwick, every surviving soldier accepted Mokain's training offer. There were far too many of them for one man to train effectively, so Mokain decided to train his officers in the mornings, and then after the day's labors, the officers would pass on the instruction to their subordinates..

That morning's training session had been atop a rocky platform overlooking a small depression not quite large enough to be called a valley. A steady breeze had blown since dawn and swept away the fog earlier than usual.

"Very good, men. That will be all for today," Mokain said. "You're dismissed for breakfast. Meet back at the command tent in an hour for assignments."

Back in the command tent, Vivek hurried about preparing breakfast. Lord Menden had returned to Rhinegard with the rider bearing Mokain's report to

Prince Aedon. Before he left, he told Mokain to take his absence as a sign of the aged warrior's confidence in him; Mokain would still have preferred he had stayed.

"Here you are, my—Mokain," the young servant said. "Peppered eggs and lentils over flatbread."

Vivek prepared their small dining table, just as he did every morning. Nothing excessively fine, just a tablecloth and two plates with cutlery. Now that Lord Menden was gone, Mokain insisted that Vivek join him for meals. Dugald would not have approved of this, but denying his master's command would have been an even greater offense.

"How goes the training?" Vivek asked. Although Dugald would have told him to stay silent until spoken to, Vivek had learned his master preferred a more proactive conversation.

Mokain swallowed a bite of flat bread. "Every day is a little better. The men don't seem overly fond of me, though."

"But they do respect you now. That's a step in the right direction, is it not?" Vivek was slowly learning how to have an actual conversation with his master, something Dugald had taught him not to do.

"Yes, yes, I suppose it is," Mokain said. He moved his lentils about his plate in no particular order.

Vivek grieved to see his master so disheartened. "Are any soldiers showing promise?" he asked, hoping to galvanize the Mariner's spirits.

Mokain only nodded.

"Which is your best fighter?"

Mokain gave the question real thought. "Hard to say." He set down his fork. "The most naturally gifted fighter is Sergeant Shaw. He has good instincts and can improvise, but unfortunately, he is not fond of being corrected. He'll follow orders to the letter, but doesn't like to be told how to fight, so he makes the same mistakes again and again. As for which fighter shows the most promise, that would have to be Lieutenant Wyndell. He isn't the natural, instinctive fighter that Shaw is, but Conroy is teachable and has a strong work ethic, and rarely makes the same mistake twice. In the long run, that will count more than natural talent." Vivek kept a keen eye on Mokain's response. His master sat taller and returned to eating his breakfast. Vivek smiled. "What will be our orders for today?" he asked as he took another bite.

"We should arrive at the village of Camhearn by midday; we'll need to get the usual reports from the villagers. We also need another inventory on supplies, we had not prepared for so long a journey when we left Rhinegard."

Over the next half-hour, officers trickled into the command tent. All were present long before the appointed time, another sign Mokain had earned their respect, so the meeting began early. Towards the end, Mokain assigned duties for their arrival at the village of Camhearn.

"Commander, there are three other villages less than half a day's ride from Camhearn," Lieutenant Balfour called out from the back of the group. "We can dispatch squadrons and have them back before–"

"You know my policy, Balfour."

"Each squadron could be back before nightfall, sir. There would be no risk, and we'd shave several days off our journey."

Mokain shook his head. "We will not divide our forces under any circumstances. Our numbers are too depleted as it is. Is that understood?"

From Mokain's tone, it was clear that the question had been addressed to the entire group, and they all replied in the affirmative.

"Good. Balfour, select two of your squadrons to take inventory and oversee them. Sergeant Shaw, select six of your best men and send them out on a scouting run. I want them to leave ahead of the battalion."

"Ay, sir. Consider it done," came the sergeant's reply. In all the battalion, there was no better scout than Shaw. No doubt the product of a childhood spent hunting wild game for his lord. Had he been the son of a nobleman, he would undoubtedly have been a lieutenant by now; Mokain intended to promote him as soon as a commission was available.

The battalion was well on its march south to Camhearn long before the sun was fully overhead. Under Mokain's command, the men were a seamless, cohesive unit. Kailem would have compared them to a school of fish darting about the reef, Mokain thought. His heart still ached when he thought of him.

It was late in the afternoon when the battalion reached the outskirts of Camhearn. Sergeant Shaw's scouting contingent had verified there were no hostile forces for miles and had already found the most suitable ground to set up camp. Lieutenant Balfour set immediately to his inventory, albeit begrudgingly, while Mokain accompanied a small group into the village.

The village of Camhearn was no different than the half dozen or so villages they had already encountered in the basin, which encompassed the northeastern counties of Donnelin. The finer buildings were constructed entirely of timber, so large it appeared a single tree trunk was used to craft each individual beam. The remaining structures were made of wooden frames and cob walls painted white, a curious building technique unlike anything Mokain had ever seen. Residents of a cob home were proud to tell you how long their structure had stood, often for several hundred years.

"Filthy Donnelish," one soldier muttered under his breath as they walked down the village's main street. Another soldier grunted his agreement, but after a disapproving glare from Mokain, they both fixed their eyes on their boots as they walked.

A jackal trotted down the flagstone road directly toward Mokain with its tail wagging like a flag under an east wind. The animal jumped repeatedly at Mokain's side before running back to an elderly villager, likely his owner. The old man was perhaps in his early sixties, and he wore a wiry beard down to his chest. From the stained apron he wore, he was certainly the proprietor of the cobbler shop outside of which he stood. The jackal sat at his side and gladly accepted a head rub.

"Good even', good sir," Mokain said, trying to adopt the local lingo.

"Hail, good fellows. Ta what be our lit'le village owin' the pleasure of company from the capital?" the man replied in a thick Donnelish accent.

Mokain realized he had no chance of adopting their speech, so he ceased trying.

"We are here by order of Prince Aedon. We've come to collect your accounts of any raids or attacks on your village. Your welfare is of great importance to the king."

The man scoffed, not derisively, but in surprise, and the scoff quickly turned into a cough. "Norm'ly, I'd balk at such a claim, there lad, but... be ye the same band o' soldiers that repaired ta mill up yonder in Oaktown, were ye then?"

Oaktown was the last village the battalion had visited before crossing the Roserock Mountains. They too had been attacked by what appeared to be Shinda warriors, and the raiders had set fire to the town's lumber mill. Mokain's battalion had missed the attack by only a week. Fortunately, enough of the stone structure remained that his soldiers were able to restore it to working order in only a matter of days, and the villagers had responded with a much-needed replenishment to the battalion's supply stores.

This had, of course, not come without protest from Lieutenant Balfour. As the king's representatives, a battalion had the right to requisition whatever supplies they needed, and they had no mandate to aid in borderland construction. But the poverty of those villagers had weighed heavily on Mokain's mind, and as most of the town's fighting men had died in the attack, he would not take from the villagers without providing them labor in return. He had insisted his men provide similar services at each town they visited, and apparently word was spreading.

"We are indeed the very same," Mokain said. "Have these raiders made any advances against your village?"

The old cobbler coughed again before responding. "We ain't had nothin' so bad as Oaktown, bless us, thems ne'r come wit'in the village, but harass our flocks n' fields they do, ta be sure, lad."

Mokain nodded to his soldiers, a sign to spread out and gather reports. Most villagers were preparing to close their shops for the day, and the soldiers were able to catch several of them before they returned home. They all had similar reports of raiding parties on their farmland, but nothing within the limits of the village itself. The men also reported multiple instances of coughing and unusual sweating from the villagers.

The soldiers returned to camp where most of the men were preparing their supper. Before long, the sound of clanging metal filled the camp. It was the same as it had been every evening since they left Tarwick: the officers used the fading light of the sunset to relay Mokain's combat training from the morning's session to their subordinates.

The following morning, Lieutenant Wyndell rushed into Mokain's tent and stirred the commander's shoulder.

"Yes, Conroy," Mokain said, blinking. "I mean, Lieutenant, what is it?"

"Commander, an illness has spread through the camp. You must come now."

Mokain left his personal tent, still in the process of donning his coat, and went row by row, inspecting the men. Many were laid low in their beds, dizzy and delirious and drenched in sweat. The diagnosis became obvious once those who had it worst turned blue in the lips, but none had the heart to say it aloud.

The lieutenants quickly formed a circle around their leader.

"It was those rotting villagers we met yesterday," Lieutenant Lowin said. His voice dripped with fear, not anger.

"Yes, we should burn the village to the ground to prevent the spread. It has worked in the past," Lieutenant Balfour said.

"Calm yourselves, both of you," Mokain said. "Symptoms of blue fever do not appear after a single day; the men contracted the disease elsewhere. Do you have a count of how many are ill?"

Mokain tallied the count from each of his five lieutenants. Altogether, 103 of his remaining 416 soldiers had fallen ill, and that number was likely to grow.

"Sir, with respect," Lieutenant Balfour began, "I've been in this situation before, and the protocol is clear. We must separate the ill from the healthy at once and leave them behind. We'll leave instructions for where to meet us if they recover, although few men ever do so."

Mokain's eyes narrowed on the heartless subordinate. "We do not leave men behind, Lieutenant." The rest of the men lowered their eyes, unsure how to react.

"Separate the ill from the sick and leave a wide barrier between the two groups," Mokain continued. "We will remain until the sick recover or decease."

The lieutenants paused long enough to be sure the commander's orders were complete, then set out to do as instructed. Balfour hissed a curse under his breath, not loud enough for anyone to make out the words, but the tone made his sentiments clear.

The next three days were spent tending to the ill. As they were under strict orders not to mingle the ill with the healthy, water and provisions were delivered across the barrier by the healthy and then distributed by the few among the sick, who were still well enough to walk.

During those first three days, an additional 74 men fell ill and were taken across the barrier. Every morning, they searched for those who had died during the night, and every evening, a new pyre was constructed to burn the bodies of the deceased. So far, the blue fever had sent 55 men to the Great Unknown. Mokain frequently walked the rows of the camp, looking for signs of the illness and taking in the morale of the men. Fear had tightened its grip on both sides of the cap. The ill feared for their lives, but it seemed that the fear of the healthy, that each of them might be the next sorry wretch to cross sides, was even worse.

On the morning of the fourth day, Mokain awoke in a sweat pool of his own. He tried to sit up but had not the strength to do so. It was half an hour before Vivek found him. Mokain could speak no louder than a whisper, and his words were difficult to discern through lips tinted blue, but his intent was clear. He was taken across the quarantine barrier and laid with the others.

***

Lieutenant Balfour called a meeting of officers, those who remained on the side of the healthy. Vivek sat in the corner of the command tent and sulked.

"It is clear this plan was folly from the start," Balfour began. "And now it has cost our commander his life. Thus, it falls to us, next in line of authority, to take action. Proper protocol must be followed. I vote we break camp immediately."

"We will do nothing of the sort," Lieutenant Wyndell said. Conroy was the most junior of the lieutenants, but that did not grant him any less authority. He had been timid at first, given that his promotion came after serving so little time as a sergeant, but the prospect of abandoning their leader revealed his mettle. "We have our orders, and we will carry them out."

"That's right," said Lieutenant Lowin. "When a commanding officer is incapacitated, their most recent orders remain in effect."

Balfour squared his shoulders. "Don't quote protocol at me, boy. I knew the book before you knew how to piss. Besides, when a commanding officer is incapacitated, his most recent orders can be rescinded by the acting commander if an emergency arises."

Lowin's posture withered.

"But an emergency hasn't arisen," Conroy countered. "It arose before our command officer was incapacitated. He gave us our orders for how to handle the emergency, and nothing has changed since then, so we stay the course."

Balfour scoffed, but he had no retort. "You lot do what you wish, but I'm taking my regiment and heading south. We'll not stay here to die blue lipped with the rest of you."

"Try it and I'll arrest you for desertion," Sergeant Shaw said. He moved his hand to the hilt of his sword and stared Balfour in the eye. His battle-hardened face, with a scar on his chin visible through his trimmed beard, was enough to give any rational man pause.

"Bah," Lieutenant Balfour finally replied. "I know for a fact, your squadron has suffered more losses than any, and you're going to arrest a whole regiment? I'd like to see you try."

Lieutenant Wyndell stepped forward. "He won't be alone."

Seeing a resistance had formed, Lieutenant Lowin found the courage to stand tall again. He said nothing, but stood shoulder to shoulder next to Shaw.

"Sarding idiots!" Balfour cursed as he stormed out of the command tent.

Chapter Thirty-Four

Tai'veda

48th Day of Summer, 897 G.C.

Osmund ran and ran and ran. Then he ran some more. He ran so much that his feet swelled and his sides cramped and his lungs burned. His once pristine linen clothes were soaked in sweat. He was certain he would vomit soon, and even worried his leg bones might shatter. Then he ran some more.

After another stride, his legs gave out from under him, and he tumbled to the ground. Pebbles and pine needles embedded his palms where he broke his fall. His sweat-soaked clothes were now soiled by dirt and dead leaves as well.

Farther up the "trail", if so it could be called, Kailem ran with ease. Emerald was just behind him, straining to keep up. How was this training him to become a sage, Osmund wondered? They had been "training" with Elwin for a week, but so far all they had done was alternate between exhausting themselves physically and sitting in the Aether Room doing absolutely nothing. And for all his efforts, he was no closer to becoming a sage.

Three times a day, they ran a specific route around the mountainside, which took Osmund well over an hour to complete. Their days also included lifting heavy objects for no apparent reason, balancing on one leg, also for no apparent reason, and demeaning themselves with manual labor in the orchard.

The only times they were allowed to "rest" were the times they sat in the Aether Room for hours on end, but these were hardly restful. Elwin had them sit upright on their floor pillows, and they were supposed to think about nothing but how it felt to breathe, of all things. To say it was painfully boring would not do it justice. Osmund was convinced that truly thinking about nothing but one's own breathing was a metaphysical impossibility. His mind would drift between how badly his body hurt, to what the point of all this was, and how badly he would rather be doing anything else. More than once he had drifted off to sleep sitting up.

The worst part was he appeared to be the least competent of the three at every task. He had assumed — in his mind, justifiably — that he would excel at anything related to sagecraft. After all, he was the one who introduced Kailem and Emerald to the very idea of the sages. He was the one who had studied them for years. He had read the Codex Andala cover to cover multiple times. He should be the gifted one, the teacher's favorite, the one the others relied upon. Instead, he was constantly behind, constantly failing, constantly the one needing the most guidance and correction.

This run had been no different.

With prodigious effort, Osmund lifted himself back to his feet, his oath to follow all of Elwin's instructions with exactness replaying in his mind. Perhaps he had been too hasty. He was so exhausted his vision blurred. He forced himself to continue running, despite his body's spirited objections. After a time, he arrived back at the monastery and entered through the door hidden by ivy.

He found Elwin, Kailem, and Emerald in the kitchen, eating a meal of boiled lentils and freshly baked bread. Osmund was sick of lentils. They were too pedestrian and bland, but he was painfully hungry. He sat down and drank nearly an entire carafe of well-water before breaking off chunks of bread and using them to shovel lentils into his mouth.

After lunch, they had time to bathe and change their clothing — which they would later have to wash themselves — then met Elwin in the Aether Room. Their teacher was already sitting on a pillow in the meditative position, his face towards the doors, his eyes peacefully closed.

Osmund didn't want to do this again. He sat down in the meditative position facing Elwin, just as Kailem and Emerald were doing. He tried to focus on his breath, but his frustrations were boiling over. He couldn't take it any longer.

"Why are we doing all this?" he finally blurted out. "What does any of this have to do with sagecraft? This doesn't make any sense. I hate this!" His outburst shattered their serene silence. Osmund's eyes went wide, and he wished he could stuff the words back in his mouth.

The others all opened their eyes. Kailem and Emerald were stunned, speechless, while Elwin looked at him with an expression that was entirely unreadable. Silence again took hold of the room, but it was far from serene.

Then a smile spread slowly across Elwin's face. He gestured with his head for them to follow him into the corridor.

While Osmund followed last in line, he thought of all the ways Elwin might punish him for the outburst. More running? More lifting? More balancing? Maybe he would make him go without food this time. Then he recognized where they were going. Of course, more orchard duty. Osmund hated orchard duty more than anything. Elwin knew exactly how to punish him.

When they arrived at the orchard, Elwin didn't stop for them to collect the farming equipment or harvesting baskets like he usually did. The three students shared puzzled looks with each other. They continued walking through the rows of trees, farther into the orchard than Elwin had ever taken them before.

On the far side of the orchard was a clearing, and in the middle were nine stone monoliths spread evenly apart over a large circle of polished stone tiles. Osmund grazed his hand across the massive stone as they entered the circle. The monoliths were tall enough that he would have had to jump to touch the top of them. The tiles on the ground were made of two types of stone. Most were pale marble, but around the center were three dark granite circles roughly three feet in diameter; the same circles were under each of the nine monoliths.

Twelve sacred circles, Osmund realized. They formed the same pattern as the symbol on the cover of the Codex Andala.

Elwin sat cross-legged on the stone circle and invited them to do the same.

"I must admit, young Osmund, you lasted longer than I expected you to," Elwin began as the three became situated on the tile floor. "I'm proud of you."

Confusion took over Osmund's face.

"There are several reasons for your exercises this past week," Elwin continued. "Would any of you care to venture a guess?"

Kailem spoke first. "I assume that physical endurance is somehow connected with sagecraft."

"It is, but there was a far more important reason. Tell me, how did it feel after all that running, lifting, and balancing?"

"It was horrible," Osmund said, invoking another grin from Elwin.

"Can you be more specific, Osmund?"

"It was painful. Every part of me hurt. You were demanding more than I was capable of. Everything inside me was screaming for me to stop, to surrender and lie down."

"Yes, your body wanted you to quit. But you didn't quit. In fact, Osmund, you completed every task I gave you, no matter how difficult. So I shall ask you again, do you still believe I asked for more than you were capable, or did I ask more of you than you *thought* was possible?"

Osmund paused for a moment, then nodded.

"You see, your will is your most powerful faculty, more than your strength, your speed, your creativity, even your intelligence, because every other faculty obeys your will. Even when your body wishes to take the easier path, or your thoughts wish to meander aimlessly, each will ultimately bow before the power of your will, if it is strong enough. That is the first lesson of sagecraft, and it is not a lesson I could have explained to you in words. It's something you must experience for yourself. And now you have."

Elwin paused to let them consider his words before continuing.

"And now for some explanations. Before you can understand sagecraft," he explained, "you must first understand the aura. The aura is a unique type of energy that exists inside us. It is an intelligent energy, and it is found in every living thing. The aura makes life possible. All living things sustain it, and all living things depend on it. Life and aura are inseparably connected. While we are alive, our aura flows through us, and it can vary in strength.

"When someone's aura becomes diminished or obstructed, their body begins to decay. It becomes unable to repair itself or to ward off disease, and eventually, it dies. But the aura can also become so great that it can no longer be contained within the body. When that happens, the aura emanates from us, encapsulating us in a sphere of energy, an energy that cannot be seen or touched, but can nevertheless exert a force on anything within its reach."

To illustrate his point, Elwin stretched out his hand towards a nearby apple tree. Three apples pulled themselves off their branches and floated towards him. His three students were awed at the sight of it. The apples danced in the air around them, like hummingbirds hovering above flowers, before resting, one at a time, in each of their laps. Emerald took a bite of hers as Elwin continued the lesson.

"Many people feel invigorated when amongst the trees — it is because they are basking in the aura emitted by all the living things around them. Others are energized when surrounded by a crowd — this is because they feel the auras emitted by so many people.

"When we are injured, we all have the same instinctual reaction. Kailem, if you were to injure your shoulder, what would be the first thing you would do?"

Without thinking, Kailem raised his left hand to his right shoulder.

"Precisely," Elwin said. "Your instinct was to place your hand on the wounded area. That is because a part of you instinctively knows you will heal more swiftly if you concentrate your aura to that area of the body."

This was a sacred moment in the relationship between teacher and pupil, the moment when genuine knowledge passed from one mind to another. Seeing the understanding in their eyes was a feeling Elwin had missed, more than he had realized, until that moment. It had been over a millennium since he last taught this majestic art. It felt right to finally be teaching again.

"Sagecraft is the art of cultivating and controlling this aura, and your mind is key. If you cannot control your mind, you have no hope of controlling your aura. I would sooner expect to see a legless dog run than see an undisciplined man use sagecraft. That is why your training will involve so many extremes, like pushing yourself to the limits of your body and mind, both through exhaustion and boredom, because it is only in those fringes of your capacity that your will can truly be tested."

Osmund understood Elwin's lesson perfectly, but he harbored serious doubts that working them to the bone all week was the best way to teach it. He decided it would be best to keep those doubts to himself.

Elwin continued. "To help you control not just your mind, but specifically the aura that flows inside each of you, I'm going to teach you an ancient practice we call 'Tai'veda'."

Elwin stood and gestured for them to do the same, then instructed them to follow his movements. As he moved, he explained that Tai'veda was more than the movements he performed. The key was his awareness of how his aura was affected by them. His aura concentrated between his hands as he moved it back and forth and all around him.

The movements were like a peacefully flowing river, fluid and graceful. They reminded Kailem of how a person moves while standing weightless on the ocean floor.

Elwin moved slowly at first, then gradually gained speed. He would dip down low and raise himself up again, stand on one foot and then shift his weight to the other. Nothing was hurried or haphazard. Every motion was deliberate, every part of his body moving in a specific, controlled manner.

His breathing was deep and cleansing, his gaze soft and kind. Although he never stopped moving completely, he often became so slow he appeared to be standing still. Other times his movements became so fast they should have looked erratic and chaotic, but even with speed, he maintained his grace and control. His body stretched into peculiar positions, positions his students wouldn't have imagined possible.

He came to rest in the same position he had begun, his shoulders square over his feet, his hands resting gently on his lower abdomen.

The three students were speechless. Elwin didn't have to read their thoughts, their feelings of inadequacy shone on their faces. He explained a simpler, modified version of his movements for them to practice.

Each of them struggled in their own way. More than once, Osmund lost his balance and fell to the polished stone. Kailem became so focused on one part of his body's movements, he ignored the rest. Elwin reminded him repeatedly that each movement involved the entire body as a whole.

To Elwin's surprise, Emerald proved the most adept. He had assumed Kailem would have excelled, given his extensive physical training. And to his credit, Kailem was better than most of Elwin's students had been on their first day. But Emerald moved as if she had practiced Tai'veda all her life. The only weakness in her movements were her own insecurities — she frequently stopped in the midst of a perfect movement because she felt silly or to ask if she was doing it correctly.

Although Kailem was too focused on his movements to notice anything around him, Emerald's grace was not lost on Osmund. The last time he fell, he stayed on the ground and watched her move. Her golden copper hair lay in waves against the white linen tunic, her green eyes sparkling like the gemstone for which she was named.

She was perfect. Every motion was elegant and refined, which he never would have expected from the disheveled, gruff young woman he had first met that day on the docks. In that moment, Osmund didn't mind that he wasn't the best at sagecraft if it meant it allowed him to watch Emerald.

Elwin cleared his throat. Osmund realized he had been caught staring and returned to his practicing. Fortunately for him, Emerald hadn't noticed.

The tranquil monastery suddenly shook under the sound of a thunderclap. The birds in the surrounding trees took flight in unison. All four looked to the sky; there were no clouds above them. They stood frozen in place, waiting.

It sounded again.

"What in blessed Iria is that?" Kailem asked.

"Something I have never heard before," Elwin admitted.

"I imagine that doesn't happen often," Osmund remarked.

"No, young Osmund, it does not," came the reply. There was obvious worry in Elwin's voice.

The strange thunderclap sounded again.

The three students followed their teacher out of the orchard and through the main door.

They heard it again.

"It sounds like it's coming from down in the valley," Kailem said. Elwin agreed with him.

They waited, eyes fixed towards the origin of the mysterious sound, but it never returned.

CHAPTER THIRTY-FIVE

TO WAR

62ND DAY OF SUMMER, 897 G.C.

Aedon stood in the king's chambers at the top of the Palace of Rhinegard. Through his balcony doors he could see legions of Cavander soldiers assembled on the outskirts of the city, preparing to march to Shinda. The new king had recalled every battalion within a week's march of the capital in preparation for the largest offensive campaign Iria had seen in generations. But Aedon's attention lay elsewhere.

The hilt of the Fang of Rhinegard fit perfectly in his hands, as if they were made for each other. This sword was perhaps the most precious and coveted heirloom in the royal family, more than even the crown itself. Aedon itched to swing it about, but his servant was busily securing his new armor.

Dugald stood on a short stool and lifted a shirt of mail over the King's head. He too could see the massive gathering of soldiers from out the balcony doors, and it demanded attention.

"I wasn't aware our military was so large," Dugald admitted.

Aedon's head emerged from his mail shirt and Dugald adjusted the ends of it to his hips.

"Most battalions are not stationed in Rhinegard, for obvious reasons," Aedon explained. "And what you see there are not all trained soldiers. I've enlisted most of the aristocracy's private militia, even conscripted villagers from the nearby countryside."

"Is that customary, Your Majesty? To enlisted untrained men on the eve of battle?"

Aedon held his chin high. "It is a new day with a new king, Dugald. What was once customary is no longer relevant."

Dugald nodded as he hefted the King's breastplate into place. The same seal from his signet ring was emblazoned across the chest. The black steel armor was immaculate, and in the opinion of most soldiers, absurdly ostentatious. It had neither scratch nor dent and was so excessively polished it glistened like obsidian in the sunlight. There were excessive flourishes carved all throughout, looking more like a work of art than a suit of armor.

Now fully arrayed in resplendent armor, the ancient Fang of Rhinegard secured to his side, Aedon descended the maze of stairs and halls in the palace. Since his coronation, he could scarcely leave his quarters without flocks of noble ladies squawking for the newly single King's attention. The general consensus from the Court had been that he had handled Kyra's betrayal as a true King, strong but fair. Kyra had committed treason, and the King had been merciful in sparing her life. The thought of her still filled Aedon with rage, so he pushed her from his mind whenever possible.

While passing through the Grand Corridor, Aedon winked at a young noble lady frozen mid-curtesy. A tint of blush bloomed on her cheeks, and she averted her eyes before looking up at him again. *What was her name again?* He wondered. She was Lord Clayton's daughter, maybe Marian? Or was it Mortima? He decided it didn't matter; he would have Dugald learn her name before he called on her.

They marched to the stables and rode through the city gates to his army encamped just outside the city walls. As Aedon marched into the command tent, the crowded gathering of officers stood at attention.

"Your Majesty," General Torvon said with a nobleman's bow. "Shall I brief you on the war plan?"

Ademar Torvon had been a close childhood friend of King Byron, and although he technically had no more authority than any other general, they all recognized him as the de facto commander of the Cavander army.

General Torvon stood with the other generals around the map table. On the table was a map of all of Iria, with tokens placed on strategic locations. King Aedon scanned the tent for his closest advisor.

"Where is Leonin?" he asked.

Lord Arturri emerged from the crowd of officers and stepped forward. "At your service, Your Majesty." He spoke with his head down and his voice low.

Without a word, Aedon extended his hand for the Devonian lord–and father of a traitor–to approach the map table. Lord Arturri took his place at the King's side.

"Proceed, General," the King said.

Ademar Torvon scowled at the King's advisor. It was a common sentiment in the command tent; a foreigner, not to mention the father of his Majesty's disgraced fiancé, had no business being in the King's inner circle. Despite his fervent objections, the general wisely held his tongue on the matter.

"Our armies will march south through Devona, then west into Shinda," General Torvon explained. His voice was a low rumble as he outlined their precise route, including where they would cut off Shinda supply lines, which cities they would take by force, and which they would place under siege.

A messenger was permitted entry to the command tent.

"General Torvon, our squadron just arrived," the messenger began.

General Torvon interrupted. "Corporal, you are not addressing the ranking officer." He stepped aside to reveal King Aedon in his shining new suit of armor. The messenger saw the crown on Aedon's head and collapsed to his knee.

"A thousand apologies, Your Majesty. I beg your pardon, I did not see you, and I would never have...."

"Your lapse is forgiven, Corporal," the King assured. "Deliver your message."

The messenger, still on one knee, explained, "our squadron is with the Fifth Battalion of the 1st Legion, Commander Roka's unit. Lord Menden returned with us bearing this report from the Commander."

Aedon received the scroll with a frown. "*Commander* Roka?" he asked the General.

General Torvon waved a dismissive hand. "The men probably didn't know what to call him."

King Aedon broke the seal and read the report aloud. It spoke of raids on the border villages, an attack by a Shinda regiment at Tarwick pass, and a most distressing revelation after the interrogation of a Shinda warrior.

"I've never heard of this 'Blackbird Society'," General Torvon said after the king had finished. "Can we trust the information?"

"It seems First Officer Roka has the same concern. He will let us know what he learns in the Basin," Aedon said. General Torvon nodded.

"Should we abandon the war plans until we receive word?" the rumbling general asked.

Lord Arturri stepped forward to interject. "I think that would be unwise, Your Majesty. Any delay on our part would show weakness and give our enemies time to prepare. The prudent course would be to—"

"The prudent course would be to leave the war planning to the soldiers, *Lord* Arturri," the general said.

Leonin's earlier timidity was fading. "A good soldier follows orders, general. The role of the advisor is to develop strategy. Keep to your task and I will to mine."

General Torvon narrowed his eyes. "The King has no need for the strategies of a failed traitor."

Leonin squared his shoulders. "I will believe it is the King's prerogative to–"

"That's enough," Aedon said. The men halted like scolded children. Aedon's eyes were still on the scroll, and he was silent for a time.

"Either the Shinda prisoner was telling the truth, or he was lying," the King began. "If he was telling the truth, then this new rebellion needs to be crushed before they gain any more strength. If he was lying, then the Shinda really did attack the borderlands and we must respond. Either way, we need to move our men south, so there's no call for delay."

"Excellent decision, Your Majesty," Leonin said. "Let us begin our march forthwith. I suggest–"

"Nay, Lord Arturri. This plan no longer serves us," Aedon interrupted. There was a brief pause as Aedon finished planning, then he spoke. "We shall proceed under the assumption that my First Officer's suspicions are accurate, which means we must extinguish this Blackbird Society with the greatest haste. We will transport our soldiers south by ship to the port in Barrowfort, and from there march west to this Riverkeep."

"Do we have enough ships for such a voyage?" General Torvon asked. He knew they did not.

Lord Arturri spoke before the King could answer. "More importantly, Your Majesty, what will we do if there is, in fact, no rebellion, which I strongly suspect will be the case?"

"If this story does prove an artifice of the Shinda," the King said, "our troops will still have moved half the distance to our target, and we will continue our march as planned."

"Your Majesty," Leonin began, "I fear this is not a wise course. Might I suggest—"

"Lord Arturri," the King interrupted. He turned to face his advisor directly. "You proved to me your loyalty on the day of your daughter's betrayal, and for that, I have allowed you to remain in my council. But do not mistake my leniency for leave to question my judgment. I have given my word, and it is final."

The command tent fell silent, but if a smile could have made a noise, General Torvon's would have been singing. Lord Arturri lowered his head and stepped back from the table.

Aedon turned to General Torvon. "The harbor is full of merchant ships. If we commandeer enough to transport all our troops, how soon can we begin the voyage south?"

With his head held high, General Torvon replied, "at dawn."

Chapter Thirty-Six

Ninety-Two Men

60th Day of Summer, 897 G.C.

When Mokain finally opened his eyes, it took them a full minute to find their focus. His joints ached, his breathing was shallow, and his head had its own heartbeat. The cot creaked as he sat up, which took far more effort than it should have. Once stable, he assessed his surroundings. He was alone, in a tent that wasn't his, and a light breeze caused the tent flaps to swing back and forth.

He noticed a ladle sticking out of a bucket of water at the tent door, and he became suddenly aware of how painfully parched his mouth was. He collapsed to his hands and knees and crawled for the water, sipping back ladle after ladle.

Across from his tent was another, and inside was a fellow soldier laid low on a cot. The man was awake, staring longingly at the bucket of water. Taking a deep breath, Mokain heaved himself to his feet, and using a combination of lifting and dragging, was able to get the bucket into the soldier's tent. He lifted a full ladle to the man's lips and helped him drink.

Outside the tent, he found another soldier sitting on a stool with his head back against the tent pole. This man looked well enough to lift the bucket.

"You there," Mokain called.

The soldier looked, and seeing his commanding officer, stood at attention.

"Come distribute this water to anyone who needs it," Mokain ordered. The soldier immediately set about the task.

After wrapping a blanket around his shoulders, Mokain ambled about the quarantined area inspecting his men. It appeared there were more men in the infirm side of camp than on the healthy side. Many of the men were unconscious, lying on cots, sweating in the chill Donnelish air. Those who were able gave him a salute as he passed, although many were too weak to lift a hand. There were, however, a precious few able to walk around with him.

At the far end of the camp, he arrived at the ashy remnants of the funeral pyres. There hadn't been enough wood for each man to have his own, as they deserved, so they piled all the men who had died on a given day onto a single pyre. Mokain counted five piles of ash and bone. When he had fallen ill, there had only been three; he reasoned he must have been asleep for two days. He walked by the charred remains of his men and reverently bid them a private farewell.

"My lord, you're awake," a voice said.

Mokain turned to see Vivek hurrying to his side. Mokain lifted his hand to stop him.

"Stay back, Vivek. You mustn't come near me."

Vivek halted as ordered, but he was already close enough to assess his master. "Your lips are no longer blue, my lord. They are pale and cracked, but not blue. It should be safe. May I?"

Mokain relented, and his personal servant came to his side. Lieutenant Wyndell was several yards behind Vivek, coming to join them as well.

"You've been unconscious almost four whole days now," Vivek said.

"*Four* days?" Mokain frowned at him. "I count only two extra pyres." He looked back at the ashes to see if he had miscounted.

Vivek looked to the ash as well, then explained. "No one else has died in two days, my lord. We haven't needed any more pyres. It appears everyone who will die from this fever has already passed; the rest should recover."

"Oh, thank Iria," Mokain muttered. Lieutenant Wyndell arrived a second later.

"Good to see you on your feet, Commander."

"Indeed. What is the status?" Mokain asked with a weak voice.

Wyndell stood with his hands behind his back. "The blue fever has fallen on two hundred thirty-five men, Commander, over half the camp. Ninety-two have perished."

Ninety-two men, Mokain repeated in his mind. That was more than they had lost in the Battle of Tarwick. He set his jaw as tears welled in his eyes.

Seeing the despair on Mokain's face, Lieutenant Wyndell added, "The rest of the sick are poised to make a full recovery, Commander. That's a hundred forty-three men. Men any other commanding officer would have left behind."

Mokain nodded, leaning on Vivek for support. "And what of the other lieutenants?"

Lieutenant Wyndell seemed almost happy to report. "Only Balfour has taken sick." Then he added, "it appears he will recover with the rest of them."

Mokain nodded again, electing to save his voice for when strictly necessary. He attempted to walk to the command tent, but after the first step, his leg gave out.

"Whoa there, Commander. Easy, easy," Lieutenant Wyndell said as he kept him from falling. Vivek hurried to Mokain's other side, and together they helped him through camp.

"Bring us some food and fresh water," Wyndell ordered another soldier just before they reached the command tent. Multiple men responded, and soon Mokain was seated at a table with a bowl of sweet potato soup, freshly baked bread, and a pitcher of cold well water.

"These aren't our rations," Mokain noted. "Where'd this come from?"

Vivek leaned forward. "Villagers have been coming to camp every morning with food and supplies. Please, eat, my lord."

Mokain's hand shook as he lifted the spoon to his lips.

The battalion remained camped outside Camhearn for another week while the sick convalesced. More villagers arrived each day, and not just to bring supplies. They nursed men back to health, cooked their food, and ate meals with them. Their children even played in the camp. It was a most peculiar sight to see in a land that normally would not take kindly to Cavanders, let alone the King's army.

On the 68th day of Summer, Mokain held an officer's meeting in the command tent. He labored to sit tall, though his strength had mostly returned.

"We need to return to Rhinegard," Lieutenant Balfour insisted. "We are in no condition to continue. Our men are exhausted."

"We're Mokain's men," Sergeant Shaw said. "We can continue if he says we need to."

There was a general murmur from the men, both in favor and in opposition to Shaw.

"It's more than just exhaustion," Balfour continued. "The men want to see their families. And we owe it to our dead to bring word to their wives and children."

Lieutenant Lowin joined in. "Wasn't our mandate to investigate attacks in the borderlands and return our report? We've done that. What else is there to do?"

"All that's left to do is go home," Balfour said. Several men agreed.

Mokain listened calmly to the debate. When the men drew silent, he turned to Lieutenant Wyndell and asked, "Do your men feel the same?"

Wyndell looked to his sergeants, then turned back to Mokain. "Of course, they are eager to return to their homes and families, but they understand the importance of our mission. Learning of these revolutionaries changed everything. If you say we should continue on, we're with you."

Mokain considered their options, then stood from his padded chair.

"Tell your men to be ready to break camp in the morning. Tomorrow, we march south to Veydala."

Chapter Thirty-Seven

CANDLELIGHT

48th Day of Summer, 897 G.C.

Kailem lay on his bed with his hands behind his head, staring at the ceiling. He had blown out his candle hours ago and his eyes had fully adjusted to the dark.

The mysterious thunderclap still rang in his mind, but that wasn't what kept him awake. How could he sleep with his parents' murderers so close? Could he stay in the monastery while leaving the world to itself, and worse, letting his parents' murderers go free? Or should he abandon the priceless opportunity Elwin had given him and fight the Blackbirds, possibly ending his own life in the process?

All hope of sleep had vanished.

With his candle relit, he left his room and found his way to the kitchen. He sat at the table and pulled his necklace over his head. The pearl shimmered beautifully in the candlelight. His mother would have loved it.

The pearl was supposed to have been a good omen; that idea seemed laughable now. Everything had changed that day. Life as he knew it, as it was supposed to be, had disappeared with two strokes of a blade. Had any good come from it?

He thought about Elwin's vision. Had it all happened just so he could find Elwin and become a sage? But why did his parents have to die for that? Had there been no other way? And what good was becoming a sage if he couldn't use that power to stop the Blackbirds and avenge his parents?

Candlelight shined through the kitchen doorway. A moment later, Osmund walked in, slumped over and shuffling his feet. A lengthy yawn escaped his mouth.

"Couldn't sleep?" Kailem asked.

Osmund nearly dropped his candle. "By Iria, Kailem! You nearly killed me. What are you doing just sitting there in the middle of the night?"

Kailem shrugged, and Osmund understood. "I was hoping to make myself some tea. I do not suppose you know how to light a stove?"

Kailem shook his head.

"Well, it can't be too difficult, I'm sure," Osmund said.

Osmund searched the kitchen for a tea kettle, but in the process, he found his way into the cellar. He emerged a full ten minutes later carrying a bottle of wine.

"I just found what is undoubtedly the most robust collection of wines in all of Iria," Osmund said. "I've selected a 45-year-old magenta wine from Tarwick. I believe our stay here will be most enjoyable."

He placed the bottle and his candle on the table across from Kailem and went to fetch some wine glasses.

Emerald walked in, shuffling her feet just as Osmund had done moments earlier, her hair a rat's nest in flames. She carried a candle of her own that she set on the counter, then waved to the men absently as she walked past them to the pantry.

Osmund poured himself a glass. A moment later, Emerald emerged carrying a basket of bread rolls they had baked that afternoon. She also had a butter tray and a jar of blackberry jam in the basket.

"'Tis beautiful," Emerald said, motioning to Kailem's pearl as she set the basket on the table. Kailem hadn't realized he was still rolling the pearl between in his fingers.

"You don't seem the type to wear jewelry." Osmund said.

Emerald spread butter and jam on a roll and gave it to Osmund.

"I found it while pearl diving with my brother on the day my parents were killed," Kailem explained. "We were going to fashion it into a ring as a gift for my Amma. She thought finding a pearl was a good omen."

Emerald and Osmund shared a look.

"But... that sounds like a sad memory," Emerald said. "So why keep it 'round yer neck?"

Kailem took in a breath. "When Mokain and I were exiled, we weren't allowed to bring much with us. This is all I have left of them."

Osmund handed Kailem the wine, and he drank straight from the bottle.

"Plus," Kailem continued, "there was something my father used to say. He said, 'some of our greatest fortunes seem like tragedies in the beginning. You just need to let time reveal the good in them.' I guess I keep hoping something good will come from that day."

Osmund nodded, and a moment of silence passed before he said, "This training is nothing like I thought it would be."

"What'd ye expect?" Emerald said between bites of her bread roll.

"Well to start, I never in a thousand years would I have imagined that just *anybody* could become a sage. I thought at the very least you would have had to be born with the gift, or have a parent who was sage. And then to learn the art, well, I confess I had supposed more potions would be involved."

"I find the implications of that... distressing," Kailem said.

"The potions?" Emerald asked.

Kailem shook his head. "Not the potions. That just anyone can be a sage. Think of what that means." He paused to fill his wine glass. "Every person we've ever known, every person we pass on the road or speak to in a tavern, even the lowest beggar in the street, all of them had limitless untapped potential inside. But none of them realize that potential because they simply don't know how. They don't even know it's there.

"But Elwin knows. He could teach them. He could end poverty and disease and even death. All suffering in Iria could vanish, but instead we hide away in the mountains. How is that right?"

Emerald and Osmund shared a look and nodded. The same thought had been on their minds as well.

A glow of candlelight shone through the kitchen door as Elwin walked in.

"Honestly?" Kailem said, mostly to himself. He had come to the kitchen to be alone with his thoughts, not for the whole monastery to join him. He wondered how much Elwin had heard.

"You three aren't nearly as quiet as you presume," Elwin said. He walked throughout the kitchen, lighting the candles on the wall sconces, then sat at the table. "Tell me, what pressing matter has summoned you all in the middle of the night?"

"Nothing of importance," Kailem said.

Osmund refilled his glass. Emerald spread butter and jam on a roll and offered it to Elwin, but he declined, so she took a bite.

"Are you troubled by the disturbance we heard?" Elwin asked.

The three friends nodded, and technically, it was the truth. The mysterious thunderclap had been one of their many concerns, albeit not the most distressing at the moment.

"I know of nothing natural that can make such a sound, do you?" Kailem asked.

Elwin shook his head.

"We must assume the Blackbirds are the cause," Kailem said, "and whatever their motive, it cannot be good."

Elwin thought on Kailem's words.

"I agree with your assessment," he finally said. "But we must not engage. Remember the oaths you three have made."

Emerald and Osmund seemed resigned to accept Elwin's policy of noninterference, but Kailem was not. He sat still and said nothing, his eyes staring blankly at the candle's flame.

"This angers you, Kailem?" Elwin asked.

Kailem looked up and met Elwin's eyes. His first instinct was to assure him it did not, but he knew Elwin saw through him.

"You promised never to read our thoughts," Kailem said.

"And I have kept that promise, Kailem. But your anger screams so loudly I could no more block out your emotions than I could a southern storm."

Kailem hated feeling so transparent.

"I can't understand you. When you found us in Glendown Forest, you said you were tracking outlaws. Then you found us on the road to Oswyn because you were tracking the Blackbirds. You mauled all three of them and turned them over to the constable. How is that not getting involved? But now, when it would actually matter, you do nothing? You're a hypocrite."

Emerald and Osmund shifted in their seats.

Elwin took a breath. "I've explained this to you, Kailem. My work is to suppress any knowledge of the sages. We infiltrated their leadership in the Riverkeep and I found no indication of sagecraft, so that is where my involvement ends."

Kailem shook his head. "It still doesn't feel right," he said. "Even if I ignore what they did to my parents, which I cannot, but even if I could, how can we turn a blind eye to all the cruelty and havoc the Blackbirds will cause?"

"I know it is difficult, Kailem, but your perspective is too limited for you to understand. I have fought in many wars, all of which seemed a just and noble cause, and I've seen what it does to the people and the land. We must be separate from them. The common men have their affairs, we have our own, and they must never mix."

Kailem's jaw clenched. He closed his eyes and forced himself to relax.

"I understand your anger, young Kailem. I truly do. But in time, you will see the wisdom in this course."

"I will never see wisdom in cowardice," Kailem said. The words had burst out of his mouth on their own. He had not planned to say it, but neither did he regret doing so.

Emerald's hand rose to her mouth while Osmund's eyebrows shot up to his hairline. Kailem braced for an outburst from Elwin in retaliation. Instead, Elwin locked eyes with him, letting the seconds stretch into eternity.

"There is no greater coward than the one who bows to his own hatred," Elwin said. His words were calm, controlled, and calculated. "If you would be brave, Kailem, then rise above your anger and be better than the men who took your parents. Vengeance brings no honor to the dead. But to become the man you are destined to become, for a parent, there is no greater honor."

Kailem was silenced. His anger still screamed inside, but he had no retort against Elwin's words. He was not afraid of facing the Blackbirds, and thus there was no bravery in attacking them. But the anger inside him, his potential for violence and destruction, that terrified Kailem more than anything. Facing it would take more courage than he could muster. He thought back to that brief moment where he had considered taking his revenge out on Osmund, and the shame returned. The pearl slipped from his fingers onto the table.

"Please help me," he said. His words were less than a whisper. The others weren't sure he had even spoken.

"Say again," Elwin said, leaning forward to hear him.

"Please help me," he repeated aloud. "What you ask is more than I have to give."

"Is it more than you have to give, or more than you believe you have?"

Kailem looked to Osmund, recognizing the same lesson Elwin had given the day prior. He looked back to Elwin, then dropped his head. "I... I don't know what to do."

"Do you believe that I do?"

Kailem avoided his eyes, but nodded.

"Then swear your oath again."

At first, Kailem said nothing. He recalled the words of the oath, considering each one carefully. Elwin waited silently for his response.

When he was ready, Kailem met Elwin's eyes. "I swear to maintain the secrecy of the Sages, to follow all your instructions exactly, to use sagecraft only for good, to protect the weak and defend what is right, and... and to stay out of the affairs of the common man."

Never had the ancient Sage heard words more sincere than these.

"Your oath is accepted, and I will teach you."

Chapter Thirty-Eight

THE HOUSE WITH THE RED DOOR

54TH DAY OF SUMMER, 897 G.C.

K yra was dead.

At least, Kyra the noblewoman was. This new person was someone else entirely. Someone damaged and broken and defeated, someone who had been maimed and abused and discarded.

After her first night in the tavern alleyway, she struggled to her feet, leaning on the wall for support. Her cheek was scabbed over. Her only clothing was her stained and soiled slip. Every inch of her was in pain. She stumbled out into the street, looking like she had been dragged through the sewer.

She stood in the shadow of the palace looking up at her former home, and the events from the previous day flooded her memory: the murder of the king, her pleading for Aedon not to go to war, her fiancé striking her across the face with hot iron, her parents disowning her, being thrown out of the palace into a puddle on the street, being attacked by drunken men in the alleyway. She had thought Aedon loved her. She had thought her parents loved her. But it was all a lie. They were all using her, keeping her around while she was useful, and disposing of her when she was not. She laid her head against a shop's wall and slid down to the floor, weeping into her knees.

"Shoo! Shoo!" someone yelled at her.

Kyra looked up to see an elderly woman hobbling toward her.

"You cannot sit in front of my shop. Go on now," the woman scolded.

The old shrew drew close enough to see Kyra's glossy, bloodshot eyes. She looked the young girl over from head to toe, shaking her head.

"Sarding Iria," the old woman said under her breath. She walked back to her store and returned a moment later with a threadbare dress of coarse fabric. "There, now put it on and go. Go!"

She continued shooing until Kyra took her dress and fled. The brown dress fit her figure like a bed sheet with a hole cut in it. She slid the dress over her head, intent on walking as far away from the palace as her feet would carry her.

She spent the next week wandering aimlessly through the streets of Rhinegard, somehow finding her way to Central Square. The city's main plaza was a mingling of the rich and poor, and the difference between the two was even more staggering when seen from the other side of the spectrum. She saw several homeless children begging for food and tried to join them, with little success. People were less sympathetic to a disfigured woman in her twenties than they were for a helpless orphan.

The Royal Guard had accosted her for harassing the good people of Rhinegard. They pulled her away from potential benefactors and threw her to the ground, bruising her shoulder in the process. But what hurt even worse than their gauntleted hands throwing her down to the Central Square flagstones, was the fact that none of the royal guards even recognized her. She had been completely forgotten by everyone that mattered. That was the moment she knew her old life was gone forever. It was the moment that Kyra Arturri, fiancé of Prince Aedon and future Queen of Cavandel died, and Kyra the destitute vagrant was born.

She left Central Square and found her way to increasingly poorer areas of the city she hadn't known existed. She felt less out of place there. The nights were cold, and finding a place she felt safe enough to fall asleep proved impossible. She spent most nights wide awake and shivering under a lamppost, then would find an alley to sleep in once the sun arose. When she slept, she dreamt the events of the coronation had gone differently.

Most nights she dreamt she had held her tongue. In those dreams, she was wed to Aedon and crowned queen of Cavandel. She even dreamed she had children and was madly in love with her husband. Other nights, she dreamt Aedon had a change of heart. In those dreams, she saw him coming down the alleyway, scooping her up in his arms and taking her back to the palace where she belonged. Regardless of the dream, she woke every afternoon to her new reality, and the roots of her hatred for Aedon and her parents grew deeper and stronger.

It took five days of an empty stomach before she was willing to eat something off an alley floor. She spent the entire night vomiting nothing but acid and bile, but after three more days of an empty stomach, she was willing to try again.

In the alley behind the market, adjacent to one of the many taverns in Rhinegard, discarded bits of food were cast into barrels before they would be carted out to cesspits at the end of the day. Kyra learned to join the other derelicts in searching through the rubbish for the most edible bits.

Her heart leapt when she found a half-eaten apple with several bites of flesh still on the core. She brushed off debris and held the precious gem to her chest as she fled around the corner to eat her treasure in privacy.

The apple core was brown and starting to shrivel, and the flesh had begun to turn sour. She gnawed at her prize anyway. When she had swallowed the entire core, she became painfully aware of what had become of her, and she wept, wondering how it had come to this. She had been destined to be Queen of Cavandel; she was meant to dine at royal banquets in extravagant gowns that made her the envy of the Court. She was supposed to have a team of handmaidens serving her every whim.

Now she scavenged for half-rotted food in a rubbish heap. She couldn't bear to go on living like this. She let the apple fall from her hands and wept. She had cried so much since the coronation it was a marvel she had any tears left to shed.

Light glinted through the shards of a broken brandy bottle by the back door of the tavern within reach of where she sat. Kyra pinched a glass shard between her fingers and sat with her back against the tavern wall, rotating the shard between her fingers. A steady stream of pedestrians passed by the alley, but no one noticed her; she might as well have been the only person in Rhinegard.

The glass shard was about the size of a salad knife, but far sharper. She pressed the sharpest point of the shard against her fingertip, and a droplet of crimson blood emerged. She stared at the red dot for a long, grim moment. There were multiple places on her body where a small cut would end her suffering. Why shouldn't she end it, she asked? What was she living for? Just a little pressure and a moment of pain, and all her problems would be over.

She let the shard drop from her hands and wept yet again.

Something deep inside her insisted she stay alive, but for what reason, she couldn't say. And frankly, she no longer cared.

A rustling came from a crate nearby. Some vermin was scavenging through the rubbish. Two weeks ago, she would have been disgusted; now she barely blinked.

Then a fox peaked its head above the crate. Its fur was matted with grime, and her body was thin beyond recognition, but her face was unmistakable.

"Ember?"

The fox leapt from behind the crate and rushed into Kyra's arms, whining a high-pitch cry as she did so. Kyra held the fox tightly against her cheek. They must have thrown her pet out of the palace the same day they threw her out. It was a mercy they hadn't just killed her, or maybe the fox had escaped before they could. From that moment on, the fox never left her side.

One evening, Kyra noticed several women walking the street together. They were well-dressed for commoners, albeit scandalously indecent, and they moved together like a clowder of cats roaming the streets. Men yelled out lustful solicitations, and the women responded with coquettish calls of their own. One by one, the women would take a man by the hand and lead him to a building on a dark corner of the street, the building with the red door.

Seeing the harlots adorned in glamorous dresses reminded her of the red gown she had worn to her betrothal feast. The wealthiest, most important women in Iria had looked at her with envy that night, and only days later there had been replicas of the dress all throughout the royal court. She thought of the dress Norman Frode was currently making for her wedding day, also according to designs she had drawn for him. Her parents surely would have already written to him, canceling the order. She looked down at the sweat-stained potato sack of a dress she wore now and made herself smaller.

For days, Kyra watched the brothel from the street. Men and women came and went at all hours. Some men entered excited and left looking satisfied, other men entered cautiously and left looking ashamed. The women only wore a smile when they were next to a man, but they never looked hungry, or poor, or scared.

It took seven days of watching the house with the red door before the thought of becoming a harlot even became a consideration. At first, she judged these women. Low lives with no dignity, no virtue. No self-respecting woman would sell herself for money.

She had recoiled at the very thought of it. She would never stoop that low, no matter how grim her prospects. But as the days passed, watching the women from afar, her disgust began to fade. Who was Kyra trying to fool? She wondered.

Who was she saving herself for? What virtue was she trying to protect? She was damaged goods; she knew it, and anyone who bothered to look at her knew it. But the harlots, they were well-fed and had beautiful dresses, warm beds, and friends looking out for them.

By the eighth day, which happened to be the First Day of Autumn, the last of her dignity had disappeared. Actually, mustering the courage to enter the brothel took the better part of the day, and included several failed attempts that stole her nerve. After instructing Ember to wait outside, an order the fox somehow understood, she opened the red door and stepped through the threshold.

She stood in the entryway, her arms folded across her abdomen, not knowing what to do next. The foyer was dimly lit by oil lamp sconces burning at their lowest setting, and the walls were painted the same shade of red as the front door. There was a bartender to the left serving drinks to gentlemen in overcoats and black hats that obscured their faces. To the right was a staircase where women led customers up and down. Men and women passed by her like she wasn't even there.

Kyra identified the woman who seemed to be in charge. She stood behind a desk, taking men's money and handing out assignments to the posh ladies who stalked the brothel. Kyra approached the woman with her head down and stood there motionless, awkward, and silent.

"Did you need something?" the madam finally asked.

Kyra whispered her request.

"Speak up, girl! No one's going to hear a pipsqueak voice like that in here."

"I'm looking for work," Kyra repeated louder.

"As one of my girls?!" the madam asked.

Kyra nodded.

"Ha! You think you can just walk in here and be put to work, do you? Let me look at you."

The madam looked her over. Kyra's hair was matted and greasy and she stank of urine — nothing that couldn't be fixed with a good bath and strong soap. As for her body, well, it was difficult to assess her figure under that potato sack she wore, but she could tell the girl was malnourished just by her sunken cheeks.

Then she took Kyra by the chin and moved her head to the side, just as the tall man had done on her first night on the street. She leaned in close to examine the wound. It wasn't infected, but would certainly leave a scar nasty enough to turn the stomach of any customer who came through, and the corner of her lips had been melted by whatever had struck her face.

When the madam was done, Kyra's eyes dropped to her bare feet, which were now cracked and soiled.

"Listen, girl," the madam said, "you're filthy, covered in dirt and grime, and your face is... well, grotesque. No one is going to pay a single copper penny for you. I have no use for you."

Kyra nodded. She wiped a tear from her cheek. What else had she expected to hear? This had been a mistake, a delusion of grandeur. With her arms still folded across her abdomen, she turned and walked toward the front door. Once on the street, she stepped aside for passing brothel patrons.

The night was unusually calm. They never lit the streetlamps on this section of the street, so Kyra stood in the dark next to Ember, not knowing what to do with herself. Her chin quivered. She fought to remain strong, but tears and sobs flowed all the same.

As she stood there failing to muffle her cries, the madam walked to her side.

"You got a name, girl?" the madam asked.

She composed herself enough to reply, "Kyra, ma'am."

"Madam Delia," the woman said. When Kyra said nothing in response, Delia continued. "Listen, Kyra. You can't be one of my girls, but that doesn't mean I can't put you to work. Do you have a place to stay?"

Kyra shook her head and wiped more tears from her cheeks.

Madam Delia nodded, having suspected as much.

"It ain't much, but I've got a few spare mattresses stored in the attic. In our business, it's always good to have a few extras on hand. You can stay in the attic if you're willing to work as a maid and clean the place. I can't afford to pay you any coins, but I can give you room and board. The attic is warm and safe, and I can promise you three hot meals a day. Do we have a deal?"

Kyra nodded absently.

"Good. Now come inside and grab a bucket. A customer just vomited on one of my girls. Can't have dirty merchandise now, can I?"

Chapter Thirty-Nine

The Might of Cavandel

21st Day of Autumn, 897 G.C.

Mokain studied their map of the Valleys of Veydala over breakfast with his lieutenants.

"Shouldn't we have found it by now?" Lieutenant Lowin asked.

"We're too far west," Lieutenant Balfour insisted. "We need to backtrack and go around the last ridge we passed."

Mokain shook his head. "We're on track. We just need to press forward."

Lieutenant Balfour dropped his fork with a huff, but a glare from Mokain kept him silent.

"What's our plan when we get there?" Lieutenant Wyndell asked. "We haven't had any confirmation the Prince received our message."

"There's too much we don't know right now," Mokain replied. "We'll assess the situation when we arrive and make our plans from there."

The lieutenants all nodded their agreement, even Lieutenant Balfour.

After breaking camp, they continued their march south through the Valleys of Veydala. Mokain marched at the head of his battalion with scattered mountain peaks in the distance around them. When he reached the top of a small hill that looked no different from the dozen other hills they had climbed that week, he abruptly stopped. Lieutenant Wyndell came to his side, and both stood speechless as they took in the view.

The valley before them was the largest they had seen since entering Veydala, and yet both ends of the valley were packed with soldiers. The northern end of the valley was occupied by at least fifteen thousand soldiers bearing the king's banners. Banners sprouted from the many divisions among the troops; most banners indicated they were legions of Cavander infantry, but others were noble house militia and units of mounted knights. This was the entire might of Cavandel.

At the southern end of the valley, nearly at the horizon's edge, was the fabled Riverkeep. An army camped around it. At first glance, Mokain estimated there were more than five thousand of them.

"This I was not expecting," Lieutenant Wyndell said, taking in the sight before them. "I think it's safe to assume the Prince got your message."

Mokain nodded. "Seems we were right about the Riverkeep as well. Tell the men to raise our banners for our approach. We need to find the command tent and see who's in charge."

Mokain's battalion descended the hill with banners of their own bearing the Cavander colors and seal, this granted them entry to the camp. While the rest of the battalion found a space to set up camp, Mokain and his five lieutenants found their way to the command tent. As they moved through the camp, Mokain felt a great weight fall from his shoulders. He was no longer the highest in command, the burden of decisions and the lives of his men were no longer his to bear alone.

The command tent was overcrowded with soldiers and servants. Aedon and his generals were around the map table, and all turned their heads when Mokain entered.

"First Officer Roka," Aedon said, relieved. He left his generals and embraced Mokain as an old friend. "You were right about everything," he said as they separated.

"I'm glad to see you received our report," Mokain said in return.

"Indeed," Aedon said, placing a hand on Mokain's shoulder. "And now you arrive on the eve of battle. You continue to impress me, Mariner. Or should I call you the Lion of Marin? Quite the epithet you've earned yourself. The lion was the sigil of the Kohel tribe, you know."

"You honor me, Your Grace," Mokain said, frowning at the crown on Aedon's head. "Or should I say, 'Your Majesty'?"

"Oh yes," Aedon said, adjusting the crown on his head. "My father took ill. I regret to report it proved fatal. It was as unexpected as it was tragic."

"I'm sorry for your loss, Your Majesty," Mokain said.

"Yes, thank you. Much has transpired in your absence, in fact. We shall have you briefed on the particulars. In the meantime, allow me to introduce Lord Theobald Gylden."

Lord Gylden stepped forward. He was a small, middle-aged man with a bulging gut and a short ribbon of hair around his otherwise bald head.

"Theobald has just been promoted to colonel; he will be taking command of your battalion for you."

Mokain snapped his eyes back to the King with a frown. "Excuse me, Your Majesty?"

"I'm sure you're anxious to be done with military life, so no need to thank me," the King said.

Mokain searched for what to say. "I serve at your pleasure, Your Majesty, of course. But is it wise to change leadership the day before a battle? This battalion has been together for months. It may serve Your Majesty to wait until—"

Colonel Gylden interjected, saying, "A Cavander battalion is a Cavander battalion, no matter who is at their head; the formations and calls all remain the same." His voice sounded like gravel in his throat.

"Indeed, Colonel Gylden," the King said. "That's the power of uniformity. But more importantly, I need you at my side leading the Royal Guard."

Mokain looked to the troubled, silent faces of his lieutenants trying to think of a way to stay their commander.

"Am I to assume these are my lieutenants?" Colonel Gylden grumbled.

Mokain could think of no way to dissuade the King. "They are," he said reluctantly, then added, "good men, every one of them."

"Very well, come with me then. No doubt you've developed some bad habits I'll need to break before the battle," Colonel Gylden said.

The five lieutenants looked to Mokain. Their pained expressions asked for confirmation, and he nodded for them to go with him. With Mokain's leave, they followed their new colonel out of the command tent.

King Aedon placed an arm around Mokain's shoulder. "My friend, I had high expectations for you, but I must say you have exceeded every single one of them. Defeating those Shinda when you were so outnumbered, discovering these traitors, leading your troops all the way south in time for the battle, I couldn't be more pleased."

"You are too kind, My King," Mokain replied.

Aedon grinned. "You are certainly a man of few words, Roka. I have found that men of action usually are. Your predecessor, Lord Menden, was the same way. I suppose it makes sense then why men in court talk so much. Here, come with me. I have a gift for you."

King Aedon led Mokain to the back of the command tent. On a reinforced cedar trunk sat a newly forged suit of steel armor shining with fresh polish. "I had it made by the same armorer who forged my new suit. I was going to have a new sword made for you, but I know how fond you are of those twin leaf blades of yours, so I decided on this instead. You won't match the other guards anymore, but it's good for a leader to stand out among his men."

Mokain inspected the armor. It was a full suit, just as he had worn in the tournament, only thicker and heavier. He lifted the breastplate; emblazoned on the chest was the stylized face of a lion surrounded by a thick, flowing mane.

"Oh yes, that was my idea as well," the King said. "That moniker of yours has taken deep roots in the Capital, so I thought we might as well embrace it."

It was flashier than Mokain would ever have selected for himself, but was a fine gift, nonetheless. "I thank you, Your Majesty. Truly. I shall wear it with pride." He left the armor there; he would have Vivek come retrieve it later.

The King gave a single pat on Mokain's back. "My pleasure, my friend. It must be a relief to be liberated of your command. And I'm sure you're anxious to return to your duties in the Royal Guard. You won't mind. I selected ten of your best men to serve as my honor guard in battle and left Lord Menden in charge of the remainder of the guard in your absence."

King Aedon walked Mokain to the map table, which was far larger and more elegantly carved than his own had been. In fact, everything about their command tent was larger and more elegant. They even had a small chandelier hanging just above their heads.

On the table was a map of the region. There was a figurine of a castle to mark the Riverkeep, and all around it were blocks to represent the Blackbird soldiers.

"According to our count, they have a little more than six-thousand men, but more are arriving by boat every day. We are eighteen thousand strong, but the longer we wait, the greater their numbers grow. The good news is they are blocked in by the Vondal River, and they haven't enough boats to evacuate their forces by water. Once we launch our attack, they'll have no way to flee."

Mokain shook his head. "I disagree, respectfully, Your Majesty. I do not believe that is the good news you think it is. An animal is never more dangerous than when it is backed into a corner with nothing to lose."

The comment earned him the ire of the generals around him.

"That is an interesting point, Roka," King Aedon said, "but ultimately irrelevant. We have not the provisions for an extended siege, nor are we prepared to keep ships from bringing them reinforcements. We're not even sure where their recruits are coming from. But if we are to attack, and attack we must, then it must be now. We are preparing to make our charge in the morning. Cornered or not, we have them outnumbered three to one. We should make quick work of them."

Something troubled Mokain. The Blackbirds surely knew they were vastly outnumbered by a force of superior training and weaponry. Any commander with even basic tactical knowledge would have already called for a full retreat, not enlisted more soldiers into a death trap. Then again, he had been outnumbered by what he thought was a superior force of Shinda, and had emerged victorious. Things were not always as they seemed where these rebels were concerned. What did they know that he did not?

Mokain kept his concerns to himself. The last thing he wanted was to upset every general in the Cavander army. There was, however, one question he could not keep to himself.

"How many men do you reckon we shall lose in this battle?"

The generals chuckled as Aedon explained. "These Blackbirds aren't trained soldiers. My generals anticipate we'll lose one man for every four we kill in the beginning, then once their lines are routed, we'll lose maybe one for every seven. When the dust settles, our casualties will most likely be no more than a thousand. Not bad for taking out six thousand of theirs."

Seven thousand men dead by tomorrow night, Mokain thought. "Have we tried everything else?"

Aedon frowned. "How do you mean?"

"I mean to avoid bloodshed, Your Majesty. Have we tried sending terms of surrender? Have we considered besieging the Riverkeep until they agree to surrender their swords?"

Aedon turned to face him. "Where is this coming from, Roka?"

Mokain thought for a moment. "I just want to make sure we're on the right side. That we're not throwing away men's lives needlessly."

Aedon placed a hand on Mokain's shoulder. "I assure you, my friend, we are on the right side. An uprising like this, if not snuffed out early, will throw all of Iria into war and chaos. And I've been over every option with my generals. The best course is to sacrifice a few thousand lives today to spare a few hundred thousand lives a year from now."

Mokain nodded thoughtfully.

"Now," the King said, "why don't you have yourself some food and some sleep? I'm going to need you at your best tomorrow. You're the one making sure I stay alive."

With the King's leave, Mokain left the command tent and found Vivek constructing his personal tent. Some of the men from his old battalion assisted, while others built a fire for him in front of the tent. Mokain met with the Royal Guard to arrange guard assignments for the night and the following morning.

After nightfall, a crowd of soldiers gathered outside his tent. Mostly members of the old battalion as well as several of the royal guard. They sat around a fire eating plates of beans and rice with thin strips of salted lamb chops.

"Oi, what's that, then? The saucy stuff you got there?" Sergeant Shaw asked.

"Creamed curry," Lieutenant Lowin said through a mouthful of beans.

"Well, how come I didn't get no creamed curry?" Shaw asked.

"Was just for us senior officers," Lieutenant Balfour explained. "Sergeants are junior officers."

Shaw slumped back on his stool and moved his dry beans about with his fork, muttering a vulgar complaint under his breath.

Mokain leaned over and scraped some of his curry onto the sergeant's plate. Shaw frowned, then the corners of his lips curled up slightly. The gesture had surprised him, but it shouldn't have. The men in their battalion had come to expect such generosity from their commander.

Seeing the gesture, Lieutenants Wyndell and Lowin did the same for the junior officers sitting in their circle. Lieutenant Balfour scooped a plentiful helping of rice dripping in curry and shoveled it into his mouth.

The men were in high spirits, given the weight of tomorrow's battle looming over them. Mokain couldn't help but recall the horrors of the battle of Tarwick, and he grimaced at the prospect of repeating it. Something to distract his mind was in order.

"How's the new colonel?" he asked his former lieutenants.

The men grumbled in unison.

"That bad?" Mokain set down his fork to listen.

"He's a noble. Never had to work his way up the ranks," Wyndell said. "When he first enlisted, his father saw to it he was made a sergeant in a battalion assigned to patrol near the capital, never saw any action until he was promoted to lieutenant and could watch from the safety of his horse."

"He talks down to us like we're imbeciles," Lowin added. "And he's undone all the changes you made."

"Wish you were still in command, sir," Shaw said.

The men all voiced a similar sentiment.

"As much I appreciate that, men, he's your commanding officer now."

"Should we be worried?" Wyndell asked.

"Naw," Balfour said. "Word is they're just a bunch of peasant farmers in uniform, and we outnumber 'em three-to-one."

"Never underestimate your enemy, Balfour," Wyndell said. He then looked to Mokain for confirmation.

"He's right," Mokain said. "Something's off about all this; I can't say how. Just remember your training and watch out for each other tomorrow."

A somber mood fell over the circle.

Chapter Forty

The Might of Iria

21st Day of Autumn, 897 G.C.

Edric Baylor stood in the Riverkeep bailey reviewing the latest report from his scouts. The Cavander army had already far outnumbered their own, and another battalion had arrived that day. The itch to turn tail and run was spreading through their ranks.

He took a moment to assess the morale of his men. The Riverkeep bailey was a hive of untried recruits sweating anxiety and dread. The full might of Cavandel had been camped in their valley since the previous morning, and every hour the Cavanders remained chiseled away another chip in the men's valor. The sun had long since fallen, and only a sliver of the gilded moon shined overhead. It was fortunate their pants were black so as to not betray which men had already wet themselves.

Edric climbed the narrow spiraling stone staircase and made his way to the council room. Oil lamps hung on the walls, but the room was still darker than Edric was used to. Their council table, which was usually surrounded by empty chairs during even their most crowded meetings, was now engorged with crotchety old lords and ladies doing their best to mask their trepidation.

At the head of the table, sitting in the chair that was usually his, was Lord Leonin Arturri. His wife, Avalina, sat at his side. Edric's parents, Lord Reginald Baylor and Lady Boudica Baylor, sat near the head of the table. The meeting was scheduled to discuss their campaign on the southern Devonian border; no one expected the Cavanders to find them.

At the opposite side of the table sat Edric's officers, along with several captains from neighboring sectors. Standing behind Lord Arturri was his personal guard, Daron. The man's face was as warm and comforting as a blizzard. Edric was always on edge around him.

"I say this respectfully, Lord Arturri," began the Captain from the Roserock Sector, "but it was my understanding you had the young king under control." The man spoke without first asking leave to question a superior, a lapse which did not bode well for Leonin's leadership.

"'Like a well-strung marionette' I believe had been your exact words," continued the captain. "So perhaps you will not object if I demand an explanation for what the entire Might of Cavandel is doing on our doorstep." The Roserock Captain's voice had grown progressively louder as he spoke.

Edric stood frozen near the doorway as all eyes were fixed on Leonin, wondering how their leader would handle the outburst. Even though the captain's words and tone had been offensive, even seditious, the question itself was a valid one.

Leonin simply stared at the man, a stare that lingered in discomforting silence. If one could generate heat with just a glare, the Roserock Captain would have burst into flames then and there. Instead, his hostile face wilted, first to passivity, then to fear, and finally into a docile man staring at the table.

Content that the man had remembered his place, Lord Arturri turned to Edric. "Captain Baylor, I trust you have the scout's report?" The leader extended his hand for Edric to sit in the empty chair next to his mother, Boudica Baylor.

"I do, Lord Arturri," Edric said as he sat in the chair. "Another battalion from Cavandel arrived late this afternoon. That brings their total to more than eighteen thousand."

A general murmuring arose from the table.

"Eighteen thousand," Leonin repeated, "against our six thousand." He tapped his fingers rhythmically against the tabletop.

The Roserock Captain said what nearly everyone at the table was thinking. "We're doomed. The Society is finished."

"Be silent, Captain, or you'll be fodder for the dogs before sunrise," Leonin said coldly. The Roserock Captain said nothing more the remainder of the meeting.

"Our new weapon will tip the scales in our favor," Avalina said. She clasped her hands on the table, flicking her thumbs together. "Believe me, once you see it in battle, you will all feel foolish for having doubted it."

Leonin's eyes were fixed on an empty section of the ceiling. His fingers pressed against each other while his chin rested on his index fingers. "How many weapons are ready for battle?"

"Nearly one thousand," replied the master-at-arms.

Leonin gave him the same stare he'd given the Roserock Captain, his lips slightly pursed, his eyes boring a hole into the man. The master-at-arms interpreted the stare immediately — Leonin was not asking for an estimate.

"Our last count was nine hundred sixty-seven, my lord, but I have men continuing to assemble more as we speak."

Leonin then turned to his wife. "And what of the alchemist who invented this weapon?"

"He had an unfortunate accident," Avalina explained. "We have his notes and schematics. No one else will have a weapon like this for the foreseeable future."

"But how confident are we that one thousand of these devices will tip the scales in our favor?" asked Lord Reginald Baylor.

Before his wife could defend her pet project any further, Leonin spoke. "This weapon has never been tested in battle, so we cannot be certain of anything. And what of training? The weapon serves nothing if our men don't know how to use it. Will they be ready?"

"The men have been training, sir, but we thought we'd have more time before actual combat was attempted."

Edric looked around the table and found not a shred of confidence among them. These were the highest-ranking officers in the Blackbird Society, and each of their faces dripped with fear; even his own parents were losing faith. If even their leaders had abandoned hope, what chance did his men have on the battlefield, he wondered?

But no, these weren't the highest-ranking officers, he remembered. There was one leader missing, the head and founder of their Society, a man only Edric's parents and Lord and Lady Arturri had ever met personally.

"What about the sage?" Edric asked.

All eyes in the room turned towards him. The silence was palpable. Although it was common knowledge they were led by a sage, there was an unspoken rule that they did not mention him unless Lord Arturri himself broached the subject.

Edric continued in spite of the stunned looks from the other officers. "Is there any way we can send a message to him? Surely, he would come to our aid if he knew the very existence of the Society was at stake."

"We do not contact him. He contacts us," Leonin explained. "Even if we were to send a message, I don't know where we would send it. He keeps his whereabouts private."

The heavy silence again overtook the room. It was clear that Leonin was searching his mind for a plan that could save them. Everyone else was doing all they could not to lament their imminent destruction. The sight of it angered Edric. Their faith meant nothing if it failed in the moment they needed it the most.

"Our plight is not as hopeless as it appears," Edric began. "Yes, the full might of Cavandel is at our front door, but those Cavanders have no cause. They believe in nothing, they fight for nothing, they merely obey the word of their king without passion or conviction."

"But not us. We fight for our freedom, for the better world we will create when the monarchies of Iria come toppling down. Conviction is what will save us. Yes, the full might of Cavandel may be at our door. But the full might of the people is within our walls. Just a single soldier with conviction is worth more than twenty soldiers without it. Our enemy stands for nothing, while we fight for everything, and that is why when the dust settles on the morrow, we will be victorious."

Leonin looked around the table. Edric's words had an effect on the captains, each of whom had been chosen because they had at one point shared Edric's passion for the Society. They were not leaping from their chairs with battle cries, but their pessimism had at least been abated.

"Well said, Captain Baylor," Leonin said. "And I happen to agree with you; if our men fight with half the passion that you have, there is not an army in Iria that could stand against us. I want you to share that message with your men. And that goes for each of you captains. Go to your men and inspire them, as Captain Baylor has inspired you. Let your men know a glorious victory awaits them in the morning."

Edric wore a proud grin as he and the other captains shuffled out of the council room. After a moment, only the Arturris and the Baylors remained.

Reginald shook his head. "The poor boy actually believes all that nonsense. Perhaps we were a little too convincing."

"It is good he believes it," Leonin said. "He is exactly what we need right now."

"But it won't win us the battle tomorrow," Boudica said.

Leonin exhaled. "No, no, it won't. So, we will need a contingency plan. If the battle turns against us, we'll ride south and sail for the Marin Islands. Lord Vanua will give us safe harbor there."

The other three voiced their agreement.

"It is absolutely paramount that no Cavender sees us here," Leonin said. "Our access to the Cavander King is the main reason he chose us; we cannot risk our positions in the Cavandel Court for anything. We will ride south the moment the battle starts to turn, long before the Cavanders have a chance to pursue us. I will see that the horses and provisions are made ready," Reginald said.

"I can spin the loss with the remaining members across Iria," Boudica added. "We can make them into martyrs, stir up some sympathy, even outrage in potential new recruits. We should be able to recoup the losses quickly."

"That is good, Boudica. See to it," Leonin said.

Boudica sat a little taller after Leonin's praise. Avalina opened her mouth, ready to defend her new weapons again, but she couldn't think of anything to say. Leonin was right, no one had ever proven the weapon in battle; she had no idea what would happen tomorrow.

Leonin turned to Daron, standing behind him. "You can't be seen here either, Daron. If anyone recognizes you, they'll know we were somehow involved. Ride back to the estate in Devona and wait there until we return."

Daron gave a nod and left to do as instructed. The man walked with all the grace of a grizzly bear in a porcelain shop. Everyone sat more at ease once he was gone.

"While it is just the four of us," Reginald said, "I would like to express my deepest sympathies for your daughter. What a ghastly ordeal that must have been for you both."

Leonin looked at Reginald with ice in his veins. "We have no daughter."

CHAPTER FORTY-ONE

THE BATTLE OF RIVERKEEP

22ND DAY OF AUTUMN, 897 G.C.

Mokain awoke with the first rays of sunlight, alert and restless. Multiple soldiers were emerging at the same time. Most were officers walking from tent to tent rousing their men. There was a heaviness in the officers' faces. Mokain was sure they could see the same in his own face.

"Good morrow, milord," Vivek said, arriving at Mokain's tent. Mokain returned the greeting while Vivek set himself to helping his master don his new set of armor from the King. Mokain felt silly being helped with his armor, especially as the men around him put on their own armor, but he had learned not to resist when Vivek carried out his duties.

Mokain watched his young servant securing armor over his shins and said, "You're a good man, Vivek." It was an offhand, spontaneous comment that Mokain hadn't planned to say and didn't give much thought after he said it.

Vivek paused and looked up to his master. Not knowing what to say, he lowered his head and went back to work. He hadn't known it at the time, but Mokain had given Vivek a compliment of no small significance. In Iria, servants were not referred to as men by their superiors. They were male, to be sure, but a servant ranked somewhere between a boy and man on the unspoken scale of manhood, and for Mokain to call someone as young and lowly as Vivek a man, that simple recognition carried the weight of an entire castle's worth of stone for the youth.

With his armor in place and his twin swords at his side, he assembled the ten other Royal Guards and led them to the command tent. It took him a moment to remember their names after so much time had passed. He met the eyes of several army regulars as he walked through the camp. The officers were adept at hiding their fear. The same could not be said for the infantry. Each bore the look of a man who didn't know if he'd live to see the sunset.

"Ah, First Officer," the King said, "come here, I want you to see this."

Mokain joined the generals around the map table. The command tent was positioned on a small rise in front of the foothills on the opposite side of the valley from the Riverkeep. Mokain could see men in black uniforms forming ranks in front of the tents that surrounded the castle.

Aedon handed him a spyglass, and Mokain raised it to his eye. The Blackbirds' vanguard were holding what appeared to be poles or staffs, with some contraption fastened on one end. Something wasn't right, and it gave Mokain a sinking feeling.

"What are they holding?" Mokain asked.

"Most peculiar, is it not?" the King said. "We can't say for sure, but it doesn't matter. The battle will be quick. We should be celebrating our victory by lunch hour."

Mokain scanned the front lines with the spyglass. On either side of the vanguard were several devices he had never seen before. They looked like iron barrels on wheels, and they were pointed toward the center of the battlefield.

The King turned to his generals. "Have your men form ranks. I want to launch the first wave within the hour."

The generals bowed and left to relay the orders. The King turned to Mokain.

"You and your men will stay by my side. You have one responsibility and one only: to keep me alive at all costs."

***

Lieutenant Conroy Wyndell barked orders at his men as they marched to the Cavander vanguard. Sergeant Shaw marched at his side. Wyndell tried to sound confident and authoritative, just like Mokain always had, but he felt like a child out of his depth.

Their battalion was assigned to the vanguard of the first wave. Men in their position rarely survived, but their morale was high. They were brave men, each with substantial battle experience, and they were marching into the most favorable conditions a soldier could hope for in a battle, but in the vanguard, they would need more than morale to save them.

Wyndell needed to say something to rouse their confidence, to inspire them to remember all that Mokain had taught them. He considered what Mokain would say if he were still their commander, but he couldn't remember if Mokain had said anything before the Battle of Tarwick. He looked to Sergeant Shaw, but the sergeant's eyes were fixed on the enemy ahead. Wyndell then looked back at Colonel Gylden. The fat man was atop his horse, leading his battalion from the rear. Wyndell wished Mokain still led them.

This waiting was the worst part. Waiting for the call to march forward. Waiting to attack. Waiting to kill or die. And all they could do was stare forward at the men across the battlefield, the men who wanted to kill them. His men stood bravely at attention, but they shifted their feet nervously, regardless.

Come on, Conroy. Think of something. Think! he ordered himself.

His mind remained empty.

The silence was broken by the sound of a bugle blaring from the command tent. It echoed through the valley, sending a chill up their spines.

"Cavanders, advance!" Colonel Gylden yelled.

Lieutenant Wyndell marched forward at the head of his men, remembering the valiant sight of Mokain at Tarwick running headlong and alone into a Shinda regiment.

The fading mist swirled around their feet as the army tramped through the valley. Wildflowers were crushed under every footstep. Despite his trepidation, Wyndell had to fight the urge to run at the enemy. Somehow, he knew his men were having the same struggle. Something inside of them was desperate to move. Perhaps it was nervous energy needing to burst out of them, or maybe the anticipation was simply worse than the battle itself.

The Blackbirds weren't marching towards them, as Conroy had expected. Instead, they remained in place, motionless statues in front of the castle. Apparently, they were going to make the Cavanders walk the entire distance of the battlefield.

Arrows were loosed by the Cavander archers behind them. The arrows sailed over their heads and fell on the Blackbird shields. The Blackbirds had enough training to stay in formation, and although a few arrows managed to penetrate their lines, they were mostly ineffective.

When they were within one hundred yards of the Blackbirds, Colonel Gylden called for a charge. All the energy building inside of them erupted. With his sword held high, Lieutenant Wyndell let out a battle cry and broke into a mad dash. His fellow soldiers ran at his sides with pointed spears, ready to crash into the Blackbirds' front line with the force of a charging rhinoceros. The enemy had some kind of stick pointed at them, like spears without a tip. It didn't make sense; something was wrong.

Within fifty yards of the front line, a foreign and unexpected sound exploded from the Blackbird's line, a sound like thunder clapping all around them. It was so loud it drowned out the Cavanders' war cries entirely. The air moved as something small and invisible whistled past him. One of the flying objects grazed his right leg just above the knee, stinging with white hot pain and sending him crashing to the grass underneath him.

Grey smoke billowed from the Blackbirds' front line, a smoke with a pungent stink like sulfur that stung the nostrils. He looked behind him and saw a horror he couldn't comprehend. His men lay bleeding on the valley floor by the dozens, as if overwhelmed by an attack, yet they hadn't even reached the front line. They were covered in puncture wounds, shot with a volley of invisible arrows. Wyndell could see the men screaming in agony, but all he could hear was the incessant ringing in his ears.

The Cavander ranks behind them pressed forward around them, running past Wyndell like he was already dead. A part of him wanted to stay there, to survive by riding out the battle playing dead. The thought shamed him. Mokain would never cower on the ground during a battle; he would fight until there was no life left in him to fight with. And Wyndell's men were dying.

Sergeant Shaw appeared at his side and helped him to his feet. Wyndell fought through searing pain and leaned on Shaw as climbed to his feet.

"What manner of sorcery was that?" Shaw yelled over the clamor of war.

Wyndell shook his head. "I've never seen it's like," he yelled back.

The Blackbirds met the charging Cavanders and fell on them like farmers harvesting wheat, cutting down everyone in their path. They employed no technique or fighting style to speak of. They didn't need one. The Cavanders were too consumed by chaos to defend themselves.

Those who hadn't been wounded in the explosion halted their charge. They were as horrified as Wyndell was, looking around like young children separated from their parents.

"What do we do?" Shaw asked.

"Regroup," Wyndell replied. "Regroup!" he shouted for all to hear. "Re—"

A Blackbird thrust his sword at Wyndell. The lieutenant deflected the blow while Shaw sliced through the enemy's side.

"Regroup!" Wyndell yelled again. He repeated the order again and again, each time louder than before. Soon, his men surrounded him in the standard formation Mokain had taught them. Mokain's lessons on fighting with a wounded limb flashed through Wyndell's mind. With his weight on his good leg, he parried each of the advancing Blackbirds. He fought better than he ever had, and with each passing moment, he was increasingly amazed he was still alive.

Despite the surprise attack, the enemy was still outnumbered. Death was administered on both sides, without restraint and without mercy. The screams of the dying echoed around them. Soon Wyndell was unaware of the pain in his leg. His muscles had been trained by the greatest fighter he'd ever seen, and he killed man after man as they again advanced towards the Riverkeep.

"Ready!" came a yell from behind the Blackbird lines.

Without warning, every Blackbird in the melee dropped to the ground in unison. The Cavanders were bewildered, but before they could plunge their swords and spears into the enemy, another explosion of smoke and invisible arrows assaulted their ranks. Men fell in agony.

Wyndell was twice hit, once in the left side below the ribs and again through the right clavicle. He again collapsed to the valley floor, this time unconscious, his blood soaking into the dirt beneath him.

***

Kailem, Emerald, and Osmund followed their teacher's Tai'veda movements in the stone circle. The sun shined overhead without a cloud in the sky, and a delicate breeze rustled the leaves in the orchard nearby. The trio's motions were slow and fluid, and in perfect harmony with one another.

The tranquil morning was pierced by the same sound they heard before, the thunderclap on a cloudless day. This time, however, the sound was so loud it made the very trees quake around them. Every bird on their side of the mountain took flight at once. Kailem saw the blood drain from Elwin's face.

"Follow me," Elwin ordered.

None of them could have imagined the full speed of a sage. Elwin's feet were as light as an ibis airing along the shoreline, and yet somehow, he ran faster than a thoroughbred stallion. The way he moved was more than inhuman. It defied reason itself.

They ran from the monastery toward the rocky outcrop. Within moments, Elwin was so far ahead he disappeared around the bend, but the three students knew the way. As they ran, the thunderclap sounded again.

Kailem arrived second and stood beside his teacher, breathing heavily. Elwin lowered his spyglass and gave it to the Mariner. Below him in the valley were two massive armies locked in the throes of combat.

Elwin was carved from stone, the sight of war recalling the battle that had ended his people. Kailem could feel the agony inside him somehow.

Emerald arrived next. She saw the scene in the valley below, and the sight overwhelmed her. She turned and buried her face in Osmund's neck just as he arrived. He wrapped his arms around her, comforting her without knowing why. Then he looked to the valley and understood.

"What is happening!?" King Aedon yelled.

His generals stood speechless and stupefied, their mouths agape.

"Well?!" the King yelled again.

"Your Majesty, none of us have ever seen a weapon like this," General Torvon said. "We..." his voice trailed off. They were entirely unprepared. They had no battle strategy, and without even knowing what weapon was used against them, they had nothing useful to offer.

"It must be sorcery, Your Majesty," said a short colonel in the back.

Aedon would not dignify the remark. Instead, he growled and turned away from them. "Useless sards," he muttered.

General Torvon's pride was sundered in two, but he had no retort, and thus he continued to remain uselessly silent. Out on the battlefield, another explosion of the new weapon sent more of their men collapsing to the ground.

Aedon turned to Mokain. "Roka, what would you do?"

Mokain was watching through the spyglass. "It appears that just before they use their weapons, they send a signal to their men, and they all fall to the ground.

I believe it is to avoid being hit. If there was some way we could relay the signal to our men so they could fall to the ground at the same time, perhaps we could neutralize the weapon."

King Aedon's nostrils flared at the suggestion. "Well, we have no signal that would tell every man to fall to the ground at the same time, and it's the height of battle, so we have no way of sending a message to every single soldier." He turned to a nearby messenger. "Order the cavalry charge!" he yelled. The young soldier saluted and ran off to relay the order.

The impotence Aedon felt from atop the incline watching the battle unfold was not one he was familiar with, nor did he care for it. Even he began to wonder if these Blackbirds weren't employing some form of sorcery. He growled again as it took far too long for the messenger to reach the cavalry and for the charge to begin.

The Cavander cavalry finally began to gallop at the enemy, making their approach from the left flank. Through the spyglass, Mokain saw the Blackbirds reposition the iron barrels, and his stomach dropped to his knees.

Fire and smoke exploded from the barrels, propelling lead balls the size of melons faster than arrows at the approaching cavalry. Some hit the horses directly in the chest, killing them instantly. Others rolled across the valley floor, breaking the horses' legs out from under them. Others hit the riders directly, removing heads and limbs like petals off a flower, blood and viscera spouting from the victims.

The few horses that escaped the carnage halted and reared on their hind legs, throwing several of their riders. Not even a seasoned warhorse could adapt to this level of chaos and tumult. Some turned and rode back to camp, others made for the safety of nearby trees. In mere seconds, their entire cavalry of over two hundred warhorses had been reduced to scattered limbs on the battlefield.

The King let out a scream that was equal parts rage and petulance. He kicked the map table, but it was too heavy to turn over. He then grabbed a nearby messenger and threw him tumbling from the command tent. The generals and guards stood motionless. Those who had been at the coronation ceremony were reminded of the brutal attack on his fiancé.

Aedon looked again at the battlefield. "It takes them several minutes to fire those weapons," he said. "Our only chance is to overwhelm them with numbers, cut down as many as we can between blasts. Send in the second and third waves together."

"Your Majesty," General Torvon began hesitantly, "perhaps we should sound the retreat. We don't know what we're—"

The General was cut off when the King grabbed him by the throat. There was hatred in the King's eyes that frightened even the hardened general. After a moment, the King released him, and the general sucked in a breath and coughed. Aedon turned to one of the messengers, who jumped back instinctively.

"Order the second and third waves together," he commanded.

The messenger was so eager to flee the command tent that he forgot to salute. The King watched as the messenger ran from colonel to colonel, relaying the order. None of the battalions moved. Several colonels looked back at the command tent in disbelief. The men were all frozen with fear.

"Useless, every single one of them," Aedon ranted. He donned his helmet and turned to leave the tent.

"What are you..." Mokain started, but the King was already climbing into his saddle. "Rotting sard," he cursed as he grabbed his own helmet. "Follow your king!" Each of the royal guards, Mokain included, leapt into their saddle and galloped with the king into battle.

***

Elwin turned away from the unending bloodshed. "Come, we must find a better vantage."

His students followed him away from the rocky outcrop and down towards the foothills. There was no running with the speed of a sage this time. Elwin marched down the mountainside at a steady yet cautious speed, and the three students were able to remain at his heels as he did so.

They reached the foothills just as the Blackbird weapons fired again. They were on the Blackbird's side of the battlefield facing the Cavander lines and were close enough now to see the blood spray from men's chests as they were cut down. Emerald was close to fainting; Osmund nearly vomited.

Kailem hated to admit it, but what tore at him more than the death and carnage before him was that the Blackbirds were nearing victory. He instinctively reached for Malua at his side. He longed to enter the fight, to slash his way through their ranks until they all lay dead on the battlefield.

Instead, he turned to Elwin. "What should we do?"

His teacher was slow to answer.

"Nothing," Elwin finally said. "We do nothing. We will stay here and observe, but not interfere."

The valley cried with the sounds of steel, black powder, and dying men.

"Ain't there nothin' ta be done??" Emerald asked, nearly in tears.

Elwin looked at her. "I cannot take on an entire army by myself," he said.

Kailem doubted that was true. "But shouldn't we fight for the side that is right?"

Elwin shook his head. "Remember your oaths, Kailem."

All three turned to Kailem, worried how he would respond.

"If you tell me to stay, I will stay," came the reply.

The response should have pleased Elwin. Kailem had learned to trust his teacher. Now the boy could finally be trained as the Aura of Iria had directed. So why was there a pit in Elwin's stomach, he wondered? Doubt crept into his mind. Doubt that he had given the right council. Why was he so adamant to do nothing in the face of such atrocities?

On the battlefield, a dozen soldiers on horseback galloped into the fray. Their leader wore glistening black armor that stood out from the rest of the army. Kailem held the spyglass to his eye. He didn't recognize the man, but he was young. Certainly, a nobleman of some kind. Then he recognized the face of the man riding beside him, and the air rushed from his lungs. It was a face he hadn't seen in months, a face that filled him both with joy and dread. It was Mokain, and he was riding directly at the Blackbird's new weapon. Kailem was about to watch his brother die.

The sight of their fearless king riding triumphantly into battle, the Fang of Rhinegard drawn and pointed at their foes, had exactly the effect Aedon had counted on. The men yelled their battle cry, their swords and spears raised high as he rode past them, then charged into the fray behind him. Nearly every soldier in the first wave was dead, and the Blackbirds aimed their weapons at the King.

Aedon and his guard rode headlong toward a sudden wall of fire and grey smoke. Massive lead balls ripped through their ranks, cracking through armor and bone as they bounced along the valley floor. One ricocheted off the King's helmet, sending him rolling backward off his horse and dropping his sword in the fall. Another ball hit the King's horse in the neck, and the beast collapsed to the ground at the same time as its rider.

Aedon landed flat on his back and the air rushed from his lungs, leaving him gasping in vain. Two of the Royal Guards took balls to the chest and collapsed to the dirt, motionless. Mokain was thrown when his horse took a ball in the shoulder.

The King scrambled about the harrowed ground, looking for the Fang of Rhinegard. The Blackbird infantry broke through the wall of grey smoke lingering on the battlefield and charged towards him. The screams of a thousand dying men blended like the monotonous hum of a beehive. Accompanying that hum was the sound of metal striking metal; that cacophony of tings and clanks that reverberates through your bones. It was the chaotic clash of weaponry, sword against sword, ax against shield, mace against chainmail, hammer against helmet.

This was not the sweet sound of glory and conquest Aedon had imagined. This was a waking nightmare, and a mortal fear penetrated his very bones. Unable to find his sword, Aedon curled himself on the ground and braced for the imminent assault.

Steel suddenly flashed all around him. Aedon looked up to see Mokain with both swords drawn facing down four Blackbirds alone. His blades were somehow everywhere at once, a spiraling windmill in expert form. A spatter of blood flew through the air and only three Blackbirds remained. Another spatter, and another Blackbird fell, this one only inches from the cowering King. The dead man's eyes stared lifelessly through him. After the third Blackbird fell, the surviving members of the Royal Guard arrived to join the fray.

Mokain knelt by the King. "Your Majesty, you need to pull back!" he yelled over the clamor of war.

Aedon found his sword among the trampled wildflowers and climbed to his feet.

"Hogshite!" the King yelled back at him. "We must charge the vanguard before they discharge their weapons again!"

Mokain started to protest, but the King was already running in step with the other soldiers.

Battle raged all around them. The Cavanders had begun the battle with a force several times greater than the Blackbirds; now, they somehow found themselves woefully outnumbered, and their ranks swiftly dwindling by the minute.

***

Kailem watched in horror as a blast from the Blackbirds' weapon threw Mokain from his horse. He waited with bated breath for Mokain to reemerge, but keeping track of a single man through a spyglass in the chaos of war was like trying to keep track of a single fish in a school of mackerel while still in the boat. He finally exhaled when he found Mokain on his feet, racing to the side of the man in glistening armor.

"Who is Mokain?" Elwin asked.

Kailem hadn't realized he said his brother's name aloud.

"He is my brother. He's all the family I have left," Kailem said. He strained to keep his voice from quivering.

Elwin nodded but said nothing. He stood with hands clasped behind him and turned his eyes back to the battle.

"Why is your brother fighting in the Cavander army?" Osmund asked.

"I have no idea. But he needs my help, Elwin. I have to go."

Elwin looked to the ground and shook his head. "You know my answer, Kailem."

"But this is different, Elwin! This is not vengeance. It's to save my brother!"

Elwin wouldn't look at him. "You made an oath, Kailem."

"Not to leave my brother to die!" Kailem yelled.

"To obey all my commands with exactness," Elwin said calmly.

Kailem snarled while he searched for the right words to say. No words came. He looked to his teacher, eyes pleading.

Elwin set his jaw, his eyes fixed on the battle, and said nothing.

Kailem turned to leave, thrusting the spyglass into Osmund's chest as he walked by.

"Kailem!" Elwin called. He was far more adept at masking the emotion in his voice than his pupil was. "If you go down, you are forbidden from returning."

Kailem looked to Osmund and Emerald. Their faces screamed with emotion, pleading with him to stay. Leaving them meant he might never see them again, and certainly meant he'd forfeit becoming a sage. But even with so high a cost, the choice was an easy one.

He looked back to his teacher and said, "I know," then hastened down the hillside.

CHAPTER FORTY-TWO

BROTHERS IN ARMS

22ND DAY OF AUTUMN, 897 G.C.

A wall of spears held by soldiers in black advanced on the Cavander lines. Mokain swung his swords in sweeping strokes, deflecting every sword and spear that sought his life. These were not seasoned soldiers. Mokain could see that from the start. But they fought with passion and now had the advantage in numbers.

A Blackbird thrust his spear at Mokain, aiming for the chest. Mokain deflected the spear with Koa, then swept Tao across the spearman's throat. Another spear made for his head, and he leaned back just out of its reach. The spear came again for his gut. Mokain deflected with Tao and slammed Koa down on the blackbird's helmet. The blade cracked through the helmet's thin steel and lodged in the man's skull.

Another Blackbird, this one wielding a two-handed longsword, swung his blade, intent on removing the Mariner's head. Mokain didn't have time to dislodge his sword from the spearman's skull. He abandoned Koa and with Tao parried blow after blow from the longsword. His single 14-inch blade was no match for the nearly four-foot sword.

The Blackbird fought not with courage, but with hatred. There was venom in his eyes and madness in his screams. The longsword came down at Mokain's head, aiming to bury itself in Mokain's skull just as his own blade was still imbedded in the spearman. Mokain deflected the longsword into the dirt, then spun toward the Blackbird and buried his blade in the man's chest. He pulled Tao out, and blood pulsed from the open torso. The man collapsed at Mokain's feet.

Two spearmen thrust their spears at the King. Aedon swung the Fang of Rhinegard frantically like he was swatting at flies. More than once, the tip of a spear bounced off the King's armor and would have claimed his life had its aim been true. His Royal Guard, those still with their feet under them, were likewise outnumbered and overrun. A spear thrust at the King's helmet knocked him onto his royal backside. In moments, his life would be over.

Mokain removed Koa from the dead man's head, then threw the sword at the King's attacker. The sword buried itself in the man's back.

Before Aedon realized what had killed his attacker on the left, Mokain thrust his second sword through the belly of the attacker on the right, making it the seventh time Mokain had saved the King from certain death that morning.

"Are you alright, Your Majesty?" Mokain yelled. He pulled the King to his feet, keeping his sword raised toward any Blackbird who might rush in on them.

"Keep pressing forward!" Aedon yelled back like a madman. Before Mokain could object, the King, deranged with fear, ran headlong into the Blackbird line. Mokain gritted his teeth and followed.

"Ready!" came a yell from behind the Blackbird line.

Without a word, Mokain grabbed the King and threw him to the ground just as the Blackbirds dropped as well. Another explosion of smoke and fire blasted over their heads, sending hot balls of lead into the Cavander soldiers behind them.

How could anyone fight against such a weapon? The battle was hopeless; despair was leaking into Mokain's heart. He had to find a way to remove the King from the battlefield. But what would happen to their men? And what would happen if the King refused to leave?

***

Kailem reached the base of the foothills and ran through a bloody field of dead and dying men, both Cavander and Blackbird alike. The greater part had stopped moving, their eyes staring blankly into oblivion. Those who still clung to life writhed upon the ground, holding open wounds and missing limbs, screaming, weeping, pleading for help.

Kailem ignored their pleas. As he approached the melee, his run slowed to a swift walk. He couldn't have appreciated the true horrors of war until he was embedded it. This wasn't where he wanted to be. Everything inside told him to run in the opposite direction. But Mokain needed him.

Don't be a pike, he told himself. *The sooner I start, the sooner I'll finish.* He bent down and pulled a cross-hilted broadsword from under the body of a fallen Cavander officer. With two hands on the hilt, he charged headlong into the fray.

He had only a general idea of where to find Mokain. He struck down any Blackbird who attacked him, but his purpose there was not to kill, only to find and protect. The Cavanders left him alone, likely assuming he was on their side by the white linen tunic he wore. It took only moments for the pristine clothing to become soiled by dirt and viscera.

The soldier in glistening black armor caught Kailem's eye. There, fighting at his side, was Mokain. Even in his Cavander armor, he recognized him. His brother fought off three swordsmen at once, attacking one after another to keep them at bay, but they were swiftly closing in. Not even Mokain could maintain this pace for long. Kailem sprinted towards him.

A Blackbird stabbed at Mokain's exposed back, aiming to penetrate between the armored plates. Kailem deflected the blow, and the force of the heavy sword knocked the soldier's blade from his hands. Kailem front-kicked him in the chest, knocking him to the ground. In one fluid motion, he rotated the broadsword in his hands and slammed it down tip-first into the soldier's heart.

Mokain sliced Tao across the second swordsman's throat and rammed Koa through the third man's belly. He looked over at his protector in soiled white linen.

His eyes went wide, nearly bulging from their sockets.

"Kailem?!" he cried out.

Joy, confusion, and disbelief all seized him at once, followed quickly by a thousand questions. His little brother gave him the briefest glance before engaging the next Blackbird to charge at him, cutting the enemy down with a skill that rivaled his own. Mokain raised Tao to parry the thrust of an enemy's broadsword before jabbing Koa through the man's neck, but between each foe that attacked, Mokain snuck a glance at his brother in disbelief.

Kailem was alive!

With his brother beside him, Mokain fought with a renewed vigor and a smile that stretched from ear to ear. The other guards surely thought him mad. How could anyone smile in the throes of such carnage? What joy could be had amid the horrors of war and the hand of death that would soon claim them? But no amount of slaughter and bloodshed could overcome the elation of having his brother back.

The brothers fought side by side, slaying one man after another. Together, they were an unstoppable force on the battlefield. Their mere presence gave each other courage and strength, and they fought with unparalleled skill and ferocity as dozens of Blackbirds fell upon them. Every enemy that swung a blade or thrust a spear at them met a swift and bloody end.

The Royal Guards at his side were the best warriors in Cavander, but even their numbers were dwindling; already five of the twelve lay dead in the grass. All the colonels were dead, and the left-side of their front line was collapsing. Soon they'd be in a full rout, and the Blackbirds would completely surround them.

***

Osmund watched through the spyglass as Kailem felled one Blackbird after another. He had known his Mariner friend was a skilled warrior, but he hadn't imagined anything like this. Kailem's fighting was more than masterful. It was beautiful, even amid the ugly brutality of war. He moved with astonishing speed, and yet he was fluid and precise, like a dancer performing to a rapid tempo. His skill with the blade was unmatched on the battlefield save for his older brother fighting at his side.

The endless expanse of dead bodies on the field sickened him. The fact that his family was involved only intensified that sickness. How could his parents be responsible for so much death and destruction, he wondered? And how could he not have known about it? A part of Osmund felt responsible, as if the sins of his parents now rested upon his head. Perhaps Edric was down there as well. He scanned the battlefield with the spyglass but couldn't find him. He moved the spyglass to focus again on Kailem.

"What be hap'nin' now?" Emerald asked, her voice trembling.

"He fights unlike anything I have ever seen," Osmund said. "But he is surrounded and heavily outnumbered. And he is the only one on the battlefield without any armor. I... I do not reckon he will last long."

Emerald turned to Elwin. "We oughta do somethin', Elwin."

Elwin said nothing. His eyes remained fixed on the battlefield.

"I will help," Osmund heard himself say.

"Don't be a fool," Elwin returned calmly. "You'll throw your life away for nothing, just as he has done."

Emerald winced at the harsh words. How could it be nothing to rescue his brother?

"But... it's Kailem," Osmund said, bewildered. "We cannot leave him to die."

Elwin finally took his eyes off the battle. He looked at Osmund. There were years in Elwin's eyes, but not confidence. Osmund saw him struggle with the decision.

"Kailem made his choice," Elwin said. "We do not meddle in the affairs of common men."

Emerald could be silent no longer. "Elwin," she began, failing to sound calm and controlled, "ye call e'ryone who ain't a Sage a 'commoner'. But ye know who else calls us that? The nobility. They oppress us, and tax us, keep us 'neath their thumbs, and then they call us 'common', and worse things, 'cause we ain't as dignified as they be."

Osmund shrank at the indictment of nobility.

Emerald continued, "'Tis that treatment why them Blackbirds draw so many to their cause. And it ain't right, Elwin. Ain't right when nobles call us 'common', and ain't right when ye do it neither. We ain't need ta be noblemen or sages for our lives ta matter. Me life matters, Kailem's life matters, and the lives of all them soldiers down there matter, just as much as any sage or nobleman. And stayin' 'way when ye have the power ta help, well, it ain't right."

Elwin was dumbfounded. He had never heard the young girl say anything half as passionately. Neither had Osmund.

"Emerald, I—" Elwin began, but Osmund cut him off.

"What use are all these powers you have if you only use them for small deeds, but ignore the greater needs of the people? You keep mentioning our oath; well, our oath was more than to simply not intervene. We also swore to do good, to protect the weak and defend what is right. Kailem is doing what is right, and he's willing to sacrifice his life to do it. He is breaking one part of his oath to keep another, and he, his brother, and thousands more will all die without your help. What about your oath, Elwin of Andil?"

Osmund couldn't believe he had spoken that way to a sage. He had gone too far, had pressed too hard, he was sure of it. There would no doubt be a penalty for his insolence. He waited for the inevitable rebuke to come.

Elwin dropped his head and sighed, giving Osmund and Emerald a spark of hope. After a moment, Elwin lifted his head and looked Osmund in the eye.

"Mother would be quite fond of you, Osmund Baylor," he said in a soft tone. He looked at Emerald. "All three of you, actually."

He then looked back at the battlefield. "Remain here," he ordered.

Leaving his students behind, Elwin bounded down the hillside, moving ten, even twenty yards with every stride. His linen tunic flapped in the wind as he moved adroitly down the terrain. He took the opposite course that Kailem had, moving toward the back of the Blackbird army rather than the Cavander side. When he was within a hundred yards from the base of the hill, an auratic leap sent him sailing through the air like an eagle in flight, and landing behind the Blackbird ranks with an explosion of grass and dirt around him.

***

The Riverkeep tower held Lord Leonin Arturri with his wife, Avalina, and Lord and Lady Baylor. From the tower's vantage, they could see the full breadth of the battle through the castle parapets. The battle lines spread the entire width of the valley.

"The Cavander lines on the right are in retreat. We'll soon have them surrounded," Reginald observed.

"We have them outnumbered as well," Leonin said. "This invention of yours is proving even more formidable than expected, my darling."

Avalina shone like the sun. By Leonin's standards, that had been a gushing display of affection. Boudica was visibly jealous, which made the moment all the more delicious for Avalina. She moved to hold his hand, but then thought better of it.

Footsteps sounded behind them. The four of them turned, expecting to see a messenger with news of the battle. Instead, they saw a regal man walking towards them, tall and lean, with a face full of harsh angles. He was dressed head to toe in raiment that resembled the Blackbird uniform but for the finer textiles and flourishing embroidery. He wore a fitted silk shirt and a jerkin of crushed velvet and leather. His boots clicked against the stones as he walked.

The four noblemen immediately dropped to one knee, their heads bowed. Only Leonin was permitted to speak unless spoken to.

"My liege, you honor us. Had we known you were coming, we would have prepared a proper greeting," Leonin said. All four of them kept their eyes on the stones beneath them, waiting for permission to raise their heads. Before them stood Torin of Errigal, the sage who had founded the Blackbird Society, the sage whose plan they had devoted their lives to executing.

"Arise," Torin said.

All four obeyed.

"Report," Torin commanded.

Leonin extended his hand, inviting Torin to view the battlefield. "We began the battle outnumbered 3-to-1, my liege, but now our forces outnumber the Cavanders. The musket is a singular asset, performing remarkably. The Cavanders' right flank has collapsed, and we have them surrounded. The battle will soon be ours."

"That is good," Torin said. He stood looking through the parapets at the battle, his hands held behind his lower back. All was as Leonin described.

"You have done well," Torin said. Leonin stood a little taller. "And Reginald, how fares your son, Edric?"

Reginald was overcome. Not only had the Sage remembered his name and that he had a son, but he even remembered his son's name as well.

"He leads a company on the battlefield, my liege. Just there, left of center." Reginald pointed to his son's company, cutting down the enemy on the front.

Torin observed Edric in battle. "He does you credit, Reginald. A worthy son is an honor to his parents. Should he survive the battle, it would please me to meet him."

Reginald bowed from the chest. "It would be our honor, my liege."

As Torin observed the battle, a figure in white ran down the nearby hillside with inhuman speed. The man leaped into the air and landed with a crash behind their men, most of whom fell to the dirt in surprise. Even after all these centuries, Torin recognized him instantly.

"Oh, dear cousin. You choose this of all moments to finally reveal yourself?" Torin said to himself. His thumb brushed against the silver ring on his left hand.

"Did you say something, my liege?" Leonin asked.

"The battle is lost," he said for all to hear.

"But, my liege," Leonin stammered, "we have the greater force. The Cavanders are surrounded. And we still have the muskets."

"The battle is lost," Torin repeated. His words were slow and sharp. The four noblemen exchanged looks like children who'd had their cake taken away, and their eyes moved to the battlefield as they wondered what they had missed that Torin hadn't.

"Are the horses ready?" Torin asked.

"They are, my liege," Leonin said.

"Good. We must leave at once."

Torin turned from the tower. The four noblemen stood baffled, then followed quickly after him.

***

Elwin rose in the cavity of his landing. A fine mist of dirt settled around him. The men nearest him had fallen to the ground, their weapons forgotten at their sides. Elwin stepped out of the depression onto level ground, a lion rising from the brush, and the fallen Blackbirds scrambled away from him on all fours.

One brave man, a behemoth in black, approached Elwin from the side. He ran at full stride, blade drawn, and swung his longsword at Elwin's head with both hands. The man was a full head taller than Elwin, and the longsword was nearly as long as Elwin was tall. Elwin stepped back, the blade passing inches from his neck.

The behemoth stepped forward and thrust his sword at Elwin's chest. Elwin leaned to his left, and the blade passed him by. He grabbed the double-edged blade with his right hand and thrust his left palm into the behemoth's chest. The man flew back like a leaf caught in a storm.

"Take aim!" a lieutenant called.

Elwin turned to see the Blackbirds had formed a line and were pointing their mysterious weapons at him. The soldiers behind him were fleeing to either side.

"Fire!"

Elwin crouched with his forearm across his face just as an explosion of grey smoke shot out a volley of hot iron. The light around Elwin rippled and warped as the balls averted from their natural course, sailing off into the distance behind him. Elwin stood again, unharmed and fierce.

"Reload!" the lieutenant yelled, his voice aquiver.

Elwin was upon them in a heartbeat, swinging the behemoth's longsword in a single hand. He cut down Blackbirds two at a time, performing the work of death with an inhuman efficiency. Corpses began to dot the ground around him.

He was soon beset by enemies on all sides. Elwin extended his hand, and a second longsword rose from the grip of a fallen Blackbird to meet it. Swinging both swords in concert, he kept the men surrounding him at bay. The screaming of steel upon steel rang out unceasingly.

Man after man attacked, and each was met with a swift and bloody end. They could not have known their opponent could hear their thoughts, that he knew their every move before their first muscle fiber twitched. They could not have anticipated the impossible speed of his blade, a speed that no muscle could produce, no matter how well-trained.

One man lunged at Elwin and met his death upon the sage's sword, the same as his comrades had before him, but not before the tip of his spear cut a gash through Elwin's cheek. Pain jolted the sage's mind, and in that briefest of seconds, the Blackbirds came upon him like water flowing from a broken dam.

Elwin crouched, one knee in the blood-soaked earth. A dozen Blackbirds covered him in a torrent of blind fury. They thrust their swords and spears over every inch of their foe, sparing no effort to kill him, but the tips of their blades met an impenetrable resistance within an inch of Elwin's skin. The light around the sage distorted with each thwarted stab, like the surface of a pond under a light rain. A line of blood trickled down his cheek and dripped from his chin. He closed his eyes and focused.

The pile of enemies burst off the sage like the top of an erupting volcano. Men flew in all directions, propelled by an unseen force with the strength of a tempest. Elwin was left alone, gripping a sword in each hand.

The wound on his cheek began to re-knit.

Elwin was surrounded by the bodies of dead men, and his heart wept. Why must it be this way, he thought? Why was there so much evil and hate in the hearts of men? He felt heavy when he stood, weighed down by the lives he had taken.

The gash on his cheek took several seconds to reseal itself, soon closing without the faintest hint of a scar. Elwin wiped the blood from his cheek, then resumed the loathsome work of death.

***

Tower bells rang in Mokain's skull. His men lay on the ground around him, peppered with inexplicable puncture wounds. He had pulled the King to the ground just as the Blackbirds' weapon discharged only feet in front of them, enveloping them in grey smoke and terror. Next to him, Aedon was lost in a haze of confusion and fear.

Before Aedon could reclaim his senses, the tip of a spear descended at his chest. His sword was nowhere to be found. Just as his life was about to end, Mokain deflected the spear into the ground. He was on his knee, his sword in hand. He swung the blade at the Blackbird's leg, separating the shin from the knee. The young spearman collapsed, screaming more in fear and disbelief than in pain. The surviving royal guards quickly surrounded them.

With the King safe, at least for the moment, Mokain looked around for Kailem. He hadn't known to drop at the signal. Had he been hit? Had his brother been returned to him only for Mokain to watch him die moments later?

After a pair of agonizing seconds, Mokain spotted him. Kailem was crawling on the ground towards his broadsword, his legs dragging uselessly behind him. Mokain raced to his brother.

"Where are you hit?" Mokain asked.

The answer was obvious. Kailem bled from his left hip and his right thigh, but based on the wounds' location and degree of blood loss, it appeared the major arteries had been spared.

"Can you stand?" Mokain asked.

Kailem nodded. He stuck the tip of the broadsword into the grass and leaned on Mokain as he rose to his feet. Mokain waited as his brother steadied himself.

"I am well, I can fight," Kailem insisted.

Mokain didn't believe him, but he had no other choice. The Blackbirds were again charging towards them. Mokain had trained his brother in fighting with a wound. Now he had to trust that the training would save him.

"Stay near the Guard," Mokain told him.

Kailem nodded. The sun was high overhead, and the heat was punishing. The sweat dripped from his brow, stinging his eyes and making his palms slick. *Pain is not your enemy*, Kailem recalled his brother teaching him. *Pain is simply a messenger; greet it as you would an old friend, then dismiss it.* He gripped his broadsword with both hands and fell into something resembling a battle stance.

Mokain turned back to the King's aid just in time to fight off the advancing Blackbirds. His guards fought valiantly, but they were outnumbered. Their remaining forces were dwindling fast, and they had no reliable defense against the

Blackbirds' secret weapon. Their lines were collapsing all around them. Their cause was hopeless.

Mokain forced the thought from his mind, cutting down every soldier who came near the King. He fought with singleness of mind, without regard for the greater battle strategy.

It was in this, the gravest of moments, that a commotion came from behind the Blackbird line. It was difficult to see through the mass of soldiers in black and the lingering grey smoke, but something was causing chaos in their ranks. As they turned to meet this new foe, Mokain was able to see the new threat behind them.

A man dressed in white linen was cutting through the Blackbirds from the rear of their formation. He wielded a longsword in each hand, swinging them back and forth like they were light as the air itself. Stranger still, some invisible force seemed to throw soldiers through the air, like an unseen giant was making a game out of tossing them about. Some men were thrown towards the man in white, meeting their end on the edge of one of his longswords. Others were thrown away from the man and rolled along the ground like discarded rag dolls.

Whatever this man was, he was engaging the entire Blackbird army by himself. He was a force of nature, a hurricane in human form. The frightened rebels didn't know whether to attack or retreat; many were frozen stiff on the battlefield.

The Cavanders were equally dumbfounded, although whoever he was, the man in white was clearly on their side. But of all those who saw Elwin's manifestation of sagecraft, there were none more staggered than Kailem. What had changed, he wondered, since the sage had told him that fighting in this battle meant he could never return? What could have caused his mentor to abandon a policy he had dogmatically adhered to for centuries? Whatever the reason, seeing Elwin on the battlefield wielding the full power of a sage, Kailem found hope they might live to see tomorrow.

After his moment of shock passed, Mokain turned to his men. "Charge!" he yelled. He raced forward to cut down the distracted enemy. His men followed him, but their charge shook the languid Blackbirds from their stupor, and the enemy turned to meet them.

As the battle raged, King Aedon saw five horses riding south from the Riverkeep.

"Roka!" the King yelled. He pointed with his sword, and Mokain saw the horses riding south. "Their leadership, they must not escape!"

"I must remain with you, Your Majesty," Mokain called back, thinking more of his brother's safety than the King's. He had lost track of him in the chaos of battle, but in his soiled linen clothing, he was easy to spot. His eyes found him just as his brother rammed his broadsword through a Blackbird's neck, then dropped to his knee to deliver a fatal cut to another Blackbird's leg. He did not appear to be in danger.

"It is an order from your King," Aedon screamed. "Go now!"

Mokain had to trust in his brother's skill. He turned from the battle and ran to the horses that had sought shelter near the tree line. Once in the saddle, he broke into a full gallop after the Blackbird leaders fleeing on horseback.

***

The longer Elwin fought, the more the scales tipped in favor of Cavandel. There were now less than two thousand soldiers alive on either side of the battle. The fighting had endured for hours, and neither side showed any willingness to surrender. Every part of Kailem's body ached, and his broadsword must have gained thirty pounds over the course of the battle.

Both of the Royal Guards, who had fought at Kailem's side, now lay dead on the ground. As best he could tell, only one Royal Guard remained, not including Mokain, who fought at the King's side. Regular infantry continued to fight around them. Kailem ignored the wounds screaming for his undivided attention and forced his mind to stay in the moment.

After slicing his blade deep through the side of an enemy soldier, Kailem came face to face with the first Blackbird he recognized. He had dark blue eyes and short loose curls of light brown hair, with a chiseled yet heart-shaped face. It was Edric, the captain he had met in the council chamber only weeks prior. This was Osmund's elder brother.

He could see in Edric's face that he recognized him as well. This was the man who, by his own admission, had orchestrated the murder of his parents. Meeting this man on the battlefield was no accident. This was justice.

Kailem gripped the hilt of his broadsword with both hands so tightly his knuckles turned white. A strength that had been buried deep within him rose to the surface, propelling him forward. He swung his sword with savage precision, delivering blow after blow. The Blackbird captain took a step back with each strike he managed to deflect. Kailem saw fear in the captain's eyes, and that fear gave him strength.

The broadsword reverberated in Kailem's hands as he swung it again and again. Edric stumbled to the ground, then managed to block Kailem's next strike as he fumbled to his feet, only to stumble again moments later. Against the Mariner, Edric looked like he had never before held a sword. Kailem heaved massive gusts of air and was saturated in sweat under the fierce Veydalan sun, but he otherwise showed no sign of fatigue.

Edric screamed for two of his men to come to his aid, and the men rushed to his side. The three of them moved into position around Kailem, preparing to come at him from all sides at once.

Kailem didn't wait. Before they could coordinate their attack, he struck like a viper, driving the tip of his broadsword through the neck of the guard on his left before the man knew what happened. The man's eyes bulged, stung with shock and fear. He collapsed to his back as blood gushed from his throat.

Kailem dropped to a knee as the guard on his right tried to lop off his head, and in the same motion, cut a gash in the guard's inner thigh. The second guard collapsed from the fatal wound next to the first. Edric was again left to defend himself, and Kailem struck repeatedly with barbaric force. With each strike, Kailem drove Edric back a step. This fight would soon be over.

Then Kailem's strength gave out.

Osmund's eye was fixed to his spyglass, alternating between Elwin and Kailem.

"What be happin' now?" Emerald asked yet again. She cursed that they had only one spyglass between them, but a part of her was glad she didn't have to look at the slaughter.

"No human could do the things Elwin does," Osmund said. He had no words to adequately convey what he was witnessing. "There's nothing any man can do against him. He wields a longsword in each hand. In *each hand*, Emerald. Those swords are so heavy even the strongest men need two hands to wield it, and he swings them back and forth as if they were but daggers."

"Ay, but what of Kailem," she asked. She had not worried for the safety of the ancient sage, but Kailem was a different matter.

Osmund scanned back through the battlefield to where Kailem fought. "It appears the battle has separated him from his brother." Osmund had been stunned by how the two brothers had fought in tandem, protecting each other in what nearly appeared to be a choreographed dance. Now Kailem fought alone, surrounded on all sides.

"He just killed two men within seconds," Osmund continued, "and now he engages the third man. It almost looks as though... it can't be."

Osmund recognized for the first time the face of his brother on the battlefield. Edric barely managed to block Kailem's blow, each of which had the power to cleave Edric in two. *This can't be happening*, Osmund thought. He was awash in more emotions than he knew how to handle, and in his heart, he pleaded for Kailem not to kill his brother.

It seemed Kailem had heard his plea, for his vicious onslaught had ceased. Osmund watched through the spyglass as Kailem remained motionless, the tip of his broadsword resting in the dirt. He looked barely able to stand, and Edric now stood tall in a battle stance. Osmund's heart began to pound.

***

Kailem dug deep within himself, to the very bottom of his soul, searching for any reserve of strength to continue attacking. There was none to be found.

He barely managed to raise his sword as Edric went on the offensive. He blocked one strike, then another, but couldn't raise the sword in time for the third. Edric sliced a gash the length of Kailem's shoulder a full inch deep. The young Mariner howled in pain.

Edric swung again. Unable to raise his sword, Kailem dodged the blow. Edric thrust his sword forward, and Kailem dashed to the side to avoid it. The pain in his shoulder was agony, and the pain from the wounds in his leg and hip had returned as well.

He managed to block several blows by holding the broadsword with the hilt high and the tip low, thereby relieving the muscles in his wrists and forearms, but Edric managed to slice a gash on Kailem's left leg. He howled again and hobbled on his one usable leg. The fatigue and blood loss were taking their toll.

Edric swung his blade like an ax at Kailem's head. He raised his blade just in time to block it, but the blow knocked the sword from his hand. He could see the hunger in Edric's eyes; the Blackbird was savoring the moment. Kailem winced in pain and fear, blood still pulsing from his wounds.

With both hands on the hilt, Edric raised his sword high above his head. With all his weight on his right leg, Kailem had no chance of dodging to either side. He had but one response, a maneuver Mokain had taught him years ago as they sparred on the beach.

As Edric swung his sword down at Kailem's head, Kailem lunged forward with every ounce of strength left in his right leg. With his left hand, he caught Edric's fists, while at the same time his right hand retrieved Malua from his side. He thrust the dagger through the soft tissue beneath Edric's chin and up through the skull.

Edric's body immediately went limp, its weight and momentum falling into Kailem. Both men collapsed to the valley floor, each as lifeless as the other.

Chapter Forty-Three

PURSUIT

22ND DAY OF AUTUMN, 897 G.C.

No soldier would engage Elwin, and anyone the sage approached simply ran away. In their haste to escape him, the Blackbirds ran headlong into enemy lines and were cut down like cattle. No longer needed in the fight, Elwin ran towards the Cavander side, searching through the dead and dying.

After a diligent search, he found his student unconscious and half-covered by a bloodied Blackbird. Kailem's dagger was embedded under his chin.

Elwin waved his hand and the Blackbird's body was thrown from the motionless Mariner like a feather caught in a gust of wind.

"Kailem, Kailem!" Elwin called. The boy didn't move. Elwin felt for a pulse. He waited, pleading for any sign of life.

There.

It was faint, but Kailem's heart still beat.

Elwin placed his hands on Kailem's wounds, healing him just enough to stop the bleeding. The rest would have to wait. More than one soldier had seen him levitate the Blackbird's body, and even though the battle continued, others were beginning to look as well.

Elwin whistled for one of the horses standing near the tree line. The horse obeyed, galloping through the battlefield towards them. Elwin retrieved his student's coronation blade from Edric's head and leapt lithely into the saddle. When he extended his hand, Kailem's body floated off the dirt and over the saddle. The soldiers who had been staring all gasped and retreated several steps. With Kailem laying across the front of the saddle, Elwin signaled for his horse to canter up the foothills to where Emerald and Osmund waited.

He slowed, but did not stop as he passed his two students. "Meet me at the monastery, and hurry," Elwin ordered. He didn't wait for a response. Within seconds, he disappeared among the trees, cantering up the mountainside.

Torin and his four subordinates rode south following the Vondal River for half a mile before climbing toward the pass through the southern hills. Once to the pass, they slowed to a trot, the ghastly sounds of war fading behind them. The journey to the harbor was far too long to exhaust their horses at a full gallop.

Before they rounded the last turn where the battlefield would become lost from view, Boudica pulled on her reins and looked behind her. The soldiers were tiny dots in the distance. Her aging eyes could no longer distinguish Blackbirds from Cavanders.

One of those dots was Edric. Boudica had sworn to sacrifice everything for Torin's cause, even her children, if necessary, but no oath could dissolve a mother's affection. Had he been killed? Had he been taken captive? Had he escaped to live out his life in peace? Something inside her said her son was already gone; a mother's intuition, perhaps. But no, it was probably just her anxiety; she decided. She chose to believe he was safe, that he had escaped and had a happy life ahead of him.

She whipped her horse's reins and quickly joined her companions.

The road south connected the Veydalan farmlands to the port towns on the Sea of Beydal. It was a winding road, but well-kept, and any travelers they might happen upon were likely to be simple farmers transporting the fruits of their harvest. In a few days, they'd reach the harbor and be on their way to safety in the Marin Islands.

A sound came echoing through the trees behind them.

Torin reared his horse to a stop, and his subordinates did likewise. In their silence, the unmistakable rapid pounding of hooves sounded from the trail behind them. Their stomachs sank to their saddles.

"Is it the Cavanders?" Avalina asked. "They could not be so close so soon, could they?"

"Who else could it be? Can we outrun them?" Reginald asked.

"No, that's too risky. We need to hide," Leonin said.

"Calm yourselves," Torin commanded. "Listen closely."

The five of them became silent again. The galloping grew louder.

"Only one set of hooves; we have nothing to fear," Torin said. "Leonin, lead them to the harbor and secure us passage. I will meet you there."

Leonin nodded, and the four of them broke into a gallop.

Torin dismounted and drew his sword, a basket-hilted rapier with golden inlays. He stood in the middle of the road, waiting for Elwin to come galloping around the corner. It had been over a five centuries since he last saw the man. Had he maintained his skill with a blade? Torin was keen to find out.

When the man on horseback came around the bend, Torin was dismayed to see it was not his cousin, but a man in Cavander armor with olive-toned skin who rode toward him. The man reared his horse mere feet from the sage.

"You are under arrest, by order of King Aedon of Cavander," the man said.

Torin laughed at the curious turn of events. It appeared his reunion with Elwin was still yet to come. He looked up and met the man's eyes.

"What's your name, son?" he asked.

"I am Mokain Roka, First Officer of the Royal Guard of Cavandel."

Torin cocked his head. "Roka, you say? Of the Marin Islands?"

Mokain nodded, and Torin laughed again.

"Iria can certainly have a sense of humor," Torin said aloud. Mokain didn't know what he meant, but he would not be distracted from his task.

"Very well, Master Roka, I am Torin of Errigal. You may come and arrest me, if you choose, but know this: I will not submit willingly. So come and take me, if you can."

Mokain dismounted. He took out one blade and then the other, marching towards Torin with a deserved air of confidence. Torin stood on guard with one hand behind his back.

At first, Mokain and Torin traded half-hearted blows, testing each other. Torin was a skilled swordsman, with subtle peculiarities in his technique that Mokain had never seen before. He could also tell the man was holding back.

Mokain swung his swords more aggressively, breaking from common strike patterns to catch the man off guard, but Torin had a response for each of Mokain's attacks. The man was impossibly fast, faster than anyone Mokain had ever fought.

"Good, Master Roka, very good," Torin said with a grin. Everything about this man was casual and calm, even as Mokain fought with the fury of a lion.

"Your form is impeccable," Torin commended. "It is clear you have devoted your life to the sword."

He spoke so flippantly, his breathing normal despite the lightning speed of the duel. Mokain, however, breathed heavily and fought through pain, still suffering the effects of his previous battle.

Steel flashed as Torin went on the offensive. His blade was a blur, and he attacked with an unpredictable sequence of strikes that kept Mokain's assault in check.

Mokain fought faster, and Torin responded in kind. Mokain swung harder, but Torin parried with ease. The man was toying with him; no one could possibly be this skilled with the sword.

Mokain had to improvise. After a backhand swing with Tao, followed predictably with a side slash with Koa from the right, he simultaneously attacked again with Tao from the left. His sword master back home would have condemned such a maneuver, it left his chest exposed with no means to parry a counterattack. But the gambit paid off. Torin did have a clear strike for Mokain's chest, but not before the tip of Koa would pierce his neck. Torin was now powerless to block it.

Then the impossible happened. Mokain's blade inexplicably stopped inches from Torin's neck, as if it had struck some invisible layer of clay. Light rippled around the blade. Before Mokain could comprehend what happened, he was thrown by an unseen force some fifteen feet into the air. He sailed across the road into the forest, his body ricocheting off one tree before slamming into another. Had he not been wearing armor, it would have surely collapsed his rib cage. Instead, he fell to the forest floor, unconscious.

Torin stood over him. "You certainly are a curious one, aren't you, Master Roka? You nearly bested me; few men in history can say the same. Farewell for now. I'm sure our paths will cross again."

CHAPTER FORTY-FOUR

AFTERMATH

22ND DAY OF AUTUMN, 897 G.C.

Mokain lay in the dirt, a tree root pressing into his thigh. Iria spun erratically around him. Even after his vision stabilized, it was several minutes before he could push himself to his hands and knees, and he remained in that position for some time.

His memory returned to him in scattered, disorganized chunks. He could recall the battle, and he had told a man he was under arrest. He remembered the King telling him to chase after five men on horseback. He remembered a duel with a man dressed in black, and he remembered... had he been thrown through the air? Impossible. Surely, the blow to the head corrupted his memory.

Kailem.

Mokain remembered his brother on the battlefield. Kailem was alive, or at least he had been. How had the battle ended? Mokain leaned on the tree as he climbed his feet. He stumbled through the forest to the road like a drunkard leaving a tavern. He had hoped to find his horse, but it must have fled after the duel.

He retrieved Tao and Koa from the dirt and set off north on foot towards the Riverkeep.

When he rounded the final bend and the valley opened before him, it was a scene of carnage unlike anything he could have imagined. From this vantage, he could see the full extent of the battle's devastation.

At least twenty thousand men lay butchered on the once serene valley floor. The stench of death assaulted his nostrils, causing him to retch. It wasn't the stench of decay and rotting flesh; the corpses were too fresh for that. This was the fetid, metallic stench of warm blood, of viscera spilled from men's abdomens, of urine and excrement expelled by dying men.

Cavandel had won the day. Their soldiers roamed through the fields, finding those who a surgeon might have a chance of saving. A group of several hundred unarmed Blackbirds sat in one corner of the field, guarded by several dozen armed Cavanders.

A battlefield is not a quiet place. That may be obvious during the fighting, but it is equally true after the fighting has stopped. You see, it takes time for a man to die. The body clings to life long after all hope is lost, and in the meantime, he yells, and screams, and cries, and pleads, and moans, and coughs, and gurgles, and not until his eyes glaze over is he finally silenced.

Mokain raced through the field of corpses. Severed limbs lay scattered about the valley floor, the bodies from which they had so recently been separated not easily identified. Bones protruded from mangled flesh and skin, their white surfaces glinting in the afternoon sun. Limbs twisted in unnatural ways that sent a chill down the spines of the living.

Had Kailem been standing, Mokain would have easily spotted him. That he hadn't seen him yet was not a good sign. He spent nearly half an hour looking for his brother, his head still in a daze after colliding with the tree.

He scoured the area where he had last seen Kailem fighting. His brother's white linen clothing should have made him stand out. Perhaps he was under someone. Mokain turned over one body after another, dreading he would find Kailem dead underneath.

He turned over the corpse of a Blackbird, and his heart stopped. He recognized the face of the Cavander underneath.

"Conroy, Conroy!" Mokain yelled, shaking the fallen lieutenant.

Lieutenant Wyndell didn't move. Mokain assessed his body for injuries. There was a strange puncture wound at his right clavicle, another below the ribs on the left side, and a third just above his right knee. Blood slowly trickled out of each wound.

Mokain ripped off his gauntlet. With his fingers bare, he felt Wyndell's neck for a pulse. It was slow and weak, so faint he almost missed it, but somehow Wyndell was alive, at least for now.

"Surgeon!" Mokain cried out. "I need a surgeon now!"

Men with sacks full of bandages, ointments, and surgical tools came running, and Mokain stepped back to let the men work.

The surgeon was covered in blood spatter from tending to prior patients; based on the amount of blood on him, it did not appear those surgeries had been successful. The surgeon used shears to remove Lieutenant Wyndell's leather armor and cast it aside.

Mokain retrieved the discarded armor. One of the metal plates that was riveted to the leather vest had a circular puncture clear through the metal. It was the plate that fitted just below the right clavicle, and the hole went through the blood-soaked leather as well. Mokain ran his finger through the hole; the metal around the edge was jagged and curved inward.

The surgeon worked a set of forceps into Wyndell's shoulder wound. The unconscious lieutenant winced; that was a good sign. The surgeon pulled back the forceps to reveal a lead ball pinched at the end.

"Give that here," Mokain said. The surgeon released the lead ball into his palm. It was roughly the size and shape of a pearl.

"So, you've seen it too, then," King Aedon said from beside him. Mokain hadn't heard him approach. The King held a lead ball of his own pinched between his fingers. "Remarkable, is it not? These little beads decimated the most powerful army in Iria. I witnessed it with my own eyes, and even I can scarcely believe it."

"Apologies, Your Majesty. Have you seen my brother?" Mokain was searching in all directions, afraid of what he might find. But not knowing would be far worse.

"You have a brother?" Aedon asked with a frown.

"He fought beside us in the battle. He was in a white linen tunic."

"Why would you have had a brother fighting—"

"Your Majesty, please. Another Mariner wearing a white linen tunic. Has anyone seen him?"

"Wasn't that the wounded man that was carried off on horseback by the Rescuer?" said one of the soldiers attending the King.

"The Rescuer?" Mokain asked.

King Aedon sighed in frustration. "That is what the soldiers have begun calling that mysterious man who came to our aid," he said, clearly vexed that another was given credit for the day's victory.

"And yes," the King continued, "he did carry off a man who matches your brother's description. They went up that hill and disappeared among the trees, but that was over an hour ago. Later, you'll explain to me why you had a brother I didn't know about fighting beside you in battle. But first, tell me what happened with the leaders I sent you after. Are they in custody?"

"They escaped," Mokain said, his eyes still scanning the battlefield.

"You let them escape? What happened?" Aedon demanded.

"Please, Your Majesty. Allow me to form a search party and go after them," Mokain said.

"No, no, I need you here. Now what do you mean they—"

"Your Majesty," Mokain interrupted for a second time. His voice was sharp and desperate, and he looked at Aedon with pleading eyes. "Give me leave to go find them. Please."

Aedon looked at his troubled friend and took time to consider the request. "Normally, I'd say we had far too much to do for you to go off on personal concerns, but I too am interested to know who this Rescuer was. Form your search party, Roka. But return by tomorrow nightfall."

Mokain left him with all haste, forgetting to bow as he took his leave.

***

It was nearly dusk when Emerald and Osmund arrived back at the monastery. They found Kailem unconscious on the kitchen table, stripped to his undergarment. Elwin's hands rested on Kailem's thigh wound.

They stepped close to the table and watched reverently as Elwin worked. Elwin's garment had been sliced and punctured in several places, each of them stained with blood, but there was no trace of wounds underneath. Still, he was clearly in pain as he performed his work. Kailem's body, on the other hand, was bloodied and broken, like a corpse pulled from a collapsed building.

It pierced their hearts to see Kailem in such a state. He was more than a friend to them; exactly what to call him. They didn't know, but they loved him. Emerald wrapped her arms around Osmund's right arm and held it tight.

Elwin's eyes were closed, and he winced as Kailem's wounds resealed themselves under the sage's touch. It was a slow process, almost imperceptibly slow; his friends wouldn't have noticed had they not known to look for it. But once they saw it, they could not divert their eyes from it.

It occurred to Osmund that he was standing over the man who had killed his brother. He wondered if he ought to be angry with Kailem. His brother was dead, and here was his killer. He should be plotting his revenge, should he not? Or at least be heartbroken. That was simply the way of things. Yet, as he watched his friend teeter on the edge between life and death, he felt none of the emotions he knew he was supposed to. What was wrong with him, he wondered, that he could be so indifferent about Edric's death? That he could feel no animosity for his brother's killer?

In the few months he had known him, Kailem had been more of a brother to Osmund than Edric ever had. He felt no ill-will towards his brother, and certainly had not wished him harm, but if it were only possible for one of them to have survived the battle that day, he was glad it was Kailem.

"Too many saw me today," Elwin said, breaking the silence. "They will come looking for us now. It will be only a matter of time before they find the monastery."

"What should we do?" Osmund asked solemnly.

Kailem's thigh wound was completely healed, without a hint or trace of a scar. Elwin moved his hands to Kailem's shoulder wound.

"Begin packing provisions, anything we might need for a long journey. When I finish with Kailem, I will assist you. We leave after nightfall."

"Kailem'll be aright, won't he?" Emerald asked.

Elwin exhaled. "I cannot be sure. He has lost a great deal of blood, I'm afraid; I scarcely felt a heartbeat when I found him. But I shall do all I can."

"Where will we go?" Osmund asked. He looked around the sacred haven he had come to love and was sorry to leave it.

Elwin looked up from his work. His two students looked at him like lost children. In many ways, that was exactly what they were. He searched his mind for a place he could take them, a place where they could not only be safe and hidden from pursuers, but also a place where they could blossom in the sacred training that was to come. A place all four of them could call home. And try as he might, his mind could deliver only a single prospect.

Resolved, Elwin met Osmund's eyes and replied, "to Andalaya."

The End

ANDALAYA UPDATES

Want updates on future Andalaya Books and Projects?

Signup for Corey Rusick's Newsletter to stay informed about future book releases and all things Andalaya.
Join Now at
www.CoreyRusick.com

Made in the USA
Middletown, DE
02 September 2024

60260518R00241